FORGOTTEN

AND *Remembered*

THE DUKE'S LATE WIFE

Also By Bree

Historical Romance:

<u>Love's Second Chance Series</u>
#1 Forgotten & Remembered - The Duke's Late Wife
#2 Cursed & Cherished - The Duke's Wilful Wife
#3 Despised & Desired - The Marquess' Passionate Wife
#4 Abandoned & Protected - The Marquis' Tenacious Wife
#5 Ruined & Redeemed - The Earl's Fallen Wife
#6 Betrayed & Blessed - The Viscount's Shrewd Wife
#7 Deceived & Honoured - The Baron's Vexing Wife (2018)

<u>A Forbidden Love Novella Series</u>
#1 The Wrong Brother
#2 A Brilliant Rose
#3 The Forgotten Wife
#4 An Unwelcome Proposal
#5 Rules to Be Broken (soon)
#6 Hearts to Be Mended (February 2018)

Suspenseful Contemporary Romance:

<u>Where There's Love Series</u>
#1 Remember Me

Middle Grade Adventure:

<u>Airborne Trilogy</u>
#1 Fireflies (Now perma-free in ebook format!)
#2 Butterflies
#3 Dragonflies (Coming 2017)

Paranormal Fantasy:

<u>Crescent Rock Series</u>
#1 How to Live and Die in Crescent Rock

FORGOTTEN AND *Remembered*

THE DUKE'S LATE WIFE

(#1 LOVE'S SECOND CHANCE SERIES)

BY

BREE WOLF

Forgotten & Remembered
The Duke's Late Wife
By
Bree Wolf

This is a work of fiction. Names, characters, businesses, places, brands, media, events and incidents are either the products of the author's imagination or used in a fictitious manner.

Any resemblance to actual persons, living or dead, or actual events is purely coincidental.

Cover Art by Victoria Cooper

Copyright © 2015 Sabrina Wolf

www.breewolf.com

ISBN-13: 978-1518723292
ISBN-10: 1518723292

To Second Chances

ACKNOWLEDGEMENTS

All my thanks goes to my family, who continues to be supportive and encouraging, inspirational and challenging. You have no idea how glad I am to have you in my life.

A great big thanks to my beta readers, Cindy Ulrich, Tray-Ci Roberts and fellow author Laura Masciarelli. Your honest words gave me the most wonderful ideas. Please never stop.

FORGOTTEN

AND *Remembered*

PROLOGUE

1801 England (or a variation thereof)

Wind whipping through his hair, Edmond Dunsworth, Duke of Cromwell, leaned forward, urging his horse to greater speed. Almost flattening himself to the stallion's body as they flew over the hedge bordering Westmore Manor to the east, he still marvelled at the new light that had come to his sister's eyes since he'd last seen her. Crashing through the underbrush, he spotted her up ahead, her golden hair sparkling in the sun, that reached tentative rays through the foliage overhead as though hesitant to touch her.

"Edmond!" Her voice travelled over the distance and the thundering of their horses' hooves as though she was right beside him. "Will you forfeit?"

"Never!"

A sparkle came to her eyes as her lips curved upward. "I shall be lenient if you surrender now."

"Never!" he repeated, pulling his stallion around another thickly growing monster barring his path. "The Duke of Cromwell does not surrender!"

Her delightful laughter, like a brook babbling in the early morning air, reached his ears, almost making him reconsider. As much as he loved her, he had never granted her an easy victory. So he urged his horse on and soon pulled up alongside her.

Seeing him next to her, she too spurred her horse onward. "Dear brother, for sure you will not make me lose face."

He laughed. "It is only us. And I swear I will not breathe a word should you lose this once, Leonora."

Biting her lower lip, she leaned forward as the wind whipped through her hair and caught in her long skirts. "Leonora Astor, Duchess of Kensington, does not lose!" Her eyes twinkled as she glanced at him. "Never! Not even once!"

Although he knew how furious she would be with him if he allowed her to gain ground, his heart just wasn't set on winning this race but on seeing her win instead.

As the distance between them grew once more, she called to him over her shoulder. "Do not disappoint me, Edmond. Have you no honour?"

Her playful insult burned in his heart, and he once again urged his horse on. The path soon levelled out, leaving behind bordering trees and opening up to green pastures, glowing in the early sun. Edmond felt his horse's flanks move as he pursued her. Soon, she was almost within his reach, and he playfully swatted her horse's behind.

Laughing, she looked at him. "Not bad, dear brother! But will it be enough?"

As they flew across a sea of grass, swaying softly in the breeze, Edmond's gaze softened, seeing her slender figure clinging to her mare's back, moulded together as though one. Her blue eyes sparkled with mischief as she turned to look at him. For a moment, a long moment, they flew onward, side by side, eyes fixed on the other. A perfect moment. A moment that would stay with him until the end of his days. A moment that he would curse all the same. A moment so dear that it hurt to think of it. A moment he would see in his dreams. Again and again, hoping for a different outcome.

Before Edmond knew what had happened, she suddenly disappeared from his view, his eyes gazing into nothing, searching for a matching pair.

Then, a shrill scream reached his ears, freezing the blood in his veins.

Instantly, Edmond reined in his horse. As he turned to look for her, his eyes swept over the green stalks, still swaying in the breeze—as though nothing had happened—until they came upon the carnage his ears had told him about a moment before.

His heart stopped beating. If only for a moment.

The white mare lay on her side, completely still, left foreleg bent in an odd angle. Dropping off his horse, Edmond rushed around the dead horse and gasped as he found his sister only a few feet away. Although the gash on her forehead seemed minor, the way she lay in the grass almost disappearing from view swallowed up by thin hands reaching from the earth seeking to pull her under, he knew the truth.

Lunging forward, Edmond almost bumped into her. His eyes frantically searched for injuries to tend to, but he found none. None except for the small cut on her forehead. Tentatively, he put a hand on her cheek and almost died of shock when she opened her eyes.

"Leonora?" he whispered, bending over her so she would see him. "Can you hear me?"

For a moment, her eyes closed, and he held his breath. Mesmerized, he watched her chest, rise and fall, slowly, ever so slowly. The strength that had always radiated from her was gone, and like never before, he felt the desperate need to protect her.

But it was too late. Seeing her lying in the grass, broken beyond repair, Edmond hung his head as tears spilled forth.

"Georgiana," she whispered and opened her eyes. "Georgiana."

Carefully, he took her hand in his. "I will take care of her." His voice caught. "I promise."

Her eyes stared into nothing; she didn't see him, but her hand seemed to relax. "I promise," he repeated, not knowing what else to do.

"Graham," Leonora said, her voice growing weaker. Leaning closer, Edmond put his ear next to her mouth to catch the last words he would ever hear her say. "Tell Graham, I…," she swallowed and drew in a ragged breath, "I—"

"What?" he whispered, but as he raised his eyes to her face, he realized her light had vanished for good. He was alone.

Burying his face in her hair, the Duke of Cromwell wept.

1

A NEW WIFE

One Year Later

 do not understand why you insist on coming along?" Graham Astor, Duke of Kensington, asked. He barely looked at his brother-in-law, keeping his gaze on the scenery passing before his eyes. "I do not need assistance."

"I disagree," the Duke of Cromwell said. Shifting in his seat to get more comfortable, he leaned forward, squinting his eyes. "Do you have a young lady in mind?"

In turn, Graham's eyes widened. How dare he suggest such a thing? Keeping his mind focused on the rumbling of the carriage's wheels on the country lane, Graham continued to stare out the window.

"So, this is like going to the market and purchasing whatever strikes your fancy?"

Once more shocked beyond comprehension, Graham finally turned his eyes to the man sitting across from him. His blond hair slightly unkempt, one boot propped up on the bench beside him, his brother-in-law crossed his arms as though in anger, but his blue eyes twinkled as his lips curled into a mischievous smile. "So," he said, "then tell me, what are you looking for in a wife?"

Graham swallowed. Was he looking for a wife? No, most definitely not. He'd had a wife, the only one he'd ever wanted. Replacing her seemed as impossible as the sun not rising in the east.

"Do you wish for a blond?" Graham flinched. "Or a brunette maybe?" Edmond asked. "With blue eyes, or rather green?"

Setting his jaw, Graham once more turned to the window. "I am not looking for a wife."

"I see," Edmond said, and there was something in his voice that made Graham look at him. "Do you?" he asked.

Edmond nodded. "You're not looking for a wife, but for a mother for Georgiana."

Smoothing down her dress with shaking hands, Rosabel Lander climbed the steps to the stately manor hosting today's engagement celebration. Finally, Viscount Davenport had selected a wife. While some voiced honest congratulations for the future couple, there were a few who viewed the spectacle with mixed feelings. Especially the mothers and daughters who had vied for his hand...and lost. It was all a game, Rosabel thought. Once more, she felt her resolve strengthened to stand aside and not partake.

While her aunt and uncle, Lord and Lady Harlowe, paraded their children around the room, introducing their eldest daughter Elsbeth to yet another eligible bachelor, Rosabel withdrew into the corners of the large hall. Eyes traveling about the room, she found many straying outside into the gardens where large tables, weighted down by enormous amounts of food, had been set in the shades of the giant oak trees. After taking a deep breath, Rosabel tiptoed passed a number of her uncle's acquaintances and pushing open the French doors, finally found her way outside, enjoying the calm breeze brushing over her face. Out of the corner of her eyes, she spotted her youngest cousins amongst a crowd of children rushing to the banquet table, inspecting the food with hungry expressions on their little faces. Feeling a smile tuck at the corners of her mouth, she watched them, their carefree spirits lighting their eyes. Oh, how she wished she could join them.

"Cousin Rosabel!" six-year-old Lydia called, her cheeks flushed with excitement. "Did you see the cake?"

"Four tiers!" Beatrice exclaimed, her own face beaming brightly. "But we have to wait until they cut it," she informed her younger sister earnestly. "Is that not true, Rosabel?"

Smiling, Rosabel nodded. "It certainly is. Why do you not play a game before you eat? I believe, by then, they will have cut the cake."

Both nodded eagerly. "But you must play with us!" Grabbing her by the hands, the girls drew her away from her shady spot of solitude and out into the sun. Reluctant at first, Rosabel heard laughter rise from her own throat as she chased after them. Her young cousins had an uncanny ability to make her forget everything around her. Today, however, she should have shown some restraint as she was so harshly reminded by her uncle's voice a moment later, "Rosabel! Do come here!"

Feeling the slap of his words, Rosabel stiffened. Before turning away from her cousins' smiles and facing her uncle's scowl, Rosabel drew in a deep breath.

"Yes, Uncle," she breathed, seeing the disapproval clearly edged in his face. "Is there something that you require?"

Robert Munford, Baron Harlowe, snorted. "I require you to behave like a well-brought up lady." He shook his head. "At the very least do try and do your mother justice." Without another word, he turned and walked away.

Following him with her eyes, Rosabel found some of the other guests casting disapproving glances in her direction. She was sure they had overheard him lecturing her, and so she decided to withdraw into the shade once more, cheeks aflame with embarrassment.

"Do not mind him," she heard her eldest cousin's voice speak from behind her. "He does not know the meaning of fun."

A faint smile crossed her face. "He is right. I should not have behaved as I did. It was unladylike."

Ellie's eyes searched her face. "Do not fret. No one saw."

Rosabel glanced about. "I am certain I saw a few look at me as he did. After all, I am my mother's daughter."

Ellie snorted. "But you are not your mother. It was not you who disobeyed your father and shamed your family. They have nothing to hold against you."

Rosabel nodded. Ellie was right. She was not her mother, and yet, hearing her cousin judge her mother so harshly in order to defend her stung. What had her mother done that had been so wrong? She had followed her heart. Unfortunately, her heart had led her, a baron's daughter, into the arms of a commoner of little fortune. The former Lord Harlowe had never forgiven his daughter for disrespecting him, and his son carried on the torch, extending the blame from mother to daughter. After all, her mother could not be lectured anymore. Death had freed her at last.

"Who is he?" Ellie spoke, tearing Rosabel from her inner turmoil. "Have you seen him before?"

"Who?" Glancing across the lawn, eyes searching the terrace as her cousin's nod indicated, Rosabel found herself looking at a young man of almost golden hair. An easy smile on his face, his eyes twinkled in the sun as they swept across the people gathered before him. "I don't believe I've ever seen him before."

"Mmmh," Ellie mused. "He is quite handsome." Her own eyes glistened as she observed him from afar. "He seems very amicable, unlike his friend."

"His friend?" Rosabel asked, redirecting her gaze from her cousin back to the new-comer. By his side now stood another gentleman, and while the fair-haired young man had reminded her of a gentle summer day with the sparkling sun shining brightly upon the face of the earth, his companion appeared like a black hole. His dark hair and cold, calculating eyes spoke of a monster hiding in the dark, preying on the innocent, waiting for the right moment to strike.

A shiver went down her back as his eyes met hers, and she averted her gaze without another thought as though afraid the cold in his eyes could turn her to stone. "There is something unsettling about him," she whispered.

Ellie nodded, giving a slight shake herself. "He does seem unpleasant. Why do you think he is here? He does not seem to enjoy himself."

Rosabel shrugged, hoping she'd never find out.

Letting his eyes sweep over the gathering of people on the lawn by the oak trees, exhaustion washed over Graham like a heavy rain. He did not see the sun or the smiling faces nor could he smell the delicious odours of freshly prepared food or hear the delighted giggles of the children chasing one another through the gardens. All Graham saw were people he didn't know, people he didn't care to know. And in that moment, he was grateful for Edmond's presence.

"So?" his brother-in-law asked. "Do you see anything you like?"

Graham frowned. "I hope you are referring to the food."

Winking, Edmond chuckled. "Do try and look a little at ease. This is a garden party, not your last meal before you meet the gallows in the morning."

"I know."

Edmond shook his head. "Are you certain? Your face seems to disagree."

"I'd be much obliged if you would refrain from finding such joy in my misery," Graham whispered, his eyes fixed on the horizon in the distance. How was it that some days seemed to never want to end? Sometimes, he felt like the sun was doing its utmost to burn the life from him.

At his words, Edmond turned to look. "Because you seem to believe that misery is all there is." Graham felt a hand settle on his shoulder as his friend turned to look at him. "You can't live in the dark forever."

Graham shrugged, shaking off his friend's attempt at comfort. "I did not bring you here for your ill advice."

Edmond grinned. "You did not bring me at all. I came."

Graham shrugged.

Once again returning to his cheerful self, Edmond turned back to the spectacle in the gardens. "So, let's find you a wife."

Although he felt he ought to, Graham didn't protest. The sooner, the better. The sooner he found a new wife, the sooner he could return to the shadows.

As Edmond pointed out every young lady to pass before their eyes, Graham barely listened. He didn't care how brilliantly their eyes shone or how golden their hair glistened in the sun. After all, he wasn't really looking for a wife.

Giving his eyes free reign, he found himself drawn to the children and their easy laughter. Laughter untainted by loss. The laughter of youth and innocence. His tense muscles relaxed as he watched them, only to be reminded of the daughter he hadn't seen since her mother's passing.

18

As Georgiana's face, conjured by the dark corners of his mind, appeared before him, he closed his eyes, trying to shake every thought of her. Considering why he had come to this festivity in the first place, he wasn't surprised when his attempts were thwarted. Her deep blue eyes smiled at him as she threw her wild, golden curls back and flung herself into his arms. The knot in his stomach tightened, and he felt ill.

Opening his eyes, Graham found himself looking at a young woman behaving quite unladylike as she chased a group of children across the lawn. She was quite petite, barely taller than some of the older children, and her easy smile matched theirs every step of the way.

As the smile died on her lips, he turned to see an older man approach her from the terrace, a scowl on his face. Her father? He wondered. A muted conversation followed causing the young woman to drop her head and sink into herself. Her eyes rested on the ground and barely glanced up at the man clearly lecturing her. The smile that had only moments earlier illuminated her soft face had transformed into a serious and collected expression, darkening her eyes.

Graham watched the man walk away and re-join his lady when another young woman approached the one he had been observing. Clearly a confidant, she tried to raise her friend's spirits, but to no avail. As they suddenly looked up, Graham averted his eyes. However, when he took another quick look, he met the petite ones gaze for a second before she looked away.

Adding up all the many details he had been able to glimpse of her personality, Graham decided that today hadn't been in vain after all. It had brought him a good step closer to choosing a wife

2

ON BECOMING A GOVERNESS

Still feeling his cold eyes linger on her, Rosabel shivered. "He seems to be most unpleasant," she whispered, eying her cousin through lowered lashes. "Do you not agree?"

Ellie nodded. "There is something dark about him. Something…," she put a finger to her lip, "…I'm not sure. Maybe—"

"Elsbeth!" a whispered shout rang from down the lawn and made them turn around. As they exchanged quick remarks, faces somewhat tense, Lord and Lady Harlowe hastened toward them.

Abandoning her observational post, Ellie turned to her parents. "Yes, Mother. Father. What seems to be the matter?"

As Rosabel peeked around Ellie's tall frame, she felt herself unwillingly shrink into the shadows. Wringing her hands, she dearly hoped that she had not given affront again. Her aunt and uncle, however, only seemed to have eyes for their eldest daughter, not even glancing in their niece's direction, and Rosabel let go a breath she wasn't aware she'd been holding.

"Elsbeth, now do not be too obvious about it," Rosabel's aunt whispered, as her quick hands brushed down her daughter's dress, flattening any ruffles their might be, "but do you see the two gentlemen standing up on the terrace?"

Without turning her head, Ellie shifted her eyes briefly to the two young men she and Rosabel had been observing not a minute ago. Eyes on her mother, she nodded. "What about them?"

Taking his daughter's hand, Lord Harlowe said in hushed tones, "We were just informed that the one on the left with the blond hair is Edmond Dunsworth, Duke of Cromwell, while the one on the right with the dark hair is Graham Astor, Duke of Kensington." His eyes glowed as though Christmas had come early this year.

Watching her aunt and uncle closely, Rosabel knew immediately that a new matchmaking scheme was afoot and that her cousin was the unfortunate victim. Unable to see Ellie's face as her father pulled her forward while her mother rearranged an escaped lock of her hair, Rosabel took a deep breath, relieved at being overlooked once again. "Come, come," she heard her aunt whisper, "put on your most dazzling smile. Viscount Davenport has promised to introduce us. Just think about it; a duchess. You could be a duchess." As though floating on air, Lady Harlowe glided down the small hill, almost dragging her daughter behind her, eye on the targets standing on the terrace, who were as of yet, unaware of their impending doom.

Clasping a hand over her mouth at such a thought, Rosabel chastised herself. Either one of them would be lucky to have her cousin for a wife. Having Lord and Lady Harlowe for parents-in-law, however, was a different matter.

"So? Are you betrothed?" Rosabel whispered after they'd arrived home, retreating to Ellie's chamber for privacy.

Her cousin's eyes flew open. "Of course, not. Viscount Davenport merely introduced us." She shrugged. "Who knows, what will come of it?"

Sitting on the small divan, Rosabel fingered the hem of her sleeves. "Do you wish to be betrothed?"

"Certainly." Observing her cousin through narrowed eyes, Ellie sat down beside her. "Not necessarily to one of them, but in general, yes, of course."

Again, Rosabel felt her cousin's gaze resting on her. She took a deep breath and met her eyes.

"Do you not wish to be betrothed?" Ellie asked, and Rosabel could see in her eyes that she was observing her carefully, trying to detect any hint that her words would not be truthful.

Rosabel shrugged. "I do not know."

"Why? Do you wish to be a spinster?"

Knowing that her cousin's words were not meant as an insult, she drew in a deep breath, hoping to find the right words to explain the turmoil going on in her heart. "I am not sure what I want. But marriage seems...undesirable."

"Really? What makes you say that?"

Again running her fingers over the hem of her sleeve, Rosabel's eyes turned inward. "My parents."

Ellie frowned. "Because it ruined your mother? And by extension, you?"

Rosabel shook her head. "No, what scares me is the love they shared...and lost."

"How do you mean? I thought love was a desirable benefit in a marriage. Those who eventually come to love their spouse consider it a blessing. Would you not agree?"

"I'm not sure." Eyes drifting out the window, Rosabel tried to remember the moment her life had changed. The moment her world had come crashing down around her. The moment everything was lost. The moment her mother had died.

After Rosabel had been born, her mother had miscarried a couple of times, until finally she seemed to be able to carry another baby full term. Only mere weeks before the baby was due, her mother had gone into labour. Days had passed. Days of pain and suffering. Rosabel, barely six at the time, had heard her mother's pain and just as clearly seen the answering emotions on her father's face. In the end, the child had been stillborn, and her mother had died moments later.

That alone, losing her mother, a mother she had loved more than anyone in the world, would have made Rosabel hesitant about giving her heart to anyone. But what she didn't know in that moment was that she was still falling, that she hadn't hit rock bottom yet.

Madly in love with his wife ever since he'd first laid eyes on her, Rosabel's father lost a piece of himself that day. And as it turned out, without that piece, he could not go on.

In the beginning, after the initial shock and disbelief had worn off, he had tried. Rosabel remembered the effort to be cheerful she had sometimes detected on his face, to give her back her smile by finding his own. But it had all been a mask. He could never recover from the loss of his wife. Barely two years later, he had followed her to the grave. Pneumonia, the doctor had said. But in her heart, Rosabel had known that he had given up, that there had been nothing left that would have kept him in this life. Not even his daughter. She hadn't been enough.

A love as all-consuming as theirs scared Rosabel. Giving yourself up to such pain seemed too great a risk. While at the same time entering a marriage without love would be a betrayal of her parents and everything they'd gone through to be together.

Marriage just wasn't an option, not for Rosabel. But if not marriage, what then?

Stepping down from the carriage that had taken them to Whitmore, Rosabel and Ellie scanned the small market place where merchants had set up stall after stall, offering a variety of sugary treats as much as exquisite fabrics. People bustled about, blocking their view, and Rosabel hastened to grab a hold of her younger cousins. "You must not run off," she warned, looking from Beatrice to Lydia to Stephen, the youngest and only son of Lord Harlowe. "We would not want anyone to snatch you off and demand a ransom of your father for your return, now would we?" As she winked at them, the girls giggled while Stephen, at the ripe age of four, bowed his head with all the sincerity instilled in him by his father.

"Should we go over there first?" Ellie pointed across the square and past the water fountain to a stall that held the most brilliant colours. "Mother said I ought to find something fit for a duchess." Her eyes twinkled.

"What if you do not become a duchess?" Rosabel asked, seeing the light-heartedness of her cousin's comment.

Ellie shrugged. "Then at least I'll have a pretty new dress." She smiled and grabbed Rosabel by the arm, pulling her along. "Let's go, you little rascals," she called over her shoulder.

While Ellie spent the next hour browsing the stall she had indicated and had the merchant show her every roll of fabric he had brought, Rosabel kept a fixed eye on her younger cousins as they threw pebbles in the water fountain or played tag on the square. Every now and then, she offered her opinion to Ellie on a particular colour or texture of a fabric, but other than that was left to her own devices.

Around her, people walked back and forth, from stall to stall browsing, buying and bargaining, their voices a vibrant cacophony of life. There was no place like a busy market to gather gossip on one's neighbours and learn new titbits here and there. Apparently, the future Viscountess Davenport had the largest dowry of any girl in the county, which was precisely why the Viscount had chosen her as his bride-to-be. No, on the contrary, another woman argued, it was her beauty that had ensured her the match.

Slightly hushed voices, as though betraying a secret, whispered of a newcomer to the neighbourhood, taking up residence at Camden Hall. A tall, stately man with hair as dark as night and eyes as cold as the ice on a frozen winter's lake. However, since he had a title—another argument broke out over whether he was a duke or an earl—those defects were easily overlooked. Rosabel disagreed; those eyes had followed her to her dreams the night before, and she had awoken with a cold sweat and an eerie sense of foreboding.

"Mrs. Garner is ailing," a woman standing slightly off to the side by the next stall spoke. "The family will be looking for a replacement soon."

"Are you certain?" the young woman standing shoulder to shoulder with her, surveying the stall's display, asked. "This world sure is harsh. To be replaced like that."

The older woman nodded. "Certainly. But what are the Comptons to do? They have three daughters. They need a governess."

"True," the younger woman agreed, turning her attention back to the display of fabrics before her. "It is just so sad."

Although Rosabel felt for Mrs. Garner unbeknownst, her heart skipped a beat as her mind took the information she had just overheard and went one step further. If not marriage, then what? Could she be a governess? Rosabel wondered, once more ensuring that all three children were still playing safely by the water fountain. As Beatrice saw her looking, she waved.

Yes, Rosabel's mind said. Why not? She loved children, and they adored her. Being a governess; nothing would be simpler. A smile spread over her face but died abruptly as her uncle came to mind. Would he allow her? Would he consider her working as a further disgrace to the family?

After her father had joined her mother in death, Rosabel had come to live with her uncle's family, but from the beginning, she had felt unwelcome. She knew they had only taken her in because they considered it their duty; she was, after all, family. Unwelcome family, however. Both, her aunt and uncle never missed an opportunity to remind her of her status. She was the black sheep of the family, and her dark hair only seemed to confirm that their opinion of her was correct. More than once, Rosabel had looked at herself in the mirror, wondering if a lighter hair colour would have made a difference. But as so often, she shook her head at such a foolish thought. Knowing that it was rooted in the deep desire to be accepted by her own kin, Rosabel thought of it no further.

A burden to her family, Rosabel often felt the need to repay them for their kindness; the kindness they showed by not sending her from their house. Always on her best behaviour, Rosabel never declined a request, never argued and never questioned her uncle's authority. And yet, to this day he had never looked at her with an emotion akin to affection. Nor had her aunt. Only her cousins were able to see past the scandal with a child's carefree and forgiving spirit, and Rosabel loved them for it all the more.

So, if she became a governess, would her uncle be relieved to be rid of a responsibility he did not ask for in the first place?

Descending the stairs of his carriage, Graham found himself in hell. As crowded as the market place before him appeared, he couldn't help but wonder how people could stomach it. One could scarcely set one foot before the other without brushing someone's shoulder or stepping on someone's shoes. Withdrawing to the less crowded side of a building situated behind the water fountain, Graham took a deep breath, already feeling the lump in his stomach harden. A scowl on his face, he looked at his friend. "Why on earth did you insist on coming here?"

Edmond shrugged, an impish smile playing on his features as he watched the children playing by the water fountain. "It's a beautiful day, and you had to get out of the house."

"Says who?"

"Graham, as much as you love your dusty, old books, they are not adequate company."

Graham returned his gaze to the children, now throwing pebbles into the water.

They'd had this discussion many times. It never led anywhere. Edmond did not understand the comfort books could give, and Graham could not explain without raising their relationship to a level that he was not comfortable with. The heart had no purpose, not one he cared for, at least. Again, for the millionth time, he wished he could tear it from his chest and bury it with his wife.

Chasing after two girls, who shared many of his features, a little boy slipped when running through a small puddle and crashed to the ground. His little face distorted painfully, he began to howl, holding his knee. Instantly, a young woman rushed to his side, and Graham recognized her as the one he had been observing at the Davenport's engagement celebration.

Gathering the boy up in her arms, she carried him to the water fountain where she sat down and rocked him back and forth. Cooing into his ear, her lips moved as though she was singing. Slowly, the boy relaxed until his tears stopped. Peeling his hands from his leg, she checked his knee and then turned around to wash his skinned hands in the water fountain. She dried his hands on her dress, tenderly patting the fabric to the sore skin, and then splashed some water on his face. The little boy shrieked, but laughter shook him a moment later, and he threw his little arms around her. Again, she hugged him tight, rocking from side to side.

"A handsome, young woman," Edmond said, and Graham flinched, his friend's voice ripping away the quiet peacefulness of the scene before him. "Is she not the one you observed at the party?"

Graham didn't answer.

"She will make a beautiful duchess," Edmond continued, his eyes carefully fixed on his friend's face.

"That is of no importance to me."

"I see." Edmond's gaze shifted to the young woman, leading the boy and the two girls he had chased after through the throng of people. Before long she vanished from sight. "If not her beauty has caught your eye, then what recommends her to you?"

Again, Graham didn't answer.

For a moment, Edmond looked at him, and Graham tensed under his friend's scrutiny. Finally, he said, "Georgiana will like her."

Graham turned to look at his brother-in-law and nodded. "I hope."

"A governess?" Ellie exclaimed as the carriage rustled along the dry lane, softened by the beginning of fall. "This is the first I've heard of this!"

"Naturally," Rosabel replied, brushing a hand over her sleeping cousin resting his head in her lap. "It's the first I've thought of it."

Ellie looked at her as though she had declared her decision to join a gypsy clan on the morrow. "What made you think of it then?"

"I overheard two women talking at the market. They said the Comptons will be in need of a new governess soon." Rosabel took a deep breath and looked her cousin square in the eyes. "I thought I could apply."

Ellie shook her head, glancing at her sisters resting their heads against the carriage wall, sleeping as only young children could. "Then you were serious about what you said about marriage?"

Rosabel nodded. "Do you think Uncle will allow it?"

"I have no way of knowing. But I doubt he will be pleased."

Rosabel sighed. "Surely, he knows that my chances of making a favourable match are slim. I have no dowry, no family name, only a scandal attached to my person. A scandal that to this day, people are unwilling to put behind them." Taking a deep breath, Rosabel tried to steady her nerves. Not until this moment had she realized how much her neighbours' disapproval hurt her.

"Then you are determined?" Ellie asked. "When will you speak to Father?"

Rosabel shrugged, her palms feeling clammy. "As soon as I can find the courage. Hopefully before the Comptons hire someone else."

3

THE PROPOSAL

ifficult business was best taken care of without delay, and so Graham Astor, Duke of Kensington, found himself in his carriage at the break of dawn. He ordered the coachman to maintain a slow pace, giving him the time he needed to prepare himself, lay down the words he was to say. After all, he could not offer his heart, nor depend on a long-standing acquaintance with the family.

Graham knew the desired outcome of this endeavour and felt fairly certain that the baron would not refuse him. After all, had he not paraded his own daughter before him and Edmond at the Davenports' engagement celebration only two weeks ago?

Giving his name to the butler who opened the door upon his arrival, Graham observed with satisfaction the slight widening of the man's eyes. Consequently, after seeing Graham to the study, the old man hurried away to inform his lord of his guest.

Mere moments later, Lord Harlowe burst through the door, eyes aglow, as he hastened to welcome Graham to his humble home. "Your grace, this is an honour. What can I do for you?" He gestured to a serving girl waiting by the door. "Can I offer you anything?"

After Graham declined, Lord Harlowe bade him take a seat and once more inquired after the purpose of his visit. Watching him closely, Graham assumed the baron's excitement stemmed from the hope that he had come to ask permission to court his daughter.

"My visit is of a personal matter," Graham began, watching with some amusement as Lord Harlowe ever so slightly fidgeted in his seat like a school boy before summer holidays. "To be frank, I have come to ask for your niece's hand in marriage." At his words, the baron's smile slid off his face and upon hitting the floor, burst into a million pieces.

"My…my niece?" Lord Harlowe stammered.

"Your niece," Graham clarified. "Miss Rosabel Lander."

For a long moment, silence hung in the air as Graham was sure Lord Harlowe considered whether or not his hearing was impaired. Then his eyes refocused on his guest, and some of the colour returned to his cheeks. "I mean no disrespect, your grace, but the young woman you were introduced to at the Davenports' engagement celebration was my daughter, The Honourable Elsbeth Munford."

Graham scoffed. "I am aware of that, my lord."

"Certainly, certainly," the baron hastened to agree. He cleared his throat. "My niece then." Still squirming in his seat, he seemed to contemplate asking the next question, lest he should make the Duke withdraw his proposal. "May I ask why…what led you to ask for my niece's hand?"

Face collected, Graham leaned back in the chair. "My reasons are my own, my lord."

"Certainly, certainly."

As Graham rose to his feet, the baron shot up too, eyes frantically looking at him. "If you intend to refuse my offer, do say—"

"Of course not, your grace," Lord Harlowe hastened to clarify. "I wouldn't dream of it. We are most honoured, and I have no objections to the match. Be assured of that."

Graham gave a slight nod of the head and sat back down. The baron followed. "I would prefer a short engagement. With your permission, I will obtain a special license for the wedding to be held within a fortnight."

Lord Harlowe's eyes strained to pop out of his head. "A fortnight?"

"A fortnight."

The baron's head bobbed up and down. "Certainly, certainly. If you have no objections, Lady Harlowe will make all the necessary arrangements for an announcement as well as an engagement affair."

Graham nodded. "I suppose it cannot be helped."

"Good, good."

Rising to his feet, Graham fixed the man across from him with an icy stare. "Do as you feel appropriate as long as the wedding will take place within a fortnight. Time is of the essence." Seeing the baron's uncomprehending face, Graham thought of Georgiana. She needed a mother. Now, not in a year. Finding a suitable wife had taken him long enough.

Walking down the winding staircase to the lower floor, Rosabel's nerves jingled. She was summoned to her uncle's study. Why? What had she done? Although terrified of being the cause for yet another scandal—as everyone around her seemed to expect of her sooner or later—, Rosabel often had minor slips of judgment, like when she had played tag with her young cousins at the Davenports' engagement celebration. Her uncle had not been happy. What had drawn his disapproval now?

Tentatively, Rosabel knocked on the heavy door. As her uncle's stern voice ordered her to enter, she stepped into the room, eyes cast down. "You asked to see me, Uncle?"

"Yes, my dear, come in." Her uncle rounded his desk, waving her forward, his face bright, eyes glowing. Rosabel froze. What was wrong? Had he just called her *my dear*?

"Please, sit." Taking her hand, he led her to the armchair set by the window overlooking the park. As he sat down opposite her, his eyes flowed over her in a calculating and very unsettling way. A shiver ran down Rosabel's back. "I have wonderful news." He clasped his hands together, looking at her in a way that made her feel like she should know what he was talking about. "The Duke of Kensington just paid me a visit," he said at last, still looking at her with questioning eyes.

Rosabel averted her gaze. "That is wonderful," was all she could think to say.

"Indeed, it is." When she remained silent, her uncle continued, "I am glad to say there will be a wedding soon."

"A wedding?" Rosabel asked, a catch in her voice as she spoke. Instantly, she feared the worst. Had he asked for Ellie's hand? Would she soon be his wife?

Leaning back in his armchair, her uncle smiled. "Did you have any idea that he would make an offer?"

"No, Uncle, I did not."

He shrugged. "Well, it does not matter now. The reason behind his proposal is secondary. What is important now is that His Grace wishes for a speedy wedding. It is to take place in a fortnight."

Rosabel froze. "A fortnight? So soon?" She couldn't believe that in a mere fortnight her dear cousin would be lost to her. A large boulder had suddenly come to rest on her chest.

Her uncle nodded. "It is soon. It will not give you much time to prepare, but do not be alarmed. Lady Harlowe shall guide your hand at every step."

For a moment, time stood still. Rosabel's gaze froze, locked on her uncle's delighted face. Hearing his words again and again play in her head, she strained to force air into her lungs lest she pass out. Slowly, time sped up again, and Rosabel heard herself say, "Me? He wishes to marry me?"

"Indeed, he does."

Stars started to dance before her eyes. "But why? I have never even spoken to him."

Her uncle shrugged. "He would not say. It does not matter after all."

Through the slight blur settling on her vision, Rosabel once again found herself staring at her uncle. "You agreed?"

Now, it was Lord Harlowe's turn to stare. Shaking his head in disbelief, he snorted, "Of course, I did. He is a duke."

"But...but—"

"Do not worry yourself. I am most confident that you will make him a good wife." Again, he shook his head, amazement giving his eyes a most unbecoming glow. "Never would I have thought to procure such a good match for you." He chuckled. "And you did not make it easy on me. After all, you never seemed to encourage any gentleman who appeared to fancy you. Lady Harlowe and I feared you would never make a connection and become an old maid." Now he was laughing, slapping his knee and shaking his head. "Wonderful how things turned out, isn't it?"

Desperately trying to focus, to keep from blacking out, Rosabel stammered, "But…Uncle, I do not wish to marry." His laughter died. "Just a few days ago, I thought a governess position would be the perfect solution."

"A governess position?" her uncle blurted, all cheerfulness gone from his face. "What nonsense is this?"

"No, nonsense. I just−"

"No, no, no." He shook his head vehemently, almost wagging his finger at her. "Nonsense, you'll marry the duke. No one in their right mind would decline such an offer. Especially a girl in your position should be grateful to have her future in safe hands."

"A girl like me?"

Her uncle nodded vigorously. "After the shame your mother brought over this family, it is only right that you do your utmost to restore our good name to its rightful status. Marrying the duke will elevate all of us." His eyes narrowed, fixing her with an unyielding stare. "Do you understand?"

Unable to look away, Rosabel nodded, feeling tears in the corners of her eyes. "May I be excused?"

Lord Harlowe waved her off. "Certainly, there is much to do."

Holding on to her emotions for as long as she could, Rosabel fled from the room, almost ran up the stairs and, after closing the door to her chamber, threw herself on the bed and wept.

Rosabel spent the entirety of the morning crying her eyes out, the desperation of her situation sinking to the core of her being. When no more tears would come, she realized that all spirit had left her. She had resigned herself to her fate, knowing that ultimately she had no say in the matter. Yet, she was no closer to understanding it.

To clear her head and chase away the dense fog that was clouding her thoughts, Rosabel splashed some water on her face, brushed down her dress and went outside into the garden for a walk.

Even though autumn was well on its way, the sun shone as brightly as though it were the height of summer. The green oasis surrounding her glistened as the sun's rays were reflected in the morning dew still clinging to the individual blades of grass.

Rosabel's eyes, however, were blind to the beauty around her. As she walked down the small gravel path leading her away from the house and into the back of the garden where a small pavilion stood in an isolated area hidden behind a tall hedge, she almost dragged her feet, feeling the weight of her situation acutely. She sat down on the bench and burying her face in her hands, sighed, "Dear God, what am I going to do?"

For a long time, Rosabel sat; the wind rustling the leaves around her the only sound to reach her ears until a soft step echoed along the gravel path, leading toward her. "Oh, please do not let it be my aunt or uncle," she whispered into her hands; then raised her head. Had they come after her?

Glimpsing Ellie's blond curls through a slightly less overgrown area in the hedge, Rosabel breathed a sigh of relief. Rubbing her hands over her swollen eyes, she turned to her cousin.

The moment Ellie spotted her sitting in her hiding place, a relieved smile lit up her features before she lifted her skirts and hurried to join her in the pavilion. "I was looking all over for you. Are you all right?"

Rosabel shrugged. "I hardly know."

"Father told me." Her voice a mere whisper as though it could reverse the truth, Ellie took Rosabel's hands in hers. "Did you have any idea he would ask for your hand?"

Staring into her cousin's eyes, Rosabel shook her head. "None. I never thought…I still do not understand. Why would he want to marry me?"

"I agree." Ellie shook her head, making her curls bounce from side to side. "You have never even been introduced. He has never spoken to you, has he?"

"Not once. After all, I only saw him the one time at the Davenports' engagement celebration." The afternoon replayed in her mind as though it might hold the answer to the all-consuming question, why? "When you pointed them out, standing up on the terrace, I looked and…"

"And?" Ellie prompted.

Rosabel's eyes narrowed as she looked at her friend. "And he looked back at me. Just for a second, but his eyes were so cold. They made me shiver." The memory alone sent a chill down her spine.

Ellie frowned. "Did he seem to be taken with you? Maybe it was love at first sight. It happens, not often, but every now and then…"

"No!" Rosabel interrupted. She wasn't sure of much these days, but she was absolutely certain that the Duke of Kensington had not asked for her hand because his feelings had suddenly run away with him. "The way he looked at me held nothing affectionate, nothing…nothing that might suggest he would…" Again, Rosabel buried her face in her hands. If only it made sense, she pleaded with fate. If only she could understand.

"All right." Ellie slowly peeled Rosabel's hands from her face. "Talk to me. Do not hide how you feel. Do not ignore it. Talk to me."

A sob escaped Rosabel's throat, and she was glad no one but her trusted cousin was near. "What can I say? Nothing I say will change what is. Nothing I say will explain what is."

Again taking her hands in hers, Ellie scooted closer on the bench. "All right, if he did not ask for your hand because he fancies you, then he might simply believe you would make him a good wife."

"But why would he? He knows nothing about me." A million thoughts raced through her mind. "I have no fortune, no connections and no family name to throw in the bargain. All I have is a plain face and a past born out of a scandal. Why would he choose me?" Rosabel raised her eyes to her cousin. "Why not you? Not that I wish him on you, not with his cold countenance, but you would be a good match. You come from a respectable family, have a sizable dowry and…and you're beautiful."

Ellie pressed her lips together, shaking her head. "You're doing it again. You only think of yourself as full of defects. What your mother did was not your fault. People are wrong to hold it against you. But all your life, you have accepted the notion that because your mother went against her family's wishes somehow that has tainted you as well." She squeezed Rosabel's hand. "Maybe he saw past it. Maybe he saw you for who you really are."

A fleeting smile crossed Rosabel's face as she looked at her cousin, the sister she never had. "I love you for saying this, but we both know it is not true. Even if my face appealed to him, it would not be enough to tempt him. His station is far beyond mine, and there are many reasons that speak against a union between the two of us. No, I am sure there is a reason, but I am equally sure that we will not discover it. And that's what scares me." Remembering the cold grip that had settled upon her heart as his eyes had stared into her soul, Rosabel shivered. "I fear there is some evil to him."

Ellie gasped, but Rosabel held up a hand to silence any objection.

"I don't mean to think ill of people, and maybe there is nothing to it. It's just a feeling I have. A feeling I cannot shake, and it terrifies me."

Pulling her close, Ellie put an arm around her cousin's shoulders, holding tight. "Do not think like that. You are just scared because all of this is happening so fast and so unexpectedly." An encouraging smile tucked up the corners of her cousin's mouth. "Look at the bright side. You are going to be a duchess. You will have everything you could possibly want." Ellie's smile grew bigger. "Children. You will have children. Children of your own. That ought to cheer you up."

Feeling the heat crawl up her face, Rosabel looked at her hands. "I do want children." Her gaze lifted ever so slightly to look into her cousin's eyes. "I'm just not sure I want his." Her gaze dropped. "Am I an awful person to say this?"

Ellie shook her head and smiled. "No. You could never be an awful person. I love you dearly, and I know you like no one else on this earth does. And I tell you now, the only fault I see in you is your readiness to think ill of yourself." She brushed a hand over Rosabel's cheek as fresh tears threatened. "You are nervous, and you have a right to be. This is all happening very fast, but after you've had some time to get used to this situation, you will see its benefits."

"Do you really believe that?"

"I do." Ellie nodded. "Have faith. Everything will sort itself out. Who knows why he seems so cold? Maybe there is pain in his past just like there is in yours. It will be up to you to discover what kind of a person he is."

Rosabel nodded. "Maybe you're right." Again remembering his eyes, she hoped her cousin was, indeed, right. She desperately hoped that at least one day, their marriage would hold something akin to affection. "I still wish things were different. I never dreamed of being a duchess."

"Then what did you dream of?" Ellie asked, patting her hand.

Rosabel shrugged. "I can't say." Dreams were dangerous. Dreams promised nothing but disappointment. Rosabel had never entertained the notion. Never had she dared to dream of dreams.

4

THE WEDDING

*T*he fortnight passed much faster than Rosabel could have ever anticipated, and only once in all that time had she laid eyes on her betrothed; at their engagement party held in her uncle's home. He had kept to himself though and not spoken a word to her. To this day, she had no idea what his voice sounded like. His eyes, however, she knew well by now. While the blue they held might have reminded her of a calm lake glistening in the morning sun in another man, the blue in his eyes only brought to mind the icicles she sometimes found hanging outside her window in the deep of winter.

Ever since that morning when the Duke of Kensington had asked for her hand, her aunt had been busy tending to all necessary preparations in anticipation of her upcoming nuptials. And while Rosabel herself received the occasional instruction to tend to a minor item on her aunt's list, she was never consulted when it came to the actual event and what it ought to be like. Never once did her aunt wonder what flowers she would like to see that day? Or what dish she might care for that morning? In a strange way, Rosabel felt like none of it concerned her, like she had no connection whatsoever to the upcoming wedding. If she only didn't have to attend, Rosabel thought. If only the past fortnight had been a dream, and all she had to do was wake up and find herself in her room, the bright morning sun shining in, promising a day of leisure spent in her cousin's company.

If only.

Her hopes were dashed though, when Rosabel woke once more in her own bed and realized that her wedding day had come at last. Only a shell of herself, she went through the motions. After breakfast with her family, she was led upstairs to her room, where the maids had already laid out her wedding dress. Seeing it, Rosabel's eyes filled with tears, but she blinked them away before her aunt could lecture her.

"You will be a beautiful bride," Ellie beamed, giving her hand a slight squeeze. "Smile for me, will you?" she whispered.

Feeling the corners of her mouth tuck up at her cousin's emphatic words, Rosabel tried her best. "Thank you."

Rushing into the room, her aunt took charge immediately, and before Rosabel knew what was happening, she was looking at herself wearing a wedding dress in the tall mirror brought in from her aunt's room. Busy hands tucked here and smoothed fabric back there. Her hair was drawn back and pinned up in the latest fashion, a few strands forced into bouncing curls, softening the somewhat rigid structure.

"Well, you look handsome enough," her aunt mused, looking her up and down. "Do try to smile. This is a happy occasion after all," she reminded her. "As unexpected as this is, we could not have hoped for a better match. He is quite amiable, and you are lucky to have caught his eye although I still cannot fathom why."

"Mother!" Ellie chastised.

Lady Harlowe completely ignored her daughter's words but, instead, looked at her and said, "You have to admit that you would have made a more desirable bride. How any man can favour Rosabel over you, I cannot understand."

"Mother!" Ellie exclaimed, a deep red creeping up her cheeks as she looked back and forth between Rosabel and her mother.

Rosabel, however, was used to her aunt's attitude toward her and had expected nothing less. "Do not worry yourself, Dear Cousin. I have wondered the same thing myself."

Her aunt's face brightened. "There you have it, my child. At least Rosabel has enough sense to see the truth."

Before Ellie could intervene on her behalf once more, Rosabel put a hand on her shoulder and slightly shook her head. Nothing her cousin would say could change the impression her aunt had of her. They would never be close. Rosabel had accepted that long ago. She was all the more thankful for her cousin's affection.

Looking at herself in the mirror, Rosabel saw the slight tremble in her hands as she brushed them down the front of her dress. The face that smiled back at her didn't seem genuine, and she hoped her betrothed would not hold it against her. He could not expect her to go into this marriage with a joyous heart, could he?

As another thought struck, Rosabel closed her eyes to maintain her composure. Before she had gone to bed the night before, her aunt had come to her room. At first, Rosabel had been surprised to see her, but then her feelings had quickly changed as her aunt had begun to speak. In but a few, short, clipped sentences, that showed no consideration for Rosabel's feelings, she had informed her of what her future husband would expect of her on their wedding night. Sinking deeper into her seat, Rosabel had listened, fighting the deep desire to put her hands over her ears. Terrified beyond compare, she had barely slept a wink. The thought of allowing that man into her bed had purged all breath from her body, and the shivers had started anew. Would his hands be as cold as his eyes?

In the carriage, Rosabel clung to her cousin, squeezing her hand as though she would be swept away if she didn't hold on tightly. But Ellie didn't mind. Gently, she held her hand, here and there stroking her arm and murmuring words of comfort. Pointing out the window, she tried to draw Rosabel's attention away from her jittery nerves and to the beautiful flowers growing by the side of the road and across the meadows they passed. But Rosabel could not appreciate what she saw. Her gaze was focused at what awaited her once the carriage came to a standstill. At times, she did her best to raise her own spirits, lecturing herself harshly for entertaining all these gloomy thoughts. Giving in to her fear and allowing it to surround her, extinguishing every rational thought, every chance of calming herself was a child's way of dealing with a world she didn't understand. And she was anything but a child. From a young age, she had been forced to deal with a reality as harsh as any she could have imagined in her mind. And she had persevered. She would persevere again.

Thoughts like these made her feel strong; if only for a moment. Then the dark fear returned, stronger than before, and Rosabel once again succumbed to it, feeling her hands tremble and a sickening sensation settle in her stomach that threatened to expel the meagre breakfast she had eaten that morning. In these moments, Rosabel thought she would not be able to get through the day. She thought she'd pass out any second. Strangely enough that thought seemed desirable. Then at least, she would be free from her emotions; if only for the moment.

Was life only about moments? She wondered. One changing into another, turning your life upside down, defying gravity and setting everything ablaze. Closing her eyes and taking a deep breath, Rosabel hoped that the moment her heart would finally stop tormenting her would come sooner rather than later. She longed to feel at peace again. The past fortnight had taken its toll, and Rosabel wasn't sure how much longer she could force herself to function and play the role everyone, most of all her aunt and uncle, expected of her.

As the carriage wheels churned to a stop, Rosabel's head flew up. Peeking out the window, she found herself at Camden Hall, the estate her betrothed had let when coming to the county. When would she see his real home? She wondered, realizing she didn't even know where it was located. Would she soon be forced to leave her friends and family behind? At the thought, another shiver ran down her spine.

A footman opened the door, and Ellie stepped outside. For just a second, Rosabel felt frozen to the spot and thought that no force on this earth could persuade her to move. But then her uncle's voice reached her mind, "Rosabel, may I escort you inside?", and suddenly years of complying with everyone's wishes and expectations took over. Rosabel felt herself move from the carriage and step outside into the late autumn sun.

Although she had seen Camden Hall before, even if only from a distance, Rosabel drew in a breath at the stately home that was to be hers by the end of the day. Grand and magnificent, the manor loomed into the sky before her, and Rosabel wondered if only the way her own fate was tied to this house made her consider it with unease. She couldn't help but see something dark hiding in the shadows, behind the rows upon rows of windows, and even the door opening to the small chapel seemed like a doorway into hell itself.

"Don't be absurd!" she called herself to reason once more. "Take a deep breath! Your fears are running away with you again!"

As her uncle tucked her onward, Rosabel fell into step beside him. Watching Ellie and her aunt enter the small chapel without being struck down or sucked into the earth, Rosabel glanced around, trying to see inside and spot the man she was to marry in a matter of minutes.

Her uncle led her through the door, and they proceeded down the aisle. To her right and left, the few guests that had been invited to observe the ceremony did not fill the pews facing the altar. More were to arrive to the festivities later.

Rosabel's eyes glided over her family; her aunt's distant smile, the shining eyes of her young cousins fidgeting in their seats, unable to keep still, and Ellie's encouraging smile, anchoring Rosabel to the here and now. Then she saw people she had known all her life, people who had never quite looked at her with open, unprejudiced eyes. Then there were those, only a few, she had never seen before and assumed them to be family or friends of her betrothed. One of them she recognized as the tall, blond gentleman she had seen in her future husband's company at the Davenport's engagement celebration.

As they proceeded further down the aisle, Rosabel's eyes met his, and a charming smile lit up his face. Through her veil, Rosabel saw his head bow ever so slightly, and she was touched by this simple, yet most welcome gesture of kindness. Again, he reminded her of the sun. A sun that shone so brightly, not even the night could subdue it, and for a moment, just a moment, Rosabel wished he were the one awaiting her by the altar.

Instantly, she chastised herself for such a terrible thought, reminding herself that he was her betrothed's friend. Wasn't he titled as well? A duke? She tried to remember but couldn't quite recall his name.

Taking another deep breath, Rosabel reluctantly directed her gaze to the front where the Duke of Kensington stood tall and expressionless by the altar. His dark hair smoothed back, he looked at her with the same cold eyes she had seen in her dreams for many nights now. And again, they did not fail to conjure all the apprehension she had felt the first time she'd seen him.

Once more, Rosabel wondered why he wanted to marry her for it clearly did not contribute to his happiness. If anything at all, he looked about as miserable as Rosabel felt herself. Coming to stand beside him, she wondered if there was something pressuring him into his marriage as well. Had he not chosen freely? Did he resent her because unknowingly she was the means to force his hand?

As her uncle released her arm and stepped back to sit down with his wife and children, Rosabel suddenly felt the loss of the only family she had remaining. Standing beside a stranger, she barely heard the priest's words as he bound them together. Her sense of loss was too acute, and tears pooled in the corners of her eyes. Grateful for the veil hiding her emotions from her husband and the few people gathered to celebrate their union, Rosabel tried to compose herself. Blinking back her tears, she took a deep breath, but as much as she tried, her heart would not slow down, hammering in her chest as though she was prey hunted by a fierce predator, desperately seeking to escape.

Murmuring her 'I do' as though some unseen force had taken control of her, Rosabel watched in utter shock as her new husband turned toward her and lifted her veil. As she fought to put a smile on her face, Rosabel saw no answering expression on his countenance. The breath caught in her throat, and the lump in her belly grew heavier and heavier as the Duke of Kensington slowly leaned toward her for the celebratory kiss, sealing their marriage vows. His breath brushed over her cheek, and as though an icy chill had caught hold of her, Rosabel closed her eyes, hoping for it to pass as quickly as possible.

When his lips brushed hers, Rosabel was surprised to find them soft and warm. As she opened her eyes, however, he had already turned toward their audience. Then he took her hand, drew her arm through his and led her out of the chapel and into the light of day.

The wedding celebration was short-lived. For all the impact it had on Rosabel's life, it appeared a mere trifle to everyone else. Her new husband kept to the shadows whenever possible, occasionally nodding to people, accepting their congratulations with a quick and not at all heart-felt smile, and seemed to avoid his new bride at all cost. Her aunt and uncle looked mildly pleased that she had made a good match after all. However, whenever they looked at her, Rosabel still saw the resentment on their faces that her new husband had not taken their daughter for his bride, instead.

Nonetheless, her uncle made a gallant speech, wishing the

newlyweds a lifetime of happiness. The other speaker was her husband's friend, Edmond Dunsworth, Duke of Cromwell, as he introduced himself to those who were not familiar with him. A sparkle came to his eyes as he raised his glass and offered his congratulations. For a second, his gaze turned to her, and for a moment, Rosabel thought that he had winked at her. However, her eyes had to be deceiving her for nothing could have been more ridiculous. Nonetheless, Rosabel thought him a pleasant, young man. Why? She did not know. But whenever he glanced in her direction, there was something in his eyes that suggested that he saw her pain and felt for her. Whenever their eyes happened to meet, Rosabel glanced away quickly, unsure how her husband would react to such behaviour. The Duke of Kensington, however, did not notice since he was paying his new bride no attention at all.

When the orchestra began to play, the groom led the bride to their first dance as husband and wife. While a courteous smile was plastered on his face for the duration of the dance, Rosabel could feel in the stiffness of his hands how much he resented having to touch her. A shiver ran down her body as she realized how much her husband detested her. What had she done wrong? He had asked for her hand after all. Had she somehow encouraged him? It wasn't possible. They had never even spoken to one another. How could she have possibly forced his hand?

Deep down in the core of Rosabel's being, under layers and layers of obedience and complacence, a tiny spark of anger ignited. How dare he blame her for anything that had happened?

As he led her around the dance floor, reluctant though sure-footed, she glanced at his face from under her eyelashes and saw that his eyes were distant. He was not looking at her. He seemed to have forgotten that she was in his arms that very second. Looking at him more openly, she wondered where his mind had wandered off to; on his wedding day of all days.

Before long, the dance ended, and while their guests heartily engaged in the festivities, her husband remained seated for the rest of the day, not even glancing in her direction. After her uncle asked her for another dance with her as was tradition, Rosabel thanked him and followed him to the floor again. Never having been a talented dancer, she was relieved when the music ended once more. She intended to return to her seat at the table when the Duke of Cromwell suddenly appeared before her as though he had shot out of the floor.

A gasp escaping her lips, her hand flew to her chest. "My," she exclaimed. "You startled me."

He bowed low, a charming smile on his lips. "My apologies, your grace." Rosabel's heart skipped a beat as she heard her new address for the first time. *Your grace*, how strange it sounded. Not at all right. "May I ask for this dance?"

Seeing the slightly mischievous twinkle in his eyes that made him so endearing, she dared not decline. Again, he bowed to her and taking her hand, led her back the way she had tried to escape.

As they stood up together, Rosabel's face broke into a smile, and for the duration of their dance, she forgot the occasion that had them all gather under this roof. The Duke of Cromwell was all politeness and looked at her as though she was the answer to his most fervent prayers. Feeling a slight blush creep up her cheeks, Rosabel more than once felt the need to avert her eyes.

When the music stopped, he led her off the dance floor but remained by her side, offering her a glass of punch. "You make a lovely bride," he said, reminding Rosabel of a reality she had all but forgotten. "My friend is in a most fortunate position to call you his wife."

Turning her eyes to the floor, Rosabel didn't answer, didn't know how.

"Do not worry," the duke continued. "He growls, but he does not bite."

Observing him carefully, Rosabel again detected a faint twinkle in his eyes as though he was jesting with her. "What makes you say that?"

The duke laughed. "The sour countenance he cannot seem to shake." His eyes turned to his friend, still sitting in his seat at the table, scowl still on his face. "I believe I am not revealing a secret by stating that he does not yet appreciate you becoming his wife, but−," his eyes sought hers with an intensity that made her catch her breath, "but he will. Give him time."

Feeling herself nod, Rosabel was tempted to ask why on earth his friend had chosen her for his bride if so obviously he did not want her. But she didn't. The words wouldn't come. After all, it was not proper to ask such a question, and besides, it would not change the fact that she now was married to a man who did not want her.

Not long after the sun had taken its leave for the night, most of the guests departed, once again offering their congratulations to the *happy* couple. Her uncle and his family were the last to leave. After a few curt words from them, Rosabel turned to Ellie, clinging to her as though afraid to drown. "I wish you didn't have to go," she whispered, squeezing her cousin's hand in a way that had her sinews stand out white. "I wish I didn't have to stay."

An apologetic smile on her face, Ellie drew her into an embrace. "Do not worry. Nothing is ever as bad as it might seem at first. Who knows? He may be the most gentle of men, and it's only large crowds that make him uncomfortable." She stepped back and looked into Rosabel's eyes. "I am certain everything will turn out all right. Have faith."

Rosabel nodded, but her cousin's words seemed a hopeful wish at best, and deep down, she did not believe them to be true.

After waving their goodbyes, her uncle's carriage soon vanished from sight, and when the door closed, Rosabel turned around...and was alone with her new husband. Swallowing hard, she raised her chin and looked at him, waiting for him to give her any clue as to what would happen next.

For a second, he held her gaze, though she felt like he was looking right through her at something only he could see. Then he cleared his throat and rang the bell to call the housekeeper. "Mary will show you to your room," was all he said, before he turned around and without a look back, walked away in the direction of his study.

Rosabel remained alone in the dimly lit hall until a middle-aged woman appeared and begged her to follow. Walking up the winding staircase, they turned to the east wing, walked down a long darkened hallway, decorated with landscape artistry, until the maid stopped before a heavy-set door. Gesturing to the left at a door farther down the hall, she said, "This is the master suite." Then, without any further remarks, she opened the door to Rosabel's new bedchamber.

Were the circumstances different, Rosabel would have enjoyed the simple, yet elegant furnishings of the room. The windows looked to the east, so she would be able to wake with the sun. A four-posted bed stood at the back wall. Smooth rugs were laid out across the floor, leading up to two armchairs sitting snugly under the bay windows. She would have felt at home here.

If only.

Without a word, the maid, a mildly sour expression drawing down her eyebrows, helped her undress and slip into her nightgown. The saying *Silent as the graves* echoed in Rosabel's mind, and a shiver ran down her back. The room felt like a tomb, and the moment the maid took her leave and closed the door behind her, Rosabel's hand went to her throat. She couldn't breathe.

Sinking into one of the armchairs, Rosabel closed her eyes, focusing all her thoughts on drawing the life-sustaining air into her lungs. How had she ended up in this place? How had her life changed so drastically in a mere fortnight?

As her gaze fell on the bed, Rosabel instantly looked away, her hands shaking. When would he come to her? Glancing at the door that connected their two bedchambers, Rosabel rose to her feet and before her nerves could dissuade her, tiptoed across the room, pressing an ear to the door. Everything was quiet on the other side. Her husband was probably still in his study, avoiding her. Should she get under the covers? Should she sit down to read while waiting for him? How much time would he give her before he made his way upstairs? Her aunt's instructions had not been that detailed, and Rosabel was at a loss.

After wandering the room, here and there picking up decorative artefacts, turning them in her hands and putting them back down, Rosabel sat down at her vanity, combing out her hair. As she looked at herself in the mirror, she hardly recognized the woman she saw. In a way, her old self had disappeared the second her lips had uttered the words 'I do'. Who was this woman who now looked back at her? A stranger? What would her life be like?

As time ticked by, Rosabel's mind was tormented by all sorts of questions, and before long, a headache started pounding behind her temples. Placing a wet cloth on her forehead, she lay down on the bed and closed her eyes. The thought that her husband might object to finding her this way crossed her mind but was instantly pushed aside by the tiny spark once more igniting within her. If he didn't like it, he shouldn't have kept her waiting this long!

Eyes still closed, Rosabel heard the grandfather clock in the hall chime. Counting the strokes, she found that it was already midnight. What was he doing?

Annoyed, she snuggled closer into the covers, trying to relax, and before long was fast asleep.

Opening the door connecting his chamber to his wife's, Graham stopped in the door frame when he saw her curled up under the covers. For a moment, he stood there, eyes focused on the sleeping woman upon the bed. Gone was the sour disposition he'd held on to all day. He felt drained, his eyes heavy, not with sleep though.

All day he had spent fighting the memories that lurked on the horizon. Doing his best to keep them locked up had taken all his concentration, and most of what had passed before his eyes had eluded him.

Seeing her now, lying there, sleeping peacefully, Graham took a deep breath, fighting down a sense of guilt and betrayal. Her mere presence in this house felt wrong. She ought not to be here.

Silently taking a step into the room, he looked at her face, dark hair spilling over the pillow. Slowly, Graham unclenched his hands. There was no resemblance. He had chosen well. His new wife would not be a constant reminder of what he had lost. At least, he very much hoped so.

Returning to his own room, he closed the door and retired.

5

A JOURNEY IS ANNOUNCED

As she never drew the curtains, come morning the warm rays of the early sun touched her face, warming her, and Rosabel awakened with a smile. Her headache was gone, and she rubbed a hand over her face, smoothing back her hair.

There had been a moment of unaware bliss before her mind reminded her where she was. Looking about the room as though searching for something, Rosabel saw no sign of her husband, concluding that he had never come to her bed. Though grateful beyond expression, she couldn't help but wonder why. Did he not want an heir? If that hadn't been the reason for marrying her, then what had? More questions rose, questions to which the answers eluded her.

Shortly after, a knock sounded on the door, and Rosabel bid them come in in a shaky voice. Relieved, she saw a young woman in a maid's uniform enter. She curtsied, a warm smile on her face. "Good morning, your grace. May I assist you with dressing?"

Rosabel nodded and slid out of bed. "Thank you. What is your name?"

"Bridget, your grace." Opening Rosabel's trunk standing by the

47

foot of the bed, still unpacked, she retrieved a lovely, purple gown, that highlighted Rosabel's dark hair and fair skin, matching the violet sparks in her hazel eyes perfectly. "I am to accompany you on your journey."

"My journey?" Seeing her face in the mirror shift into a frown, Rosabel glanced down as Bridget placed her shoes before her. "What journey?"

Looking up, Bridget's eyes narrowed. "The journey to—"

In that instant, the door flew open, and Mary rushed into the room. "Make haste!" she called to Bridget before quickly curtsying to Rosabel. After ushering the other maid out the door, she turned back, eyes quickly assessing Rosabel's appearance, and with a hint of disapproval in her expression, said, "Let me escort you to the dining room, your grace."

Once again, Rosabel followed the sour-looking woman down the stairs to the back of the house towards the gardens. Not even by daylight did her new home look appealing to her. Dark corners remained, and longing for the company of someone familiar, Rosabel felt her loneliness acutely. This was her first day as Duchess of Kensington. How would she be able to live like this for the rest of her life if she was even now ready to give up?

A footman opened the door and bowed to her as she entered. Feeling more than just a little uncomfortable at such a treatment, Rosabel gave him a quick smile and stepped toward the long table. Her hands trembled even though she did not see her husband sitting at its head. Nor was there a table setting laid out for him. She spotted only one at the downward end to which the maid beckoned her.

Taking her seat, Rosabel looked about. "Will his grace not be joining me?"

The maid shook her head, gesturing to one of the footmen to bring in Rosabel's breakfast. "His grace eats at the break of dawn." After watching the footman's every move like a hawk, she turned back to Rosabel. "However, he requested to see you after you have eaten."

Then Mary left, leaving a much younger and rather insecure looking maid to watch over the breakfast proceedings. Rosabel found herself alone in a room with a maid who barely glanced at her, let alone spoke a word. From the slight tremble in her hands, Rosabel guessed that this was a new position for her as well.

Forcing every bite down her throat, Rosabel felt her heart hammering in her chest. Would this ever stop? Would she ever feel safe again? Content? Happy even?

When she finally decided she could not eat another bite without knowing what the duke wished to talk to her about, Rosabel rose from the table. Instantly, the maid approached. "Will you show me to his grace's study?"

The maid paled. "Your grace, I...I do not know...I mean, I—"

A smile on her face, Rosabel lifted her hand. "Do not worry yourself. I am sure I will find it," she said with more confidence than she felt. In a way, she felt better seeing that she was not the only one forced into a new situation that made her hands tremble and the breath catch in her throat.

Stepping out into the hall, she turned back to the west of the building until she came upon the entry hall, where only last night she had said goodbye to her family. Remembering that the duke had walked away toward the west end of the house, she followed his example. As Rosabel set one step before the other, the confidence she had felt only moments before seemed to evaporate into thin air. Her nerves got the better of her again, and by the time she found herself outside a heavy oak door that she suspected led to her husband's study, her hands were shaking and the cold of the morning air raised goose bumps on her skin.

Her knock sounded weak, even to her own ears, and when his voice called for her to enter, Rosabel was ready to bolt. Instead, she took a deep breath and entered, a part of her curious to finally exchange words with the man she was married to.

The Duke of Kensington sat behind a massive oak desk but stood upon her entering. Bowing slightly, he indicated the chair opposite him and took his own again after she had seated herself. "I bid you a good morning, my lady," he forced out through slightly clenched teeth, and Rosabel felt reminded of a lion ready to attack.

"Good morning, my lord," she replied, her voice wavering.

His dark blue eyes seemed guarded as he opened his mouth to speak. "My lady, I will be frank. I intend for you to travel to Westmore Manor tomorrow morning. The carriage will depart an hour past daybreak. Ready your things accordingly."

Rosabel's eyes widened. The journey. That was what Bridget had been talking about. He meant to send her away? But why?

"Westmore Manor?" she all but whispered.

"My main residence," he explained, eyes now focused on her. "About a two-day journey north."

Uncomfortable under his scrutiny, Rosabel averted her eyes before gathering her courage and lifting her chin again. "Why do you wish for me to go there, my lord?"

His eyes still fixed on her, he leaned back in his leather armchair and placed his elbows on the armrests, fingers touching as though in deep thought. "Since I am detained by business and shall be for the foreseeable future, I intend for you to act as Lady Georgiana's guide in every way that she requires."

Rosabel's face settled into a frown. "Lady Georgiana?"

Staring at her as though trying to read her thoughts, the duke simply said, "My daughter."

To Rosabel, his words were like a slap in the face. Her eyes flew open, and she stared most unbecomingly back at him. Had this been the reason he'd married her? So she would take care of his child?

"I expect you to treat her with as much respect and kindness as you bestowed on your cousins."

Had he been watching her? Rosabel wondered, feeling her mind zone in and out, trying to focus on something tangible. If he needed someone to take her of his daughter, surely he could have hired a governess. "How long am I to remain at Westmore Manor?" she asked, knowing the answer full well but needing to hear it nonetheless.

He shrugged as though she ought to know. "Permanently."

Retreating to her room, though temporary it was, Rosabel once more sank into the armchair under the bay windows. How many more surprises would she have to handle? Would she continue to be moved across the chess board like a pawn? Would it ever be her turn to decide on a move?

His daughter. He had a daughter. He had been married before. What had happened to his wife?

Entangled beyond hope, Rosabel's thoughts raced through her mind, setting the world a-spin. Her eyes closed, hoping to regain some sort of quiet, of balance. But it wouldn't do. She hadn't even thought to ask her husband how old the girl was. Was she almost grown up? Or still a child? A babe even? Had her mother died in childbirth? How long ago had it happened? Was this the reason for his cold eyes? Was he grieving?

Rosabel shook her head. There would be time for all these questions later, and hopefully at some point, she would receive some answers. But today, today she had to go see her family. Fortunately, her husband had not denied her this last shred of comfort. If she was to leave the county for good, she had to at least say goodbye.

The thought of never seeing Ellie again, her friend and confidant, brought fresh tears to her eyes. How was she to go on all by herself? No! Rosabel commanded herself. She would not cry, not now. Now, she had to make herself presentable or she would lose the only chance she had of saying her goodbyes and confiding in her friend one last time.

As the carriage stopped in front of her uncle's house, Rosabel could almost imagine that all had been a mere dream. A nightmare from which she had finally awoken.

Upon entering the front hall, her little cousins flew into her arms, showering her with hugs and kisses. Smiling at them, Rosabel blinked away tears, brushing her hand over their little heads, trying desperately to memorize their faces.

"What is the meaning of this?" Her aunt strode into the hall, eyes scanning the scene before her. "What are you doing here? Is there a problem?"

From the tone in her voice, Rosabel could tell that her aunt was more concerned for herself and the effect any scandal would have on her family's reputation than for her niece's well-being.

Rising to her feet, Rosabel faced her aunt. "Do not worry yourself. I am only here to bid you goodbye." Her aunt's eyes narrowed. "My husband sends me to his estate up north. I do not know when I will be returning." If at all.

Her aunt nodded. "I see. Well then, have a safe trip." A curt smile came to her features but vanished as quickly as it had appeared. "I am sure you wish to see Elsbeth. She is in the gardens."

Rosabel nodded her thanks and strode outside in search of her cousin.

As expected, she found her sitting in the pavilion, their pavilion, their hiding place, the place where they had spent many hours in their childhood and beyond, sharing secrets and talking about their dreams and fears. These carefree days seemed to have been a lifetime ago.

"I thought I'd find you here," Rosabel said as she approached.

At her cousin's voice, Ellie lifted her head, and Rosabel saw her eyes were red-rimmed. She had been crying. Worried, she hastened over, putting an arm around her cousin's shoulders. "Is something wrong? Why are you crying?"

Brushing away her tears, Ellie tried to smile. "Do not worry, Dear Cousin. It is nothing. I was only sitting here, remembering all the many days we spent together." Her eyes swept over their surroundings as Rosabel's had only a moment before. Then she turned to look at her. "I am going to miss you. I'm going to miss seeing you every day." Ellie took a deep breath, her smile growing deeper. "I'm being silly. You still live only a moment away. You did not move to the end of the world."

At her cousin's words, Rosabel's expression turned grave, and she looked away.

"What's the matter?" Ellie's eyes narrowed as she searched Rosabel's face.

Taking a deep breath, Rosabel lifted her gaze off the ground. "I am sorry to be the bearer of bad news, but...," she hesitated until Ellie's eyes urged her on, "my husband is sending me away."

"Sending you away?"

Rosabel nodded. "To his estate up north."

Ellie scooted away a little, facing her cousin with a confused frown on her features. "Why? Is he not going with you? Why would he take up Camden Hall and send you away? That does not make sense!"

Rosabel shrugged. "Honestly, I understand his motives in this regard as little as I understand his motives in marrying me." Brushing imaginary lint off her dress, Rosabel continued, "All I know is that he is sending me to his estate because he wants me to...take care of his daughter."

The last words flew out of Rosabel's mouth, and it took Ellie a moment to comprehend them. Then her eyes bulged. "What? He has a daughter?"

Rosabel nodded, not knowing what else to say.

"He was married before?" Ellie mumbled as though to herself. "Did you know this?"

Vehemently, Rosabel shook her head. "I had no idea. But I am guessing that his wife died not too long ago and that his remarrying so soon after her death is only for the sake of his daughter. That is the only thing that would explain why he married me even though he can't stand being in the same room with me."

"Unbelievable!" Ellie muttered. "Although I feel for him, he is not being fair to you. What are you going to do?"

A short laugh escaped Rosabel. "What can I do but do as he says? He is my husband now, whether I like it or not. I cannot disobey him."

Staring at her friend, Ellie's eyes once more filled with tears. "So you're leaving? When?"

"At daybreak tomorrow." Sniffing herself, Rosabel brushed the tears from the corners of her eyes. "I do not know when I will be back. From what he said, I believe I shall never return." And with that, she threw herself into her cousin's arms, clinging to her as much as Ellie held on herself. Their shared sobs mingled with the joyful chirping of birds and crickets.

When they drew apart again, dabbing at her eyes, Ellie wondered, "Why would he be so secretive about everything? Why did he not talk to you before his proposal?"

Rosabel shrugged. "He does not seem to be the kind of man who shares his thoughts with others. He has every right to act this way, and I have no right to question his decisions."

"I never thought things would turn out like this," Ellie said, placing her hand on her cousin's. "I am still hoping that one day you'll be happy in this marriage."

Rosabel shook her head. "I doubt it." She forced a smile on her face. "But, at least, I get to be a mother."

"How old is the girl?"

"I didn't think to ask."

For a second, Ellie's face remained grave until it suddenly split into a grin. "No matter how old she is before long you will have children of your own. Surely, that is something to look forward to."

Feeling herself blush, Rosabel looked down at her hands. "We'll see," was all she could mumble.

"Was your wedding night not to your liking?" Ellie wondered, trying to glimpse at her face. "I hear it is not all that pleasurable for women, but it is our duty and it makes us mothers."

Wringing her hands, Rosabel glanced at her cousin, not knowing what to say.

Ellie shook her head. "Do not say a word if you do not wish to."

Grateful, Rosabel smiled at her. She didn't know what to say, much less wanted to. While she had been relieved that her husband had chosen not to visit her bridal chamber, this decision, like many others, only brought more questions, more complications. Sure enough, Rosabel was married. But would the only good thing that a woman could hope for in a marriage be denied to her? Would she ever be a mother?

6

A NEW HOME

The carriage seemed to sway in tune with the fields of grass, tall stalks dancing to the symphony of a calm breeze. Everywhere colours grew in intensity as autumn approached on fast heels, painting the world in reds and browns.

Departing Camden Hall at daybreak, Rosabel had not felt a hint of regret at leaving her new home. After all, she had scarcely had had time to make it so. She had wondered if her husband would see her off, but the Duke of Kensington had not made an appearance.

Now sitting in the carriage, Rosabel was grateful for Bridget's presence. She had liked the young maid immediately and was dying to learn more about her new husband as well as his daughter and former wife. Unsure of how to introduce such a sensitive topic, Rosabel slightly fidgeted in her seat, stealing glances at the woman sitting across from her.

A small person herself, Bridget did not appear shy but rather content to sit in silence. Her eyes faced out the window, taking in the landscape flying by. Her hands lay folded in her lap as she rested her head on the backrest and looked, for all intents and purposes, at ease.

When the sun finally climbed higher, Rosabel bundled all her courage and said, "It is a beautiful day, is it not?"

Bridget nodded, looking at her, an awed smile on her face. "It certainly is, your grace." She hesitated, but seeing Rosabel's eager face, she continued, "I've never been far from home. Coming to Camden Hall was the first and only trip I've ever taken."

Rosabel nodded. "I have never been anywhere myself." Glancing out the window for a moment, she returned her attention back to Bridget. "So, you worked at Westmore Manor before?"

Bridget nodded. "And my mother before me. The family has always been good to us, which is why I was particularly glad when I was taken into service at the duke's estate."

Filing away every bit of information she could obtain, Rosabel asked, "Is your mother still in service?"

Bridget shook her head no. "You see, I am the youngest of ten."

Rosabel nodded and taking a deep breath asked, "And did you know the Lady Georgiana?" Feeling her nerve endings tingle, she waited, all but patiently.

Again, Bridget nodded. "I came into service maybe two years before she was born."

Georgiana cannot be that old then, Rosabel thought. "Can you tell me a little about her?"

Bridget shrugged. "Not much. She was but five when we set off for Camden Hall. But I remember she was a delightful child, her mother's image." Eyes suddenly jerking up, Bridget looked at her. "I beg your pardon, your grace."

Rosabel shook her head. "Do not worry yourself. I do not consider the former duchess a forbidden topic. She was Lady Georgiana's mother and as such deserves to be held in high esteem."

A smile lit up Bridget's face. "Your grace is most kind. Lady Georgiana will be delighted to have a new mother such as yourself."

An embarrassed smile played on Rosabel's lips at the young woman's compliment. After all, since she was not tied to the duke on an emotional level, speaking about his former wife did not pain her. She felt no jealousy. Instead, she pictured the woman's little girl, left all alone at only five years old. Instantly, Rosabel's heart went out to her.

The rest of the journey passed in a pleasant manner. Occasionally, Rosabel dared to ask another question but could not learn any more material information. The night they spent at an inn, resting their travel-weary bodies. Only Rosabel's mind would not give her any repose. The little girl's face, based on Bridget's description, hovered before her, bright blue eyes, a button nose and a dazzling smile framed by golden curls. Every now and then, the pictures shifted, and the golden curls turned black, and Rosabel recognized herself in the face before her.

The loss of her parents had changed her in more ways than she could name. What had this little girl felt when her mother had suddenly died? And when her father had left her to grieve alone? Tears came to her eyes, and from a day's distance away, Rosabel vowed to be everything she could, to heal the wounds inflicted on such a young soul.

When they set off the next morning, Rosabel was surprised to discover her spirits were indeed heightened. Though still apprehensive about the situation at large, she was looking forward to meeting Lady Georgiana as well as her new role in the little girl's life.

However, when the sun began to set and the carriage finally drove down the lane, passing through expansive gardens, leading up to the manor, a slight shiver ran down Rosabel's spine. Looming like a giant in a darkening world, the house held nothing friendly in the way it peered into the dark. Remembering that same feeling from when she had first laid eyes on Camden Hall, Rosabel wondered if it was her state of mind which only allowed her to perceive her future home as a threat, or if her husband had an uncanny taste of dark obscurities.

Imposing on the sky, the pastoral manor slightly resembled an ancient castle, surrounded by a well-trimmed hedge and a moat-like creek pooling into a small lake on the eastern side of the property. Some windows glowed with light, which only served to remind Rosabel of a monster's glowing eyes, instead of promising warmth and the comfort of human companionship.

Her shoulders back, and taking a deep breath, she stepped from the carriage and approached the steps, leading up to the front door. Bowing deep, a mostly bald man in spotless uniform stood on the upper stair. "Welcome, your grace. Welcome to Westmore Manor. I am Lawrence, the butler."

Giving a quick nod, Rosabel followed him inside, eyes flowing over her new home, trying to determine if her first impression had been correct. Unfortunately, it had. Rosabel couldn't quite tell what gave her the impression, but looking around, she felt reminded of a place untouched by life. A museum or rather a tomb. Darkness lived in every corner, and Rosabel couldn't help but doubt that the darkening sky was its only source.

Turning her attention to Lawrence once more, she found him standing before a long line of servants gathered to welcome her and be introduced to the new mistress. A new shiver came over Rosabel, and she took a deep breath to keep her hands from trembling. *They must not see how unqualified I am to fill this position.* She thought. The former duchess had probably done a marvellous job of running this household. Irrationally, Rosabel wished she were here right now.

From the corner of her eyes, Rosabel saw Bridget get in line with the other maids, one of whom squeezed her hand slightly, giving her a warm smile. Lawrence then proceeded to introduce the staff by stating their name and position within the household. Rosabel was sure she would not remember everything she was told, but she still smiled and slightly bowed her head at each and every one of them.

After dismissing the staff, Lawrence turned back to her. "I will show you to your chamber, your grace."

"Thank you," Rosabel said, still feeling her hands tremble. "But I was hoping to be introduced to the Lady Georgiana tonight. Is she still awake?"

"I believe so," Lawrence said. "If you will follow me, your grace."

After ascending the winding, marble staircase, Rosabel found herself walking down a wide corridor, walls adorned with portraits of people she presumed to be family of generations past, at least, most of them. Among them, she spotted a painting of a young boy, whose features struck her as familiar, but it wasn't until she met his eyes that realization found her. As a young boy, her husband's eyes had been just as blue, but not as cold. She saw laughter in them and joy and couldn't help but wonder what had hardened him so. Had it been his wife's passing?

Finding herself in the east wing, Rosabel waited as Lawrence came to a stop at the very end of the corridor. He knocked, and after a voice called for them to enter, he opened the door, stepping inside.

Her heart hammering in her chest, Rosabel took a deep breath, trying to be as unobtrusive as possible. Then she placed one shaky foot before the other and stepped over the threshold.

In the corner by the window stood a small table, and there on a chair much too tall for her short legs sat Lady Georgiana, barely six years old.

Her wild, golden curls had been brushed back and pinned up in proper fashion, giving her otherwise soft features a strained expression. Her eyes, a deep shade of blue, almost bubbled over as they came to rest on her. For a moment, Rosabel thought she saw the impulse to jump off the chair and rush over to her play on the girl's face. But instead of giving in, the little girl glanced at the stern-looking woman standing across from her and remained seated, her legs dangling excitedly.

"May I introduce, Lady Georgiana Astor," Lawrence said and turning to look at the woman beside the table added, "and her governess, Mrs. Rigsby."

"It is a pleasure to meet you, your grace," Mrs. Rigsby said, though from the tone in her voice Rosabel could tell it to be a lie. Eying her with open perusal, Mrs. Rigsby stood with her hands on her hips, head slightly angled, and looked Rosabel over.

Although her promotion to duchess was a mere two days old, Rosabel instantly objected to the woman's open disrespect and would have liked nothing better than to put her in her place. Instead, she smiled and said, "The pleasure is mine." Then she turned back to the little girl.

"Lady Georgiana, it is a pleasure to meet you," she said, walking over to the table. "I am sorry to be interrupting your dinner."

A shy smile came to the girl's face, and a red blush crept up her cheeks. "Would you like some?" she whispered, fingers working to lift up the heavy plate.

Rosabel smiled, instantly taken with the child, but before she could utter a response, the governess interfered. "Nonsense, the duchess has been on the road all day. Lawrence!" she called, gesturing at the butler who instantly stepped forward. "Take her grace to her rooms, and see to it that she is adequately provided for."

"Certainly," he mumbled, a hint of disapproval in his eyes. However, when Rosabel did not object, he added, "If you will follow me."

Stunned, but unable to speak up, Rosabel took her leave of her new step-daughter, seeing a similar disappointment on her features that she felt in her own heart.

Tucked into bed, Rosabel felt her eyelids heavy on her face. Though beyond tired, sleep just wouldn't come. A month ago, she hadn't even known her husband, and now she was married, had been shipped off to a northern estate, had a step-daughter to care for and a position to fill that felt like a shoe ten times too big. Rosabel knew she would not wear it well. She would stumble and fall, and she would do so under the eyes of everyone watching. Mrs. Rigsby would love to see her falter, Rosabel was certain. For some reason, the woman had taken an immediate dislike to her.

Outside the window, a heavy storm raged, rain drumming on the window as though mimicking her own emotional state. Thunder crashed, and a moment later, lightning sent a bright spark, illuminating her room. Shadows danced, and the old wooden panels creaked as if a thousand hell hounds were trying to burst through the door.

Just as Rosabel closed her eyes, forcing herself to give slumber a fair chance, a sound reached her ears that, even on such a night, seemed out of place. A slight screeching, barely audible, came from the direction of her door, and when another bolt of lightning zigzagged across the sky, she saw the handle of her door turning downward.

Heart speeding up until Rosabel felt its beats pulsing in her ears, she swallowed hard, trying to keep her wits about her. Who would come to her room this late at night? She wondered. And without announcing themselves? It couldn't possibly be her husband asking for his marital rights. The thought made her shiver nonetheless.

When the door slid open ever so slowly, Rosabel sat up, and before her wits could abandon her called, "Who is there?"

Instantly, the door froze.

"Who is there?" Rosabel called again. "Show yourself!"

When no answer came, Rosabel reached for the oil lamp on her bedside table, increasing its flame. Not bothering to dress, she approached the door, still standing ajar.

As she peeked out into the corridor, more shadows danced along the walls although no one was there. Slowly, her heart settled down. Then, when she was about to turn back, the sound of a door closing echoed all the way from down the hall.

"Georgiana," she whispered, unsure how she had come to this conclusion.

Shrugging on a robe, Rosabel hastened down the corridor until she found herself outside the little girl's door. After a soft knock elicited no response, she took a deep breath and put her hand on the handle.

Slowly stepping into the dark room, Rosabel hoped she wouldn't wake the child in case her hunch would prove wrong. However, the second she came around the bed, her eyes fell on a pitiful creature cowering in the corner of the room, knees drawn up, arms hugging her legs. Her eyes were wide like those of a cornered animal, and when another roll of thunder sounded in the deep, a frightened gasp escaped her small lips, her chest rising and falling with her rapid breathing.

In that moment, Rosabel's heart opened and she became Georgiana's mother.

7

A MOTHER AFTER ALL

Seeing the numbing fear in Georgiana's face, Rosabel rushed to her side. She tried to scoop the little girl into her arms, but fear had frozen her in place. Limbs rigid, she gripped her own arms as a lifeline to hold on to. Her skin felt cold. Goosebumps, whether from the chill in the air or fear of the raging storm, covered her arms and legs. She shook all over, the tiny teeth chattering despite her jaw being clenched shut.

At first, she didn't look at Rosabel, her eyes fixed on the window, showing the madness burdening this night. Mumbling soothing words, Rosabel brushed a hand over Georgiana's hair, down her arms and over her cheeks. Slowly, she felt the distance Georgiana had put between herself and the world around her melt away. She blinked, and her head slowly turned from the source of her fear to the young woman kneeling before her. "Mummy?" she whispered.

The words felt like a stab to the heart, and Rosabel clearly saw the loss that still haunted her step-daughter. Smiling with all the reassurance that she could find within herself, Rosabel cupped the little girl's face and looked into her dark blue eyes. "Do not be afraid," she whispered. "You are not alone."

Again, Georgiana blinked, and Rosabel saw recognition flicker in her eyes. The girl took a deep breath, never moving her gaze from Rosabel, and her small hands reached up to rest on the ones holding her face. "Don't leave," she pleaded, tears pooling in the corners of her eyes.

Before Rosabel could answer, another round of thunder shook the house as though the earth was moving. Georgiana flinched, squeezed her eyes shut and all but jumped into Rosabel's arms.

Sitting on the floor, holding the small, fragile body and soul of her new step-daughter in her arms, Rosabel felt tears of her own stream down her face.

Unable to sort through her own feelings in that moment, Rosabel acted on instinct. Rising from the cold floor–her feet had turned to ice a while ago–she carried the precious load in her arms back to her own room. The storm raged more strongly on the side of the house where Georgiana's room was located while her own was relatively quiet in comparison. She closed the door and pulling back the covers slid inside while Georgiana still clung to her.

Small sobs rose from the little girl's throat, and while the storm raged outside, Rosabel held her. She stroked her hair, whispered words of comfort in her ear and noticed with relief that the cold slowly left and a soothing warmth spread through her body.

As Rosabel rocked from side to side, her blanket wrapped around them both, Georgiana's sobs became quieter and quieter until her rapid breathing turned into the quiet rhythm of sleep. Then Rosabel leaned back, relaxing against the pillows, and stole a glance at her step-daughter's face, resting on her shoulder.

Her wild curls looked like a tangled mess, hair matted against her forehead and temples. Her eyes were red-rimmed and a little swollen, and even in the dim light, Rosabel could still see the dried paths her tears had taken down her cheeks.

However, Rosabel's heart saw none of that. Her heart only saw the little angel sleeping in her arms, abandoned by those who had loved her, and responded to it the only way it could; with a mother's love.

Rosabel could almost feel her heart grow as it swelled with the love that suddenly invaded it. So unexpected. So overwhelming. And yet, so simple.

Brushing a hand over Georgiana's cheek, Rosabel wondered why her husband kept his daughter at such a distance. How could he bear to be separated from his child? Did he not long to hold her? Was his heart truly made of stone? Or ice? Cold as ice?

That night, Rosabel did not sleep a wink. She just sat there, resting against the headboard of her bed, holding Georgiana in her arms, and watched the storm subside and eventually the night give way to a new day.

There was nothing she could do about her husband's relationship to his daughter. For whatever reason, he seemed determined to ignore her. And as she most certainly could not bring the girl's mother back from the dead, the only thing she could do was to offer her own heart and hope that in time Georgiana would come to love her back and feel comforted by her presence.

As the early morning sun slowly ascended the horizon, Georgiana began to stir. Her breathing returned from the shallow rhythm of sleep, her arms began to move, and not long after her eyelids started to twitch, her eyes opened.

Smiling at her, Rosabel whispered, "Good morning. I hope you slept well."

Her face only two inches from Rosabel's, Georgiana blinked and then lifted her head off Rosabel's shoulder. Staring at her, she rubbed her eyes. "Who are you?" she asked. "You arrived here last night, did you not?"

Rosabel nodded. "I did. My name is Rosabel." She brushed a strand of hair from the girl's forehead, but Georgiana didn't seem to notice, instead, her eyes wandered around the room. "This is my mummy's room."

For a second, Rosabel froze. "I did not know that. Maybe I can sleep somewhere else."

Georgiana turned to look at her again, her gaze gliding over her eyes, down her nose to her mouth. Rosabel felt as though she was being weight. Then Georgiana shrugged. "You can stay if you like. My mummy doesn't need it anymore."

Ignoring the hint of sadness in the girl's voice, Rosabel said, "Thank you. Maybe later after breakfast you can help me unpack."

A shy smile came to Georgiana's face. "I'd like that. Do you have many beautiful gowns?"

Rosabel laughed. "Some. But you must decide for yourself if they are beautiful. What is your favourite colour?"

Georgiana put a finger to her lips. "Well, I like purple." A smile came to her face. "My mother used to wear purple a lot."

Brushing a hand down Georgiana's arm, Rosabel said, "Purple is a wonderful colour. I can see why your mother loved it."

Georgiana's grin grew bigger at the compliment, showing off her tiny white teeth, and her eyes began to sparkle.

Asking a few more questions, Rosabel watched with contend as the little girl came to life. She talked animatedly about her mother, her favourite horse and the lessons she so disliked. Rosabel was careful to tread lightly, but as much as the loss of her mother was still felt by the little girl, speaking about her also brought delight to her heart.

As the sun slowly climbed over the horizon, reaching inside the room, the whole world seemed aglow. Everything looked brighter and far from gloomy as Rosabel had thought the night before. Maybe it had been her state of mind through which she had seen the house before her. Her room at the very least had been turned into a place of laughter and happiness, and Rosabel looked forward to many more days passed in such delight.

"I love visiting the horses in the stables," Georgiana continued her narration with glistening eyes. "Peter sometimes lets me feed Shadow an apple or a carrot. It tickles." She giggled.

It was the most wonderful sound Rosabel had ever heard. "Who is Peter?" she asked.

"One of the stable boys. He is very nice. He understands about wanting to be outside." Instantly, her eyes dimmed.

Observing her step-daughter closely, Rosabel asked, "And who does not understand about wanting to be outside?"

Georgiana's shoulders slumped, and the last remnants of a smile vanished from her face. "Mrs. Rigsby. She always wants me to–" There she clasped a hand over her mouth. Jerking her head to the window, her eyes opened wide. "It's morning. I forgot. I need to get back to my room." Scrambling off the bed, she raced for the door.

Rosabel was dumbfounded. Before she could utter a single word, Georgiana's footsteps echoed down the hall. Mrs. Rigsby, Rosabel thought. That woman made her shake in her shoes as well. What would she do if she found Georgiana out of bed? And above else not in her room?

Getting out of bed, Rosabel shivered and rang the bell to call for Bridget.

When Rosabel stepped out of her room, everything was quiet down the hall. Maybe Mrs. Rigsby had not noticed Georgiana's absence.

Heading downstairs, Rosabel entered the breakfast parlour and was surprised when she found only one table setting. One of the footmen pulled out her chair, and she sat down.

Having a number of staff standing by, watching her eat, made Rosabel uncomfortable and self-conscious. As the footman poured her tea, she asked, "What of Lady Georgiana? Does she not come down to breakfast?"

The footman declined, stating that Lady Georgiana always ate in the nursery. Rosabel frowned but soon concluded that without a parent in the house there probably was no need for the girl to head down to the breakfast parlour to take her food. Upon rising from the table, Rosabel instructed the footman that from now on Georgiana would eat with her. For a second, the footman seemed to hesitate but then nodded and returned to his position by the door.

Not having anything to do, Rosabel decided to have a closer look at her new home. From what her husband had said, she concluded that her stay at Westmore Manor was of a more permanent nature and, thus, did her best to see the future in as bright a colour as possible.

The manor had housed many a generation before her, which became most obvious when Rosabel walked the many corridors connecting the different wings, up and down the stairs and into the great hall; all were adorned with portraits of people that now were considered her kin.

Ornate rugs and tapestries decorated the marble floors and wood-panelled walls. The furnishings were simple, yet elegant, many of which appeared to have been acquired in previous generations. Artefacts were displayed proudly, and Rosabel came across more than one maid with a duster in her hand, tending to the upkeep of the house. All in all, Rosabel did not dislike what she found. The rooms had high ceilings, and tall windows allowed a maximum of sunlight to reach inside the stone walls and brighten her day. However, there was something about this place, something that bothered her, something she couldn't quite make out.

However, remembering her earlier comparison of Westmore Manor to a museum or even to a tomb, Rosabel finally understood what was lacking. While the house itself was beautiful and inviting and had everything money could buy, there was no life in it. No laughter. No smiles. And without conscious thought, Rosabel found her feet ascending the stairs, turning toward the east wing and approaching the door to Georgiana's nursery; the only place where there was still a resemblance of life.

As she knocked on the door, waiting for someone to bid her enter, a tingling ran through her body, and she realized how excited she was to see her step-daughter again.

Hearing Mrs. Rigsby's voice, Rosabel stepped inside and found Georgiana with a book on her head, walking up and down the room. A small grin spread over her face as their eyes met.

"A lady does not show her teeth," Mrs. Rigsby reprimanded. Then she turned her cold eyes to Rosabel, who instantly understood that she was not welcome here. "What can I do for you, your grace?"

Since Rosabel had not come with a specific purpose in mind other than to spend some time with Georgiana, she didn't quite know what to say. "I have come to…observe your lessons."

At her words, Mrs. Rigsby's eyes narrowed, clearly displeased at the suggestion that her methods might be in need of supervision. Rosabel, however, pretended not to see the woman's scowl and sitting down by the small table where Georgiana had taken her dinner the night before said, "You are doing a marvellous job, Georgiana. How do you manage to keep your head up with such a heavy load upon it?"

The girl beamed with pride. "It is not all that difficult. Just keep your head level to the floor."

Mrs. Rigsby huffed. "If it is not difficult, why did you drop the book three times this morning?"

A bit of the twinkle left Georgiana's face, but her eyes remained fixed on Rosabel. "Would you like to try?" Taking the book from her head, she held it out to Rosabel.

Before Rosabel could take it though, Mrs. Rigsby once more interfered. "Nonsense! Her grace does not need to be bothered with childish games."

Again unsure of what she ought to do, of what her role was in this, Rosabel's heart broke when she saw the light vanish from Georgiana's face. Without another thought, she stepped forward and took the book. "I'd love to. Now, again do explain how to do it."

Georgiana's face lit up from the inside, and like a dedicated teacher, she carefully instructed Rosabel how to balance the heavy volume on her head. Before long, both were walking up and down the room, laughing when a book hit the floor with a loud *bang*. All the while, Mrs. Rigsby looked like she would be sick.

8

THE LATE DUCHESS
OF KENSINGTON

After spending the afternoon with Georgiana in the stable and meeting her favourite horse, Shadow, a black stallion of immense size and a scary temperament, Rosabel slipped into a deep slumber the minute her head touched the pillow at the end of the day. The night passed quietly. No storm. No nightmares. And when the new day began, the world looked a brighter place.

With a smile on her face, Rosabel went down to breakfast, careful not to skip down the corridor like a little girl. The excitement, however, coursed through her veins without hindrance, and she had some trouble maintaining composure in front of the staff. Upon entering the breakfast parlour, Rosabel's smile died on her face.

Like the day before, there was only one place setting to be found on the long table, and Georgiana was nowhere to be seen. Sitting down, Rosabel turned to the footman. "Where is the Lady Georgiana?"

Keeping his eyes averted, the footman all but whispered, "Mrs. Rigsby insisted she take her breakfast in the nursery so as not to lose time on her lessons."

Rosabel felt like someone had slapped her in the face. Not so much did she feel the humiliation of her governess negating her orders but rather the loss of company. In that moment, Rosabel realized that if she wished to spend time with her step-daughter and have any say in how she spend her day, she would have to fight Mrs. Rigsby, who was clearly unwilling to relinquish the control she'd had so far. What scared Rosabel most was that she wasn't sure if she had the courage to do so. She knew everyone else would have relieved Mrs. Rigsby of her position immediately especially since the rest of the staff had already grown accustomed to heeding her orders, even if it meant defying the lady of the house.

However, Rosabel couldn't.

Barely touching her food, she stared out the window at the lush gardens outside Westmore Manor. Ever since her parents' death, her life had been marked by absolute obedience. Afraid to be rejected by the world around her, Rosabel had done her best to be agreeable, to follow orders, to not question her superiors (or anyone else for that matter) until it had become second nature.

Could she undo what years of necessity had forced her to become? Could she return to being the girl her parents had set on the path to self-respect? Could she hold her head high in a confrontation?

Rosabel shook her head. There was no spark that gave her fire. Instead, a heavy boulder rested on her shoulders, bending her to its will.

About to ascend the winding stairs leading to the upper floor, Rosabel stopped and turned her head at the rapidly approaching footsteps echoing along the hall.

In long strides—although not running as his dignified position would never allow for such behaviour—Lawrence hastened toward her. "Your grace," he called, just a touch out of breath. "The dowager duchess requests your presence in her chambers."

At his words, all blood drained from Rosabel's face. "Excuse me?" she whispered.

Not surprised at her ignorance, Lawrence nodded. "His grace's grandmother. Due to an ailment, she is unable to leave her bedchamber, but she would very much like to make your acquaintance." Without waiting for her reply, he took to the stairs. "If you please follow me, your grace."

Rosabel felt her hands tremble as they turned down the west wing, passing door after door. Her husband had not mentioned a grandmother. How could he have not told her? She was so very unprepared to meet this woman, especially on short notice.

Lawrence stopped in front of a heavy-set door. After giving a quick knock, he slid it open and beckoned her to enter.

With shaking hands, Rosabel stepped across the threshold into a darkened room. Looming shadows rose from the floor to her left and right, and she had trouble picking her way across the room toward a massive four-post bed at the far wall.

Against the white bed clothes, the small woman looked like a ghost, her skin almost translucent and her hair barely visible. Her eyes were closed, and Rosabel stopped, unsure what to do.

She ought not to be here! Clearly the woman was sleeping and would probably have a fit if Rosabel disturbed her rest. Lawrence had not mentioned what ailment she suffered, but Rosabel suspected that it was simply an ailment that came with age.

Turning back to the door, Rosabel silently placed one step in front of the other, afraid to trip and wake the woman. When her hand touched the door handle, a remarkably strong and clearly irritated voice spoke from amidst the covers. "The moment I doze off, these people sneak in here and close the blasted curtains again!"

Rosabel froze, drawing in a sharp breath at hearing the anger in the woman's voice. Not what she had expected.

"Ah! Someone's here," the dowager duchess observed. "Do be so kind and open the curtains."

Not knowing what to say, Rosabel did as she was asked. Once she had pulled back the heavy curtains, sunlight flooded the room, temporarily blinding her as her eyes had slowly grown accustomed to the dimness.

When she turned around, Rosabel found soft, green eyes looking at her. They travelled down her frame, took in her trembling hands and unsteady gaze. Then a smile lifted up the corners of the woman's wrinkled mouth. "Welcome, my dear."

"Th-thank you," Rosabel stammered.

"Would you be a dear and come a little closer," the dowager

duchess asked, squinting her eyes. "I promise I will not bite, and I wish to see your face."

"Certainly," Rosabel mumbled, slowly approaching the bed. Under the woman's scrutinizing eyes, she grew more and more uncomfortable, wringing her hands and casting the occasional longing glance at the door.

"What did my grandson tell you about me that has you trembling like this?" she asked, and her eyes narrowed.

Rosabel quickly shook her head. "N-nothing, Duchess. He did not mention...I mean—"

A chuckle rose from the old woman's throat. "You mean to tell me he did not even mention me." She shook her head, but a warm smile played on her features. "Graham, dear boy, how very unbecoming of you."

Rosabel just stood and stared.

"My dear, would you mind sitting down?" the dowager duchess asked, pointing to the chair beside her bed. "You look as white as a sheet. Believe me, if I could get up, I'd offer you the bed." Again, she chuckled.

Sinking into the soft armchair, Rosabel was grateful for the woman's observing eyes. As her hands still trembled, she took a deep breath, trying her best to look more comfortable with the situation she found herself in so unexpectedly. "Is there anything I can do? Do you need anything?" she whispered as the silence stretched too long.

The dowager duchess smiled. "A little company would be nice."

Rosabel nodded, not sure what to say. How was she to converse with this woman? If she said a wrong word, would her husband's grandmother recognize her low station and send her from the room?

"Relax, dear," the dowager duchess interrupted her thoughts. "I am not the evil step-mother in this story." A devilish grin lit up her face. "I would just like to learn a little bit about the woman my grandson chose for his bride." Rosabel stiffened. "Here, I'll start. I'm an old woman, which is fairly obvious, and since my body is slowly failing me, I am tied to this bed day in and out, and quite frankly, I'm bored to death." She nodded her head vigorously. "I swear. It is this," she waved her hand at the lonely room, "that will put me in the grave. So, when my grandson wrote to me about his impending nuptials and his intention of having you here at Westmore, I was delighted." A genuine sparkle came to her eyes, and Rosabel felt herself relax, returning the woman's smile whole-heartedly. "So, before the Season starts and he'll whisk you off to London, please brighten up an old woman's quite dreary days."

Smiling, Rosabel nodded, feeling the sun in her back, warming her limbs and stilling their trembling. Yes, London. Her husband had informed her of his intention for a quick introduction into society. However, instead of focusing on life's unpleasantries, Rosabel felt herself bewitched by the old woman's charms. Maybe there was more life in Westmore than she had first thought.

Despite Mrs. Rigsby's interference, Rosabel grew more and more attached to the little girl over the next few weeks. The cheerfulness of her spirit amazed her, and she realized that not the sun but Georgiana's presence had brought light to her room that first morning. Wherever the little girl went, smiles followed her. The only one who seemed immune to her powers was Mrs. Rigsby, the governess.

In many ways, the dowager duchess was very much like Georgiana. Both open and welcoming, Rosabel felt completely at ease in their company within a matter of days.

"What's bothering you, my dear?" the dowager duchess asked one morning while they were sitting together in her room, sipping tea. The curtains were pulled back and allowed the warm fall sun to reach inside and chase away the chill that seemed to linger these days.

Rosabel shrugged, eyes focused on the amber liquid in her cup.

The dowager duchess sighed. "Talk to me, dear, and preferably today. Who knows if I will still be around tomorrow?" A chuckle rose from her throat, and Rosabel stared at her open-mouthed. "Don't look so shocked, dear. Can't an old woman make a joke? Now! Say what's on your mind."

Putting down her cup, Rosabel folded her hands in her lap. "I…I don't know how to be a duchess. Not a day passes when I feel unsure of how to express myself, how to address the servants, what to say and what not to say. Every time someone addresses me as 'your grace', I almost flinch."

"Dear, I know you're a bit on the shy side of the world, but these things take time. Be patient and do what feels right. I'm sure you're doing a fine job."

Rosabel nodded, forcing a smile on her face. "I will."

The dowager duchess narrowed her eyes. "Now, even with my impaired hearing, I could hear the lie in your voice." Rosabel's eyes opened wide. "And stop looking so shocked all the time. My goodness, what happened to you that instilled such fear in your heart?"

Looking at her hands, Rosabel recounted the sad story of her life, hoping that the dowager duchess would not regard her with pity in her eyes from now on. However, her fear proved unfounded. For when she looked up, a warm smile played on the woman's lips, and she gently placed her hand on Rosabel's clenched fists. "We all have our pasts, dear. I do not mean to belittle yours, only to remind you that your past is your past. The future is still unknown, and we need to make the best of it. Do not allow your past to hold you back or a time will come when nothing but regret fills your days."

Facing the green eyes that so imploringly looked into hers, Rosabel nodded; and this time, the dowager duchess looked pleased. "Good," she whispered, gently squeezing her hand. "Now, tell me, what brought on this worry?"

Rosabel took a deep breath. "I'm afraid Mrs. Rigsby does not like me."

Instantly, laughter echoed through the room, and Rosabel had to blink to assure herself of what her ears had perceived. Wiping a tear from the corner of her eye, the dowager duchess said, "Dear, that's not your fault. The woman does not like anyone, and from what I've gathered, the feeling is mutual. Do not worry about her. Walk down your path, and if she gets in your way," a twinkle came to the old woman's eyes, "push her aside."

Rosabel couldn't help but smile, and yet, she was unsure if she could ever find half as much courage as the dowager duchess possessed. Rosabel doubted it very much and was proved right later that afternoon.

As she sat down with Georgiana in her nursery, having a tea party with her dolls, Mrs. Rigsby stormed into the room and demanded to know the meaning of this. Georgiana froze, and Rosabel swallowed, feeling her own nerves jump. "We are having tea," she responded, unable to comprehend for what reason this seemed to give offense. "I see nothing wrong with that, Mrs. Rigsby."

Mrs. Rigsby huffed short of steam coming out of her ears. "I most certainly do, your grace. I mean no disrespect," Rosabel doubted that very much, "but I must insist that Lady Georgiana continue her lessons. His grace insisted that she be prepared to take her mother's place." A wicked gleam came to her eyes as they settled on Rosabel.

"I see," Rosabel mumbled, wondering once again why the duke had married her. From what Mrs. Rigsby said, Georgiana's education was well taken care of and in the sure hands of the governess. Why had he insisted on providing his daughter with a new mother if there was no room for her here?

Although Georgiana looked at her with sadness in her blue eyes, Rosabel could not help herself. "We will continue this later," she said, rising from her chair. "Your father is right. You should not neglect your lessons." With a smile for Georgiana and a curt nod for Mrs. Rigsby, Rosabel left the room, guilt flooding her heart at her own weakness.

Going for a walk by the duck pond, Rosabel was delighted to have Georgiana with her. After the girl's lessons, they'd escaped Mrs. Rigsby's controlling eye and stolen away as fast as they could. Skipping with each step, Georgiana approached the pond, tossing bread crumbs into the water, as she watched the ducks with bubbling delight diving after her offered treats. She jumped up and down, clapping her hands. "Did you see that? That one dove under all the way."

Rosabel smiled and brushed a hand over Georgiana's golden head. Instantly, she stopped as the familiarity of the gesture struck her, but Georgiana didn't seem distressed at all. Her eyes shone as she leaned against Rosabel, watching the pond come to life when a quick toss of bread crumbs hit the ground or the water.

"Mummy always took me here," Georgiana said, gaze fixed on the commotion before her. "She loved books, duckies and horses." She looked up at Rosabel, and although there was a hint of sadness in her eyes, her face shone with pride. "Mummy had a very big, white horse. Her name was Lightning because she was so fast. But mummy wouldn't let me near Lightning because she was wild," Georgiana giggled, "like her. She always told me so."

"I believe you," Rosabel quickly assured the girl. "Your mother sounds like she was a lot of fun. Did you always spend a lot of time together? Was Mrs. Rigsby here back then?"

Georgiana nodded, and at first, Rosabel wasn't sure how to

understand her answer. "Mrs. Rigsby never liked me going outside. She always tried to make me stay in my room and study." She lifted her head, and her face scrunched up in disgust. "All kinds of boring stuff." Then the radiant smile returned to her face. "But mummy always took me outside anyway, and Mrs. Rigsby got so angry. But mummy just shrugged and said, 'Take it up with the duke.' And then Mrs. Rigsby would stare." Her little body shook with laughter.

Trying to picture the late Duchess of Kensington, Rosabel looked out over the duck pond at Westmore Manor, looming tall into the sky. Had her predecessor been able to handle Mrs. Rigsby? From what Georgiana had said, she had. Apparently, the little girl's mother had been a strong woman. Gazing at Georgiana, Rosabel could see that same spirit shine in her eyes. At six, she could not help but submit to Mrs. Rigsby. But Rosabel doubted that the governess would easily subdue Georgiana once she grew older. Feeling her chest swell with pride, Rosabel looked at the little girl, who would undoubtedly follow in her mother's footsteps and find her own way, no matter the obstacles.

A frown drew down her eyebrows, and she turned to Georgiana. "What was your mother's name?" So far, she had only heard people talk of her as the late Duchess of Kensington.

"Leonora," Georgiana whispered almost in awe. "Uncle Edmond sometimes called her Leo, because she had the heart of a lion." Again, pride rang in her voice, and Rosabel couldn't help but feel a sting of jealousy. The late Duchess of Kensington had been a great woman in every way, and Rosabel herself was a lacking substitute, only reminding those who had loved her what a great loss they had suffered.

Rosabel spent the rest of the day locked in her mind. Almost as though in a trance, she wandered the halls, not seeing anything before her, but, instead, imagining Westmore Manor when Leonora had been its mistress. Had it seemed so dead then? Had her life taken everything that had made this huge house a home?

Rest wouldn't come that night. Rosabel tossed and turned, and once again, as though to mimic her inner turmoil, a raging storm assaulted her windows; this time rolling in from the south-west. Rain pelted on the panes, drumming into her mind the thoughts that wouldn't leave her alone.

Pushing back the covers, Rosabel shrugged into a robe and tiptoed out of the door and down the hall. Slowly opening the door to Georgiana's room, she peeked inside, relieved to see the little girl in her bed, eyes closed, breathing evenly. A small golden-haired doll was clutched in her arms.

This night, Georgiana's room was not the centre of the storm and the muffled sounds had not yet disturbed her sleep. However, fearing that Georgiana might wake up and be frightened again, Rosabel drew up a chair and settled in for the night, watching over the sleeping child.

As she sat there, her eyes ran over Georgiana's features, and she tried to imagine what her mother had looked like. As many portraits as she had found in almost every part of the house, Rosabel thought it more than just a bit odd that there appeared to be not a single one of the late Duchess of Kensington anywhere in Westmore Manor. Had there never been one? Or had it been removed? Hidden away to not be a constant reminder of what had been?

Georgiana didn't wake that night, and when the storm calmed down and the early rays of a new day slowly climbed the tree line outside the window, Rosabel withdrew to her own room, lest she run into Mrs. Rigsby. Her gloomy thoughts, however, were still with her. Unable to shake the nagging feeling of merely being an insufficient substitute, Rosabel kept to her room for the next few days. She only ventured downstairs to take her meals and spend an hour here or there with Georgiana or her husband's grandmother. Apart from that, she remained in her prison cell, sitting by the window, gaze fixed on nothing specific, wallowing in thoughts that she knew served no purpose.

Thinking of the governess and the disdain in her eyes as she had looked over Rosabel the night of her arrival at Westmore Manor, Rosabel couldn't help but shiver. No one else, not even her aunt and uncle, had ever been able to make her feel as little as Mrs. Rigsby did without effort on a daily basis. Rosabel couldn't even tell what it was that the governess did. There was something in the air with which she entered a room and appraised those within, as though her opinion was a ruling universally accepted as the truth. And that ruling had fallen on open ears with Rosabel. She knew it to be wrong to believe her, but she did nonetheless. Feeling smaller and smaller every day, Rosabel soon cowered in her room, barely feeling any strength to leave her bed in the morning.

Until one day when Georgiana came to her room, tears running down her rosy cheeks. She sobbed so heart-breakingly that Rosabel took her into her arms. Trying her best to comfort her, she felt her own concerns melt away at the sight of this little angel in pain. Anger ignited then because deep down Rosabel knew the source of Georgiana's pain even before the little girl opened her mouth.

Mrs. Rigsby had taken Georgiana's favourite doll, a gift of her mother's, when she had failed to recite a five-verse poem.

Heat boiled in Rosabel's veins and rushed through her body. Before she knew what she was doing, she found herself hastening down the hall, pulling Georgiana behind her. With more force than necessary, she pushed open the door to the nursery and found Mrs. Rigsby by the window, hands on her hips glaring at them. "There you are!" she hissed, cold eyes fixed on the little girl half-hiding behind Rosabel's skirts. "A lady does not sniffle! And a lady most certainly does not run off just because—"

"Mrs. Rigsby!" Rosabel interrupted, her voice radiating the anger she felt. Instantly, the governess fell silent, confusion clouding her eyes. "Where is Lady Georgiana's doll?"

Straightening her posture, Mrs. Rigsby met Rosabel's burning eyes. "Forgive me, your grace, but I am merely trying my best to teach Lady Georgiana to be a lady," she paused for a second, "like her mother."

Rosabel swallowed, understanding the words the way they were meant, as an insult. Fighting down the urge to run from the room and hide, Rosabel took a deep breath as her eyes shifted to the little girl, her tiny hand still clutched in her own. Hiding behind her skirts for protection, Georgiana barely glanced at her governess, small frame shaking as the tears continued to run down her cheeks.

In that moment, Rosabel's heart sped up. The blood pumped through her veins as though running a marathon, and as though a flame had been ignited that could never be subdued, a fire stronger than anything she had ever felt rushed through her body. She felt it burn in the tip of her toes as much as in the tip of her hair. It burned, and a fever took control, suffocated her fears and discarded their ashes.

In that moment, Rosabel was not herself anymore. In that moment, she was a mother protecting her child, and nothing scared her more than the threat of new tears running down her daughter's cheeks. Knowing she'd do anything in her power to prevent that, Rosabel stepped forward.

"Mrs. Rigsby, where is Lady Georgiana's doll?" The governess held her ground, but Rosabel thought to detect a hint of weakness in her eyes. "I will not repeat myself," she hissed, her own eyes unwavering as she fixed her opponent.

A moment of silence hung in the air, lasting a short eternity. All that could be heard were Georgiana's soft sobs, spurring Rosabel on, giving her the kindling she needed to keep her fire burning.

Then Mrs. Rigsby turned and strode from the room. In a moment, she returned, holding in her hands the doll with the golden hair. For the first time, Rosabel recognized its resemblance to Georgiana.

A scowl on her face, the governess extended her hand. As Georgiana was still hiding behind Rosabel's skirts, eyes longingly staring at her precious doll, Rosabel took it from Mrs. Rigsby's hand and passed it on to its rightful owner. A small breath of relief escaped Georgiana as she clutched the doll to her chest and closing her eyes hugged it tightly as though it was her mother. In that moment, Rosabel understood what the doll meant to the little girl.

Tearing her eyes from the heart-breaking scene partially hidden by her skirts, Rosabel turned to the governess. "Mrs. Rigsby, I feel the need to remind you that, as Lady Georgiana's governess, it falls to you to provide her with the education she requires to lead a successful life. You are, however, not her mother," Rosabel could almost feel Leonora speaking through her, "and you will refrain from punishments such as these in the future. Am I understood?"

As much as her own eyes burned, Mrs. Rigsby's were cold as ice, and for a terrifying moment, they reminded her of her husband's. But then the governess looked away, and Rosabel heard the disdain in her voice as she mumbled, "Yes, your grace," before walking out of the room.

9

THE ATTIC

"Georgiana told me, dear," the dowager duchess beamed at her. "I cannot tell you how proud I am of you!"

Rosabel felt the heat rise in her cheeks as she took her regular seat by the old woman's bed. "It was nothing. I—"

"Nothing?" The dowager duchess shook her head. "Now, now, this is not a moment for false modesty. I know how much courage it must have cost you to put that woman in her place. It was about time."

"But will she not be angry?"

The dowager duchess shrugged. "Certainly, but what is it to you?"

Wringing her hands, Rosabel rose from the chair and started pacing the room. "I'm afraid she will direct her anger at Georgiana. What if she takes it out on her?"

The old woman's eyes turned serious. "Then you will do as you did before. You will step in front of the child and protect her from that lunatic woman."

"I'm not sure I can."

"But I am."

"How?" Rosabel asked, shaking her head. Staring at the small, old woman in the enormous bed, she felt her own limbs tremble. "How can you possibly know?"

A smile illuminated the dowager duchess' face. "Because you're her mother. It's what mothers do."

Sinking back into her chair, Rosabel looked at the old woman. "I do love her," she whispered, feeling a wrinkled hand embrace hers, giving it a gentle squeeze.

Still contemplating her options later in the afternoon, Rosabel followed Georgiana down a long corridor in the west wing. Eventually, they met with heavy-set double doors. When she gave them a slight push, they slid apart as though made of air.

"This was my mother's favourite room in the entire house," Georgiana whispered as though not wanting to disturb the rows upon rows of books filling the library from floor to ceiling. "She always said every book was an adventure waiting to happen." Taking Rosabel's hand, she drew her deeper into the room lit by arched windows running along the entire length of the west wall. Sunshine spilled inside, touching the massive stone fireplace in the back fronted by a number of armchairs and a Persian rug running all the way to the double doors.

Craning her neck, Rosabel did not know where to look first. "This is wonderful!" she gasped. "Oh, so wonderful! Did you spend a lot of time here?"

Georgiana nodded. "She would always read to me. At night, she would read to me in bed, but during the day, we would come here. This is where she taught me to read."

Rosabel's eyes turned to the quiet, little girl, holding on to the dearest treasure she had, the memories of her mother. "You miss her a lot."

Meeting her eyes, Georgiana nodded. "I do." A tear ran down her cheek, but she brushed it away. "I wish she would come back."

Pulling the little girl into her arms, Rosabel held her tight, gently stroking her back. "I wish that too."

In the coming weeks, Rosabel and Georgiana spent many wonderful hours tucked away in the library, going on one adventure after the other. As the air outside grew chilly and had a more and more distinct nip to it, they would huddle in front of a roaring fire, watching the late afternoon winds carry around the coloured leaves of late autumn on their never-ending journey. Hot tea and Cook's delicious biscuits with a touch of cinnamon would keep them warm and well-fed, and they would often forget to return downstairs for the evening meal.

Rosabel loved these weeks.

While Mrs. Rigsby refrained from any further attempts of sabotaging Rosabel's position in the household–apart from the occasional, thinly-veiled insult–Rosabel herself felt like a heavy weight had been lifted off her shoulders. Step by step, she found her way around Westmore Manor and its people. Always having an open ear and a kind word for her staff, Rosabel was delighted to see that most of them curtsied with an honest smile whenever they would come upon her. Bridget and Lawrence were dearest to her; both openly showed their affection for Georgiana and hardly missed an opportunity to sneak her an extra biscuit or a treat for Shadow.

Whenever Georgiana was stuck with Mrs. Rigsby—her lessons being the only time she could not escape her governess—Rosabel would sit with her husband's grandmother or explore Westmore Manor and its grounds. Riding Shadow, at Georgiana's request, she found that the horse's temperament stemmed from a skittish and frightful nature. So she took her time, bribing the black stallion with treats and stroking behind his ears whenever she visited the stables. Soon, the tall horse greeted her with a friendly neigh when she drew near, and Rosabel delighted in his affections. Taking him outside into the grounds almost every day, Rosabel felt freed of the last chains that simply wouldn't dissolve. Although she felt more or less at peace in Westmore now, there always was that tiny voice whispering in her head warning that life would not remain as it was. There was a danger to her happiness on the horizon, and Rosabel only knew too well what danger that voice spoke of.

Her husband.

Not having heard from him even once since her departure from Camden Hall, Rosabel often all but forgot he even existed. Only when people referred to her as the duchess in name did she remind herself that she was indeed a married woman. Nevertheless, Rosabel hoped with all her heart that her husband was equally contend with their arrangement and disinclined to ever make any changes to it.

Returning from a long run across the grassy plain to the west of the manor, Rosabel handed Shadow's reins to Peter, the stable boy, and hurried toward the house as the first heavy drops of another rainy afternoon announced themselves. Lawrence took her hat and coat, and Rosabel hurried upstairs, desperate to run a brush through the entangled mess that used to be her hair. The fresh air still in her lungs, Rosabel climbed the steps with ease, energy almost giving her wings. Humming under her breath, she turned right and walked down the corridor toward her room when something caught her attention.

Set off to the side, another, smaller corridor broke off to the left, usually hidden behind a door; a door that looked like every other door. Only now, this door stood ajar and slowly moved open as Rosabel swept passed it.

Stopping, Rosabel peered past the door into the dark hallway. Curious, she took another step forward, pushing the door all the way open. Except for walls, a floor and a ceiling, there was nothing much to see, nothing but another door, just as ordinary, at the opposite side of the small corridor.

Wondering what lay beyond, Rosabel approached the door. It wasn't locked but stuck at first and only slid open after a vigorous pull, screeching so loudly that Rosabel was sure the whole household would be upon her in a second demanding to know what unholy sound had disturbed their existence.

Beyond the door, stairs led up into an attic. Although Rosabel was sure to find nothing exciting up there but old furniture and cobwebs, her feet would not turn to leave. With a mind of their own, they steered her up the stairs into a dimly lit space. Small round windows here and there hung with cobwebs as though fashioned into curtains allowed some of the dark afternoon light to enter.

Bulging shapes covered with white linen cloths resembling tables, chairs or a chaise stood here and there. The walls were adorned with antique cabinets and commodes and trunks of all sizes were stacked covering the entire floor, creating small pathways and forming a labyrinth.

When her eyes had adjusted to the dim light, Rosabel stepped forward, unsure what to look at. The scene before her reminded her of a dungeon in an old castle in a ghost story her father had told her when she was young; before her life had changed so abruptly. Her pulse beat in her chest, partly with excitement and partly with fear as the old stories caught up with her.

Entering the labyrinth, Rosabel ran her finger across the lid of one of the trunks, and it came away with a thick layer of dust covering it. No one had cleaned here in a while. Of course, there was no need to clean an attic that lay all but forgotten. Keeping right at the next turn, Rosabel walked on, her eyes gliding across the ancient possessions along the wall as though searching for something. Once her eyes had found what Rosabel herself had not known to look for, she could not help but stand and stare.

Against the very back of the wall, hidden by crates and trunks, an old frame, glistening golden in the few rays of light dancing over its ornaments, rested among companions. This one frame, however, was not completely covered. The white linen had slid aside a little, revealing the upper left corner of a woman's portrait. And although Rosabel could see mere strands of her golden hair held back with a blue clip, she did not doubt for a second that she would finally lay eyes on the woman so dearly missed, the woman who had left a hole that could not be filled, the woman whose place she had been forced to take but failed to fill.

Leonora.

Georgiana's mother and her husband's beloved late wife.

10

A VISITOR

osabel felt as though she was about to disturb Leonora's grave as she carefully set one foot before the other. Approaching the corner of the room with the greatest of care, she tried her best not to make a sound, moving away crates and trunks, feeling their weight in the trembling of her arms and the pearls of sweat springing up on her forehead. But as much as Rosabel's skin filled with goose bumps cautioning her, she could not turn back.

Ever since the day she had made her vows had she been walking in this woman's shadow. To everyone around her, Leonora had been the perfect wife, mother and duchess. Compared to her, Rosabel felt more than just a little inadequate but like a failure at life. And she was compared to the former Duchess of Kensington every step she took.

In a strange way, facing Leonora now gave Rosabel a first glimpse at her competitor for everyone's affections and good opinion. But as much as she guessed was her right to, Rosabel could not feel resentment for the woman whose face she was about to finally lay eyes on. Leonora had had a life she had loved, and she had been loved by those around her, only to be torn out of this life for no good reason. Was there ever a good reason? Rosabel wondered. If anything, she felt her heart go out to Leonora, hoping the woman would not mind her presence in her home.

Tenderly, Rosabel placed a hand on the edge of the portrait's frame, feeling the smooth surface of the polished wood under her fingertips. Pushing the linen aside little by little, Rosabel found she was holding her breath.

Slowly, the linen fell away, revealing golden hair pinned up, with loose curls dancing down Leonora's temples and resting on her slim shoulders. The blue clip in her hair perfectly matched the startling blue of her eyes, pale and pure as a summer sky and yet, deep as the ocean on a stormy day. Her lips were the tiniest bit curled at the corners as though she was doing her best not to laugh. Head held high, chin lifted, Leonora looked the duchess Rosabel knew she could never be. Looking her in the eyes, Rosabel felt awed by her presence as though Leonora's spirit had risen from the painting and now stood beside her.

Involuntarily, Rosabel glanced to her left. Although she saw nothing but specks of dust floating through the air, a shiver went over her.

Absorbed in the connection she felt, Rosabel flinched as the sounds of hooves on gravel reached her ear, tearing her away from the wonderings and musings of her ever-trembling mind.

As she rushed to the small window, Rosabel prayed that it was not her husband, who had decided to pay them a visit after all. Standing on her toes, she still could not see the path leading up to the front hall. The sky, however, hung heavy with rain-filled clouds, threatening to drench those unwilling to heed its warning any second.

Casting one last glance at the portrait, Rosabel straightened her dress and only then remembered that she had been on her way to fix her hair. Frightened to have her husband or any unknown visitor lay eyes on her in such a state of dishevelment, Rosabel rushed down the stairs, carefully closing the door to the attic behind her, and hastened to her room.

By the time, she had managed to disentangle her hair and pin it up in an orderly fashion, there came a knock on her door. Lawrence entered and bowing to her, said, "You have a visitor, your grace."

A visitor? Rosabel wondered. Then it could not be her husband. A wave of relief washed over her, and she could feel the knot in her stomach dissipate. Taking a deep breath to steady her nerves, she asked, "Who is it?"

"Edmond Dunsworth, Duke of Cromwell, your grace."

Although the name sounded familiar, Rosabel could not conjure up a face to go with it. Nodding to Lawrence, she followed him downstairs toward the front drawing-room. He opened the door and stepping inside, announced to her visitor, "Her Grace the Duchess of Kensington."

Still at odds with her address, Rosabel took a deep breath and stepped forward, eyes straining to glimpse her visitor. Not knowing what to expect, she was relieved to find a welcoming smile on his face.

"Duchess," he said, bowing to her, but his eyes sparkled with mischief. "I hope you do not mind my intrusion upon your hospitality."

"Not at all," Rosabel said, bowing her head in greeting to her husband's best friend. Oh, how inconvenient this connection was! Remembering how she had wished he could be her husband instead, Rosabel felt herself blush.

"Are you unwell?" he asked, although from the expression on his face she could tell that he was jesting with her. "Do have a seat."

Following his suggestion, Rosabel was relieved to be off her feet and not in danger of swooning any time soon. Her heart hammered in her chest, and she could hardly concentrate on what to say. "What brings you to Westmore?"

A smile on his face, he leaned back comfortably. "I am passing by on my way to Camden Hall."

"I see," Rosabel nodded. He was on his way to see her husband. Was he to report on how she managed herself in her new role? Did her husband ask him to spy on her? A shiver ran up and down her arms.

As she looked up, Rosabel found his eyes observing her. However, when she took a deep breath, readying herself to face any accusation or shortcomings he could lay at her door, a grin spread over his features that once again displayed his easy-going nature. "There is no need for concern, your grace. Even if Graham had asked for a report, I could not deliver one that would paint you in a bad light."

Rosabel felt herself tremble, embarrassed at how easily he had read her thoughts. It would prove well to be more guarded in the future.

"I assure you I have no such concerns."

"Good," the duke nodded. "Then let's talk of pleasanter matters.

How is Lady Georgiana?"

Rosabel's face instantly transformed at the change of topic. She noticed his eyes watching her, and yet, the words spilled from her mouth without thought as to how her eagerness would be received. She talked of Georgiana's delightful nature, her fondness of Shadow and the many wonderful hours spent upstairs in the library.

"The library?" the duke mused. "Yes, Leonora often read to her there. I am glad that Georgiana remembers so much of her mother." His face grew darker. "She was so young when it happened."

Seeing his face, Rosabel couldn't help but ask. "Did you know the late Duchess of Kensington?"

Meeting her eyes, the duke nodded. "I did, yes. She—"

In that moment the door flew open.

Rosabel flinched, expecting something terrible, but was relieved to find Georgiana fly into the room, the biggest smile on her face. Her eyes barely glanced at Rosabel as she instantly flung herself into the duke's arms. "Uncle Edmond!"

Uncle Edmond? Rosabel wondered as she watched him spin her around and around, his laughter mixing with hers. Then he set her down again, and both took a seat across from Rosabel.

A feeling of forbearance settled over Rosabel, and the words flew out of her mouth. "Uncle Edmond? Is that an honorary title? You are not my husband's brother, are you? Does that mean you are...?"

He met her eyes without flinching. "Yes, Leonora was my little sister."

Rosabel gasped, afraid to see a new cold settled in his eyes as well. How he must hate her for taking his sister's place!

11

MY LOVE LEONORA

After a quick excuse, Rosabel all but ran from the parlour. Her feet echoed in the marble hall as they carried her away, up the stairs and down a corridor. Before she had formed any coherent thought, she found herself pushing open the door to the attic, the stairs creaking under her shoes. Climbing to the top, Rosabel turned to the still uncovered portrait sitting in the back of the room. She hurried over as though someone was after her and feeling her knees wobble, sank down onto the floor in front of it.

Tears dropped from her cheeks and onto her hands, and Rosabel realized that she was crying. The realization drew heavy sobs from her throat, and for a moment, she buried her face in her hands, unable to look at the woman staring back at her from the portrait.

"Wherever I turn, there you are," she cried, glancing up at the woman who had to face her accusations with nothing but silence. "How am I to make a life here if all they want is you?" She shook her head, knowing that she was being unfair.

Leonora had not been the one responsible. She had not been the one to put Rosabel in this impossible position. She had simply died; died and left a hole impossible to fill. And yet, here Rosabel was. Here she was, forced to live a life not meant for her. And at every twist and turn, people reminded her of it, intentionally or not; it made no difference. Rosabel couldn't help but feel she was the one who had robbed Leonora of her life and the people who loved her of the woman with the kind eyes and the affectionate smile.

Looking at Leonora's portrait, Rosabel's gaze travelled over her blue eyes, full of kindness and devotion, down to her mouth curled up in an attempt not to laugh and wondered how she had not seen the resemblance to her brother before. Whenever she had seen him, his face had held the same joy of life, the same kindness that she had instantly felt comfortable in his presence.

She stopped.

He had smiled at her, always. Why? Did he not resent her for taking his sister's place? Although Rosabel knew he must, she could not remember anything in his eyes that had held blame or accusation directed at her. The only one who made her feel like this was her own husband.

And while the Duke of Kensington had the same blue eyes as his late wife and brother-in-law, his froze her heart. Whenever he had looked at her, a shiver had spread down her back and arms as though warning her of an evil in her vicinity. Never before had Rosabel realized how someone's eyes held the secret of their souls.

What was she to do? Rosabel wondered, brushing the tears off her cheeks. She could not hide in the attic for the duration of the duke's visit. She had to face him, at the very least, to save face.

Determined not to let him see how much his connection to her predecessor had rattled her, Rosabel rose to her feet. As she steadied herself with a hand on an oak chest, stacked on top of two crates, the lid creaked, and the key fell from the lock, hitting the floorboards with a dull thud.

Staring at it for a second, Rosabel bent down and picked it up. As she inserted it back into the lock, however, her hand, as though moving on its own, did not release the key but, instead, turned it. Instantly, the lock sprang open, and the lid stood ajar, inviting her to explore further.

"This is wrong," she whispered, knowing that whatever these crates and trunks held had once probably belonged to Leonora. Rosabel had no business going through the woman's possessions. And yet, Rosabel couldn't help herself.

Opening the lid all the way, she found a small jewellery chest engraved *My Love Leonora*. Next to it, neatly stacked, were leather-bound books held closed by a small golden thread. Running her finger over the spine, turning it in her hand, Rosabel suspected that these were Leonora's diaries. Her fingers itched with curiosity, but Rosabel called herself to reason.

Putting down the diary, she turned to a small wooden box. The lid could be slid sideways, and as it came off, a small draft caused one of the letters inside to tumble to the floor. Rosabel placed the box back in the chest and bent down to pick up the envelop. As she grabbed it by the edge though, a single sheet of paper slid out and once again fell to the floor.

Although Rosabel knew she ought to put it back, her fingers unfolded the paper and her eyes turned to the words written there. It was dated April 1793, eight years ago.

My dearest L.,

I am counting the days until I will lay eyes on your beautiful face once again. Without you, my days are spent in darkness as though the sun is absent, but I pray it will not be absent for long. I am hopeful that all will be settled in due time. I beg of you to put your trust in me and not despair. Brighter days will come when my father will see the beauty of your soul and whole-heartedly agree to our union. Of that, I am certain.

I remain yours with all my heart,

G.

Entranced, Rosabel stared at the slightly fading words on the gilded piece of paper. As short as the letter was, it gave her a unique, while undeserved, insight into her husband's life. Apparently, his father had not approved the match, at least, not at first. "Why would he reject her?" Rosabel mumbled. "She must have been a duke's daughter, considering that her brother is now the Duke of Cromwell." Had there been a feud between the families? According to everyone who had known her, she had been such a lovely woman, perfect in the eyes of many; surely her husband's father could have had no objections with regard to her character.

Obviously, he had later agreed to the marriage. Rosabel frowned.

Or had they gone against his wishes? Maybe he had died before they had gotten married, thus, freeing his son to choose as he wished.

Whatever the obstacles, they had overcome them. They had stood by each other through dark and light and had been rewarded. At least, for a time.

Sipping her tea, Rosabel stared out the window, aware that the dowager duchess had her watchful eyes on her. Millions of questions assaulted her mind, and yet, she had never spoken to the woman about her grandson and his first wife. At times, the dowager duchess had inquired after their courtship and the circumstances of their hastened wedding. Rosabel had always eluded such questions though. Nevertheless, she had no doubt that the dowager duchess had her suspicions about the nature of their marriage.

"It is not Mrs. Rigsby, is it?" her husband's grandmother asked.

Rosabel shook her head, lifting her eyes to look upon the woman regarding her with heart-felt concern. "I…I cannot help but wonder about…my husband's first wife." For a second, her eyes returned to the soft rain drumming on the window pane before returning to the woman in the bed. "What was she like? Did they love each other?"

Eyes not leaving Rosabel's face, the dowager duchess took a deep breath, collecting her thoughts. "My grandson, he has always been a bit of a closed book." She smiled ruefully. "I am convinced that there are a great many things I do not know about him, and so I cannot answer your questions with certainty. But although he never said a word, I do know that he loved her dearly. Her loss shattered his heart." Her lips thinned as she looked at Rosabel. "That's when the cold came to his eyes."

Rosabel's head snapped up at the old woman's words.

"He does not have kind words for you, does he?" the dowager duchess asked. "Yours wasn't a love match, was it?"

Rosabel shook her head, feeling a lump in her throat. She took a deep breath, and some of the weight on her shoulders fell to the floor. With shy eyes, she glanced at the old woman, whose sad eyes observed her carefully. "I did wonder whether I could have come to care for him, had I met him before; before her loss shattered his heart, as you say. Was he very different then?"

The dowager duchess shrugged. "He was always guarded, rarely revealing deep emotions, not because he did not care but because he was afraid to care too much." A sad smile danced across her face. "It is difficult to know someone who will not look at you with an open heart.

I always wondered if one day there would be someone he would allow to see him." Her eyes focused on Rosabel's. "All I can tell you is that it was not Leonora."

When Rosabel came down to supper that night, her dress felt tight around her chest, and she had trouble taking a deep breath. Her hands trembled as she turned the corner and walked in the door held open by the footman.

At the other end of the table, the duke and Georgiana were just being seated. As they caught her standing in the doorway, Georgiana's face split into a grin while the duke beckoned her to sit, the same light-hearted smile on his features.

As they were all seated around the table and the food was served, Georgiana's happy chattering chased away any awkward silence that might have otherwise hung about the room like a rain cloud on a sunny day. While the girl's attention was still mainly focused on her uncle, Rosabel was free to observe their interaction. Georgiana was clearly beyond herself with happiness, and the duke followed her childish narrations with a rapt attention and delight that made his eyes sparkle. Remembering her own relationship to her uncle, Rosabel couldn't help but smile. The duke was a very different man, and she was glad for it.

Although Rosabel could not detect a hint of resentment directed at her, she still couldn't help but feel slightly uncomfortable in his presence. Whenever he looked in her direction, she averted her eyes. Any questions he asked, she answered in a monosyllabic manner, determined to keep their interactions to a minimum.

The next morning, Rosabel was on her way to the stables, deciding that a long ride in the fresh air would help clear her head, when the duke stopped her, asking for a moment alone. Unsure of his intentions, Rosabel followed him to the front drawing room. As he closed the door behind them, a shiver ran over her. What did he want?

"You are probably wondering why I wanted to see you," he opened, his eyes dancing over her drawn brows. "Well, for one, I wish to apologise for not revealing my connection to this house sooner."

Sitting down in the armchair by the window, Rosabel observed him curiously. Still, there was nothing negative about his demeanour toward her. "There is no need to apologise, my Lord Duke."

He shook his head. "Yes, there is. And please, call me Edmond." When she hesitated, he added, "After all, we are family now."

Shocked, Rosabel could do nothing but nod.

"Thank you," he continued, sitting down across from her. "I am aware how strange this situation you find yourself in must seem to you. And I am sorry I did not make it easier by not being forward with you. But I must admit I had an ulterior motive." He grinned. "I wanted to know what kind of a person you were. I wanted to know if you would be a good mother for Georgiana."

"I see." Rosabel glanced at her hands. "And what have you discovered?"

Leaning forward, Edmond placed a hand on hers. Startled, Rosabel raised her eyes to his face and found a warming smile as he nodded his head to her. "I believe that Leonora would be very grateful for what you have done for her daughter. Georgiana told me about what happened with Mrs. Rigsby, and," he shook his head, smiling, eyes distant for a second, "believe it or not, you are a lot like her. You are a lot like Leonora." Rosabel's eyes opened wide. "You will be a great mother for Georgiana. I truly believe that."

"Thank you," she breathed, feeling tears form in the corners of her eyes. "I…I never thought…"

He squeezed her hand. "You do not get many compliments, do you?"

Rosabel shook her head. "And I never would have expected one from you."

"No? Why not?"

Embarrassed, Rosabel glanced at her hands, only to realize that his hand was still covering hers. "She was your sister." Raising her eyes to his, she whispered, "I thought you would hate me."

"What happened to her was not your fault?" Edmond assured her as though knowing the intricate ways of her mind. "Believe me, I wish with all my heart that that day had never happened. That she'd still be here." He brushed his other hand through his hair. "But no matter what we wish for, that will never be." He nodded, eyes looking into hers imploringly. "So, we have to move forward, make the best of things. It took me a while to understand that, and I'm not saying it's not hard. But she would have wanted us to be happy, especially Georgiana. That little girl was her whole world."

Feeling tears spill down her cheeks, Rosabel nodded. "I know. I

94

could see it in her eyes."

Edmond frowned. "What do you mean?"

Rosabel shrugged. "I…eh…found a portrait of hers up in the attic. I don't know why it's up there, but there is that kind of unconditional love shining in her eyes as though she was looking upon Georgiana when it was painted. I remember that kind of love. I remember what it was like to be looked at like that." A sob escaped her lips, and once again Edmond squeezed her hand.

"I know it is a sad story, but we haven't read the end yet." A smile came to his face. "It'll still be a long way, and I am sure that all of our lives have taken a turn for the better because Graham chose you."

Feeling a sudden cold in the room, Rosabel withdrew her hand.

"You have to know that Graham's life has not been easy, and while there is no excuse for how he is treating you," Edmond explained, his hand settling on hers once more, "he himself is damaged. He does not know it yet, nor do you, but I believe the day he married you, he saved his own life." Rosabel's eyes opened wide, and she was about to interject when Edmond hastened on. "You are strong, stronger than you know yourself. I've seen the difference you've already made in Georgiana's life, and I'll wager everything I own that before long Graham's smile will return as well."

Rosabel shook her head. "I am afraid you are mistaken. I am nothing like your sister, and if you think of me like this, I will only disappoint you."

"I do not believe that," Edmond assured her. "You think too little of yourself."

Rosabel frowned, hearing a strange echo of his words in Ellie's voice. "How can you possibly know me this well? We have barely spoken two words to each other before today?"

Edmond shrugged. "It's my gift." A dazzling smile came to his lips. "I can see the truth. I always could. It's a gift and a curse, believe me."

As Shadow carried her in a fast gallop across the meadow half an hour later, the cold wind whipped her hair in her face, freezing the remnants of tears still lingering on her skin. Her eyes burned as the cold air assaulted them, and she lowered herself to the stallion's neck, feeling the strength of his movements carry her toward the horizon.

Distancing herself from Westmore Manor and the people within, Rosabel felt the air flow more freely through her lungs. Her heart slowed to a normal rhythm and she looked with wonder at the house, half-hidden by a grove of oak trees. From far away, slightly raised on the hilly grasslands to the west, the house looked so small, and Rosabel wondered at the history it held. Did Leonora's spirit still linger? Sometimes Rosabel was so certain to feel her presence. Was Edmond right? Were they a lot alike? Rosabel shook her head. While Leonora had been like the sun, essential to the happiness of others, Rosabel was the black sheep of her family, hidden away from society, never talked of but in hushed whispers.

Running a hand through her dark hair, Rosabel glanced at a strand. Had Leonora once sat upon her horse on this very hill glancing down at Westmore Manor in the distance, her golden curls dancing in the wind? Everywhere Rosabel stepped, she was afraid to crush the memory of this woman. How was she ever to live here and be happy?

Georgiana was her delight. She had come to love the girl in the mere weeks since her arrival and could not imagine being without her ever again. But there still was her husband to consider. He was and would always remain her husband. That would never change, not unless one of them followed Leonora to the grave. But Rosabel wondered if she should accept his indifference, his rejection and allow him to keep her and his daughter at arm's length. Or should she go against his wishes and try to…Rosabel didn't even know what the alternative was. Did she seek his affection? Certainly not. He scared her. Whenever her thoughts turned to him, her body shivered as though fighting off a cold. Could she find a way to accept him for Georgiana's sake though?

Knowing that the little girl needed nothing more than to have her father back in her life, Rosabel wondered if she could make this happen. Did she have the strength? And even if she chose to, how would she go about it? She could not simply walk up to her husband and demand he spend time with his daughter. He would laugh at her. Worse, he would look at her with those cold eyes of his and send her away. Nothing would be won by such an attempt.

Still unsure about what her future held, Rosabel returned to the house, hoping that Edmond was at least partly right. That she would be a good mother to Georgiana. That much she could give her. If nothing else.

12

FOR GEORGIANA'S SAKE

gain and again, Rosabel sneaked up to the attic. Most of the time, she stared at Leonora's portrait, trying to glimpse the woman who had sat for it; her spirit, her heart, the very essence of what made her so special. And every time Rosabel found herself up in the dusty, cobweb-covered room, she discovered something she hadn't seen before. A small scar on Leonora's left temple. Sparks of green hidden among the blue ocean of her eyes. A small freckle shining through the soft curls falling past her cheek and grazing her shoulder.

Leonora's face followed Rosabel to her dreams. Night after night, she awoke, seeing the woman's spirit stand by her bed, just as she had stood there when Rosabel's eyes had still been closed. And although her obsession sometimes felt intrusive to Rosabel, she could not direct her thoughts elsewhere. A deep desire to know the woman everyone compared her to led her up the creaking stairs again and again.

The letter she had read before, she reread many times, eyes peeking at the many more, yet unopened letters still stacked neatly in the wooden box she had taken from the chest. What did they contain? What secrets awaited her within? More and more, Rosabel was convinced that there was something about Leonora's life that was still hidden in the shadows. What gave her this impression, Rosabel couldn't say.

Running her fingers over the spine of the letters, lying neatly side by side, Rosabel debated with herself whether or not to open another. Her curiosity, unimpressed by thoughts of right and wrong, urged her on. Her decency, however, cautioned that letters were private and that the confidentiality of their content was to be maintained.

While her head still debated the question, her fingers had already snatched up another letter. Staring at it as though shocked to find it in her hand, Rosabel took a deep breath. She whispered a silent apology to the woman whose privacy she was about to violate and slipped open the sheet of paper. It was dated October 1793, five months after the last one.

My dearest L.,

The seasons are changing, but my love for you holds true. I beg of you not to question my heart. My intentions have not changed, and I am pursuing their fulfilment with a dedication born out of the greatest of inspirations, true love.

By the end of next month, I hope to be in your vicinity. Visiting a mutual friend, I shall call upon you. Await my message.

I remain yours with all my heart,

G.

Rosabel's hands trembled as the words echoed in her mind. They had faced a great deal of trouble, but they had made their way. More than anything, the letter was inspiring. It encouraged her to believe that anything could be achieved if one only believed and not wavered from one's course.

Did the same hold true for her? Could she find a way to deal with her situation and come out the victor? Could she succeed in bringing father and daughter closer to one another? To bridge the gap that Leonora's passing had somehow opened between them?

Rosabel shook her head. Maybe Leonora could have succeeded. She had been a strong and confident woman, charming those around her and achieving her goals. Rosabel, however, was as far from strong and confident as any woman she had ever met. Ellie. She thought. Yes. Ellie would have succeeded too.

She exhaled slowly, feeling defeated. Suddenly the letter only represented a reminder of her own shortcomings. Heroic deeds were reserved for the brave of this world. She could never—

"Hello?"

Rosabel flinched, dropping the letter. She spun around, heart hammering in her chest, fire creeping up her cheeks at being caught in the act of violating a sacred trust.

As her eyes searched her surroundings, small footsteps echoed on the floorboards, drawing closer. A moment later, golden curls appeared in her field of vision, and for a second, Rosabel's breath caught in her throat. Had Leonora's spirit come to seek revenge?

But then she saw the short height of the person standing in the dim light, half-hidden in the shadows of the stacked crates. It was Georgiana.

Step by step, she came forward, eyes frozen, focused on something behind Rosabel's shoulder. Casting a glance backward, Rosabel found herself looking at Leonora's portrait.

"Mother," Georgiana whispered in awe. Stopping next to Rosabel, she lifted her right hand and carefully extended it toward her mother's portrait. Tenderly, she brushed a finger over her hair.

Rosabel knelt down beside the girl, placing the letter back in the box as she did so. "Have you never seen this painting before?"

Georgiana nodded. "I have. It used to be in the Great Hall." Her eyes wandered over her mother's face. "But then, one day, it was gone."

Wrapping an arm around the girl's slim shoulders, Rosabel waited, letting her stare as much as she liked, knowing only too well what this moment meant for Georgiana. When the girl exhaled slowly, leaning into Rosabel's embrace, she said, "Your mother was beautiful. Just like you."

Georgiana smiled.

"You have the same golden hair and those eyes too." Her hand brushed up and down Georgiana's arm.

Once again extending her hand, Georgiana took a step closer. "I thought I'd forgotten what she looked like," the girl whispered, a small catch in her throat as she spoke. "I felt so bad. How could I forget what my mother looked like?"

Drawing her into her arms, Rosabel whispered words of comfort. "Do not worry. You never forgot what was important. You remembered her smile, the way she laughed, how she read to you. You remembered what made her your mother. That is what's important." Gently, she brushed away the single tear running down Georgiana's cheek. "Your mother loves you. Don't ever doubt that."

Georgiana then turned to Rosabel, wrapping her tiny arms around her and hugging her tight. More tears spilled from her eyes as Rosabel held her, soothing her fears and easing her mind. "Can I keep it?" Georgiana whispered when her tears had stopped. "I don't want to forget again."

Unsure how to respond, Rosabel held her close a moment longer.

From what Georgiana had said, the painting had once hung in the Great Hall. That meant that someone had to have intentionally taken it down and hidden it away in the attic. Who would have done so if not her husband? And if he had done so, should she go against his wishes and return Leonora's portrait to the light of day? What would he say if he found out?

Rosabel shivered, feeling her courage fail. But then Georgiana stepped back, pleading eyes looking into hers, and Rosabel knew she was lost.

"Of course, you can keep it," she said, brushing a golden curl behind the girl's ear.

"Can I put it in my room?" Georgiana whispered, casting a loving glance at her mother.

Rosabel nodded. "I'll speak to Lawrence to have it arranged."

As Georgiana hugged her tight, whispering her heartfelt thanks in her ear, Rosabel knew that dark clouds were taking up residence upon the horizon. One day the storm would come upon her.

One day was not long off. Leonora's portrait decorated the back wall of Georgiana's room a matter of minutes when Mrs. Rigsby bustled in, a stack of books in her arms, which instantly upon seeing the painting crashed to the floor in a loud clatter.

Both, Rosabel and Georgiana flinched, looking up from the painting they had been working on. It showed a black stallion, resembling Shadow as much as a six-year-old's hands could muster.

"What is this?" Mrs. Rigsby demanded, face turning red as she stared at her former mistress. "What is this doing here?"

Georgiana slipped off her chair and coming to stand by Rosabel slipped a hand through the crook of her arm, holding on. Her eyes flitted back and forth between her mother's portrait, Mrs. Rigsby and Rosabel, resting on the latter with a pleading expression that could have melted stone.

Bracing herself for what was to come, Rosabel rose to her feet. Her right hand coming to rest on Georgiana's shoulder, she lifted her chin and met the governess' eyes head-on. "I suppose what this is should be fairly obvious," she said, trying her best to add a note of confidence to her voice. "As to the other matter, Lady Georgiana asked to have it in her room, and I agreed. After all, it shows her mother." Having finished, Rosabel fought the urge to look away as Mrs. Rigsby's eyes tried to burn a hole into her soul.

The governess' hands came to rest on her mid-section, giving her an even sterner look as she regarded Rosabel with open disdain. "His grace ordered it removed," she said, her voice even and detached as though discussing business. To Georgiana, however, this was a matter of the heart. "I apologise for being so frank, but it would be advisable to inquire after his grace's orders before agreeing to Lady Georgiana's wishes, your grace." From Mrs. Rigsby's mouth, *your grace* sounded like an insult.

Rosabel knew that Mrs. Rigsby had no right to question her decision even if her husband had given different instructions. She knew how insolent such behaviour would have been seen by everyone else and how no one of her station would have allowed their governess to speak to them so disrespectfully. Rosabel knew all that, and yet, she had to fight the urge to just run from the room and hide.

Taking a deep breath, she felt Georgiana's shoulders tremble beneath her hand and drew courage from the knowledge that she was not taking a stand for herself. But for Georgiana.

"Mrs. Rigsby, do allow me to remind you that my decisions are not yours to judge," she said, her voice slowly growing from a whisper to a small echo in the high-ceilinged room. "Lady Georgiana has every right to have her mother's portrait in her room. It should never have been removed in the first place."

Watching Mrs. Rigsby's face turn a darker shade of red, Rosabel noticed the door silently slide open, revealing Edmond standing in the door frame. Rosabel drew in a deep breath, unsure how he would react and which side he might take. After all, her husband was his brother-in-law and best friend. Georgiana, however, was his niece, his beloved sister's daughter.

A questioning look on his face, Edmond did not step into the room but remained hidden from Mrs. Rigsby's view, observing the scene before him.

"His grace himself ordered it removed," Mrs. Rigsby huffed. "I merely intended to remind *you* that his word is our command." Her tone clearly suggested that this included Rosabel as well.

Unwillingly her eyes drifted to Edmond. He raised his eyebrows, eyes shifting to the governess, and Rosabel had the distinct impression that he was urging her on.

Collecting her thoughts, Rosabel turned back to Mrs. Rigsby, who had no doubt read Rosabel's feeling of insecurity on her face and now stood looking at her mistress with a victorious glint in her eyes. Rosabel, however, refused to be intimidated by this woman any longer. To hell with the consequences, whatever they might be!

"Mrs. Rigsby, this is the last time I will stoop to such a conversation." The governess' eyes widened. "His grace chose me for his wife. He made me the Duchess of Kensington and put me in charge of Lady Georgiana's care as well as this household," she stopped for emphasis, her eyes drilling into Mrs. Rigsby's whose face appeared to have lost all its colour, "which includes you." For a second, she glanced at Edmond, seeing the grin on his face as his head bobbed along to her words. "Am I making myself clear?" Her voice was harsher than she had ever heard it before.

Steam coming out of her ears, Mrs. Rigsby nodded. "Yes, your grace."

"Good," Rosabel said. "You are dismissed for today." The governess' eyes widened. "Lady Georgiana will not attend her lessons but spend the day with her family."

Swallowing the words she clearly wished to say, Mrs. Rigsby nodded, turned on her heel and stopped as her eyes fell on Edmond, still standing in the door, grinning.

After the shock dissipated, she mumbled 'your grace' and hurried out of the room.

Edmond closed the door and walked over to where Rosabel slowly sank back down on her chair, her knees feeling like pudding. "I am proud of you," he said beaming. "It was about time the old crow got

102

put in her place."

Georgiana giggled.

Feeling all blood drain from her face, Rosabel blinked, trying to chase away the bright spots suddenly appearing in her vision. "What have I done?" she whispered, not seeing the others but staring straight ahead, contemplating her doom.

Edmond knelt down in front of her and taking her hand said, "You did the right thing."

Rosabel shook her head. "You don't even know what happened here."

Edmond shrugged. "I can guess." He glanced at his sister's portrait.

Rosabel followed his eyes. "Won't he be furious when he finds out?" she whispered, casting a careful glance at Georgiana, who had returned to her painting of Shadow.

"I would count on it."

Rosabel gasped, seeing bright spots again.

Instantly, Edmond lifted a hand, begging her to remain calm. "Please, do not fear him. Dogs that bark rarely bite." His eyes shifted to Georgiana for a second, making sure that she was still engrossed in her painting. "Graham is dealing with his own demons right now. He has his reasons for what he does, as ludicrous as they are, but that doesn't mean you should back down just because he might get angry." He squeezed her hand. "Do what you did today! Stand your ground. If you're right, you're right. No amount of yelling can change that."

Withdrawing her hand, Rosabel brushed them over her face, rubbing her temples, contemplating the situation she suddenly found herself in. Then she met Edmond's eyes and shook her head. "I am not your sister. I cannot do what she did. I..."

He smiled at her then. "But you already have! You need to open your eyes and see yourself as I do."

Again shaking her head, Rosabel considered him. "What makes you say these things to me? How can you be so kind? Do you not hate me for taking your sister's place? How is it that instead of wishing me gone you come to my aid?"

Edmond smiled, taking the seat next to her. "As I have said before, I believe that you will heal the wounds of this family. As much as I wish my sister was still with us, she is not. And although she will always be with us in a way, she cannot do the things she did before. She cannot protect Georgiana anymore. She cannot hold her. Comfort her." He glanced at his niece, and Rosabel saw love in his eyes. "We need you for this." Again, he squeezed her hand. "And from what I understand of your situation before, you are in need of a family yourself, isn't that so?"

Rosabel nodded, remembering the cold detachment with which her aunt and uncle had always regarded her and the heart-felt love that had always shone in her parents' eyes whenever they had looked upon her. The memory twisted her heart. "I love how she looks at me," Rosabel whispered, glancing at Georgiana.

Edmond nodded. "She is beginning to love you. You are becoming her mother."

Although his words warmed her heart, Rosabel couldn't help but shake her head. "I know that Georgiana needs someone to love her, but I do not wish to replace her mother. That would not be right."

"I do not speak of you replacing Leonora. She will always be Georgiana's mother. She will always be a part of this family." His eyes held hers as he spoke. "But that does not mean you cannot also be a part of this family. Who says Georgiana cannot have two mothers?"

"Do you truly believe that?"

Edmond nodded. "With all my heart. I could never contemplate a life in which anyone replaced my sister. But I believe, under the circumstances, she would share her role as Georgiana's mother. Wouldn't you? If you were in her position."

Rosabel looked at the little girl; her golden curls framing her soft face, cheeks flushed pink as she bent over the paper on the table, brush in hand, a concentrated frown wrinkling her forehead. Rosabel nodded. "I would, yes. She deserves no less."

Edmond smiled. "I am glad. Then for the sake of Georgiana and ourselves, let us find a way."

13

BUSINESS TO ATTEND TO

*T*o Rosabel's great relief, after their confrontation, Mrs. Rigsby seemed to avoid her wherever possible. Putting the governess out of her mind, Rosabel spent her days with Edmond and Georgiana. They took turns around the garden, to the duck pond and rode into the bordering woods and across the grassy meadows to the west of the manor. Meals echoed with chatter and laughter. Her own face split into a heart-felt smile, and the echo of her laughter rose and mingled with those in her company. More often than not, they all had tea in the dowager duchess' chambers in the afternoon. The old woman glowed when they filled her room, their voices echoing off the tall ceiling. In these days, Rosabel felt happy, welcome, not just tolerated, and even loved.

With honest regret, she watched Edmond take his leave a week later and ride down the winding road leading away from the house. Before long, he was lost from sight, and Rosabel felt the deep loss of a friend and ally.

Returning to the attic, Rosabel no longer saw herself as an intruder, someone who didn't belong. Getting closer to Edmond had also brought her closer to Leonora. Now, Rosabel considered her husband's first wife an ally as well, someone to lean on, someone who could help her find her way, someone who counted on her to succeed. And she sought to know the woman who would walk hand in hand with her to ensure their daughter's happiness.

As she opened the crate that had formerly hidden half of Leonora's portrait, her eyes fell on the by now familiar wooden box containing Graham's letters. Taking out another one, Rosabel took a deep breath, seeking permission. As the trembling in her fingers ceased, she took out the sheet of paper, unfolded it and began to read. It was dated December 1793, two months after the last one.

My dearest L.,

I beg your forgiveness for not writing sooner.

Even though I am away from you once again, the memory of our last meeting keeps me whole. Before my eyes I still see your beautiful face wherever I go, whoever I meet. No one and nothing matters until I will be in your presence once again. At this point, I cannot say when that will be, but believe me, my love, that I will not rest until I am with you once more.

I remain yours with all my heart,

G.

Had her husband written these lines? Rosabel could hardly believe it. Edmond's words again echoed in her mind. Leonora's death had left her husband a shadow of himself. He seemed broken beyond repair. Would she be able to help him? Was Edmond right? Or did he deceive himself? Having hope when there was none?

That night, Rosabel lay awake, staring at the ceiling, and compared the two men that she knew to be one and the same, but that she also thought to be mutually exclusive.

There was the man who was her husband. He had cold eyes, which threatened to stop her heart whenever he looked at her. His lips pressed into a tight line; she had yet to see him smile. She barely remembered his voice for he had hardly spoken two words to her. It had only been an order, short and clipped, without explanation or concern for her. He had married her because he needed her not because he wanted her. He needed her to raise his daughter, but he refused to be in the same house with her. There was nothing between them. Nothing but distance.

And then there was Graham. A man who had married the love of his life. A man who spoke of love in every letter he wrote. A man who had fought for the woman he loved. Fought and won. Rosabel tried to imagine his face as he had looked upon Leonora at their wedding day. The blue in his eyes sparkled, flecks of emerald dancing upon a sea of blue, matching the radiant smile that curled up his lips as he lovingly whispered, 'I do.'.

Glancing up from the papers cluttering his desk, Graham turned to the sound of hooves echoing on the gravel path leading up to the house. He cursed. Taking care of his estate's business from two-days away was complicated enough. He did not need unnecessary interruptions.

Before he could turn to the next item on his schedule, there came a knock on the door to his study, and the butler entered.

"Yes, Stanton, what is it?"

"The Duke of Cromwell, your grace," Stanton said, giving a quick bow.

"Have him enter," Graham instructed, sorting through his papers and neatly stacking them on one side of his desk. Then he walked over to the cabinet and poured himself and his friend a drink.

Footsteps echoed on the marble floor, and then Edmond came bursting through the door, his usual good-natured smile on his face. "Ah, yes, refreshments!" he exclaimed, reaching for the glass Graham extended to him. "Just what I need." He downed the contents in one swallow.

Sitting back down behind his desk, Graham looked at his friend. "Good day to you too."

Filling his glass once more, Edmond sank into the armchair by the window, opposite Graham's desk. He stretched out his legs, crossing them at the ankles, and leaned back, exhaling slowly. "You have no idea how inconvenient it is for me to have to come all the way down here to see you. What on earth possessed you to take up residence here?"

Eying him carefully, Graham frowned. "Is there a particular reason for your visit? Or did you just come to deplete my liquor cabinet?"

Edmond smiled. "I'd say a little bit of both."

"Well, then let's get to your reason. Why are you here?"

"To enjoy your delightful company. Truly, there is nothing like it." Edmond chuckled as he toasted Graham.

"Edmond, I do not have time for your games," Graham grumbled, glancing at the stack of papers that still needed his attention. "State your business or leave me to my own."

Edmond sat up, and the impish smile slowly left his face. Graham swallowed. Whenever Edmond looked as mature as his age, his words were serious. Why had he come?

"I've seen Georgiana," Edmond said without preamble, looking across the desk, eyes intent on Graham's face.

At the mention of her name, Graham felt a tug at his heart. It had been months since he had last seen her. He didn't even know how many. He couldn't keep track. The key to peace of mind was the removal of all those who affected him.

"I assume she is well?" he asked, not realizing that he was holding his breath. When Edmond nodded, he exhaled. "Well, is there more?" Pretending that his friend's words hadn't rattled him to the core, Graham averted his eyes, turning his attention back to the papers on his desk.

"You can't ignore her forever," Edmond said. "She is your daughter, and she needs you."

For a moment, Graham stared at his friend. Jaw clenched, he forced out the next words. "You know the situation. You are one of the few who do. Why do you speak of this to me?"

Edmond leaned forward in his chair, unimpressed by the anger burning in his friend's eyes. "Because you need her too."

Graham drew in a sharp breath but did not say a word. For a long while, they just stared at each other. Having grown up together, they had reached that point in their relationship when words were often unnecessary. Graham knew how much Edmond cared for Georgiana, and while his friend had never hesitated to take his side, his loyalty to Leonora and her daughter trumped the loyalty he had for him. In a way, Graham admired that about Edmond, even though it inconvenienced him at the moment.

Then Edmond blinked, breaking the connection of their silent exchange. He leaned back and the smile returned to his face,

108

mischievous and plotting. Graham knew to be on his guard. "I've seen your wife, too."

Graham shrugged. "Is she well?"

Edmond nodded. "Better than was to be expected under the circumstances."

"What circumstances?" Graham scoffed. "I made her a duchess and demanded very little in return."

Edmond laughed. "You have no idea, Brother. And I fear that no matter what I say you will not see it. So," he rose to his feet, "I have decided that you will accompany me back to Westmore."

Graham's eyes fell open. "What? Are you out of your mind?"

Edmond grinned. "Never felt better. Thanks for asking." He leaned forward, hands resting on the desk, and the twinkle in his eyes grew more intense. "Listen, I can see that you've gotten into a nice, little habit of brooding and grumbling here, but that doesn't mean that all your responsibilities have dissolved into thin air. Wasn't that the reason why you married Rosabel? Because you thought it your duty to provide Georgiana with a mother?"

Graham didn't know what to say. Hearing her name conjured up an image of her face. Although he barely remembered details from the few times he had laid eyes upon her, the softness of her kind features had stay with him. It had been the reason he had chosen her. For her kindness. Her compassion.

Reading his friend's face correctly, Edmond continued, "You made her a duchess, yes, but do you really intend for her to walk the rest of the way alone? She was not born to this, and yet, she is doing remarkably well." He grinned, apparently remembering something entertaining. "You'd be proud of her." Straightening up, Edmond came around the desk. "Come back with me, my friend, and set things right." When Graham hesitated, he added, "I am not talking about forever, merely a few days."

As he watched Edmond's face, the determination and honest interest he saw there, Graham felt his resolve waver. After all, he had planned on taking her to London for a few days in the beginning of the Season any ways. But now that these days were approaching fast, he felt reluctant. Should he go? He had worked so hard to put this distance between them, between himself and his daughter as well as his wife. What would happen if he saw them again? And at Westmore? Would he survive? What would it be like to see his daughter again without his beloved wife by her side? To walk the halls of Westmore without Leonora?

"I will think about it," Graham mumbled, avoiding his friend's inquiring eyes. "Now, leave me to my business."

14

RETURN TO WESTMORE

Whenever Rosabel was not with Georgiana or the girl's great-grandmother, she spent her days hidden away in the attic, reading Leonora's letters, or rather her husband's letters to Leonora. In the beginning, they sounded hopeful. Although some obstacle stood in their path, Graham sounded confident that they would overcome it. He professed his love again and again, begging Leonora to place her trust in him and not despair at the troubles they faced. Over time, however, the hope that Rosabel had always felt when reading his letters slowly dissipated. Instead, hidden anger resonated in the lines before her eyes. Although he had hoped for a positive outcome, it became clearer and clearer that it would not come to that.

Rosabel was confused. After all, in the end they had gotten married. Had they almost despaired, given up, only to have fate interfere and bring them together after all?

Again turning to the letter in her hand, dated November 1794, Rosabel found her eyes once again glued to the words written there.

My dearest L.,

Although my love for you has not lost its life, these days my heart is filled with fear rather than hope. I beg you to believe me when I say that my intentions are still where they were a year ago. My heart has not changed. But I fear my heart will not be allowed to dictate the future. My hands are bound. I fear all is lost. If only…No, there is no point in wishful thinking.

Pray do not worry about your situation. I will see you safe at the very least. Trust that if nothing else.

I remain yours with all my heart,

G.

As Rosabel sank down onto one of the crates, her eyes felt moist, and tears threatened to spill forth. The emotions in those lines touched her. She knew very well the feeling of hopelessness, of being forced into a situation, of having your future taken out of your hands.

Taking a deep breath, Rosabel wiped at her eyes, blinking away the tears. She returned the letter to the small wooden box and closed its lid, feeling too emotional herself to read another one. However, when she turned to go, she spotted something out of the corner of her eyes.

From the slit between the wooden box containing the letters and a small jewellery chest, the edge of what appeared to be another letter peeked out. Frowning, Rosabel reached to pull it out. Had she dropped one? She couldn't remember but knew she ought to be more careful.

Unfolding the letter, Rosabel frowned. The letter was not one she had read before. It was dated April 1795, about a half a year after the one she had just read.

Dear Leonora,

I write to assure you that all will be well. I understand if you do not believe me now, but do not despair. The clouds will pass, and the sun shall return. I give you my word that I will keep you safe and guard your happiness as the dearest of my treasures.

I believe I do not reveal a secret if I tell you that you already possess my heart. But soon I will give you the protection of my name as well. No harm shall ever befall you. This I vow.

I remain your friend always,

Graham

Rosabel shook her head. There was something wrong with this letter. In the half a year since the last one, which had rung with hopelessness, all had turned out all right. They were set to be married, and yet, the words sounded strange. Rosabel couldn't quite grasp it, but something had changed. More than just the circumstances keeping them apart.

Still torn between the desire to understand what had happened with Leonora and Graham and the knowledge that reading someone else's diary without expressed permission, which Leonora could not give anymore, was a heinous violation of trust, Rosabel stood before the little box that contained Leonora's belongings, namely her diaries. Eying them carefully, Rosabel swayed from one foot to the other, weighing her options. More than once, she extended her hand, only to withdraw it the next instant. Minutes passed.

"I don't have to decide now," she whispered, making up her mind. "I will just take them to my room and decide later." Lifting the little box off the crate, Rosabel was satisfied at having put off her decision.

As he leaned out the window, Westmore Manor slowly appeared on the horizon. The sky was darkening, but Graham could make out a few lit windows, the entrance hall as well as the side buildings. He took a deep breath. How long had it been since he'd last been here? He didn't know. Time had lost all meaning after Leonora's death.

For a second, he closed his eyes and pretended that nothing had changed. That he was coming home to his family. That his wife would be waiting for him on the stairs, welcoming him with a smile on her beautiful face.

Then his eyes opened, and in front of the darkening sky, Westmore had never seemed more like a place devoid of life. Stone walls, cold and dead, were reminders of that which once had been. They had seen the tides of time, and yet, they could not be moved to change. Some things could not change while others refused to stay the way they were.

As the carriage came to a stop in front of the stairs leading up to the front doors, Lawrence appeared as though stepping out of a shadow. He bowed low as Graham climbed the steps. "Welcome your grace," his monotone voice whispered. "Forgive me, but we were not expecting you."

Graham waved the old man's concerns away. "Do not worry. I did not have time to send a message ahead." He stepped into the entrance hall, eyes searching. Where were they? Georgiana? And his...wife?

Graham knew he ought to send for them, inform them of his arrival, and yet, he wanted nothing more than to retire to his room and hide away.

Knowing his duty, Graham turned back to his butler. "Where is Lady Georgiana?" And as an afterthought, he added, "And my wife?"

Lawrence nodded in the direction of the staircase. "Upstairs in Lady Georgiana's room as usual."

As usual? Graham wondered, as he climbed the steps. He knew nothing of their routines, nothing about how they spent their days. In that moment, he wasn't sure if he liked that or not. Approaching the door to the nursery, he could hear Georgiana's giggles echo into the hallway. Her voice was like a melody his ears were attuned to, his lips curling upward as though on reflex. His heart skipped a beat and then started hammering as though wishing to jump out of his chest and hurry into her arms. For a moment, he stood outside the door, listening, preparing himself. How would she react? Would she be angry with him for leaving? For returning? She was so young, did she even remember him?

The moment his hand curled around the handle to push open the door, another voice reached his ears, and he stopped. A melodious laughter, not unlike his daughter's, responded with equal delight. His wife, a little voice whispered. An ear pressed to the door, he tried to hear. Again, she laughed, and he could hear the smile in her voice. Trying to picture her face, Graham remembered the kindness he had seen there before. The adoration with which she had looked at her young cousins. Did her eyes hold the same emotions now that they were directed at his daughter? Graham hoped with all his heart that it was so. If they were happy, if Georgiana had a mother who doted on her, he would be able to leave and return to the emptiness that was now his life. He would be able to return to mourning his wife.

Slowly, he pushed open the door, his pulse straining against the tight collar threatening to choke the life from him. He found them sitting on a chaise by the fireplace, absorbed in a book. Heads bent together, their eyes shone, fiery sparks reflected in them. Their cheeks rosy from warmth or laughter or both, they huddled close, clearly enjoying each other's company. In that moment, Graham felt a stab to his heart. Somehow this picture was wrong. Felt wrong. Were they not to be happy? A voice whispered. He didn't know.

Then Georgiana looked up, and when their eyes met, Graham froze. Staring at his daughter, he waited for her to turn back to her book and ignore him or to yell at him for leaving her alone for so long or to order him from her room. He was prepared to face her anger, her rejection. What he wasn't prepared for was the heart-breaking smile that split her face the second her eyes beheld him.

For a moment, she sat transfixed, staring at him. Then she jumped to her feet, and running as fast as her little legs would carry her, she lunged herself into his arms. He barely had time to catch her when her tiny arms came around his neck, holding him tight. "Father," she whispered, over and over again. "You came back." Her little chest shook with sobs. They pierced his heart, and he fought to keep his countenance. What was she doing to him? He had worked so hard to distance himself from the past. And yet, here she was; a smile and a word, and he was hers once more.

15

ON THE OTHER SIDE OF THE DOOR

*R*osabel stared in shock.

As Georgiana had turned her head to the door, Rosabel had expected to see Mrs. Rigsby or Lawrence or maybe even one of the maids, but not her husband. In the past few weeks, she had successfully put him out of her mind. At least most of the time. The man she frequently thought about was Graham, the man who had loved Leonora, not the man who now stood mere feet from her, hugging his daughter, a tortured expression on his face.

Still staring, Rosabel didn't know what to do. Time seemed to be suspended as father and daughter held each other. Then after a long while, he set her down, and her little face beamed up at him. Again and again, she hugged him.

Finally rising to her feet, Rosabel approached the two. Her hands trembled as she looked from daughter to husband, dreading to meet his eyes. When he turned to look at her, his eyes were not as cold as she remembered them to be. Maybe Georgiana's welcome had melted the ice. Would the cold return? Rosabel wondered.

"Welcome home, my lord," Rosabel whispered, barely recognizing her voice. "Did you have a safe trip?"

For a moment, he seemed to search her face, then a mask slipped over his features hiding all emotions and he nodded. "Thank you. I did. I trust you two are well?" And with that, he turned back to Georgiana.

The remainder of the night, they spent in each other's company although Georgiana seemed the only one at ease. She chatted happily, showing her father her paintings, her favourite books and dresses. She spoke of Shadow and her lessons, how she disliked playing the pianoforte but loved singing. While Graham listened and expressed sympathy where appropriate, Rosabel watched them from under her eyelashes. Never before had she spent this much time in her husband's presence.

Tall, with broad shoulders and long legs, he towered over his daughter as he followed her to the easel to inspect her latest drawing of Shadow. Hands held behind his back, Rosabel noticed how he wrung them repeatedly as though agitated. His eyes mostly remained on his daughter, but every now and then, she caught him looking in her direction. The smile that occasionally flitted across his features, however, never reached his eyes and appeared far from genuine. He seemed tense, his jaw slightly clenched, eyes narrowed.

For the first time, Rosabel did not attribute the cold in his demeanour to anger or heartlessness, but she thought she saw something brewing under the surface. Something he did his best to hide from those around him. And she couldn't help but wonder if he felt as nervous about their sudden meeting as she did herself.

Graham couldn't help but glance at the door. It was long past midnight. The wind howled outside his window, bringing with it the cold of the season. The leaves had all but disappeared from the trees, leaving only pines and firs adorned with green. A chill crept up his body as he all but felt the wind push itself against the pane of the window, almost as though trying to reach inside. Held at bay by the remaining embers in the fireplace across the room, the cold still clung to his arms and legs, raising goose bumps. Graham knew though that it wasn't the slight chill in the air that made him shiver.

Again, he looked at the door, which connected his chamber to his wife's. Was she sleeping? He wondered. Did she care that he was there? Did his presence bother her? He knew it did.

Although his outward attention had been focused on Georgiana when he had entered the nursery a few hours ago, his eyes had glanced at Rosabel. Upon seeing him, there had been a moment when her disapproval, later carefully masked, had been clear on her face. He knew that she didn't appreciate him disrupting the life she had carefully established for herself. From Edmond, he knew that Rosabel and Georgiana had settled into a routine, which seemed to benefit them both. Lonely, they had turned to one another and found comfort in the other's company.

He knew she didn't want him there under the same roof with her. And although he had only returned to Westmore upon the urgings of his friend, Graham felt a slight stab at being so negatively thought of. It called to mind all those times he had spent in this room, lying in bed, staring at the ceiling, and hoping. Hoping for what? Hoping for the life he had dreamed of ever since he had first laid eyes on Leonora. Only now, any chance for this life was gone. Buried not too far from where he laid his head at night.

His chest felt like a boulder had come to rest on it, slowly squeezing the life from him. He couldn't breathe, and rising from the bed, he turned to the window. With a soft creak, the window opened, and the freezing night air rushed into the room, chilling him to the bone. However, instead of shutting the window, Graham breathed in the fresh air, enjoying the feel as it flew down his lungs and into his body. What was he to do? How should he handle this situation?

Again, he glanced at the door. Was she sleeping? Would she deny him if he decided to visit her chamber? Not that he planned to. The feeling of rejection, of not being thought of as good enough had an iron grip on his heart that kept him confined to his room. And yet, his heart yearned. Yearned to be loved. Yearned to be thought of as worthy of love. Would he ever have that?

Throwing the window shut with a loud bang that ought to have raised the dead, Graham turned away, feeling anger boil in his veins. Anger at himself. He ought not to think like this. There was no point. It would only lead to more disappointment. His whole life he had served others, served his country, his king, with no thought for himself. He ought to stay the course. It was the only way.

Hearing a loud bang from her husband's chambers, Rosabel flinched. Ever since he had set foot into the nursery and disrupted her life, her nerves had been on edge. Why had he come? Did he mean to be a husband now? The thought made her shiver. Again, she glanced at the door, wishing for a key to lock him out. Would he come? If not tonight, then tomorrow? Not knowing kept her eyes open. Sleep wouldn't come although Rosabel begged for the sweet release of a dream's oblivion. Just for a few hours, she wanted to leave Westmore behind and escape to a place without looming threats in the next room.

Unable to stay in bed, Rosabel grabbed her robe, and carefully opening the door to the hall, she slipped out and hastened down the corridor toward Georgiana's room. Feeling the soft rug under her bare feet, she remembered her slippers but refused to return for them. Walking up to the bed, Rosabel's lips curled up in a smile at the sight of the peacefully sleeping child. The hint of a smile played on her features as her eyes moved with the dream that held her captivated. Rosabel's heart unclenched a little. At least, Georgiana was happy. She deserved to be. Knowing she couldn't keep this happiness from the child nor desiring to, Rosabel made up her mind. She would do her best to find a way through this maze. There had to be a way for all of them to live under this roof and not have it turn into a nightmare. Whatever her husband would decide for their future, she would go along with it, trying to find a way to be happy. If only for Georgiana.

Once again, Georgiana's chattering was the only thing keeping awkward silence at bay. While Rosabel and Graham offered a friendly word here and there, the little girl almost burst with energy. Only the reminder of her lessons put a scowl on her face, and she reluctantly withdrew from the breakfast parlour and headed upstairs to meet Mrs. Rigsby in her room.

Feeling her husband's presence almost like a cold shower, drenching her and making her shiver, Rosabel too rose from her chair, intend on going out to the stables. A ride with Shadow would do her good and help clear her mind. However, when she began walking to the door, her husband's voice called her back.

He gestured to the chair she had only just vacated, and when she had sat down again, he too took a seat across from her. "I apologise for disrupting your day, my lady, but I feel the need to explain my intentions in coming to Westmore."

Rosabel swallowed as the cold slowly crept up her arm, and she had to link her hands to keep them from trembling. Forcing her eyes up, she looked at his expressionless face. Did he never tremble?

"While I am glad that you have settled into life at Westmore Manor so easily," Rosabel couldn't help but laugh...on the inside. Did he truly believe that? "I thought it right to lend a hand in introducing you to local society." Sitting straight in his chair, her husband's hands gestured along to his words, his eyes not cold but disinterested. "Soon, there will be a Christmas Ball, that I usually attend, and this year, it will provide the opportunity for you to meet important people from around Westmore. In the new year, we will then travel to London to engage in the appropriate circles for a reasonable amount of time so that proper introductions can be made. Knowing others of your station, I trust that you will have no problem filling your day in the future. Whenever you are not with Georgiana, of course."

Clenching her hands even tighter, Rosabel felt as though she had lost all control of her body. Her muscles trembled as though she sat outside in the deep of winter, desperately trying to stay warm. She only hoped her husband didn't notice.

Others of her station? She thought. Did he truly believe that? She already knew that the Earl of Hampton was the one to hold the legendary Christmas Ball each year. He was an earl, and who was she? A duchess, a little voice whispered. But still Rosabel felt like a fraud. What would she say to those people? Alone at a festivity with only her husband to reassure her? Again, her hands clenched around one another.

Taking a deep breath, Rosabel tried to speak. "When will the Ball be held?" she croaked in a whisper. She already knew the answer. The invitation had come a month ago. And yet, she felt the need to say something.

"The 21st."

Rosabel nodded. A week from today. The little voice whispered again. Straightening her posture, she turned to her husband. "Will you be staying until then, my lord?" She wasn't sure what she hoped his answer to be.

120

Graham nodded. "I will." The expression on his face told her that he wasn't entirely happy with the situation either.

Taking her leave, Rosabel almost ran to the stables. Waiting for Peter to saddle Shadow, she danced from one foot to the other, unable to keep still, feeling the desperate need to get away.

The second Shadow's long legs reached the open meadow covered in deep snow and thundered along the ridge of the hillside, Rosabel closed her eyes, feeling the cold wind on her face. Tiny snowflakes caught in her hair and melted into drops of water, slowly running down her temples and pooling in the corners of her eyes. Before long, she felt them drift down her cheeks as though she were crying. Appropriate. The little voice whispered. Rosabel knew it to be true. More than anything, she felt like crying, but she knew if she gave into her fears, she might not be able to stop the floods.

Unfortunately, even two hours outdoors had been unable to perch Rosabel's fears from her heart. So upon her return, she hastened up the long staircase, knowing only too well where the only counsel in Westmore was to be found. As she approached the door to the dowager duchess' quarters, Rosabel noticed that it stood ajar, silent voices drifting to her ears.

Taking a step closer, almost pressing her ear to the gap between door and frame, Rosabel ignored the little voice telling her that this was not proper and listened.

"I thought you would never return," the dowager duchess said. "It's been a long time."

"It has," her husband answered. "How are you?"

A chuckle rose from her throat. "Dear boy, you did not come here to speak to me about my health! We both know that. Why don't you tell me what is really on your mind?"

Even through the door, Rosabel could hear her husband draw a deep breath. "How is Georgiana? Is she happy?"

"Well, she is happier, ever since you found this remarkable, young woman to care for her. Rosabel really is doing a fine job. I have to congratulate you, dear boy. You could not have chosen better."

"I am glad to hear it." Footsteps drew closer to the door, and Rosabel's breath caught in her throat.

"We are not done here, my boy," the dowager duchess called after her grandson, who stopped instantly, the echo of his footsteps vanishing into thin air. "May I ask? Why did you choose her?"

For a moment, silence hung about the room. Then her husband's voice reached her ear. "I thought she'd make a good mother for Georgiana. I told you so."

"Yes, you did. But what gave you the idea? From what I understand, you had barely spoken a word to her before proposing?"

"Did she tell you that?"

"Is it a secret?"

Her husband sighed. "Of course, not."

"Then what was it?" When no answer came, she continued. "Don't make an old woman wait!"

"Fine. I thought she was kind. I thought she would be a kind mother."

"And what gave you that impression?"

Again, her husband sighed. "You ask a lot of questions."

"I am tied to this bed. All I know is what people tell me, and you're not very forthcoming! So? Enlighten me!"

Again, footsteps echoed across the floor, but this time they returned to the bed. The chair was pulled up, and her husband took a seat. "I watched her. The way she was with her younger cousins, it was…it reminded me of happier days, of innocence; of a time in one's life when the world only holds wonder."

"I see. That certainly makes her a good mother, and I've seen the proof of your words in Georgiana's eyes." The bed covers rustled as she tried to sit up. "I have one more question though."

"Then ask it." A smile rang in his voice. "I know by now that I could not stop you even if I wanted to."

The dowager duchess chuckled. "Although it did take you a while to realize this, my boy."

"Well, then ask?"

"You looked at the mother, but did you ever look at the woman?"

Rosabel froze as she supposed did her husband, considering that he did not say a word.

"If you only cared to look, you would see that she would make you a fine wife as well. Her heart is not taken. You still have a chance, but not for long. Eventually she will close her heart to you if you keep treating her like this."

As her husband got up, the chair legs scraped across the hardwood floor. "Like what?" he snapped. "I made her a duchess. She has never been more comfortable in her life!"

Again, the dowager duchess chuckled. "How blind you are, my boy.

You do not treat her like a wife, but like a servant. For now, she may obey your command, but mark my words, it will not last forever. She may not know it yet, but a strength resides within her that will eventually break free. And believe me, as much as I love you, you are no match for her."

16

THE CHRISTMAS BALL

The week until the Christmas Ball passed in a relatively boring manner, anticlimactic in a way. While her husband mostly kept to his study, Rosabel spent her days as she usually did, with Georgiana and the dowager duchess or riding out with Shadow. Meals were taken together with her husband, but then Georgiana mostly carried the conversation, needing little encouragement to relate her day, her plans for the next and all those seemingly insignificant details that were of such importance to someone so young.

As much as her husband avoided her company during the day, he also did so during the night. Rosabel awoke each morning feeling relieved that he had not come to her. And yet, there was a tiny voice considering his behaviour an insult. Was she so undesirable?

When the day of the Christmas Ball arrived, Rosabel's nerves were on edge. While Bridget and two other maids helped her get dressed, do her hair and choose appropriate accessories, Bridget gave her a quick rundown of who would be at the ball. By the end of her overview, Rosabel's head swam. She could not remember all those names and titles. How was she to get along?

When she finally descended the grand marble staircase leading down to the entrance hall, Rosabel felt every inch of her tremble, afraid she'd lose her footing and land head-first at her husband's feet. Standing by the front doors, he looked up as her footsteps echoed down the stairs ahead of her.

Dressed in a simple, yet elegant suit, his black hair combed back, her husband looked the picture of a gentleman. Only the scowl on his face offset her impression, telling her without a doubt that having to introduce her to local society did not please him in the least and he'd rather be somewhere else. Somewhere far away.

Taking a deep breath, Rosabel approached him, eyes cast down, and took his offered arm.

Hearing her footsteps, Graham turned to the sound, and for a moment, the control he usually had over his features slipped away as his grandmother's words echoed in his ear.

For the first time, he did not see the mother Rosabel had become, but the woman she was.

And she was breath-taking!

The crimson red dress perfectly complemented her raven-black hair, accentuating her pale skin and slim figure. The stark contrasts made her glow, vibrant with colour. A rosy shine on her cheeks spoke of excitement or jittery nerves, he could not tell. Her eyes glistened in the dark, hidden under thick cast-down lashes. Nervously, she bit her lower lip, brushing a hand down the soft fabric of her dress. He could see the concern about her appearance plainly on her face. Then she looked up and for a moment met his gaze, before returning it to the stairs under her feet.

Graham barely managed to get his own features back in check before they'd give him away. He noticed his pulse had sped up, and although it returned to a more normal rhythm, he could still feel it pulsate against the tight fit of his collar.

For a moment, his eyes turned inward. Leonora had been beautiful, in a more obvious way even. Her golden hair and glowing blue eyes had enchanted anyone to ever lay eyes on her. She had been like the sun, drawing everyone near, necessary to everyone's survival. Her smile had always been given freely, true, genuine and heart-felt. Nothing about her had ever been fake. From the very beginning, Graham had loved her, loved her even before he got to know her and fell for her all over again.

Rosabel was different.

Again, he cast a careful glance in her direction as she approached and hesitantly slipped her arm through his. As he led her out the door and to the waiting carriage, their feet crunching in the snow, he felt her tremble by his side. Again, he wondered if it was the cold or her nerves. Helping her into the carriage, he took a seat across from her, noticing tiny snowflakes in her dark hair, shining like diamonds.

Avoiding his eyes, she kept her head down or faced out the window as the carriage slowly turned down the road. Pretending not to look at her either, Graham still felt her presence like a thick blanket wrapped around him. Again and again, he glanced at her. Again and again awed by her simple gracefulness. Again and again lecturing himself to redirect his thoughts. And yet, a tiny voice whispered that she was his wife after all. There was nothing wrong about the thoughts he entertained.

Too wrapped up in his own mind, Graham did not notice the silence that hung between them. Every now and then, he thought he saw her glance in his direction, but when he turned to look, her eyes were once again focused on the snowy landscape passing by their window.

Before long, they reached the earl's estate, seeing the many lights a mile off, glistening like stars in the darkening night. Cheerful laughter met their ears as the carriage came to a stop, and a footman opened the door. Stepping out himself, Graham turned and offered Rosabel his hand, grateful to feel the chilly wind on his face, cooling his cheeks.

As she slipped her hand into his, a tingle ran up his arm. Her skin felt soft and tender, yet cool and trembling. Instantly, he drew her forward, determined to get her out of the cold as soon as possible. When her hand slipped from his and linked through the bend of his arm, he felt a hint of regret.

Stepping inside, they quickly found themselves submerged in the holiday festivities. Many congratulations were offered, but also regret that no invitation to their wedding had been received. Graham did his best to manoeuvre the sea of people with ease. He knew what was expected of him and played the role that had been his long before his

126

father had passed his title on to him.

Next to him, he felt Rosabel almost clinging to his arm. Her eyes were wider than usual, taking in her surroundings with apprehension. A smile passed his lips as he realized that they had something in common after all. Neither one of them felt at home in a sea of people.

The noise. Rosabel had never heard such noise, never seen so many people in one place. The earl's estate was large, almost as large as Westmore, and in every corner, in every nook and cranny people were gathered, talking, laughing, dancing and drinking. They sounded like a beehive, only louder, much louder, and their voices held none of the soothing hum of the little honey collectors. Their voices were shrill. Like an instrument out of tune, they hurt her ears.

For the first time thankful for her husband's presence, Rosabel's hand clutched his arm tightly, afraid to be left behind. Following him through the crowd, she was introduced to her neighbours as well as guest visiting for the holidays from other parts of England. Names and titles flew at her. Some sounded familiar, some didn't, but none found a permanent place in the corners of her mind.

Playing his part with ease, Graham offered her a drink, which she accepted gratefully. Her throat felt parched, and the cool liquid offered relief. However, letting go of his arm, Rosabel soon found others drifting toward them, crowding around her husband and drawing him into a conversation. Step by step, she retreated from the throng of people until she could barely see him anymore. Her heart hammered, and her palms began to sweat as she found herself alone, unsure how to proceed.

Unwilling to wedge her way into the crowd and back to her husband's side, Rosabel decided to walk about the rooms. She thought if she didn't stand in one spot for too long, the chances that someone would try to engage her in a conversation would decrease. Slipping from the ballroom, afraid someone would ask her to stand up with him, Rosabel found her way to the front parlour. As she walked through the door, she saw a table with small refreshments by the opposite wall. Glancing at her empty glass, she headed over there, passing through small groups of ladies chatting animatedly. Keeping her head down, Rosabel avoided eye contact and after procuring another drink for herself retreated into a shady spot in the corner by the window front.

Not too far away, a group of young women stood, their backs mostly in her direction. After a while, a tall blond in an emerald dress that accentuated her green eyes and rosy lips said, "Did you see the new Duchess of Kensington?" Rosabel's blood froze in her veins. The others nodded. "She looks nothing like the former duchess. Too plain."

More nods encouraged her to go on.

"Almost like a wallflower, don't you agree?" Again, the others' heads bobbed up and down, offering their own comparison. Each word was like a stab in the heart, and tears formed in the corners of Rosabel's eyes.

"Why did he marry her?" the blond asked, shaking her head. "He could have had anyone, why her?" Rosabel supposed the tall blond herself had vied for his hand, and lost. Thus, the bitterness in her voice. "She is not fit to be a duchess. I heard her father did not even have a title."

"I heard she is the niece of a baron down south," another offered.

The tall blond shrugged. "Niece, not daughter."

Having her worst fears for the evening realized, Rosabel sneaked past the group of ladies without raising their attention. She was a fraud, and they all knew. They had seen past her masquerade and clearly identified her as someone not worthy of their company. Someone who did not fit in. Someone who was not one of them. Did her husband regret his decision to marry her by now? Even if she was a good mother to his daughter, was that enough?

"Ah, here she comes," a voice boomed not too far from her, and Rosabel looked up, seeing all faces staring at her. As her heart threatened to jump out of her chest, she saw her husband walk toward her, offering his hand. As though it was a lifeline she reached for it, grateful for his warm touch to her own chilled skin. He led her through the throng of people to the dance floor. As they stood up, he whispered, "I apologise, my lady. This spectacle was certainly not my idea." She could see the truth on his face. He was forced in this position just as she was. Society dictated the rules. It would be rude not to comply, and so they both put a pleasant smile on their faces and moved to the music, keeping in tune with the couples around them.

As he led her across the dance floor, Rosabel felt his hand on her waist, and even through the layers of fabric, she thought she could truly feel the warmth of his touch. The hand that held hers, guiding her movements, sent a tingle down her back as his thumb slowly moved over her skin. Was he doing this on purpose? She wondered. Or was he lost in thought?

Letting her feet move, Rosabel held on to her husband, feeling safe for the first time that night.

Her hand trembled as it lay in his. He could feel her breath on his skin as she forced a mask of happiness on her face. Not looking him in the eye, her gaze was focused beyond his shoulder, giving him the opportunity to observe her more freely. Her cheeks were flushed as though she had run a sprint or heard something embarrassing. Every now and then, her tongue snaked out, moistening her lips, and he thought to detect a small tear drop clinging to her thick eyelashes. What had happened during his absence? Had someone treated her without the appropriate respect? He didn't know, and he was surprised to realize that it bothered him. After all, any disrespect toward his wife was ultimately an insult toward him, he told himself.

Too soon the music stopped, and the dance ended. New couples encroached on the floor, demanding their turn. Leading his wife into the hall, Graham's mind drifted to other dances, dances with Leonora. These moments holding her in his arms had been the most wonderful moments of his life. He had cherished them like his greatest treasure, and even now, the memories put a smile on his lips.

Rounding the corner, they came upon the Earl of Hampton kissing his lovely wife under some mistletoe. Giggling, she clung to her husband, eyes gazing at him adoringly, as the crowd cheered.

Looking around, Graham noted the various places were mistletoe had been hung in the doorways and made a mental note to stay away from them. Himself deeply in love with his wife, the Earl of Hampton found great joy in ordering those caught under the wintry green to a public display of affection. Remembering his wife's fearful eyes when he had bent down to kiss her on their wedding day, Graham did not care for a repeat of that situation. He would not force himself on her, no matter the circumstances. He had forced her hand, but he would draw the line there.

17

MISTLETOE

*F*inally back in the carriage on the way back to Westmore, Rosabel breathed a sigh of relief. While not altogether pleasant, the evening had passed without further embarrassments, and Rosabel longed for her bed, feeling her limbs growing heavy with the need for rest.

Pulling up in front of the house, the carriage came to a stop and a footman opened the door. Once again, her husband assisted her the two short steps down to the slippery ground, holding her hand firmly in his and guiding her up the stairs to the front doors. Lawrence bowed and wished them a good evening. Thanking him, her husband stopped as a familiar voice echoed across the empty hall. "What a delightful couple you make! My compliments!"

Rosabel's head snapped up. Striding toward them, a big smile on his face and a twinkle in his eyes, was Edmond. His gaze shifted from her husband to her and back again. "Did you have a good time?" he inquired, but before her husband could answer, Edmond's eyes shifted upward and his hand too indicated something above their heads.

Rosabel felt her husband stiffen. The muscles in his arm grew tight, and she released her grip, suddenly realizing that there was no need for assistance any longer.

Lifting her head, Rosabel found a small twig with green leaves dangling from the ceiling. Having seen the like all throughout the evening, she instantly knew what it was and realized its implications. Her eyes shifted back to Edmond, who grinned from ear to ear, and then darted to her husband, whose face had turned into an angry scowl. Swallowing hard, Rosabel didn't know what to do. Would he kiss her? Vaguely she remembered her wedding day. Although his eyes had been cold as always, his lips had been soft and warm, and she had felt herself respond at their touch. Would this kiss feel the same?

"I believe a kiss is in order," Edmond said, a mischievous gleam in his eyes as he looked at his friend. It made Rosabel wonder if the mistletoe had even been there earlier when they'd left for the ball. She couldn't recall it had. Had Edmond put it up to force them into a kiss?

Casting a careful glance at her husband, Rosabel thought he was fuming with anger barely held in check. As his eyes shifted to her for a second, her hands began to tremble and the breath caught in her throat. Was he angry at her? Or had he figured out the same thing she had just realized and his anger was directed at Edmond?

Waiting for his approach, not knowing what to expect, but strangely curious, Rosabel was taken aback when her husband bowed to her formally, saying, "I bid you a good night, my lady." Then he walked off, heading for his study.

Dumbfounded, Rosabel stared after him. Her eyes clouded, and her head fell as she realized the meaning of his actions. How he must hate her! She was not the wife he wanted. She was but a substitute. A poor one at that. And he could not even bring himself to kiss her. Feeling a sting deep in her heart, Rosabel turned to go.

"Do not mind him," Edmond spoke up. "It will take some time. But do not give up. I beg you." His eyes were imploring, and Rosabel couldn't help but nod. Shocked, she realized that she had come to care for her husband. How could this be?

When Rosabel finally lay in bed, the tears she'd held back all night ran freely down her cheeks, wetting her pillow. Exhausted after the emotional turmoil, she only relaxed when sleep finally claimed her.

Grabbing the small vase on the mantle, Graham hurled it at the wall, watching in satisfaction as it shattered into a thousand pieces. And yet, the heat that burned in his heart did not dissipate.

A knock came on the door.

"Enter!" he barked.

When Edmond peeked his head in, Graham saw red. He grabbed the nearest item in sight, which happened to be the decanter, and hurled it at his friend's stupidly grinning face.

Barely able to duck out of the way, it hit the doorframe right above Edmond's head, glass shards and liquid hitting the wall in a deafening explosion. "How dare you?" Graham snarled. "How dare you force my hand? How dare you interfere?" His breath coming in heaving rasps, Graham's hands raked through his hair, and he felt a painful tug on his scalp as he pulled.

Closing the door, Edmond lifted his hands in surrender, carefully stepping around the shards scattered across the floor. "Calm down!" he cautioned, his usual smug smile replaced by earnest concern.

Graham couldn't stand to look at him. "Leave me alone!" he bellowed.

"So that you can destroy the rest of your study?" Edmond snapped. "No! Whatever is bothering you, tell me! What happened tonight?"

Graham spun around. "You! You happened!" Again, his hands raked through his hair, eyes frantically searching for a way to repair the damage. The damage to his life. "Everything was fine until you interfered!"

Edmond laughed, and Graham felt the desperate need to punch him in the face. "Everything was not fine!" his friend objected, unaware of the threat lying in wait. "You at Camden Hall, her at Westmore, you call that fine? I saw you tonight when you came walking up the stairs. You looked," he stopped as though searching for the right word, "untroubled. I haven't seen you like this in years. Why didn't you kiss her?"

Staring at his friend, Graham shook his head. Through gritted teeth, he forced out the words. "I do not force myself where I am not wanted."

Nodding, Edmond grinned. "But *you* wanted to, didn't you? Is she the first woman you wanted to kiss since my sister?"

Graham froze, a thick lump forming in his throat. "This is none of your business! Get out! Now!"

Edmond shook his head. "You can't scare me, Brother! I know you better than anyone else on this sodden planet, and I won't leave until you admit why you didn't kiss her tonight!"

Hands balling into fists, Graham knew if his friend didn't leave soon, it would come to blows. "I told you why!" he snarled.

"And I told you you're lying!" Edmond objected once more. "At least to yourself. I know quite well why you ran away."

Cursing the heavens, Graham slumped down in his chair, all fight leaving his body. "Then tell me. Tell me and leave!"

Leaning forward, Edmond rested his hands on the desk, gaze focused onto his friend's face. "Because you're scared. You're scared that she will refuse you. That she does not return your affections."

Graham's head snapped up. "Affections?"

A slow smile curled up Edmond's lips. "I suppose you're the only man in England who finds it highly inconvenient to be in love with his wife."

Pushing back the chair, Graham shot up. "I am not—"

"Not yet maybe," Edmond interrupted. "Give it time."

18

IN THE DARK OF NIGHT

ot knowing how to meet her husband's eyes after his open rejection the night before, Rosabel dreaded each step that took her closer to the breakfast parlour. Oh, if she could only stay in bed and pretend none of this had happened!

As the footman opened the door, she took a deep breath, squared her shoulders and with her head held high walked into the room to find Georgiana sitting in her usual place, looking at her with round eyes. Her husband's chair was empty.

Smiling at the little girl, Rosabel strode forward. She brushed a hand over her head and took the seat across from her. "Good morning, Georgiana. How did you sleep?"

As the footman poured her tea, another approached her with a silver platter in his hands, a folded sheet of paper on it. Frowning, Rosabel took it and began to read. With each word, although there weren't many, her eyes grew bigger. That coward! She thought. He had sneaked away in the middle of the night, blaming some unforeseen business that had come up. In her heart, Rosabel knew the truth. Once again, he was avoiding her. And once again, she didn't know how to feel about it.

A part of her rejoiced at being spared an awkward and highly uncomfortable meeting after the happenings of the previous night. And yet, she couldn't help but feel like he was insulting her again. He didn't even have the decency to look her in the eyes after clearly telling her that she displeased him as his wife. He had not uttered a word of apology, nor did the note contain one. What was she to do? He fled in the dark of night from his own house, and she was supposed to keep up pretences? The world was far from fair.

Remembering the little girl across from her, munching on her muffin, Rosabel felt bad. Georgiana would be heart-broken to learn that her father had abandoned her once again. How ought she to tell the child?

As the door opened once again, Rosabel looked up in surprise, seeing Edmond stride into the room, the usual gleam in his eyes. As her gaze met his, he actually winked at her. Rosabel couldn't stop the smile curling up her lips, but she shook her head at him nonetheless.

"Good morning," he beamed, taking his seat next to her. "How did you sleep?" Again, there was that twinkle as though he was referring to something highly inappropriate...and enjoying every moment of it.

"As well as expected." Her face once again serious, she handed him the note. "Then I received this."

He took the letter, and his voice dropped a little. "A love letter?" But then his eyes flew across the page, and the smile withered away and died a slow death. His lips pressed into a tight line, he brought his fist down on the table with a sudden blow that rattled the cups in their saucers. "Damn that fool!"

Both, Georgiana and Rosabel, looked up in surprise. Realizing he had an audience, Edmond regained his composure quickly. He put away the letter and smiled at Georgiana. "Care for a sleigh ride in the snow?"

Georgiana's mouth fell open, and her eyes shone like the morning star. "Oh, yes please! Can I?"

As Rosabel found her looking at her, waiting for permission to go, a sweet warmth spread from her heart into every fibre of her being. She truly was the child's mother now, and she could not have been happier! If only her husband weren't such a—

Instantly, she called herself to reason. Such thoughts served no purpose.

Instead, she returned her daughter's smile and nodded.

"Great!" Edmond clapped his hands together. "You better go and bundle up. It is freezing outside. I'll wait for you in the hall."

Georgiana ran from the room, too excited to ask why her father hadn't come down to breakfast. When they heard her small footsteps echo on the marble staircase, Edmond pushed back his chair and turned to Rosabel. "I am so sorry. I never thought he would do this."

Rosabel waved his concern away, concentrating on buttering her muffin. "Well, neither did I, and yet, I cannot help but feel I should not be surprised."

Edmond frowned. "Why?"

Rosabel turned to look at him, hoping to silence him on this subject once and for all. "Because I have never seen him or myself the way that you do. But I am hoping that after everything that happened today and before, you will find the need to alter your idealistic impression of us. It serves no purpose." Her eyes looked at him imploringly. "We are who we are. I cannot change who I am, and neither can he change who he is. It would be best for all of us to accept reality."

His shoulders sinking a fraction, Edmond leaned one arm on the table. "I admit that this," he pointed to the letter with a scowl on his face, "does not help my case, but neither does it dissuade me to pursue it. On the contrary, it strengthens my resolve."

Rosabel shook her head. "Why? Why are you so insistent? Do you truly believe that this is what Leonora would have wanted?"

Edmond shrugged. "To be honest, I do not know. But I believe that wallowing in misery is no way to live. And while you," he smiled at her, and that twinkle came back to his eyes, "seem to have found a place for yourself, a place that holds love," he glanced at the doors through which Georgiana had left, "Graham has none of it. He might not be at a loss to fill his days, but he has nothing to fill his life with. And while I understand that his recent behaviour does not endear him to you, he is like a brother to me, and it pains me to see him in such low spirits."

Rosabel nodded. "I understand that you cannot give up on him. But I feel obliged to point out the futility of your endeavour."

A boyish grin came to his face. "Duly noted." He rose from his chair and Rosabel realized none of what she had said had altered his mind in the least. "If you'll excuse me, my lady, I have an engagement to honour." And with that, he bowed to her and strode from the room to meet Georgiana.

19

LEONORA'S DIARIES

While Georgiana and Edmond faced the cold, Rosabel retreated to her room. As she entered, her eyes fell on the upper drawer of her vanity, and without thinking she walked over and pulled it open, revealing Leonora's diaries. Would they contain answers?

Settling into her favourite armchair facing the bay windows, Rosabel watched tiny snowflakes dance on the air, free to go wherever they chose. The sun caught in their minuscule crystals and had them sparkle like diamonds. Eyes gliding over the snow-capped trees and hills outside her window, the only word that came to Rosabel's mind was beauty. How could her eyes perceive something so stunning while her mind rolled over in turmoil? Would outside and inside ever walk hand in hand?

Her gaze still fixed out the window, Rosabel's fingers slowly traced the small lines running every which way across the cover of one of Leonora's diaries. The leather was soft to the touch almost like a living being welcoming her caresses. Intrigued beyond self-control, Rosabel turned the cover, her eyes settling onto the page, reading the first words without comprehension as her mind reminded her that she had just crossed a line.

... I never thought I'd find true love. I've heard people speak of it, and yet, deep down my heart never truly believed it existed. There is no other way to describe the surprise I feel at now experiencing it myself. Like a unicorn stepping off the pages of a fairy tale, one morning suddenly standing out in the gardens among the rose bushes as though it had always been there.

But it is true. I blink, and the unicorn is still there. Only thinking of him makes my heart beat faster. The sparkling blue of his eyes. The tender curl to his lips as he smiles at me. The soft touch of his hand as he helped me into the saddle.

But as glorious as this feeling is, I know it can never be. Why would love torment me this way? I, who never believed true love existed, am destined to suffer a doomed love. How cruel fate can be!

Rosabel frowned, wondering again what it had been that had Leonora and Graham both deem their love one without hope, without future. Even from the first day.

Reading on, Rosabel could not discover anything new. Leonora was torn between the glorious feeling of love in all its facets and the hopelessness it faced.

Forgetting about the midday meal, Rosabel read and read. As Bridget stuck her head in, wondering whether her mistress was suffering some ailment, Rosabel just assured her that she was fine and sent her away. Nothing in the world could tear her away from the pages in her hands. Like someone hunting for lost treasure, the fever of the chase had completely taken her over.

... His father does not approve. I always suspected as much, but hearing G. confirm it still brings tears to my eyes. Although my mind had been expectant of it, my heart had still hoped. Now all hope is lost. G. assures me that he will not give up, that he will find a way to receive his father's blessing. Although G. did not speak of it, I am aware of the match his father strives for. I cannot compete.

There was something that eluded Rosabel. As much as she had learned about Leonora and Graham's situation, she was certain that there had to be something she was overlooking. Something that would have everything make sense. Why had Graham's father disapproved of him marrying Leonora? She had been a duke's daughter. What other match could he have preferred? And besides, from what Rosabel had been able to piece together from snippets heard here and there the late Dukes of Kensington and Cromwell had been good friends, like their sons were today.

... I know I am to blame. I should not have allowed him. I should have kept my wits about me. Now I am to pay.

And yet, regret is not the only feeling within my heart. Part of me rejoices in the triumph of our love. A small triumph, one enjoyed in silence and never shared with the world, but still a triumph. Only no one else will see it as such. To the world, I will be ruined. My family will be ruined. Oh god, what have I done?

"What did you do?" Rosabel asked the words before her eyes, feeling the pulse hammer in her veins. The kinship she felt to this woman, this woman she had never met, scared her, and yet, it made her heart beat with sympathy and the need to understand. Not that she could have changed the outcome of the situation or altered Leonora's fate, but still Rosabel thought if she could only understand, Leonora would appreciate her effort.

... He promised he would find a way. A way to save me. To save us. I believe him, and yet, I do not believe such a task can be accomplished. Not without severe losses. Losses that may by far exceed the gain.

But G. insists I put my trust in him. And so I wait. Only, time is of the essence.

From the many entries, Rosabel had read so far, a suspicion arose. Deep in her mind, a small voice began to whisper, and with each page she turned, it grew louder and louder.

Leonora had been with child...before she had gotten married.

Rosabel felt for the young woman, imagined her fears and wished she could have been there to assure her all would be well.

... Today I received a letter. I still cannot believe what it said. My mind is numb. Never would I have thought G. would consider such a solution. A solution that solves but one problem and leaves the other as hopeless as ever.

How can he agree? How can he suggest such a thing? Part of me can only see the evil of his plan. And yet, there is another part, smaller but slowly growing bigger, that sees the wisdom of his words. It is a sacrifice, for us both, and yet, it will ensure confidentiality. Nothing will be revealed. I will not be considered ruined. But

I will lose the love of my life forever.
What should I do?

More confused than ever, Rosabel closed the diary as she spotted a horse-drawn sleigh approach over the far hill. Remembering Edmond and Georgiana's outing, she hastened downstairs and had warm tea prepared the minute the two burst into the entrance hall, snow falling off their clothes, leaving little puddles in their wake.

"You must be freezing," she exclaimed, pulling Georgiana's coat off and rubbing her cold hands. The girl's cheeks were rosy and snowflakes still clung to her hair. She looked like life itself, and yet, there was a sorrow to her eyes that instantly froze Rosabel's heart.

Georgiana knew.

Glancing to Edmond, Rosabel caught his eyes. As he read the question on her face, he nodded in answer.

He had told Georgiana that her father had once again abandoned her. Certain that he had not used these words, Rosabel could still see in the girl's face that no matter how Edmond had phrased the news, her heart understood its essence perfectly.

Unfortunately, not long after her husband had fled Westmore Manor, Edmond took his leave as well. Saying their goodbyes, for he did not steal away in the middle of the night, Edmond assured her that he would not give up; as though such a promise would ease her heart. She thanked him nonetheless and watched as his horse carried him down the lane and vanished soon after behind a grove of oak trees. When would she see him again?

With Edmond gone, Georgiana's smile disappeared as well. Not only had her father left without a word of farewell, but her uncle, who like no one else knew how to lift her spirits, had gone also.

As they sat over imaginary tea on New Year's Day, Georgiana's gaze clung to the horizon outside her window. Not seeing the green hills before her, the little girl's eyes were distant, turned inward at something only she could see.

Eventually tearing her eyes from the window, Georgiana's gaze met hers, and once again a small stab injured Rosabel's heart. Brushing a hand over the little girl's head, she smiled at her reassuringly. "Would you like to go to the library? We could find a new adventure."

Georgiana shrugged. The twinkle that usually came to her eyes at such a suggestion remained absent. Once again, Rosabel cursed her husband!

"Why does everybody leave?" Georgiana whispered, her innocent, blue eyes looking into Rosabel's. "Why don't they stay?"

Swallowing hard, Rosabel took Georgiana's hands in hers. "Do you mean your father?"

The girl nodded. "Father, and Mother, and Uncle Edmond." For a moment, she looked down at her hands as they lay in Rosabel's. Then her head came up, and a single tear rolled down her left cheek. "And soon you will leave to. Why can't I come with you to London? Did I do something?"

Her words were like a slap in the face to Rosabel. "No! Of course, you didn't. Please, don't think that." Pulling the little girl onto her lap, Rosabel wrapped her arms around her. "Listen, your mother didn't leave. She didn't have a choice. Otherwise, she would be here right now. She would never have left you." Georgiana's shoulders relaxed a little as she exhaled slowly. "And your father, well, he misses her too. He is very sad, and he believes it to be easier for you if he is not around. He is afraid he would make you sadder." Rosabel desperately hoped that Georgiana's innocence would accept her explanations.

"But he is wrong!" the girl exclaimed. "I'm sadder when he is not around."

"I know. You're right, he is wrong. But he doesn't know. He is too sad to think clearly. But I'm sure he will soon realize that sharing sadness heals the heart best. I'm sure he will be back soon." Rosabel couldn't help but bite her tongue. Why had she said that? She couldn't possibly know what he would do, and from experience, she supposed that he would not again return to Westmore, at least not willingly. How could she have given Georgiana false hope?

Lifting her head, Rosabel's eyes met Leonora's gazing down at them from the portrait that decorated the east wall of the nursery. Help me! Rosabel pleaded. What am I to do? How can I protect our child?

Leonora's blue eyes looked as kind and loving as ever. But as she gazed down at her daughter's bent head, Rosabel thought to detect something else. Strength. Determination. And in that moment, Rosabel knew what Leonora would do.

Leonora would fight. She would not bend to her husband's will.

She would not back down. Leonora would fight for her daughter, no matter the consequences.

The hint of a smile came to Rosabel's lips as her resolve strengthened and the decision to act became a certainty. She didn't know how. She didn't know what she would do. But she knew her goal.

Georgiana's happiness. To see a permanent smile on those soft, rosy features. Not one constantly overshadowed by grief and disappointment.

Tomorrow, Rosabel would go to war. She would fight her husband with everything at her disposal.

However, that was easier said than done. For the question remained, what were the means at her disposal?

20

LONDON

"hy don't you call me Helen, dear?"

Rosabel saw the warmth in the woman's eyes and felt herself respond. After losing her mother at such a young age and resigning herself to her aunt's rejection, the dowager duchess was the answer to Rosabel's prayers. Finally, she had a mother to confide in.

Taking her hand, Rosabel smiled at her. "I'd like that very much." Tears came to her eyes, and she quickly blinked them away.

"When will you be leaving?" the old woman asked, her own eyes growing moist. "I will certainly miss you."

Rosabel swallowed the lump in her throat. "Tomorrow."

"And my grandson?"

"According to his note, he is already there, tending to some urgent business." The dowager duchess scoffed. "The carriage will take me to his townhouse."

"How long will you be gone? The whole season?"

Rosabel shook her head. "He didn't say, but I doubt he wishes to spend that much time in my company."

145

A gentle squeeze of her hand made her look up. "Watch him carefully," the old woman implored, her eyes intense with meaning. "For years now, he has been wearing a mask, and although he has nearly perfected it, no mask is ever truly flawless. It cannot be, for it is not real. Every now and then, a mask slips, revealing the true self underneath. Look for it."

Rosabel nodded, wondering if she would ever catch more than a glimpse of her husband's true self.

The next day, saying goodbye to Georgiana broke Rosabel's heart. Not even by the time the carriage had left Westmore grounds far behind had her tears dried. Even inside, the icy air rested on her shoulders like a heavy blanket. Not long ago, the snow and ice had turned everything into a winter wonderland, and Rosabel had walked through it with open eyes, watching everything with rapt attention, seeing awe everywhere she looked. Now, the snow seemed smothering, heavy, a burden. How could things change so drastically in so short a time?

Occasionally, Rosabel slipped into a fitful sleep, exhausted after spending her nights worrying about the days ahead, and so she did not notice when the carriage finally drew up a hill and approached the city of London. Only when its sounds, the sounds of crowds of people going about their everyday business, drifted to her ears did her mind abandon sleep.

At first, her eyes cracked open a fraction and then widened as she took in the sights before her eyes. Sitting up, Rosabel stared out the window at the tall buildings and wide cobblestone streets filled with people on foot, people in carriages, people driving carts, people on horses. People were everywhere, no matter where she looked, and their voices rose into the air completely extinguishing the more familiar sounds of nature. Rosabel could not hear the calls of birds or the soft rustle of a breeze brushing through the trees. In a strange way, the world before her eyes fascinated Rosabel, and yet, it frightened her all the same. Soon, she would have to abandon her observational post and join the people of London in their crowded lives.

When the carriage stopped, Rosabel found herself facing the steps of a massive townhouse, silently standing side by side with its brothers.

A few rays found their way through the thick mass of clouds obscuring the skies and gently touched her cheek. Rosabel took a deep breath and stepped across the threshold, entering not only the house but also a life she had never wished for.

As the door closed behind her, Rosabel realized that the sounds of the street were still there. Muted, but not gone. They would never be gone. She would have to learn to live with them, hopefully not for too long.

Rosabel spent the rest of the day alone, exploring the house and being introduced to the staff. Only when supper came around did her husband grace her with his presence. Taking their seats at opposite ends of the large dining room table, Rosabel felt dwarfed by the size of her surroundings. Not that the rooms at Westmore had been smaller, but in the country everything was vast and wide. In town, however, space was limited, and the crowded streets had altered her understanding.

As the soft clatter of silverware on porcelain echoed across the room, Rosabel felt her own muscles tense, casting a careful glance at her husband.

His eyes, too, were fixed on his own hands as they moved fork and knife across the plate. Watching, Rosabel saw him take a deep breath before lifting his eyes to her. "I hope this is to your liking, my lady."

Rosabel nodded. "It is, my lord." She took another bite in order to avert her eyes.

"We will be at the theatre tomorrow."

Rosabel's head snapped up. "The theatre?"

"Yes, Covent Garden," he elaborated. "Then there will be a number of social gatherings in the following days that will represent the perfect opportunity for you to acquaint yourself with your new social circle." When they had both finished, he gestured for the footman to clear the table and bring the next course. "I have a week, maybe two before my presence is required elsewhere. I believe that ought to be enough time."

"Of course, my lord," Rosabel mumbled, inwardly rejoicing. No matter what her husband thought she ought to do after her introduction to her new social circle, Rosabel's own plans were quite specific. As soon as possible she would return home, to Georgiana.

Like a deer hunted by a pack of wolves, Rosabel stood surrounded by the ton, all appearing nonchalant while their eyes betrayed their eagerness at getting a good look at the new Duchess of Kensington. Appraising looks slid up and down her frame, and Rosabel trembled with the effort it took not to bolt and return to the safety of the carriage.

While her husband greeted friends and business acquaintances, Rosabel stood by his side, her own arm looped through his, a lifeline to keep her from drowning. Occasionally, she smiled or nodded, gave a quick greeting, desperately hoping that no one would seek to draw her into a conversation. Clutching her husband's arm, she prayed they would not be separated. More than anything, she wanted to avoid a repetition of the embarrassing scene she had witnessed at the earl's Christmas ball.

To her surprise, her husband would now and then place his hand on hers, giving it a gentle squeeze as though to reassure her. She would look at him then, and whenever his eyes would flash to hers, she would see compassion and understanding there, not cold appraisal as she had feared.

Helen's voice echoed in her head as she carefully observed her husband through batted eyelashes. *Watch him carefully. Every now and then, a mask slips, revealing the true self underneath. Look for it.*

When it was finally time to take their seats, Rosabel breathed a sigh of relief, reluctantly letting go of her husband's arm.

As her fingers slipped from his arm, Graham felt their loss acutely. Never before had he felt the desire to protect her. But as the hyenas grouped around them, preying on his wife, Graham had stood his ground, firmly redirecting every attempt at drawing her away.

Throughout the performance, Graham only had eyes for the woman by his side. While his head was directed at the stage and the actors, his eyes frequently strayed to his right, his mind occupied with only one thing: keeping his hands to himself. More than anything, he wanted to feel her again. Even through the layers of fabric, the way she had clung to his arm had touched his heart and stirred his desire. Had there been mistletoe anywhere in sight, today he would not have been able to stop himself!

Watching her every move, Graham saw her shiver again and again as her eyes occasionally shifted from the stage to the rest of the audience around them, equally unoccupied with the performance on stage. Instead, their eyes openly stared into their box.

Graham wondered why he had not noticed before.

Of course. He only had eyes for his wife. How had this happened? He wondered.

Slightly turning toward her, he leaned over. "Are you still cold, my lady?" he whispered.

As her eyes came to rest on him, he could read her answer. Before she could decline though, he placed his hand on her arm, her silky skin soft and warm under his touch, and observed, "You do feel cold, my lady."

Her eyes narrowed as she looked at him, and he saw her confusion at his lie. He smiled at her then, rose from his seat and offered her his hand. "Allow me to escort you home lest you catch cold, my lady."

For a second, she hesitated, but then a grateful smile lifted the corners of her mouth, and Graham saw the relief in her eyes as she placed her hand in his. Savouring her touch, he pulled her arm through his once more and led her away from the stares and out into the cold where their carriage waited to take them home.

When they bid each other good night, Rosabel saw something in her husband's eyes that made the breath catch in her throat. His blue eyes shone with a warmth she had never seen before, and sudden heat invaded her cheeks. She took a slow breath to steady her nerves.

As his eyes seemed to burn into hers, Rosabel watched his chest slowly rise and fall as he, too, remembered to breathe. He stepped toward her then, head lowered to gaze into her face. A small smile curled his lips as his head slowly dipped lower, his eyes flitting from hers down to her lips.

As though in trance Rosabel watched him slowly move toward her, his lips aiming for her own, until all of a sudden he froze.

His upper body snapped back up, and he drew in a sharp breath as the smile vanished from his face. Clearing his throat, he merely whispered, "Good night."

Before he turned away though, Rosabel reached out a hand and held him back. "Can I speak with you?" she asked, feeling the disappointment over the distance he once again forced between them burning in her heart.

Turning to face her, he barely met her eyes.

"I have been meaning to speak to you about something, but there never seemed to be a right moment." Drawing in a deep breath, Rosabel gathered her courage. "I know you intend to return to Camden Hall." He nodded. "What about Georgiana? When will you return to see her?"

Eyes hardening, he almost glared at her. "That is none of your concern!" Gone was the warmth that had melted her heart before.

Feeling her lips press into a thin line, Rosabel lifted her chin. "I beg your pardon! She is my daughter. Of course, it concerns me. How can you just disregard her like this?"

At her words, his muscles tensed, and he took a menacing step toward her. "As I said, it does not concern you!" He turned on his heel, about to walk away and leave her standing in the hallway.

"If you could only see the heartbreak your actions cause her," Rosabel spoke to his receding back, "you would not disregard her so easily."

He stopped, and his head slowly turned back to look at her. Then he drew another laboured breath before his jaw tensed. Rosabel could see the indecision in his eyes, but then rigid determination chased it away, and without another word, he walked down the hallway.

The next engagement on her husband's list proved less straining. For one, a ball generally offered a more engaging atmosphere with many opportunities for socializing. People talked and danced, shared food and secrets. Venturing from the ballroom to one of the adjoining rooms, Rosabel felt herself reminded of the earl's Christmas ball. However, with repetition, her own attitude changed. Not that she felt comfortable in such a crowd. Not at all, but at least her heart beat did not threaten to knock the feet out from under her.

Another reason for people's lessened interest in her person came in the form of Edmond Dunsworth, Duke of Cromwell.

Seeing his warm smile and twinkling eyes, Rosabel immediately felt herself relax. A friendly face. A little voice whispered. A face she knew. For once, she did not have to face a stranger.

He greeted her warmly, twirling her around the dance floor mere minutes later.

"You look radiant," he beamed, eyes flitting over her shoulder. "And my friend's scowl seems to have lessened as well."

When they turned about the room, Rosabel glanced at her husband's face. Edmond was right. His eyes were far from cold as he stood, drink in hand, following them with his gaze.

Turning back to her dance partner, Rosabel detected the same mischievous twinkle in his eyes she had seen there many times before. "He has that same glow in his eyes he did the night of the Christmas ball," he whispered grinning at her. "Before I…made a mess of things." He sighed, looking disgusted with himself. "Rosabel, I apologise for interfering." Once again, he glanced at his friend. "I suppose you'll be more likely to succeed on your own, without my…help."

Staring at his face, Rosabel smiled at him. "Are you truly admitting to a wrongdoing on your part? Edmond, I am shocked." A giggle escaped her, and she sighed at the lightness of heart she felt at that moment.

Edmond grinned sheepishly. "Begrudgingly, I do." His eyebrows arched up. "Do me a favour and keep this to yourself."

Rosabel nodded, smile still unwilling to abandon her lips. "This is truly a day to remember, Dear Brother?" she said, before her mouth dropped open in shock as her own words rang loudly in her ears. "I apologise." She shook her head. "I shouldn't have…"

"There is no need," he assured her, his smile less beaming but all the more genuine. "You are not Leonora, but I am proud to call you my sister."

The end of their first week in Town brought Rosabel another

insight into her husband's true self. As his grandmother had advised her, Rosabel watched him carefully whenever she could without being too obvious.

Once again attending a social gathering, Rosabel felt more and more confident to occasionally venture off on her own. Here and there, she returned a greeting or even exchanged a few words with a recent acquaintance.

In the corner by the currently unoccupied pianoforte, Rosabel saw a young woman. Though tall, her frame was slim and her ash blonde hair flowed far past her shoulders, stretching her even more. From her pale complexion, Rosabel would have thought her feeble; if it weren't for her eyes. Although pale blue like a summer's sky, they spoke of deep emotions and thoughts held in check, buried underneath a surface of pliability and acceptance. Her name was Henrietta Turner.

"Duchess," the woman smiled as she caught sight of Rosabel. "You are attending tonight's soiree as well? Well, what do you think of these gatherings? Yesterday, you mentioned you had never been to London before. Is that true?"

Rosabel nodded, feeling an instant connection to the young woman. "It is very crowded. I have to admit it does make me uncomfortable. I never know what to say."

Henrietta laughed. "The sad thing is people do not generally care what others have to say. Especially men." Frustration rang in her voice as her eyes travelled across the room, where her brother, the new Viscount Elton, stood with their uncle, Henrietta's guardian since her parents' passing. "As long as you have a pretty face, they are satisfied." As though remembering something, Henrietta shook her head. Turning her eyes back to Rosabel, she forced a smile on her lips. "I apologise. I did not mean to make you uncomfortable. Here, let us get some refreshment." She gestured to the adjoining room, where long tables groaned under the loads of food piled on top of them.

Stepping through the doorway, they stopped as a small group of men and women stood in their way, and Rosabel felt oddly reminded of the Christmas ball. Goosebumps rose on her skin, and she drew in a breath.

As though only waiting for her to overhear, a dark-haired beauty in a pale blue dress said in a rather melodious voice, "The new Duchess of Kensington is a rather plain woman, wouldn't you agree? Oh, sure she is pretty, but she does not have this air of superiority about her that dear Leonora did."

Rosabel felt her limbs grow rigid at the woman's words, echoing her own thoughts.

Henrietta touched her arm, beckoning her to follow, but Rosabel couldn't move. Hidden in the crowd she felt somewhat safe. What if they saw her?

"I suppose she had a sizable dowry to recommend her," the woman continued. "Why else would the duke have married her?" She snickered but instantly stopped when another, quite familiar voice echoed through the little group.

"Because the moment he laid eyes on her, he knew her to be the one woman who could make his life complete."

All chattering stopped, and as people drifted apart, revealing the speaker of these eloquent words, Rosabel found herself staring at her husband. A smile on his face, he looked at the small crowd before him, then gave a quick nod and walked away.

Entering the ballroom, Graham felt a small stab of regret. Tomorrow, he would return to Camden Hall.

Glancing at his wife drifting through the crowd on his arm, deep down he knew that something had changed. The only thing he didn't know was whether or not he was ready to admit that to himself.

Throughout the evening, he kept his eyes firmly planted on her beautiful smile, shy and yet, honest, the sparkle that came to her eyes when Edmond drew her onto the dance floor and the gracefulness with which she held her head high, even though he knew she wished for nothing more but to retreat into a corner.

Watching them sweep across the room, Graham noticed a strange tightening in his chest as he beheld his wife's delighted face, looking up into his friend's eyes. His jaw tensed, and he took a deep breath to still his nerves.

Instead of instantly seeking his wife's company once the music came to an end, Graham intercepted his friend. Trying to remain unobtrusive, he offered him a drink, which Edmond downed in one gulp. "You seemed parched," he observed, narrowly looking at his friend. "Was dancing with my wife so tiresome?"

Instantly, Edmond's head snapped up, his eyes narrowing as they slid over Graham's face. "Jealous?"

As his pulse sped up, Graham laughed. "Do not be absurd!"

A delighted smile broke out on Edmond's face, and Graham knew that he had lost. "She looks at me as a friend, a brother even." He nodded, placing a hand on Graham's shoulder. "You have nothing to fear." Then Edmond's eyes shifted up, staring past his shoulder. "At least not from me."

His heart in a tight grip, Graham turned around and took a deep breath. "Who is she talking to? Is that Baron Northfield?"

"It is," Edmond confirmed. "You should keep an eye on her!" Then he turned to look at Graham and another grin spread across his features. "But you've been doing that anyway, haven't you?" Laughing, he marched off.

At least partly relieved, Graham noticed that his wife did not encourage Baron Northfield's attention. On the contrary, she appeared somewhat bothered by his insistence to remain by her side. More than once did she try to take her leave without success. Graham knew that he should interfere and put the baron in his place, but he wanted to know her true feelings on the matter.

However, when he finally made up his mind and started toward her, Lord Ashton stepped in his way. His business associate vigorously congratulated him on his nuptials and was exceedingly difficult to get rid of. When Graham finally did, his wife was nowhere in sight.

His heart hammering in his chest, he searched high and low, his pulse rising with each minute that passed. Then he spotted her in the back of the room by the French doors.

Eyes again fixed on her, he relaxed as she stepped outside, only to suffer nearly a stroke when the baron hastened toward the doors as well.

In that moment, Edmond came upon him, pointing at the same doors that held Graham's attention. "Did you see—? You did. Let's go after them."

Almost outrunning his friend, Graham reached the doors in the blink of an eye, not caring in the least about the questioning eyes that followed him. He yanked them open and stepped outside, Edmond on his heels.

"Where are they?" Edmond asked.

Footprints in the soft layer of snow covering the terrace led them to the right. All the while, Graham's heart hammered in his chest as though ready to explode.

"Lord Northfield, I must insist that you let me pass," his wife's insistent, yet slightly frightened voice broke the deafening silence, and he quickened his steps.

Coming around the corner, Graham found her with her back to the wall, Baron Northfield blocking her way back. Her eyes stood open wide, and she had her hands lifted to maintain the distance between them.

Graham cursed himself. Knowing what kind of a man Northfield was, how could he have left her alone?

"I insist as well," he snarled, and two sets of eyes flew to him. While the baron looked mildly startled, instantly taking a few steps back, his wife almost seemed to sag into herself as relief flooded her face. No one had ever quite looked at him that way, and Graham felt his regard toward her deepen.

"Are you all right?" he asked, reaching for her. Her cold hand came into his, and he instantly wrapped his other arm around her shoulders, drawing her near, warming her body with his. Lifting her chin, he looked into her eyes. "Did he touch you?" he whispered, his insides twisting into knots.

When she shook her head, he closed his eyes for a moment and took a deep breath. Then, without turning his gaze from her, he said, "Edmond, if you would *escort* the baron back to the festivities."

As the sound of their footsteps had vanished, his wife took a step back. By now shivering from the cold, she looked up at him, a single tear clinging to her lashes. "I'm so sorry," she pleaded. "I shouldn't have come out here. I didn't think he would follow me."

Graham nodded, already missing the feel of her body against his. "It is not your fault," he said, trying to reassure her. "That man has no honour. And yet, you're right, you shouldn't have come out here. Not alone."

She nodded then, and he led her back inside. They said their goodbyes and returned home, the carriage ride filled with a silence that held a thousand meanings. Where were they to go from here? Graham wondered. Things definitely had changed, and yet, he could not go back. He was a man of reason. He was led by his head, not his heart. Following his heart had once before led him into a darkness that he still had not been able to leave behind. He knew what he ought to do, and yet, a little voice whispered that maybe, just maybe she could come to love him.

Finding herself in the carriage back to Westmore, Rosabel recalled the last words exchanged with her husband that morning. At least this time, he had bid her farewell. When he had asked about how she intended to pass her time in London, she had stated that she would rather return home. Hesitant for a moment, he had nodded, and Rosabel thought he had looked relieved. Did he not trust her? Did he think her foolish enough to venture into another dangerous situation? Was he afraid what such a scandal would do to his reputation?

Pushing all gloomy thoughts aside, Rosabel focused on what awaited her beyond the horizon: Georgiana.

A fortnight had passed since she had seen the girl, and Rosabel's insides clenched at the thought of being separated from her any longer. As entertaining as London had occasionally been, it was not her world.

And so when the carriage finally pulled up to the steps of Westmore Manor and the golden-haired girl flung herself into her arms, Rosabel felt at peace.

21

TO SAVE A LIFE

aving spent the night tossing and turning, Rosabel felt a painful throbbing behind her temples when the sun finally etched its way up the horizon, glistening in the new snow covering the grounds outside her window. The bright light, however, did not cheer up her spirits, instead it increased the dull pain behind her eyes, and she turned away immediately.

Although her reunion with Georgiana had proved as wonderful as she had dreamed it, new questions had arisen that had kept her awake. Who was the man she called husband? In London, he had been so different from the cold-hearted man who had chosen her for his bride without having spoken a single word to her beforehand.

Feeling the need to clear her mind, Rosabel walked down the corridor to Helen's chamber. Quietly, she knocked on the door, hoping she would not disturb the old woman. Fortunately, Helen had already been informed of her return and was awaiting Rosabel's visit eagerly.

"How have you been, child?" she asked, her own eyes glowing with vitality. "Did you enjoy London?"

Rosabel shrugged. "Too crowded for my taste. I prefer it here."

Helen laughed. "Thank god, you do. I wouldn't know what to do without you."

Taking the old woman's hand, Rosabel smiled. "I've missed you too."

"Now, my dear, tell me what happened. How did my grandson treat you?"

Blushing, Rosabel averted her eyes.

"Ah, something happened!" Helen declared in triumph, eager eyes on Rosabel's face. "Tell me!"

Relating the encounter with Baron Northfield on the terrace, Rosabel felt her own cheeks flush even deeper at her own defect of judgment. "He must think me a fool to not have seen it coming," she whispered. "He looked perfectly scandalized when he came upon us."

"Oh, my dear, sweet child," Helen laughed. "He was not scandalized. If I had to make a guess, I'd say he was jealous."

Rosabel's eyes went wide. "What? Why would you..?"

"Oh, my dear, it is so obvious. He cares about you. The only problem is," Helen snorted, "that he hasn't yet admitted that to himself. But when he saw you with our dear Baron Northfield, I suppose he finally realized what he has to lose." Clapping her hands like an excited child, Helen chuckled. "Oh, Baron Northfield, what would we have done without you?" she mused, then shrugged. "Probably died of old age before that thick-headed grandson of mine had given any indication as to his true feelings."

"But Helen—"

"No, no, no," she shook her head vehemently. "Do not argue with me. Listen." She took Rosabel's hand, drawing her closer. "I know this is not easy for you, but you must not let him get away."

"Let him get away?" Rosabel mumbled.

Helen nodded. "Go after him. Do not allow him to retreat into the shadows. He will never find a way out himself. Go to him," Helen pleaded. "And safe him from himself."

Still unsure how best to proceed, Rosabel returned to her room after breakfast, once more running her fingers over the leather-bound diaries that held the connection to Leonora. Diaries she hadn't seen in a fortnight.

Once more sitting down in her favourite armchair, Rosabel opened the book. No longer did she feel like an intruder, someone trespassing, but instead her heart swelled with warmth whenever her eyes found the by now familiar handwriting. It was as though Leonora had given her permission.

...I know his heart. I know he means well, and I agree that this is probably the only way. And yet, a part of me hates him, hates that he can be so rational about this. Is his heart breaking like mine? If it is, he conceals it well. Once, I thought I knew him. Now, I am not sure.

Rosabel's heart went out to Leonora, reading the pain that these words held. The hopelessness and desperation. And yet, Rosabel still did not fully understand what had caused it.

... My fate is sealed. I cannot escape it now. The date for the wedding is set. God help me.

Eyes glued to the words before her, Rosabel's heart stopped, too shocked to not acknowledge the simple truth it had stumbled upon. Had Leonora not willingly married Graham? Rosabel was confused. Before she had spoken of him with such affection; more than just affection, love. What had happened to change her mind? What had he done to lose her love?

Rosabel couldn't help but shiver. Her muscles began to tremble, her stomach quivered and, as though cold, her teeth began to chatter.

Closing her eyes, she felt a headache approach. The slow drumming behind her temples echoed in her heart as her head desperately tried to make sense of what she had just learned. Was there a simple answer? One that could explain everything and not paint someone's soul black? Rosabel prayed that there was although she couldn't imagine how.

... Although I can only consider myself a burden to him, Graham treats me with the utmost respect. This has doomed his life as it has doomed mine, and yet, he seems contend. After all, I am grateful that my life is tied to him. I am sure he will be a wonderful father. Of that he assures me each day, and each day, I believe him a

little more.

I feel safe with Graham, and yet, my heart does not glow the way it used to. Will it ever again?

How could Leonora see Graham as her doom on one page and then paint him as her saviour on the next? Rosabel shook her head. She was missing something vital. But whatever it was, Leonora had trusted him to be a good father. Knowing that, Rosabel felt more determined in her endeavour.

In the coming days, she watched Georgiana carefully. Although the girl smiled and laughed, clearly glad to have Rosabel by her side once more, and behaved the way she always had, Rosabel could see that something was missing. There was no spark in her laughter, no twinkle in her eyes. It was as though she was only going through the motions, but her heart remained untouched.

One night, holding a sleeping Georgiana in her arms, Rosabel lay awake and pondered her options. At first, she wasn't sure what to do. She only knew whatever she did would mean to defy her husband and go against his wishes. Feeling Georgiana's arms cling to her as another nightmare claimed her, Rosabel knew that she was willing to risk her husband's wrath. What was he going to do? Divorce her? Although she doubted he would go to such length, the thought scared her, and yet, Rosabel still had no doubt in her heart about her loyalties. Georgiana's happiness took precedence over her husband's wishes as well as her own security.

Her mind made up, Rosabel wondered what best to do. She knew he would not willingly spend time with his daughter. Well, if he wouldn't come to them, they would just have to go to him.

Helen's words echoed in her mind, but Rosabel pushed them away. This was about Georgiana.

Although a part of her feared his anger, her mother's heart currently shielded her from its intensity, allowing her to revel in the power and control she had decided to claim for her own life as well as Georgiana's.

The next morning, she ordered their things packed, had Leonora's portrait taken from the wall and carefully wrapped, knowing Georgiana could not be without it, and then joined the girl in the breakfast parlour.

Hearing about their travel arrangements, Georgiana's face lit up in a way Rosabel hadn't seen in weeks. "We are going to visit Father?

160

When?"

"We will leave after breakfast," Rosabel said, earning her a delighted squeal. "So eat up. It will be a long trip."

Eagerly, Georgiana ate her eggs and drank her tea before running upstairs to fetch her mother's doll. When Rosabel headed toward her own room to add a few more personal items to the things that needed packing, like Leonora's diaries, Mrs. Rigsby caught up to her.

"Your grace," she said, and her voice held as much disdain as her eyes. "I was just informed of your travel plans."

"Yes, I am so glad to have a word with you before we leave." Having accepted the woman's attitude toward her long ago, Rosabel felt a hint of satisfaction whenever she went against Mrs. Rigsby's idea of right and wrong. "It won't be necessary for you to accompany us. I will be taking care of Lady Georgiana's education myself."

Mrs. Rigsby's eyes narrowed. "I see. Is his grace displeased with my work?" she asked, clearly fishing for information.

Rosabel smiled. "Not that I know of."

"I see," Mrs. Rigsby repeated. "During his visit, he did not inform me of his intention to have Lady Georgiana join him at Camden Hall."

"Well, Mrs. Rigsby, I might as well tell you that he had no such intention back then. So he could not have informed you."

"I see. Did he send a communique then?"

Apparently the woman grew desperate to learn more about the circumstances of their trip to ask such a direct question.

"Let me be frank, Mrs. Rigsby," Rosabel replied with equal boldness, her smile gone, her eyes cold and calculating, an imitation of her husband's expression from when he had looked at her in the very beginning of their marriage. "It was my decision to take Lady Georgiana to Camden Hall. As her mother, it is my duty to ensure her happiness, which I am doing based on my own judgment of her wellbeing." Mrs. Rigsby's lips pressed into a thin line as she listened. "I do not appreciate you questioning my decisions. It is not your place." For a second, Rosabel thought the woman would have steam coming out of her ears, but then her lips thinned even more, and she remained silent. "Did I make myself clear?"

Without waiting for an answer, Rosabel turned on her heel and left Mrs. Rigsby standing in the hall. The feeling of empowerment whenever she put her foot down followed her all the way to her room and stayed with her as they finally stepped into the carriage. A smile on her face, she took Georgiana's hand and gave it a soft squeeze. "Do not worry. Everything will be all right." And in that moment, Rosabel honestly believed it would be.

22

UPON ARRIVING AT CAMDEN HALL

The two-day journey stretched as far as the horizon was wide, its ends hidden and unreachable. Whenever Rosabel was not busy tending to Georgiana, reading to her, chatting about the beautiful landscape they were traveling through and watching her play with her doll, her mind was occupied with one subject alone: her husband's reaction upon seeing them at Camden Hall.

Predicting his reaction would not be favourable, Rosabel had taken Bridget along. Not only to keep Georgiana and her company but also to shield the girl from the ugly truth.

Stopping at the same inn where they had spent the night on their journey to Westmore, Rosabel waited until Georgiana was fast asleep. Then she tiptoed across the hall and spoke to Bridget. Not going into details, Rosabel instructed the maid to take Lady Georgiana to the stables immediately upon their arrival and keep her occupied for as long as she could. Preferably until Rosabel came to take them to the house. Bridget listened intently, and Rosabel thought she detected a flicker of understanding in her grey eyes.

The next day, they commenced their journey, and with each mile, Rosabel grew quieter and quieter, her mind torturing her with all kinds of doomsday images. She knew without looking that her cheeks had gone pale. Feeling her hands tremble, she buried them in the folds of her dress. Slowly the courage that had led her down this road started to dissipate. Rosabel could almost see it slipping away, like the snow slowly melting, surrendering to an early spring.

When the sun once more began its descent, Camden Hall appeared on the distant horizon. Feeling a lump sink to the bottom of her stomach, Rosabel had to take a deep breath to keep her food down. Revolting as though equally reluctant to approach the forbidden place, her stomach twisted and churned, warning her of what lay ahead.

Georgiana, on the other hand, squealed with delight as her father's residence came in sight. Instantly, Bridget started talking about all the beautiful horses they would find in the stables, and as predicted, Georgiana begged to be allowed to see them first. Of course, Rosabel acquiesced.

Slowly the carriage entered through the gates of Camden Hall, stopping in front of the steps leading up to the front doors. Rosabel took another deep breath and allowed a footman to help her down. Then he tended to Lady Georgiana while Rosabel surveyed the scene before her. Trying to remember the location of her husband's study, Rosabel was shocked when she suddenly heard his voice reach her ear from just within the entrance hall. Throwing a look over her shoulder, she saw with relief as Georgiana and Bridget walked away in the direction of the stables.

Squaring her shoulders, Rosabel turned her gaze back to the entrance and came face to face with her husband's cold eyes, now ablaze with barely contained anger.

Seeing her standing just outside the doorway, Graham thought he had strayed into a dream. Her dark hair whipped about by a cold breeze, her cheeks flushed a rosy red, Rosabel's eyes shone like two dark pools. Instantly, Graham noted that there was something different about her. However, he didn't know what, and that thought unsettled him deeply.

Feeding off his anger, lest he forget his position in this affair, he stormed toward her, feeling his own face contorted into a scowl that rasped his voice. "What in the devil's name are you doing here? I gave you specific instructions with regard to…this." Blocking her path, he stared her down.

For a second, Rosabel's shoulders seemed to tremble, but then she brushed it off and lifting her eyes to his, said, "My Lord, I suggest we take this into your study." And with that, she moved past him and headed down the corridor he had come.

For a moment, Graham was too stunned to move. Yes, there was something different about her, only now he began to suspect what it was. Confidence. All of a sudden, the woman radiated confidence. Certainly, here and there, there seemed to be a slight hesitation in her manner, but that only underlined the change her personality had undergone since he had last seen her. A mere fortnight ago.

Not having another option, Graham begrudgingly followed her to his study. He stepped inside and closed the door with a loud bang. Rosabel, however, did not flinch. She merely lifted her eyes, and although she barely moved, he couldn't help but feel that she was shaking her head at him. Graham knew his behaviour was childish, and yet, he couldn't help it.

Swallowing all uncertainty on his part, he glowered at her. "We have privacy here, now speak! What is the meaning of this?"

Again, Rosabel seemed to grow taller as she squared her shoulders and lifted her chin, meeting his eyes without flinching. "This is about Georgiana."

Exhausted and unwilling to enter into the same discussion he had considered closed, Graham walked around his desk and began to shuffle through some papers. "As I told you before, there is nothing to discuss. Nothing changes. You and my daughter will remain at Westmore while I conduct my business from Camden Hall. This arrangement benefits all."

This time Rosabel did shake her head. "My Lord, it does not, and I believe you know that." Had she just called him a liar? "I brought Georgiana here because I believe that a daughter belongs with—"

"Here?" Graham croaked, hearing the blood rush in his ears. "You brought her here? Georgiana is in this house?"

Rosabel nodded. "Yes. Although at the moment she is in the stables."

Feeling his knees soften and turn into pudding, Graham sank into his desk chair. He took a deep breath and for a second closed his eyes. He could only guess what his wife would take from this behaviour, however, right then and there, he felt drained and unable to maintain his carefully constructed mask.

Taking a seat across from her husband, Rosabel once more buried her trembling hands in the folds of her dress. How handy! As she glanced across the desk at her husband's slumped figure, his broad shoulders sunken in, Rosabel experienced a hint of pity. Why did he reject his daughter in such a manner? Clearly he cared for her. Upon hearing about her presence at Camden Hall, his face had shown not only shock, but a longing pain had come to his eyes that Rosabel only knew too well. In that moment, whether she had wanted it or not, her heart had gone out to him. If only he wouldn't seek to destroy this fragile connection at the next opportunity, they could all live together peacefully. It could all be so simple.

After a short eternity, her husband took a deep breath and his gaze returned from whatever inward contemplation it had been occupied with, fixing her with yet another icy stare. In that moment, their fragile connection shattered like a vase hitting the hardboard floor.

Putting on her own mask, her armour for battle, Rosabel pressed her lips together in a thin line and narrowed her eyes as she looked at him with the same disdain she had so often seen in Mrs. Rigsby's gaze upon herself. Indeed, the governess had been an excellent teacher!

"As it is late, you may stay here until the morrow," her husband said, glancing out the window at the setting sun, "However, tomorrow morning, the two of you will return to Westmore. Am I understood?"

His voice frightened her. Nothing in its harsh, clipped tone resonated with emotion. Could he really turn off what he felt for his daughter at a whim? Had she not just moments before witnessed a near-meltdown at the thought of his daughter under the same roof as himself? What had happened?

Her fingers curled around the fabric of her dress, balling into fists, in order to keep a tight grasp on her nerves. Desperate to just run from her husband's study, Rosabel almost averted her eyes when the weight of his stare became too much. Georgiana. A tiny voice whispered, and instead of backing down, Rosabel stood her ground.

"No, I am afraid not," she answered his question in a voice that rang clear and unflinching, much to her own surprise. "We have come here to stay. For how long, that remains unclear at the moment." Watching the scowl on his face deepen, Rosabel rushed on. "I did not come to ask your permission." Now, her eyes drilled into his. "I am here," with a sweep of her arm she indicated her husband's study, "to inform you of the situation. I'd appreciate your cooperation, but I can see that, at least at the moment, this is a futile wish." As she rose from her chair, he followed. "Good night, my lord."

Fighting to control her feet, lest they take over and run from the room, Rosabel maintained her composure. However, when she reached out to open the door, hands grabbed her from behind and spun her around.

A startled cry escaped her lips as she found her arms trapped in iron grips, back pressed against the door. Her husband's looming figure stood before her, barely an inch separated their chests, and she could feel the touch of his breath on her cheeks. Looking down at her, his eyes held her immobile, the scowl on his face impenetrable. "How dare you speak to me like that?" he hissed, pressing into her. "I am your husband!"

Feeling herself tremble and tears accumulating in the corners of her eyes, Rosabel swallowed hard. Eyes not wavering from his, she squared her shoulders, feeling the restraint of his hands on her arms, and raised her chin. As she lifted her head and looked up into his face, her lips almost touched his. For a moment, he seemed to hesitate, thrown off by the proximity of their bodies. However, before his scowl could intensify again, Rosabel said, "And I am your wife."

His eyes no longer drilled into her being but, instead, roamed her face as though trying to unearth her secrets. For a second, they lingered on her lips, and Rosabel felt herself tremble. Only this time, it wasn't from fear.

"Yes, you are my wife," he whispered, and Rosabel could all but feel his words fall from his lips onto her own. She inhaled slowly, breathing in his scent. Again, his body seemed to be moving closer, pressing into her, and the air between them was filled with a promise not yet fulfilled. "As my wife, you are to obey. Do you not remember your vows?"

From whence it came, Rosabel didn't know, but a sparkling smile suddenly curled up her lips, reaching even her eyes. She could see its effects on her husband's face, and she bit her lower lip to keep it from growing even bigger. She did not wish to anger him further, but instead of a renewed anger, his eyes held something else. Something Rosabel had never seen there before. Something she couldn't quite name. And once again, his eyes travelled down to her lips, staying there as though mesmerized.

How long they stood like this, locked away from the world, Rosabel couldn't say. However, the sun was nowhere to be seen, when a sudden knock on the door shattered the illusion they had retreated to.

As though startled awake, her husband released his grip on her, clearing his throat. He stepped back, and his eyes wouldn't meet hers. Rosabel, too, took a step back, before her husband bid the person on the other side of the door to enter.

Hanson, her husband's butler, held a small silver platter with a single envelop on. "This was just delivered, your grace. It was said to be urgent."

With the seal hidden on the other side of the envelop, Rosabel didn't know who it was from. However, when her husband picked it up and turned it over, there was a slight widening to his eyes as he beheld the identity of the sender. "Thank you, Hanson, that'll be all."

When the door closed behind the butler, her husband turned to her although his eyes told her that she did not possess his undivided attention any longer. "We will discuss your presence here later. At the moment, I have important business to attend to." And with that, he returned to his desk.

Whispering a short goodbye, Rosabel left the room, looking for Georgiana. The sun had gone down a while ago and taken with it the little bit of warmth it offered in these cold days of early spring. Rosabel suspected that she and Bridget had long since returned from the stables.

As her footsteps echoed on the marble floors, Rosabel couldn't help but smile. She may not have won the war, but from this first battle, she had emerged the victor. For now, at least, they were staying.

23

ELLIE'S ADVICE

yes focused on the words before him on the sheet of paper, Graham barely knew what he read. His mind was still occupied with the sudden and completely unwelcome change in his wife's personality. An anguished moan escaped his lips, and for a second, he closed his eyes, resting his head on his arms.

Instantly, an image of Leonora flashed into his mind.

Startled, Graham jerked up, back rigid, breath panting. Rubbing his hands over his temples and running them over his eyes and down his face, he tried to chase away the memories, but they wouldn't yield. Again and again, he saw her smile, that beautiful, tantalizing smile that had nearly driven him mad since the first day he had laid eyes on her, but especially during the years of their marriage. Her soft, blue eyes looked at him, always so tender, so forgiving, making guilt surge to the surface like never before.

He was betraying her memory, and she would have hated him for it. At least, he hoped she would have.

Again, her face stole into his mind. But this time her golden curls and ocean-blue eyes slowly changed and became darker. Her hair shone like the night sky, pitch-black, and yet, sparkling while her eyes turned into soft doe eyes, darkened by memories. At first, he frowned, not recognizing his wife, but then understanding dawned, and he found himself thinking, not of Leonora, but Rosabel instead.

Again, guilt washed over him, and yet, he could not force the image from his mind. Too much did it intrigue him. What had happened to alter her personality to such a degree? She had been so timid and yielding, completely obedient. There had been no doubt in his mind that he would be able to bend her to his will. And what now? Had she not fought her way back into his life? But why?

For Georgiana, she had said.

Once more, the image changed, and he saw Leonora's face snarling at the Duke of Somerset. At a picnic his precious son had pushed Georgiana for correcting his speech, and since the duke had seen no reason to lecture his son, Leonora had charged them both, more the father than the son. By the end of the day, the duke, who was a bear of a man, had feebly asked the Lady Georgiana to apologise his son's behaviour as well as reprimanded the future duke himself. Graham had never been more proud of his wife. She had stood like a lioness to defend her cub. Just like Rosabel had done today.

What had happened? Had it really been Georgiana who had brought about this change? If so, Graham knew he would not have a moment of peace from his wife in the future. Not as long as he didn't give in to her demands and spend time with his daughter. If he could only make her understand why that was impossible.

Turning back to his letter, Graham pushed all thoughts of his wives away, determined to ride out the storm, no matter what it would cost him.

The next morning, Rosabel felt drained. After the two-day journey back to Camden Hall followed by an intense conversation with her husband, she had gone in search of Georgiana, finding her in the nursery with Bridget, unpacking their trunks. Despite the late hour, the girl had been exhilarated and wouldn't stop talking until Rosabel knew all about the horses in her father's stable. Then, as expected, Georgiana had asked when she could see her father.

Rosabel had taken her by the hand, and they had sat down on a chaise. Hoping she had found the right words, Rosabel had explained to Georgiana that her father was busy with business, would be for the next few weeks, and that she probably wouldn't see him as often as she would like. However, her father was delighted that she had come to see him.

Rosabel felt a small stab of guilt at her lie, but seeing Georgiana's face light up, she couldn't be too unforgiving with herself. Praying that in time her husband would reconnect with his daughter, she had lent a hand straightening out the nursery and then put Georgiana to bed. Tucking her in, Rosabel had sat with her for a little while, brushing the golden curls from her forehead.

Before drifting off to sleep, Georgiana had looked at her for a moment, eyes intent as though aged beyond her years. Then she had snuggled into the covers and whispered, "I am so happy you're here." She had breathed in and out, her chest rising and falling. "Mother."

Hearing that word had startled Rosabel, and for a second, she wasn't sure if Georgiana had already fallen asleep and was seeing her mother in her dreams or if she had really just now for the first time referred to her as her mother.

But then Rosabel felt a soft squeeze of Georgiana's hand, still resting in hers, and knew how deep the girl's feelings were. With tears in her eyes, Rosabel sat at her bed for hours, just watching her sleep, touched beyond words.

When Rosabel had finally surrendered to the heaviness of her eyelids and sought her own bed, the night had not been young anymore. As soon as her head touched the pillow though, she had been lost to the world.

However, these few hours of sleep were not enough to sustain her and return the energy the previous days had cost her. But the sun was up, and Rosabel could hear Georgiana's excited giggle from down the hall. Suppressing a yawn, she got out of bed, wondering what this day would bring.

Remembering that her husband generally ate breakfast at the break of dawn, Rosabel was not surprised to not see him in the breakfast parlour. While Georgiana seemed a bit disappointed, Rosabel assured her that they would go see him as soon as possible.

After running through various scenarios in her head, Rosabel decided on a direct approach. There was no use in delaying the meet between father and daughter. However, Rosabel intended to make it as short as possible, so as to give her husband a little time to get used to the thought of his daughter being under the same roof with him.

While contemplating her options, Rosabel had realized something else. Something she hadn't even thought about in coming back to Camden Hall. Not only had she returned Georgiana to her father's side, but she had also returned herself to the place she had called home for the past ten years.

Giddy as she hadn't felt in a long time, Rosabel decided to pay Ellie a visit, and she would take Georgiana. More than anything, Rosabel wanted to introduce her daughter to her dearest friend and cousin, but in addition, she thought it would ease everybody's mind to keep Georgiana happily occupied. And her little cousins would be just the ones to accomplish the task.

After breakfast, Rosabel led Georgiana down the corridor to her husband's study and knocked on the door. Desperately hoping he had not once again chosen the coward's way out and disappeared in the dark of night, she breathed a sigh of relief when she heard his voice bid them to enter.

However, before Rosabel could say anything, Georgiana pushed past her and ran into the room. Following on her daughter's heel, Rosabel saw her husband's face when Georgiana flung herself into his arms. What she saw there gave her hope.

Although his forehead was lined by furrows too deep to be of only minor importance, his eyes shone with suppressed desire as they beheld the little girl's beaming face. As her tiny arms wrapped around his neck, he hesitated only for a second. The look of uncertainty vanished quickly, and giving in to the feelings he clearly had for her, he embraced her as strongly as she did him. Rubbing his hands over her back, he held her tight, closing his eyes and savouring the moment.

Rosabel felt like an intruder, and yet, she found a smile on her own face at the beautiful scene before her eyes. Yes, she had done the right thing in coming here!

Sitting back, Georgiana looked at him, chatting without catching a breath. All the while, her husband's eyes moved over his daughter's face, his hand tucking a golden strand behind her ear, cupping her cheek and brushing over her forehead as though trying to familiarize himself with her again. He seemed oblivious to Rosabel's presence, all attention focused on his daughter.

Time passed, and in the end, it was Rosabel who ushered

Georgiana from the room, seeing the drained look on her husband's face. For whatever reason, keeping his daughter at a distance had taken its toll. He seemed exhausted after dealing with the emotions he so clearly sought to ignore. Rosabel couldn't help but wonder why? Why did he not count his blessings to have a daughter like Georgiana?

Shaking her head, Rosabel left the room, guiding the chatty girl past the entrance hall and to the carriage.

Hugging her cousin tightly, Rosabel breathed in the familiar scent of lavender and mint. "I missed you so much," she whispered, desperately trying to keep a grip on her emotions and keep at bay the stream of tears threatening to spill forth. "I've felt so alone without you!"

"Me too," Ellie agreed, her own eyes glistening with tears as well. "But now, you're back! How did that happen? I thought going to Westmore was to be of a permanent nature?"

Taking her cousin by the arm, Rosabel led her over to one of the chaises standing by the back windows. After a short and slightly cold greeting from her aunt and uncle, the two friends had retreated to the back parlour while Georgiana had joined Rosabel's younger cousins in the gardens. Beatrice, Lydia and Stephen had taken to Georgiana instantly, leading her about the house as tour guides and explaining in excruciating detail how to play hide-and-go-seek. Smiling, Rosabel had watched them depart, hoping the company of peers would do Georgiana some good, considering how isolated she often was at Westmore.

"I don't even know where to begin." Rosabel sighed, trying to collect her thoughts. So much had happened in the past few months, most of which she still could not make sense of. After a short while, she turned to her cousin, eyes unguarded, knowing she was in the company of a confidant. "You know me," she began. "I am not a fighter. I do as I am told."

Ellie nodded. "I've never heard you say no. To anyone." She reached over and squeezed her cousin's hand. "So, what happened? Does your husband know you're here?" Suddenly, her mouth fell open, and she clasped a hand over it. "Did you run away? With his daughter?

How—?"

Rosabel placed a hand on her cousin's knee to stop her. "No, of course not. Do not be ridiculous! I would never be so reckless. No." Again, she took a deep breath. "But you're right; my husband didn't want me to come back here. He was not pleased." A small triumphant smile danced on her lips that she didn't quite manage to hide.

"Oh my god, but why?"

Glancing out the window at the children playing in the gardens, their laughter echoing in the distance, Rosabel said, "Georgiana. She…I…" For a moment, she didn't know how to put into words what she felt in her heart. Lifting her gaze, she turned back to her cousin, who looked at her with wondrous eyes. "She is my daughter, now, in every way, and I came here, I defied by husband's wishes to see her happy." Again, her eyes travelled to the little girl with the golden curls, her laughter bubbling over like a small creek in early spring.

Ellie smiled. "You really love her, don't you? Your eyes shine when you speak of her."

Nodding, Rosabel said, "I don't know how it happened. Maybe we were both just so alone, without anyone to care for us that we turned to each other. But it doesn't matter. I am her mother now, and I will do whatever I need to in order to see her happy. Even if the one standing against me is my husband."

"Okay," Ellie began, scooting closer on the chaise. "You have to explain this. Why does he not want her to be happy? He is her father. That doesn't make any sense."

Rosabel shook her head. "Oh, I'm sure he wants her to be happy, and he believes that the way things are she is happy, or at least well taken care of. I'm not sure if he can even think in terms of happiness at the moment. He does not see how alone she is, and how sad." Remembering her husband's cold eyes, Rosabel shivered. But then the memory of him embracing Georgiana only this morning returned and gave her hope. "He loves her, I am sure of that. But for some reason, he feels like he cannot be around her. Georgiana, of course, misses him and wishes for nothing else but to be near him."

"Understandably," Ellie murmured, forehead creased, listening intently. "Did he really plan on not seeing her ever? Him at Camden Hall, and her at Westmore?"

Rosabel shrugged. "I honestly don't know. I don't know what his plans are. All I know is that they are not good for Georgiana. And that's why I'm here."

174

"Did you ask him?" Ellie wondered. "About why he married you? And...well, everything?"

"Let's say, I asked as much as I dared." Remembering how uneasy he had made her feel in the beginning, Rosabel realized that she had come a long way. She still disliked his cold eyes, but they did not shake her to her very core anymore. "He married me to be a mother to his daughter. I suppose he thought this way he wouldn't have to feel guilty about leaving her with no parent at all."

"What about his first wife?" Ellie asked. "Do you know anything about her? How did she die? And when?"

"About a year and a half ago. It was a riding accident." The diaries and letters had granted Rosabel a deep insight into Leonora's life, but she wasn't sure how much of it to share with her cousin. Revealing she had read them felt like admitting a crime. "I...I" She took a deep breath, lifted her eyes and found her cousin's. "I found her diaries...and some letters the duke wrote to her." She stopped, hoping her cousin would not condemn her.

For a second, Ellie didn't blink. "Did you read them?"

Holding her breath, Rosabel nodded.

Instantly, Ellie's face broke into a smile. "Oh, good, I feared you'd have thought that inappropriate."

Relief washing over her, Rosabel smiled. "I did find it inappropriate. I battled with myself for days, believe me."

"But you read them?"

"Most of them, yes. I haven't gotten to all of them yet."

"So? What do they say?" Ellie inched closer, leaning forward to listen.

Again, Rosabel took a deep breath, hoping Leonora would understand. Without going into detail, she laid down how Leonora and Graham had been in love, how something had happened—Rosabel suspected a premarital pregnancy—and then how it had all gone horribly wrong. She tried her best to explain the contradicting information she had taken from the letters and diary entries, and although disappointed, couldn't help but feel a little relieved when Ellie could not connect those satisfactorily either. There was still something missing. Something without which they would not be able to see the whole picture. Why did Leonora look at Graham with love one second and the next consider him her doom?

"So? What are you going to do?" Ellie asked after Rosabel had relayed the situation as best as she could.

"I am hoping for Georgiana to have her father back in her life. I want to see her happy. That's what's most important."

Ellie smiled. "You really see her as your daughter, don't you?"

Again, Rosabel's gaze was drawn to the window. Stumbling through the last bits of snow, the kids were chasing each other, tripping and falling. Their faces, however, shone with laughter, eyes dancing. Georgiana's cheeks were even rosier than usual as she threw the remnants of a snowball at Stephen. Her blue eyes sparkled like the sun reflected on an icy lake.

Rosabel had trouble tearing her gaze away, but when she looked at her cousin, she saw the joy over her unexpected happiness in her eyes. "I do. She is my daughter in every way."

"I'm so happy for you," Ellie said, again squeezing Rosabel's hand. "But what about your husband?"

"What do you mean?"

Ellie shrugged, but Rosabel felt her cousin's eyes linger on her face. "You only ever mention him as Georgiana's father, but he is also your husband." She sat up as a thought seemed to strike her. "What about children of your own? You are not with child yet, are you?" Avoiding her cousin's eyes, Rosabel shook her head. "But you might be soon. Sooner than you think." Ellie smiled, again taking Rosabel's hands. "Haven't you always wanted to be a mother?"

"Yes, and I am," Rosabel said, hoping to steer the conversation away from the fact that her husband had yet to visit her chamber. "I do not need any other children."

Ellie frowned. "But what about your husband? Does he not wish for an heir? After all, Georgiana cannot inherit his title."

Remembering how she had asked herself those very questions, Rosabel shrugged. "I couldn't say. He does not speak to me much, not unless he has to."

A devilish grin curled up Ellie's face. "Yes, but that is about to change. After all, isn't that why you're here?"

"I'm here for Georgiana."

"Oh, please," Ellie chided shaking her head. "Do not tell me that you wish to continue this distant relationship with your husband! You must wish for the two of you to grow closer!" Again, she squeezed Rosabel's hand. "Maybe a baby would help."

Still not looking at her cousin, Rosabel mumbled. "Maybe." Did she want a closer relationship with her husband? It couldn't possibly grow any more distant. Rosabel didn't know though.

Her thoughts up to this point had been focused on Georgiana. Living at Westmore, away from her husband, Rosabel had even been happy, almost able to ignore the fact that she was married. After all, she hardly knew the man she was married to. How could she miss him? She hadn't. And yet, their time together in London had brought on a change. Rosabel had to admit that his presence was more than welcome to her. In fact, she had begun to rely on it for her own happiness.

Shaking off these thoughts, Rosabel returned her attention to her cousin. She would take one step at a time. Right now, all that mattered was Georgiana.

24

A KISS OWED

*T*he following weeks after their arrival at Camden Hall passed in fairly the same fashion as their first day. While Georgiana was delighted to simply be in the same house as her father, her eyes beamed whenever she caught but a glimpse of him. Rosabel's husband seemed to be avoiding them, particularly his daughter, as much as he could. However, at the same time, whenever Georgiana managed to get a hold of him, his cold demeanour seemed to evaporate.

Rosabel watched in amazement.

When the little girl's arms came around her father's neck or her glowing eyes looked into his or her bubbling laughter reached his ears, the bitter mask he wore vanished, replaced by a smile that said more than words ever could.

These moments were dearest to Rosabel because they gave her hope. Hope that her husband would not send them away again, that he would finally accept and even welcome their presence in this house. Only to herself, Rosabel admitted that she was rather surprised that he hadn't demanded their departure yet. Was he torn? Did a part of him wish them gone while another desired them to stay? Whenever she saw his eyes come to life when Georgiana was near, Rosabel was sure of it.

Over supper one night, Georgiana related her adventures with the horses that day. She talked and talked while her parents listened, giving her all the attention she had craved for so long. In this relaxed atmosphere, Rosabel saw honest smiles on all their faces and her own frown lines, deep from worry, vanished, her shoulders relaxed and her stomach jumped little hoops as the delight of their conversation filled her with happiness. Step by step, Rosabel fought her way forward, battle by battle. Victory seemed to be within her reach.

Their joy seemed to be infectious. The whole house was soon caught up in it. More than usual did smiles decorate the staff's faces, and more often than not did they even reach their eyes as they gazed upon the little angel that had transformed their master's life.

Still, Rosabel could not ignore, although she tried, the sadness and exhaustion that often dominated her husband's face. Whenever Georgiana left his presence, Rosabel occasionally witnessed small meltdowns. His shoulders would slump, he would bury his face in his hands or he would just turn and stare out the window for hours, not speaking to anyone, until the little girl returned, and once again, his face would light up. She was like the sun to him, absolutely necessary for him to flourish, and without her, he would wilt and die.

In the beginning, her husband merely tried to extract himself from situations that made him uncomfortable, but the more time wore on the more his attempts seemed to be premeditated. He would leave the house early, spending hours riding about the countryside. He even took up hunting, which surprised Rosabel even more when Hanson informed her that her husband had never shown the slightest interest in it before. He was actively avoiding them, or rather avoiding Georgiana. The only time he spent at home was when the girl would sit with Rosabel and tend to her lessons. Seeing his actions as deliberate, Rosabel soon allowed Georgiana free time whenever her father was near, and they took up their lessons whenever he would leave. Still, she believed that throwing them together, not giving him the opportunity to evade his daughter altogether, was the best course of action.

Georgiana brought him cookies to his study, showed him her paintings, a book that had become her new favourite or a new dress she had sown herself for her mother's doll. Never would he tell her to leave. Never did he use harsh words with her. Never did he reject her affections. But he would still try to distract her into leaving or persuade her that he had work to do. Rosabel long since suspected that all these excuses were merely that, excuses. Her husband had always struck her as someone in control of his life. Everything was structured, planned and carried out accordingly. Few things ever surprised him, and so he usually had significant time at his disposal to spend in leisure.

But Georgiana did not know these things. Considering her father's attention a gift from above, she doted on him, never fussing, never arguing, always considerate of his needs. If he suggested he had work, she would leave him to it, only returning to make sure he had his tea and a plate of cookies. Then later at supper, she would inquire after his dealings and express her hope that all had gone well.

Often Rosabel was surprised how grown-up Georgiana seemed. Having spent most of her life with adults and left to her own thoughts, she possessed a maturity that few her age did.

One night after Georgiana had gone to bed, Rosabel returned from the library, a book in hand, and went up the stairs to her own room. Walking down the corridor, she turned a corner and stopped.

Just ahead of her stood her husband. His collar stood open, and his sleeves were rolled up. He raked a hand through his hair, and his eyes widened as he spotted her looking at him. For a second, Rosabel thought he would turn and walk away, but then he swallowed. Having made a decision he approached her.

Feeling her own hands tremble, Rosabel gripped her book tighter as he came to stand before her, his eyes looking down into hers. He didn't seem happy or sad, but merely exhausted, as though the last few weeks had depleted all his energy.

When the silence between them stretched on, Rosabel all but whispered, "Can I help you, my lord?" As close as they stood, she knew he had heard her.

At first, he didn't answer her but drew in a deep breath as his eyes trailed from hers down to her lips, touched her shoulders and travelled farther down. Feeling herself tremble under the scrutiny of his gaze, Rosabel was relieved when his eyes found hers once again.

As though fighting for every bit of oxygen to sustain himself, he drew in another breath and then abruptly stepped forward, his hands grasping her by the arms.

Rosabel gasped, feeling the heat of his touch through the fabric of her dress. "My lord?"

Once again, his eyes held hers captive. "Why are you doing this?"

His voice was hoarse as though speaking took too much out of him. "Why?" His jaw clenched, and his hands tightened. "Why?" he almost snarled.

Confused, Rosabel swallowed. She couldn't remember ever seeing him this angry, enraged even. Had he been drinking? She couldn't smell anything on his breath as it brushed over her skin. As his fingers dug deeper into her flesh, Rosabel began to squirm. "Let go, please. You're hurting me!"

As though transfixed, he just stared at her. Then instead of complying with her request, he pushed her against the wall.

Again, Rosabel gasped, more in shock than pain. His nose almost touched hers as he pressed out through gritted teeth, "Why did you bring her here? Are you trying to destroy me?"

Realization dawned, but for the life of her, Rosabel could not understand how Georgiana's presence could have possibly caused his current state. What was he hiding? "Your daughter loves you—"

The words had barely left her lips, when a menacing snarl rose from his throat.

Flinching slightly, Rosabel refused to be intimidated. Squaring her shoulders as best as she could with his hands still locked around her arms, she raised her chin and her lips slightly brushed over his, sending a pleasant tingle down her spine.

Her husband too seemed startled, but before he could speak, Rosabel said, "And I know you love her too." Another snarl echoed between them, but Rosabel chose to ignore it. "Why would you push her away?"

Lips pressed together, he stared at her. "Do not speak of things that do not concern you, *my lady*."

Hearing the insult in his words, Rosabel recognized it for what it was, a desperate attempt to silence her on the matter. She knew she had hit a nerve. She could see it hurt him, and yet, she knew she had to continue. "They do concern me. She is my daughter."

"Your daughter?" he echoed her words as his eyes searched her face. "But she is not."

Not shaken in her resolve, Rosabel's lips curled upward into a smile that touched her eyes as they looked into his. "She is. You told me I was to be her mother. Now I am, and that will never change."

The blue in his eyes seemed to grow darker, only not with anger but with emotion. For a second, Rosabel thought she saw the beginnings of a tear form in the corner of his eyes before he blinked and the moment was gone. Again he inhaled deeply, and took a step back, his hands loosening, but not letting go. "Tell her to stop."

"Stop what?"

He stared at her as though choosing his words. "If she does not keep her distance, I..."

Holding his gaze, Rosabel asked, "What will you do, my lord? Because there is nothing in this world that could keep her from you. You were too good a father to her!"

As though slapped, he suddenly released her, stepping back. His face held more than just pain, and for a second, Rosabel saw how wounded he was. What had given him that wound? She wondered before a mask of bitterness once again hid his true self from her.

Unwilling to let the moment just slip away, Rosabel stepped forward and carefully put her hand on his cheek. He flinched, and his eyes grew big, but he didn't pull away.

Rosabel felt a slight stubble under her hand and the muscles twitch as though he was holding on by a thread. "She gave you her heart a long time ago, and it is yours now to keep safe from harm." This time, Rosabel clearly saw the tear that sprang from the corner of his eyes and then slowly made its way down his cheek until it touched her fingers. "Trust her with yours. She will not disappoint you."

Gently, she removed her hand, letting it glide to his shoulder and running it down his arm, feeling his muscles tense. When she reached his hand, she gave it a tender squeeze. "Good night," she whispered and with a last look turned and walked away.

As though struck by lightning, Graham stood in the corridor, staring at his wife as she walked away and then vanished into her rooms. What had just happened?

Almost stumbling backwards, Graham was glad for the wall at his back, for it was the only thing keeping him on his feet. His eyes shifted back and forth from the wall before him to the closed door to his wife's chambers. The way she had looked at him...The way she...

Without conscious thought, his hand rose to his cheek, remembering the lightness of her touch. She had touched him, willingly, of her own accord. Did she not despise him? How could she not, after what he had done to her?

Remembering how her body had trembled under his hands, Graham once again raked a hand through his hair to keep from putting it through the wall. Had he scared her? He must have. But she had smiled at him. And those eyes! When she had straightened her posture, lifted her head, and her lips had touched his, he had almost lost control. A fire had gone through him, reminding him of desires he had thought buried for good. How could he find himself in the same situation again? Married to a woman who did not want him? A woman he loved nonetheless.

Shocked at his own thoughts, Graham frowned. Did he love her? How could he? He barely even knew her. And yet, Leonora had been in his heart from the first moment he'd laid eyes on her.

Leonora, he mused. She had been strong and determined, yet kind and caring. Just like Rosabel was now. Nodding his understanding, Graham finally saw how his new wife could possibly have affected him the way she had just now. It was Leonora, and the way she reminded him of her.

Marrying Rosabel, he had thought to give his daughter a mother who would see to her needs in a loving way. At the same time, his subconscious had rejoiced at the difference in personality between his two wives. There would be no reminders, nothing to bring back memories that would certainly torment him. And now, here he was, suffering what he had sought to avoid. How had Rosabel changed so? And what was he to do now?

Sleep just wouldn't come. No matter how strongly Rosabel willed herself to forget what had happened in the hallway, her mind wouldn't let her. Again and again, she saw his eyes, full of pain and sadness, looking into hers. She remembered his breath as it brushed over her skin and felt his hands on her arms as they held her pressed against the wall.

As much as the whole scene had saddened her, lying in her bed remembering Rosabel did not feel sad. Instead, a shy smile played on her lips, and her whole body tingled with anticipation. Of what exactly?

Although he had scared her before, he did not anymore. She had seen the depth of his pain and thought she knew that the cold she had always seen in his eyes and heard in his voice was nothing but a mask to hide the emotions that ran so deep, that had wounded him, even crippled him. In many ways, he seemed broken to her. And yet, she couldn't understand why.

Standing in the hallway, Rosabel had felt the almost desperate desire to comfort him. She had barely been able to stop herself from wrapping her arms around him and laying his head on her shoulder for comfort. Instead, she had merely touched her hand to his cheek. But it had been enough. A jolt had gone through her that she was sure he had felt too.

Again, she felt the soft touch of his lips as she had lifted her head to meet his eyes. Sweet and tender, like at their wedding. Only this time, Rosabel realized she wanted more. Once again, her lips curled into a smile as she remembered standing under the mistletoe with him after the Christmas Ball.

He still owed her a kiss.

And one day she would claim it.

One day soon.

25

UNABLE TO FORGET

After the night their paths had crossed in the hallway, her husband seemed to be avoiding her even more, if that were possible. One time when she and Georgiana were out walking in the gardens, she actually saw him stop in his tracks when he beheld them. His face frozen like a grotesque mask, he stared at them. For a moment, he seemed hesitant, but then he blinked, and with long strides and no look back, he turned on his heel and hurried away. Grateful that a tall hedge had obstructed Georgiana's view, Rosabel pretended nothing had happened.

Inside, however, Rosabel had felt the burning heat of anger slowly rush through her veins and igniting a deep place within her. Reminded of Leonora's portrayal of 'their' husband, Rosabel wondered how he could make her feel for him in one moment and then infuriate her the next. The man truly was an enigma.

One she intended to solve.

After a few days of never even glimpsing her father, Georgiana began to wonder. Turning sad eyes to Rosabel, she asked if she had done anything wrong, if she had angered or disappointed her father somehow. Rosabel immediately assured her that that was not the case, that only unexpected business was keeping him away. But in the little girl's eyes, she could see her own lies.

She had to do something. He was slipping away, and every now and then, she thought Georgiana was ready to give up hope as well.

But then one late afternoon, Rosabel walked into the library, looking for an entertaining and hopefully distracting read before bed, only to find father and daughter sitting side by side on a chaise. Leaning against her father's leg, Georgiana had an open book on her lap, her little finger tracing line after line as she read, her sweet voice barely carrying the words. Again and again, she peered up at her father, seeking approval. And to Rosabel's great surprise, he gave it willingly.

One arm around his daughter's small shoulders, he hung on every word spilling forth from her mouth. Occasionally, he pointed at a word or line and then whispered something in her ear. All the while, a shy, yet content smile lingered on his features that Rosabel had never seen before. More than that, he seemed relaxed, at ease, not at all conflicted.

Standing behind a row of bookcases, Rosabel watched them, transfixed, unable to move. A small voice whispered that she ought to discreetly leave the library, but her muscles wouldn't comply. Frozen to the spot, she watched them, her heart beating, even jumping in her chest at the silent joy she beheld.

Rosabel was sure at least an hour had passed when father and daughter put down the book and exited the library together. Keeping back, Rosabel followed them, careful not to cause any unnecessary sound that would draw their attention.

Heading upstairs, they proceeded down the corridor toward the nursery, and Rosabel caught snippets of sentences, concluding that Georgiana had invited her father to join her tea party. As they reached the door to the nursery, her husband opened it and bowing slightly held it for Georgiana to enter. Then he fell in step behind her and—

Froze.

Following close behind, Rosabel almost bumped into him as she approached the room, unable to conceal her presence any longer and determined to ask permission to join their little gathering.

As she could not see his face, Rosabel was at a loss as to what had caused this sudden reaction. Oblivious, Georgiana chattered on, but when her father didn't move from the door, she turned and looked at him. Instantly, the smile died on her lips.

Brushing past him, Rosabel saw his frozen features, eyes staring

186

ahead, lips pressed into a tight line. Every resemblance of happiness had vanished, replaced by a seething anger boiling just below the surface. Following his line of sight, Rosabel flinched.

Leonora's portrait was staring back at them.

Rosabel had completely forgotten the painting they had taken with them on their journey from Westmore. Used to sleeping under her mother's watchful eyes, Georgiana had not been able to part with it. Not even at the promise of seeing her father.

"Where did you get this?" her husband forced out through gritted teeth, his voice hoarse and menacing. "Why is this here?"

Feeling his eyes burn holes into her soul, Rosabel straightened, glancing at Georgiana. The girl looked uneasy back and forth between the two of them and her mother's portrait, aware of what had caused her father's displeasure.

"My lord, I suggest we talk about this in your study," Rosabel suggested, eyes indicating the presence of his daughter. Sensing the anger ready to burst forth, she hoped to detain it long enough to remove Georgiana from the scene. "Please, my lord."

Her husband didn't hear her though. "I ordered this painting removed," he hissed, approaching her with slow steps, like a predator circling its prey. "How did you—?"

Feeling little of the courage she hoped to portray, Rosabel lifted her hand, stopping him mid-sentence. "Not here, my lord." Then after ringing the bell, she turned to Georgiana.

"Listen, your father and I need to speak to each other. But Bridget would love to keep you company during your tea party." Gently, she brushed a lock behind the girl's ear. "Is that all right?"

Looking her in the eyes, Georgiana simply nodded, but the happiness that had been there mere moments before had vanished into thin air. Her small shoulders slumped, and her eyes had lost their glow.

As Bridget entered, Rosabel excused herself and marched out of the room, hoping that her husband would follow. Not stopping to check, she headed straight for his study, knowing that they would have privacy there. As she came to stand before his desk, the door slammed shut behind her.

Slowly, Rosabel turned around, finding her husband's burning eyes on her. The scowl on his face spoke volumes before he even opened his mouth to say a word. "How did you get that painting?" he hissed, arm gesturing to the door and Leonora's portrait they'd left behind in the nursery. "I know it was you. How dare you disobey me?"

Taking a deep breath to steady her nerves, Rosabel fought to keep her eyes fixed on his. She would not yield! Yes, he didn't scare her anymore, not like he did in the beginning, but there was something about him when anger took over that made her uneasy. Keeping her own voice as steady and unburdened by emotions as she could, Rosabel said, "I found the painting in the attic, by accident. I did not intend to disobey you. You never mentioned the portrait, did you?"

He knew she was right, she could see it in his eyes, a spark of reason, and yet, his anger could not that easily be extinguished. "You were not supposed to enter the attic in the first place! You—"

"I did not know that."

He threw up his hands, shaking his head at her. "So you find a painting of my wife in the attic and decide to hang it in Georgiana's nursery? What possessed you? Are you out of your mind?"

Trying to stay calm, Rosabel fought down the spark of anger that ignited in her own core. "My lord, I did not mean to cause affront," he snorted, "I had the painting brought to Georgiana's room upon her request. She followed me to the attic one day and saw it. Could you have denied her?" Looking into his eyes, she saw his answer.

He turned away then, and the tense anger that had held his body captive slowly dissipated. His shoulders loosened, and his head seemed too heavy to be held up.

Feeling her own muscles relax, Rosabel said, "She was her mother. You cannot expect her to forget."

Again, his shoulders stiffened, and he turned back to her, slowly, menacingly. It sent a shiver down her back. "This is none of your business!" He spoke so quietly that Rosabel had to strain her ears to hear him. "The painting will be destroyed! And you will never speak of her again!"

Shocked at his words, Rosabel's own thoughts instantly travelled to the little golden-haired girl. Losing her mother's portrait would destroy her. It had given her such peace ever since they had put it up in her room. How could he demand such a thing?

Rosabel shook her head, feeling her own resolve strengthened to the point of unyielding. "The painting will remain where it is," she said just as quietly. Upon her words, his eyes narrowed slightly, and he stepped toward her. Before he could respond though, Rosabel continued. "Your anger will not serve you, my lord. You need to make peace with the past." His eyes narrowed into slits, and she could see that his whole frame trembled with barely contained emotions, and yet, Rosabel could not stop herself. "What happened with Leonora?" Saying her name out loud, and to him of all people, felt strange as though conjuring up a ghost.

"I told you not to mention her again!" he hissed as he towered over her. "She is no more. You are now Georgiana's mother, and that will be it! Do you hear me?" His head bent over hers, the blue in his eyes seemed almost gone, replaced by a black abyss.

Feeling her body yield, Rosabel quickly shook off the urge and lifted her chin. Again, her lips almost brushed his. "Yes, I am Georgiana's mother now, and I am proud to be, but that does not make Leonora any less her mother."

A deep growl escaped his throat, and his hands closed around her arms once again.

"You cannot change that. No matter what you do," Rosabel whispered, her eyes looking into his, noting that his own occasionally travelled down to her lips. Again, a tremble went through her, and again, it was not one born out of fear. "You must let your anger go, my lord."

"Why must you always fight me?" he hissed, staring at her as though she'd just declared war. "From the day we met, I did not have a day of peace. I did what I could to protect you, and yet, it was never enough, was it?" Rosabel frowned, unable to make sense of his words. Was he talking about her? But she hadn't... No, he was talking about Leonora. Searching his face, she found his eyes distant as though he wasn't really looking at her, but at a memory of his past, at Leonora. Uncomfortable, Rosabel tried to shake off his hands, but they only held her tighter.

Lips pressed into a thin line, he looked at her, a hint of desperation on his features. "What will it take to make you forget him?" He stepped closer until the desk cut into her back. "What? Tell me!" He shook her, bringing his face even closer to hers.

Rosabel didn't know what to do. He clearly did not see her, trapped in emotions of his past. What was she to do? She tried to shove against him, but he was too strong, holding her pressed against him. At a loss for words, she searched his eyes, trying to make herself seen. But his gaze remained blind to her.

"Tell me," he demanded again, only this time his voice had grown softer. "Tell me how I can make you forget him." He slowly bent his

189

head, inching closer, his eyes traveling to her lips once more.

Seeing his intention, Rosabel's heart sped up even more. Would he kiss her? But it would not be her kiss, would it? Not really. In his mind, he was seeing Leonora. The woman he had loved his whole life. The woman who apparently had never loved him back. Knowing this, Rosabel still couldn't move, couldn't stop him.

When his lips finally touched hers, a flame rose within her, and Rosabel felt herself respond. Kissing him back, she placed her hands on his chest, feeling the rapid beating of his heart. His hands released their almost painful grip on her arms and brushing down her back settled on her waist, pulling her closer.

Rosabel could have lost herself in the sensation, but a small voice whispered that she was not the one his caresses were meant for. Fighting down her own desire, Rosabel shoved against him, hands still flat on his chest, trying to break his hold. As his mouth freed hers for a second, she ordered him to "Stop!"

Instantly, his head snapped up, and his eyes stared down at her.

Panting, she returned his gaze, her hands still pushing against him, asking for more space. "I am not Leonora," she whispered, knowing the pain her words would cause him.

He blinked, and then he saw her. Rosabel watched the realization light up his eyes and then hit him right in the chest. Recognizing her, he stumbled backwards, shock clear in his eyes. When his back finally hit the door, he spun around, yanked it open and rushed out.

Fleeing his study, Graham's head was still spinning. His feet carried him without conscious thought until he found himself in the stables. Knowing that he needed to get away, he didn't waste time to ask his groom to saddle his horse but grabbed the gear himself and went to Storm's box. The stallion pranced impatiently, clearly as eager as his master to leave the confinement of the stables behind.

Feeling the wind in his face, Graham urged Storm on as they flew across the meadow leading away from the estate. Upon entering the forest, Graham still didn't slow down, needing the rush their ride brought him, as it cleared his head, at least momentarily. He was afraid of the thoughts that would return once he slowed down, and so they thundered along a well-trodden path, trees flying past.

How long he ran from his thoughts, Graham didn't know. But the trees grew less dense and the sun dipped low on the horizon when they reached the small lake east of Camden Hall. Until recently, Graham had never been there. Only his hunting trips in the last weeks had taken him this way. As he spotted the lake, it echoed with the thoughts he was trying to leave behind. Georgiana. Leonora. Rosabel.

Oh God, what had he done?

26

LEONORA'S SECRET

*F*or a long while, Rosabel remained in her husband's study. Why? She didn't know. Her thoughts were still busy trying to make sense of what had just happened. He had kissed her, and she had to admit she had welcomed it. Her teeth gnawed on her lower lip as she remembered the touch of his, and a smile came to her face.

However, the kiss had been meant for Leonora, a small voice reminded her, and instantly the smile died on her lips. Remembering the closeness she had felt to the woman after reading her diaries and letters, Rosabel experienced a touch of guilt herself. Although he *was* her husband, had she betrayed Leonora by enjoying his kiss?

Sinking into his chair, she rested her elbows on the desk and buried her face in her hands. When had life gotten so complicated?

Replaying the scene before her eyes, his words echoed in her mind, and instantly her head snapped up. *Tell me how I can make you forget him!*

Who had he been talking about? Had Leonora loved another? Had she really never... Rosabel's thoughts trailed off as another puzzle piece suddenly fell into place.

Jumping up, she rushed from the room.

Glad that no one was around, Rosabel hastened up the stairs and cursed each step it took to reach the end of the corridor and open the door to her room. There in the top drawer of her vanity were Leonora's diaries and letters; letters that her husband had written to her or so Rosabel had thought.

After slamming the door shut, she gathered the drawer's contents and retreated to her favourite reading spot under the window. Flipping through the first diary, Rosabel scanned the entries, re-reading snippets here and there.

> *…G. assures me that he will not give up,…*
> *…Although G. did not speak of it,…*
> *…But G. insists I put my trust in him. …*
> *…Never would I have thought G. would consider such a solution. …*

And then her eyes found what she had been looking for.

> *…Graham treats me with the utmost respect. …*
> *…I feel safe with Graham, …*

Graham.

Here, she had suddenly used his full name and before only the initial. Again, her husband's words echoed in her head, *Tell me how I can make you forget him!*

The truth hit her with such force that it knocked the breath from her lungs. Panting, Rosabel leaned back, closing her eyes for a split second, before she returned her gaze to the words on the page before her.

> *…Graham adores her, and I am grateful for the father he is to her. Upon first hearing me call her by the name I had chosen, his eyes seemed to darken for a bare instance. I cannot blame him. However, I could not help myself. I feel choosing the name I did would always keep her connected to her roots since she will be denied everything else her line owes her. …*

"Georgiana," Rosabel breathed, feeling the blood drain from her face. "She is not his daughter."

Watching the sun disappear behind the horizon, Rosabel couldn't move. The truth she had sought for so long did not give her peace. All she had wanted had been to understand, but now, she wished she could forget.

Again, she re-read the lines before her eyes and shook her head. Georgiana was not his daughter. There was no other explanation. Trying to think things through, she replayed everything she had learned about Leonora in her head.

Leonora had been in love, with whom she did not know. However, his name started with a G. Although his father had been against the match, they had hoped for a happy outcome. They had to have been sure to succeed in persuading his father, considering that Leonora had risked everything by agreeing to a physical relationship in such a situation. Shortly after, she had then been with child...and then everything had fallen apart.

Instead of marrying the man she loved, he had arranged for her to marry someone else instead, Graham. And her husband had known, he had promised to take care of her and protect her as well as he could. But he had loved her too. Was that why he had agreed to marry her even though she was carrying another man's child? Because he loved her?

Rosabel couldn't believe her own reasoning, and yet, it appeared the only explanation.

Again, her thoughts returned to Georgiana and the question of her fatherhood. Why had Leonora shortened his name to an initial? Had she been trying to keep his identity a secret in case someone should read her diaries? Why did his identity need to be protected? Who was he?

Reading the lines before her eyes yet again, Rosabel suddenly knew what his name was.

...Upon first hearing me call her by the name I had chosen, his eyes seemed to darken for a bare instance. I cannot blame him. However, I could not help myself. I feel choosing the name I did would always keep her connected to her roots since she will be denied everything else her line owes her. ...

Georgiana was named after her father. That had been the reason

for her husband's reaction upon hearing her name.

So his name had to be George.

Unfortunately, it was a name widely popular.

27

A MERE REPLACEMENT

Shocked, and yet, not surprised, Rosabel read the note Hanson handed to her. Again, her husband had fled the premises. Officially, it had been urgent business calling him to Town, and yet, Rosabel knew without a doubt that the reason he had once again departed in the middle of the night lay with what had happened the day before in his study.

Desperate to kick or hit something, Rosabel tried to satisfy her anger by balling up the note and tossing it into the fire, its flames licking at it like hungry dogs. However, it did not work. Her anger still burned within her, another flame but just as hungry as the ones warming her cheeks.

Strangely following her husband's example, Rosabel decided that a little distance would help her clear her mind and douse the flames in her heart. She ordered the carriage and then went in search of Georgiana. Half an hour later, they rolled through the greening landscape. Seeing a glow fill the girl's eyes as the baron's estate came into view relieved Rosabel of at least some of her anxieties. If she was to suffer from her husband's cowardly behaviour, at least, his daughter would be spared that day.

Immediately upon their arrival, Rosabel's youngest cousins latched onto Georgiana and before she knew what was happening, the four of them scampered off to find new adventures. Watching them go, Rosabel smiled. At this age, life was still easy, still a wonder.

Again sitting in the back parlour with Ellie, Rosabel found eager eyes looking at her. "Is something wrong?" she asked. "You keep fidgeting."

Casting a glance at the footman, serving tea and sandwiches, Ellie remained silent, only her eyes seemed to be dancing. When the door finally closed and they were alone, it burst from her like a stream breaking a dam. "I know I shouldn't tell you yet, but I cannot keep it a secret." She grinned from ear to ear. "I might be married soon myself!"

Rosabel's mouth fell open as she stared at her cousin wide-eyed. "Married? But...? To whom?"

"Viscount Haston," Ellie hummed, her voice dreamy as though speaking to a loved one. "He has not proposed yet, but he will. I'm sure of it."

"Has he made you any promises?" Rosabel asked, worried that her friend might have jumped to conclusions.

Ellie shook her head. "It's the way he looks at me. I've never seen him look at another quite like this. Whenever we meet at a gathering, he stays by my side almost the whole evening." Remembering one such occasion, her eyes became distant.

"I am happy for you," Rosabel said, hoping her friend's hope would not be disappointed the way Leonora's had been. "But please do not rush into anything without thinking," she cautioned. "Be sure of his intentions before you allow your feelings to run away with you."

Ellie nodded. "I will. I promise." Rosabel hoped this was true.

"And how are you?" Ellie asked. Her eyes seemed to have abandoned their former occupation and now narrowed slightly as they observed Rosabel with curiosity. "You seem different."

Rosabel shrugged. Although she had hoped to leave her troubles behind for at least a little while, she had known that such a wish was hopeless. Her cousin saw right through her. And yet, Rosabel wasn't sure how much she ought to share with Ellie. What she had learned the day before was of such delicate and intimate nature that she hesitated to even share it with her truest friend and confidante. What if the servants overheard? Such knowledge could destroy Georgiana's future and happiness.

"Have you been able to learn more about your husband's first wife?" Ellie prodded.

Rosabel drew in a deep breath and met her eyes. "I know he still loves her." Not knowing she would say that, Rosabel clasped a hand over her mouth. Where had this come from?

A knowing smile played on Ellie's lips as though she had just glimpsed the core of Rosabel's problems. "I am sorry," she whispered. "You care for him greatly, do you not?"

Not sure how to answer, Rosabel shrugged, turning her gaze out the window at the gardens slowly coming to life with each passing day, welcoming the brilliant spring sun.

"That bad?" Ellie asked.

Feigning ignorance, Rosabel said, "What do you mean?"

Ellie shook her head. "Please, Dear Cousin, do not play me for a fool. You have come to care for him, greatly. Why do you deny it? Are you afraid he does not return your affection?"

For a moment, Rosabel contemplated pretending not to understand what her cousin was referring to, but then their eyes met, and Rosabel realized it would be a futile endeavour. Her cousin knew her too well. So, in the end, Rosabel nodded, gaze fixed on her hands playing with the folds of her dress.

Ellie nodded. "Maybe not yet," she counselled. "From what you said, he shared a great love with his first wife. Something like that is not easily forgotten. You must be patient." Rosabel felt her cousin's hand descend upon hers, squeezing it gently. "He will come to love you. I am sure of it."

Desperate to lift the burden that had been weighing down her heart for the past months, Rosabel turned to her cousin. "Oh Ellie, I wish you could be right, but I fear he will never love another. Leonora was everything to him and still is. How can I compete?"

Deep down, Rosabel wasn't sure she even wanted to. After everything, she considered Leonora a friend, an ally, and not a rival for her husband's affections. Could she live with herself if she were the reason he stopped loving his first wife? Was that right?

Again turning to her cousin, she said, "Yes, I realize now that I do want him to love me…for me. Not as a replacement for his first wife. But at the same time, I do not want him to stop loving her. She was a great woman, who suffered a doomed love." Ellie frowned but Rosabel ignored her. "She deserves to remain in the hearts of those who loved her." Hearing Georgiana's voice echo through the door, Rosabel smiled. "What I want from him is what Georgiana already gave me."

Again, Ellie frowned. "And what is that?"

"A place in her heart," Rosabel said. "Leonora was and always will be her mother. I would never dream of taking that away from them. However, Georgiana allowed me to be her mother as well. It does not have to be either or. Leonora and me, we are both her mother. And that is what I want." Feeling the burden lifted, Rosabel looked at her cousin with eyes that held hope for the future. "I know it will not be easy, and I am afraid that there might be a time that I will despair, but I will try nonetheless. I care for him deeply; how that happened I do not know. But I do hope that he will come to love me. It is my dearest wish, and yet, I do not want to rob Leonora of his love. I will not make him choose."

"It sounds like you have a plan, Dear Cousin!"

Rosabel laughed. "Not a plan, no. Yesterday, something…happened. I cannot explain further, so please do not press me, but it resulted in an unwelcome consequence."

Ellie's eyebrows rose in question.

"He left Camden Hall in the night," Rosabel admitted. "I don't know where he went or when he'll return; if he'll return. So all I can do is wait…and hope."

A fortnight passed, and her husband remained absent. No letter, no communique of any kind, nothing. Rosabel's as well as Georgiana's spirits dragged the floors. Few things could bring about a smile. They spent many days sitting in the front drawing room, waiting for the echo of hoof beats to drift up the drive.

The nights were even worse. Glad that at least Georgiana could sleep, Rosabel often wandered the halls, desperate for anything to occupy herself with. Her mind left her restless, and her eyes refused to close for more than a few hours when she neared exhaustion around the break of dawn. And so she spent her nights reading, either in bed or in the library. When a book would not hold her attention and her thoughts strayed to questions whose answers only plagued her and roused a terrible drumming behind her temples, Rosabel would seek the silent comfort of the kitchen.

While she had always loved the outdoors, early spring's cold temperatures prevented her from roaming the gardens in the middle of the night. Her chosen alternative, the kitchen, harboured scents quite unlike those of the gardens, but they nonetheless stirred feelings of warmth and contentedness. Even in the dark hours of the night, the scent of fresh bread and tea hung in the air. Sometimes she would just sit and smell preserves, savouring the concentrated smell of ripe fruit and their sweet aroma as it mingled with the spicy tea she had brewed herself. Doing small things herself, as she had not been permitted since becoming a duchess, brought great joy to her and calmed her nerves. Her mind occupied with ordinary tasks, her heart rejoiced in the simplicity of small pleasures.

One morning, after a night when Rosabel's eyes had closed later than usual, Bridget burst into her room. "Your grace, you must wake! Your husband arrived."

Rubbing the remnants of sleep out of her eyes, Rosabel yawned. "Are you certain?" At Bridget's eager nod, she jumped out of bed. "Help me dress!"

Properly attired, Rosabel had trouble keeping her feet in check lest they run down the curved staircase and burst into her husband's study fairly the same way Bridget had greeted her that morning. Although eager to see him, Rosabel didn't know what to expect after everything that had happened. Would he treat her with civility? Would he ignore her? Would he use harsh words or speak with indifference in his voice? Would he pretend that nothing had happened and they were still strangers?

Rosabel's head spun. Starting to feel dizzy, she braced a hand against the wall, breathing in deeply.

In that moment, small footsteps echoed from down the hall, quickly drawing closer. Turning around, Rosabel spotted Georgiana's golden curls bouncing up and down as the girl came running toward her. "Father is back! Father is back!"

Forcing a smile on her face, Rosabel nodded. "So I heard. You have not yet seen him?"

Georgiana shook her head. "Can we see him now?"

Not trusting her voice, Rosabel nodded. Allowing the girl to pull her down the corridor toward her husband's study, Rosabel wondered if she was making a big mistake by facing him now, when he clearly wished to avoid them or at least her. Wouldn't he have announced his arrival if he didn't?

Although reluctant, Georgiana stopped at the door and knocked. To Rosabel, it seemed like an eternity passed before her husband's familiar voice beckoned them to enter. Eagerly, Georgiana pressed down the handle and pulled Rosabel after her into the study. "Father, you're back!" she beamed. "I have missed you!"

Clearly not expecting his daughter, Rosabel's husband stared at her as though she was an apparition. Not even glancing in his wife's direction, his eyes were focused on the little girl bouncing up and down in front of him. "I am afraid I have to work," he said in a brusque tone.

Undeterred, Georgiana kept beaming at him, blue eyes shining like diamonds. "I have new paintings to show you. I practiced a lot like you said. I believe I am getting better. Will you come and look at them?" Her pleading face could have melted ice, and her father's face was no match. The corners of his mouth twitched, and a small twinkle came to his eyes as he looked at his daughter. "I will."

Squealing, Georgiana jumped up and down.

He lifted a hand. "But not right now. I still have business to attend to. Go, return to your lessons, and I shall see you shortly."

Nodding her head, Georgiana bounced from the room, humming under her breath as she skipped down the hall.

The second she had passed the door and her father's eyes could not follow her any longer, he only then seemed to realize that his wife was still in the room. His eyes flitted to her for the barest of seconds before returning to the stack of papers before him. "As I said, I have business to attend to."

His shoulders rigid and jaw clenched, her husband looked as though he was about to face the gallows. Sheer determination seemed to keep him from breaking free and fleeing the scene. The fact that he would not meet her eyes hurt Rosabel more than anything else.

Needing time to tend to her own heart, Rosabel mumbled a quick goodbye and quit the room as well. Donning a coat and scarf, she rushed from the house, desperate for some fresh air.

As she walked about the garden, her mind began to clear with each chilled breath that touched her lungs. The cold stung in the tip of her ears as well as her nose, and she rubbed her gloved hands together in order to keep her fingers from growing stiff. How were they to go on? Rosabel wondered.

For the first time since coming to Camden Hall against her

husband's wishes, Rosabel questioned the wisdom of her decision. Was there truly a way they could all live under the same roof as a family? Not as strangers merely sharing a residence?

In that moment, standing among the slowly awakening shrubs, Rosabel could not fathom a positive outcome. Every scenario led to a doomed future. Strangely, she felt reminded of Leonora's troubles, feeling a renewed connection to the woman. Was there a chance for her, Rosabel, to be happy when Leonora's hopes had so tragically been dashed?

28

A KISS CLAIMED

Although her husband remained civil, particularly to his daughter, his resolve to avoid them as much as possible seemed undeterred. Most days, he left the house before breakfast, only to return when night had fallen. What he did away from Camden Hall, Rosabel could only guess. She suspected he spent most of his time on horseback, as Storm seemed exhausted lately, and had probably taken up hunting again. Occasionally, he was accompanied by a group of men carrying rifles, and they spent the better part of the night drinking in the parlour.

Rosabel didn't know what to think. She couldn't help but despise his behaviour, and yet, something told her he was merely putting on a show.

Weeks passed, and nothing changed. Temperatures climbed, allowing a warming breeze to brush through the pines and oaks grouped in the gardens. Buds opened and soon blossomed, dotting nature's green canvas with sparkling colour. The sun shone more brightly these days, promising a brilliant summer. And yet, her husband's scowl remained.

Finding sleep still a fickle friend, Rosabel once more found herself tossing and turning, unable to find a path to sweet oblivion. After a small eternity, she finally threw off the covers and climbed out of bed. Pacing her room for a good ten minutes, she donned her robe and quietly sneaked out into the hall. Tiptoeing past Georgiana's room, Rosabel found her way into the kitchen. By now familiar with the twists and turns of the house, she moved sure-footed like a mountain goat, not even lighting a candle until she reached the kitchen.

There, she stoked the fire in the stove for warmth for nights still had a biting chill in the air. She put on a kettle of water and settled onto a chair, leaning her elbows on the table before her and resting her head in her hands. Suddenly her eyelids felt heavy, and Rosabel cursed the world and everyone in it.

Still, she remained seated, sipping her tea, and her thoughts wandered in all directions, never lingering anywhere for long.

Hours after the house had fallen asleep, Rosabel heard hoof beats coming up the drive, and she wondered if a messenger had come or if it was her husband returning from one of his late-night exploits. The hoof beats stopped, and voices rose from the dark, murmuring. Straining her ears, Rosabel could not make out what they were saying, only that they were quickly approaching, circling the house and coming around back. Before she knew what was happening, footsteps echoed just outside the door to the kitchen, and Rosabel barely had time to seek cover inside the pantry when the door flew open.

"Are you certain you do not want us to send over the physician? That shoulder of yours does sport all kinds of unnatural colours," a gruff and quite inebriated voice slurred.

"There is no need," her husband's voice answered. Although he appeared to be in need of a good night's sleep, his was not the speech of one too deep in the cups. "Now, get yourselves off."

Then the door closed, and the voices outside slowly vanished into the dark.

Peering out of the pantry, Rosabel watched her husband move about the kitchen. From his pocket, he drew his handkerchief and dipping it in a bowl he'd filled with fresh water dabbed it to his left cheek.

Frowning, Rosabel inched closer, curious as to what he was doing. Her foot, however, caught on the potato basket, and trying to catch herself, she banged into the pantry door so loudly that her ears rang.

Instantly, her husband spun around, face alert.

Upon recognizing her, the tension left his shoulders, and he exhaled. However, seconds later, his entire frame seemed to stiffen as he avoided looking at her, hand still clutched to his face.

Stepping out of the pantry, Rosabel approached her husband. "Are you injured, my lord?" she asked, pointing at the handkerchief.

Taking a step backward, he waved her away. "It is nothing." For a second, his eyes swept over her nightgown partly visible under her robe as it hung open, the strap dangling loosely at her sides. "You ought to return to bed," he said and turned away.

Retying her robe, Rosabel moved for the door but stopped before she had taken more than a few steps. As she glanced over her shoulder at her husband, something changed her mind. Without another thought, she approached him. Walking around, she placed a hand on his arm and urged him to face her.

As he glanced at her, his shoulders slumped as though in defeat. "Why will you not leave me alone?"

"Because you are injured," she whispered, moving her hand to cover his own, still holding the handkerchief to his face. Slowly, she drew it away and gasped as she saw the bruised cut covering his left cheekbone. "Oh, my goodness, what happened?"

She could feel the muscles in his arm tense, and his voice sounded strained as he spoke. "A misunderstanding, nothing more."

Rosabel's eyes opened wide. "You fought someone over a disagreement?"

Frown descending upon his face, he shook his head. "Not I. I merely sought to end the dispute."

"I see," Rosabel mumbled. "And were you successful, my lord?"

"I was, and I was awarded a souvenir as well." He gestured to his face and cringed, clasping his right hand over his left arm.

Seeing pain distort his face, Rosabel moved to withdraw his arm and pull off his overcoat. "You suffered another injury?" she asked, remembering the slurred voice speaking of a *shoulder sporting all kinds of unnatural colours*.

As her fingers moved to remove his shirt, his hands stopped hers. "I do not need your assistance. It is but a bruise and will be all healed by the morrow."

Watching him closely, Rosabel saw the slight tremble in his hand and the twitching of his muscles as he strained to maintain his composure. Unable to leave him, she shook her head. "You will not get rid of me this easily."

Upon hearing her words, his eyebrows rose, and he stared at her. "Why are you so insistent? I assure you it is nothing." Again, his eyes swept over her form then jerked back up to her face before trailing off to the iron-cast stove behind her. "You should return to your room."

Seeing a hint of red come to his cheeks, Rosabel's breath caught in her throat. Her pulse quickened, and her hands began to tremble ever so slightly. But again, she noticed that it wasn't fear that had her shiver. On the contrary, the shiver filled her whole body with a new warmth, and without thought, she reached out and placed her hands on his chest, his thin shirt the only barrier left between them.

He drew in a sharp breath and would have backed away had he not stood pressed against the workbench as it was. As his eyes shifted down to hers, Rosabel's hands moved of their own accord and slowly began to unbutton his shirt.

She could feel his chest rise and fall beneath her fingers, and her eyes spotted the traitorous goose bumps that rose every time her finger tips brushed his skin. Occasionally, he would avert his eyes and grit his teeth as though the process was pure torture.

When the shirt finally fell away, Rosabel gasped.

While his finely-chiselled chest and upper arms sported the occasional smaller bruise here and there, she could see a hand-sized bruise right below his left collar bone, shining deep blue with a tinge of purple in the flickering candlelight.

Lifting her eyes to his, Rosabel said, "You were right indeed. It is nothing but a scratch."

A faint smile played on her lips, and after a moment of hesitation, the corners of his own mouth drew up as well. "Do you not feel foolish now that you see it for yourself?" he asked, a humorous tone to his voice.

"I do indeed," Rosabel whispered, forcing her eyes from his. Turning to the stove, she poured the remaining water from the kettle into a large bowl. After soaking a linen towel in it, she carefully wrung out the towel so as not to burn her fingers, let it cool briefly and then turned to her husband. Again finding his eyes with her own, she stepped back into the spot she had vacated before, gently placing the hot towel on his shoulder. "There, this should help your muscles relax."

"Thank you," he whispered. "Now will you go to bed?"

As a smile curled up her lips, Rosabel again shook her head. "Will you never give up?"

Now, it was his turn to shake his head. All the while, his deep blue eyes gazed into hers, touching a part within her that made her want to scream with joy. Instead, she reached for another towel, this one dry, and placed it over the wet one already covering his shoulder. Then she tucked his shirt back up, turning her attention to the buttons once more. While her fingers worked, she could feel his breath brushing over her skin, from her forehead down her cheeks to the side of her neck. Goose bumps of her own rose as another shiver ran over her, making her fingers tremble.

"Are you cold?" he whispered, his right hand coming to wrap around hers.

Instantly, she jerked her head up as though lightning had struck her. Looking up, she found him staring at her with the same stunned expression on his face that she knew to be on her own.

Rosabel swallowed, again forcing her eyes away. Reluctantly, she withdrew her hand from his, finding it as heated as her own.

As she reached for the handkerchief he still held clutched in his left hand, he relinquished it without a fight. Following his example, she dipped it in the bowl containing fresh water and then turned back to him, slowly inching her eyes up to meet his.

Feeling his gaze roam her face, Rosabel dabbed at the cut on his cheek, cleaning away any remnants of dirt that might cause infection. All the while, his breath brushed over her skin, and the trembling in her hand would not cease.

Finished, Rosabel turned to the pantry to retrieve the cooking port. Putting a little distance between them, she drew a deep breath, trying to steady her nerves. Being so close to him had her rattled, leaving her unable to think straight.

When she re-emerged from the pantry, she felt his gaze on her, following her every step until she stood before him once again, their bodies almost touching.

Avoiding his eyes, Rosabel poured a bit of the port on her own handkerchief and again dabbed at his cut. The second the cloth touched the wound, he drew in a sharp breath, his body tensing. "I'm sorry," Rosabel whispered.

He didn't say a word but kept his gaze focused on the iron-cast stove behind her.

"There, done." Removing the handkerchief, Rosabel felt her eyes rise to meet his before she could stop herself. Once again, a shiver went over her, all the way down to her toes. Her heart beat in her chest, straining against her ribs.

His blue eyes sparkled in the dancing candlelight, and Rosabel wondered how she could ever have thought them cold. Right then, there was nothing cold about them. On the contrary, Rosabel felt her cheeks flush hot and her ears turn pink as they remained locked in each other's gaze.

More than anything, Rosabel wanted to reach out and touch him, feel his skin under her fingers and his breath caress her neck. But before she could, he blinked, and the spell was broken.

Clearing his throat, he averted his eyes, glancing at the door. "Well, I guess I should be going. Thank you for your help."

Then he turned away and strode toward the door.

Watching him leave, Rosabel felt the desperate need to stop him. No matter what, in that moment, all she wanted was for him to stay.

Before her mind could interfere, her heart spoke. "You still owe me a kiss."

Instantly, he stopped.

29

DESIRE

ot sure if his ears had deceived him, Graham slowly turned. As his eyes met hers, she instantly dropped them, a faint flush creeping up her cheeks. Seeing her fidget with the hem of her sleeve, Graham took a step forward.

While part of his conscious mind screamed at him to leave and not entangle himself in a situation that couldn't possibly lead to anything good, his feet wouldn't move in the direction of the door. Forward, approaching her, however, was not a problem. He needed to know.

Stopping merely an arm's length in front of her, Graham tried to peer into her downcast eyes. "I owe you a kiss?" he asked, feeling his own voice shake.

The crimson colour in her cheeks deepened as she raised her chin. Meeting his eyes, she began to gnaw on her lower lip. Her voice was barely a whisper, and he could see the hesitation in her eyes, yet she did not try to back out of it. "Yes, from the night of the Christmas Ball."

His own eyes widened as he remembered the moment Edmond had pointed out the mistletoe dangling above their heads. Although he had wanted to kiss her, he had refused, afraid to force himself where he was not wanted. But now, here she was, demanding that kiss. Did she really mean it?

Eyes sweeping her face, Graham tried to determine why she would make such a request. Did she care for him? Could that be possible?

Her eyes sparkled in the candlelight as she held his gaze, unflinching, and yet, her cheeks burned red, and he saw a slight tremble in her fingers. Although all but certain what would be the most sensible course of action, Graham felt his feet move forward until his shirt brushed her robe. Gently, his right hand cupped her cheek, his thumb brushing over her lips. A small gasp escaped her lips, and he noticed his own breathing increasing in intensity. If he kissed her now, would he ever be able to stop? He wondered.

Inching forward, he carefully placed his left hand on her waist. Still feeling a stab of pain surge through his shoulder, he gritted his teeth.

Her small frame trembled, and again Graham worried that she did not really want this. Desperately trying to contain his own desire, he spoke, his lips a mere inch from hers. "Are you certain?"

In answer, her lips curled up, and she placed her hands on his chest, careful not to hurt him. Her fingers brushed against his skin, and he sucked in a breath.

Staring into her eyes, all doubt fell from him, and he slowly lowered his head toward hers. As she closed her eyes, so did he and allowed himself to live in the moment.

Her lips felt soft, welcoming him, and before he knew it his hand moved from her face downward. His arm encircled her waist, pulling her closer to him.

When her fingers dug into his shirt, pulling her into him, he deepened the kiss, pushing her against the workbench behind her. As he tried to use his other arm to hold her even closer, a fresh jolt of pain went through his shoulder, and he cursed.

"I'm sorry," she whispered, eyes full of worry as she glanced at his injured shoulder. Letting go, she tried to step back. "I did not mean to hurt you."

Feeling the moment slip away, Graham reached out with his good arm and drew her back. "Don't. It does not matter." Before she could answer, his lips crashed down on hers again, and a soft moan escaped her throat.

In the next instant, footsteps echoed on the back stairs leading down to the kitchen.

Rosabel stiffened, and he released her, head turned to ascertain the

situation. Although it was still dark outside, Graham suspected that morning was closer than he had thought. Soon, the kitchen would be swarmed with staff preparing breakfast.

"Come," he whispered, drawing her to the other door, leading in a number of corridors to the front hall. Ascending the curved staircase, her hand still in his, Graham realized he was taking her toward their bed chambers. Feeling his heart hammer in his chest, he pushed all thoughts away and decided to live step by step.

Still breathless from their kiss, Rosabel followed him up the stairs. Eyes darting left and right, he approached the door to her bedchamber. Grateful that no one was up and about at such an early hour, Rosabel shivered as he stopped in front of the door and turned to her. What now? She wondered. Yes, she had demanded a kiss, but was she ready to take this further.

Hesitant himself, he looked at her, still breathing heavily. His hand was still wrapped around hers, and she could feel the pulse hammering in his wrist. Unable to move, suddenly feeling shy, they gazed into each other's eyes. Although she saw desire in his blue depths, he did not move forward or draw her to him.

When the sound of a door opening reached their ears, they both flinched.

Instantly, he dropped her hand, eyes searching the corridor. Although no one was in sight, footsteps approached quickly.

Rosabel knew they had to make a decision fast. Would he join her in her bedchamber? She wondered. Or would he—?

"Someone is coming," he said, eyes darting left and right before settling on hers. "You should go inside." As his eyes left hers and he leaned over to open the door for her, Rosabel's heart sank.

As though nothing had happened, he bowed to her and quickly walked away, opened the door to his own chambers and disappeared inside.

Although she considered going after him, Rosabel entered her own quarters and closed the door. Why had he not come in? She wondered, feeling a stab of rejection. Did he not desire her after all?

Tears pooled in the corners of her eyes and spilled forth as a heart-wrenching sob escaped her throat. Throwing herself on her bed, Rosabel wept until exhaustion took over and closed her eyes.

In her dreams, however, she felt the touch of his hands and the caress of his lips. Hugging her pillow, she smiled.

30

A FOOLISH WOMAN

The days following their kiss, her husband again returned to avoiding her. Usually such a treatment would strengthen her resolve and ignite the flame of anger, making her more daring. But then and there, Rosabel was exhausted. This war was costing her. She felt tired and worn out. If she could not get through to him any time soon, would she be forced to surrender? Would she forfeit and leave the battlefield?

Desperate for a distraction, Rosabel gathered Georgiana, and they spent the day at her old home. Ellie and her younger cousins were delighted to see them, and the afternoon progressed far into the evening, night had already fallen, before they finally returned home.

With Ellie's encouragements echoing in her mind, Rosabel spent the night in deep slumber, finally regaining some of the energy she had invested thus far. Waking refreshed, she ventured down to breakfast, disappointed but not surprised at her husband's absence.

However, when she returned to her room, the door stood open. Stepping inside, she found Bridget and another maid packing her things while two footmen were already carrying her trunk out the door

213

and down the corridor. "What is going on here?" she breathed, feeling an iron grip settling around her heart. "Why are you packing my things?"

Bridget looked at her with open eyes, clearly surprised she didn't know. "For the journey," she said.

"What journey?"

Clearly uncomfortable, Bridget said, "Back to Westmore."

Her knees turned to pudding, and Rosabel sank into her favourite armchair. How could he do this? Shaking her head, Rosabel snorted. How could she have been so foolish? Nothing had changed. He still loved Leonora. Only Leonora. And whatever had happened between them in the kitchen downstairs had only served to remind him that no other woman could ever replace the only one he had ever truly loved. Tears came to Rosabel's eyes, and she didn't bother to hide them.

Bridget ushered the other maid from the room. "I'm sorry, your grace. Is there anything I can do?"

Looking up, Rosabel was about to shake her head when the door flew open and Georgiana rushed inside. The little girl's face held the same shocked, tear-streaked expression that Rosabel knew was visible on her own. Rushing toward her, Rosabel took her in her arms, holding her close.

"Father is sending us back," Georgiana sobbed. "Why doesn't he like me?"

Again, Rosabel's heart broke. "Listen, I will go to your father and speak to him," she whispered, despite feeling the hopelessness of their situation as a new ache in her broken heart. "I'm sure this is a misunderstanding."

Georgiana nodded, and Bridget drew her away so Rosabel could leave. Drying her tears, Rosabel quickly smoothed back her dress. Then she took a deep breath and headed to her husband's study. However, for once, he was not there, and it wasn't after searching half the house that Hanson told her he had gone to the stables.

Hurrying outside, Rosabel hoped she would catch him before he could once again run away.

The smell of fresh hay and manure reached her nose upon entering the stables. Walking down the long aisle framed by boxes on each side,

Rosabel found herself the centre of attention as her husband's prized horses came to investigate who had come and if there was any chance for snagging a treat. Long arched necks bent over the boxes' doors, their heads stretched toward her. Patting a nose here and there, Rosabel quickly moved on. In the far back of the stable that opened to the paddock and farther down led around the outbuildings to the far-reaching grounds of Camden Hall, she spotted Storm, her husband's horse. Henry, the new groom, bowed to her and mumbled 'your grace' before lifting the saddle up and placing it on Storm's back.

From inside Storm's box, her husband appeared, eyes barely meeting hers. "Is there anything I can do for you, my lady?" he asked, his attention focused on his horse. The cut on his cheek was healing well, and since he was planning to ride out, his shoulder had to be too.

Anger flared, and Rosabel felt the desperate need to slap him. "You could tell me why you are sending us away?"

For a second, he glanced at her, then shrugged. "When you arrived, I made it clear that your staying here was only temporary. I do not understand the confusion."

Stomping toward him, Rosabel was at a loss for words. Unfortunately, he had a point. However, after everything that had happened, she had simply assumed that he accepted if not welcomed their presence. How foolish of her!

Fidgeting with the saddle, Henry looked the picture of discomfort as he pretended not to hear what was spoken. As though suddenly realizing they had an audience, her husband dismissed him, and he hurried away, almost tripping over his feet as he went.

Trying to calm her nerves, Rosabel took a deep breath. Georgiana, she thought. This was not about herself. She had to succeed for Georgiana. She could not allow the little girl to lose her father, as mule-headed as he was. Oh, how she missed Helen in that moment! The old woman would know exactly how to handle him.

"By sending her away, you're breaking her heart," she said, speaking as much about her daughter as about herself. "How can you do such a thing?"

For a moment, his eyes closed. Then he looked up and came toward her. "You have noted on many occasions that I am lacking as a father so I deem it best to remove her from my company."

Not expecting such a revelation, Rosabel stared at him. Although she wanted to argue, a part of her realized that he had twisted her words on purpose. Apparently, he was willing to use any means necessary to rid himself of them. "Do you not care what happens to us?" she whispered, feeling new tears threatening.

Not flinching under her gaze, he shrugged. "You will be provided for."

Rosabel snapped. "You know that is not what I meant! How can you not care?"

His eyes narrowed, turning a darker shade of blue. Suddenly, Rosabel felt reminded of the cold she had seen there in the beginning. He took a step toward her, pinning her with his gaze. "I told you before that the only reason I married you was to provide Georgiana with a mother."

Rosabel's mouth fell open as he spoke the words.

He shook his head. "I cannot fathom why this should bother you? You did not strike me as a woman foolish enough to seek a love match."

Again, his words felt like a slap in the face. What had happened that he now spoke to her without any emotions? The night in the kitchen, he had gazed at her almost lovingly, and now…now everything was different. If she only knew what she had done wrong, what she had done to anger him, to drive him away. Or had she been mistaken? Had it merely been a passion sparked in the moment? And gone the next?

As her emotions threatened to undo her, Rosabel drew on the small flame of anger that still burned in her chest. Eyes narrowing into slits, lips pressed into a thin line, she approached him. "I curse the day we met," she hissed, drew back her arm and slapped him hard across the face.

While he still stared at her, his hand traveling to the red mark slowly spreading across his cheek, Rosabel turned away. She was about to run out of the stables when a thought struck.

Instantly, she changed directions, ran the few steps toward Storm, swung herself into the saddle with more ease than she would ever have expected and kicked the horse's flanks. Storm reared and jumped forward with Rosabel clinging to the saddle.

In seconds, they had reached the open meadow, leaving the stable and her husband behind.

Staring after his wife, Graham stood stock-still. What had just happened? Realizing that their relationship, just like his to Leonora, was built on a shaky foundation that threatened to bury them all when it collapsed, Graham had decided to do the right thing. For weeks, he had postponed sending them away. While he dreaded their company and evaded them wherever possible, he had more and more come to depend on their presence. The house did not feel as empty as when they were not there. He could almost pretend he had a family. More than once, he had stood in the door watching Rosabel and Georgiana reading a book, chatting over tea or painting. A new warmth had spread through his chest upon these occasions, and he had wished for nothing more than to be able to join them.

However, what he wanted did no matter. He had a duty. He could not run from that, and so he had decided to run from his wife. Or rather send her away. He knew it was cowardly, and yet, he saw no other way.

Never would he have thought, she'd react in this way. Seeing her and the horse grow smaller as they flew across the meadow approaching the forest line, Graham turned and ran to the nearest box. Opening the door, he threw a bridle on Winter, didn't bother with a saddle and swung himself on the horse. While his shoulder was healing nicely, it still sent a small stab of pain down his side.

Cringing, he urged the mare on, hearing her hooves thunder on the path before entering the grassland stretching out before them. The wind whipped in his face as he drew up on the small hill leading down to the forest. For a second, his eyes focused on the dark clouds gathering in the east before he once again kicked the mare's flanks, and they flew forward.

31

A MEMORY TO BEHOLD

*T*ears blurring her vision, Rosabel clung to Storm's mane, letting him run free. He carried her through an ocean of grass stretching on both sides to the horizon in the distance. Dark clouds were gathering in the east, a looming threat, ready to descend upon her at any moment. However, Rosabel turned her head, ignoring nature's warning, and spurred Storm on.

Feeling the wind brush over her face, even nippier now that the sun was disappearing behind overhanging clouds, Rosabel had no destination in mind. She only felt the desperate need to get away. Away from Camden Hall. Away from the complications of her everyday life. And most importantly, away from her husband.

Not in her wildest dreams had Rosabel ever believed such a life would await her. Although unwelcome, an arranged marriage was nothing out of the ordinary. Few people ever married for love. However, some were fortunate to realize that the one they were bound to even possessed their heart. Eventually.

But even without love, Rosabel could have accepted a marriage built on respect and honesty. A husband who might have become a friend, someone she knew, someone she could trust.

The marriage she found herself in though was far from exemplary and not even fulfilled the basic requirements.

Leaving behind the open fields, Storm carried her into the forest. As they travelled down a well-trodden path, Rosabel realized that they were not moving at a break-neck speed anymore. Storm had adjusted his movements to the terrain, growing denser the deeper into the forest they proceeded. However, Rosabel didn't mind as her thoughts were occupied with more pressing matters than the speed of their travels.

While Rosabel had to admit that she had come to care for her husband, deeply even, he obviously held no such feelings for her in his heart. Certainly, he might desire her occasionally, but his interest in her never went beyond desires of the flesh. He did not care for her happiness or her well-being.

Admitting the truth made her heart ache, and tears spilled down her cheeks. Not bothering to brush them away, Rosabel sobbed quietly, hearing the echo of her breaking heart in the forest sounds around her.

As the sky slowly darkened, she heard an owl hoot here and there, a chilling breeze carrying its screeches to her ears. The wind picked up, tugging at her dress and blowing her hair in her face. As the chill crept up her arms, Rosabel began to shiver. Looking around, she realized how far she had travelled and that she would not make it back before the rain would pour from the heavens.

When the first drop fell, Rosabel urged Storm on. Knowing that she would get wet no matter what, she decided to put as much distance between herself and her husband as she possibly could. Where she was going she didn't know, didn't even think about. All that mattered was to get away.

Maybe he would rejoice if she left him for good.

Already soaked through, Graham squinted through the downpour, knowing that he couldn't turn back. She was his wife; he had to find her.

Following the only trail that led through the forest, he hoped that she had stayed on the path and not ventured through the thick underbrush. If she had, he knew he would never find her.

Why was she acting in such an irrational manner? Did she not see that he was doing what was best for all of them? Although there had been moments that had indeed resembled those of his happy childhood, he knew that the burden he carried on his shoulders was starting to affect them too. Not only his wife, but Georgiana as well, had grown quieter and more solemn in his presence. The light that usually shone in Georgiana's eyes had slowly dimmed each day she spent in his company. She loved him; he knew that. But it didn't matter. Ultimately, he would make her unhappy, and she would come to resent him for it. Better to make a clean cut now.

But how could he make his wife see this? She was so determined to reunite him with Georgiana. Could she not see that the happy family she clearly had in mind was not to be? How could he make her understand?

Slowly the trees grew fewer and farther apart. Leaving behind the thickness of the forest, Graham lifted his hand to shield his eyes. Peering through the sheets of rain pummelling the earth, he spotted a huge willow tree down in the small valley stretching out before him, standing like a sole sentinel on the shores of a small lake. Under that tree, a small figure huddled close to the trunk.

Surveying the terrain, Graham urged Winter on, allowing the mare to find her footing down the slippery hill. Slowly, she carried him down through the thick grass and muddy earth toward the lone tree.

As he drew closer, the figure turned. Even from a distance, Graham could see the resentment in her posture as she took a step back, shoulders squared and chin raised in defiance. If he could, he would have turned back.

Not spotting Storm anywhere in the vicinity, Graham peered at her more closely. Here and there, mud stained her dress, and a small cut ran from her forehead to her temple.

She had been thrown.

Feeling his heart beat against his ribs, Graham slid off the horse. Now, no more than a few feet away from her, he tied Winter's reins to a low-hanging branch and stepped toward his wife.

With eyes as dark as he had never seen them, she snarled at him. "Get out! Leave me alone!"

"I cannot do that, my lady," he replied, wondering how she could be so reckless. The rain still drummed down all around them. She had no horse to carry her home. And besides being soaked through and in danger of catching pneumonia, she now had a head injury as well.

220

"Do not pretend you care about what happens to me!" she hissed, regarding him with disgust. Never had he seen such dark emotions in her.

"I do care," he said, feeling his own anger rise at her complete lack of reason. "You are my wife."

She snorted. "I am your wife, yes, but only on paper. You do not care for me. If I died out here in this weather, you would probably rejoice at ridding yourself of me so easily."

Her words stung, and Graham stepped forward, brushing wet hair out of his face. "Are you mad, woman?" he snapped. "Have you lost your mind?" He glanced at the small trickle of blood running down the side of her face. "I should take you home." He reached out his hand for her, but she slapped it away, stepping back, pressing herself to the trunk of the huge tree as though seeking protection. The way she looked at him as though he was the enemy drove him mad.

Planting himself before her, his eyes narrowed. "Whether you like it or not, I am your husband, and you will do as I say, understood?" Again, he held out his hand to her, and again she refused to take it.

Shaking her head, she drew even closer to the tree, her eyes fixing him, their icy stare piercing his heart. "What kind of a man are you? How dare you treat others like this? I am your wife, but that does not matter to you, does it? Did you treat Leonora the same way? Did you try to get rid of her too?"

At her words, a chill crept up his spine. Hearing his first wife's name spoken aloud felt like a punch in the gut, and he nearly toppled over. Leaning forward, he steadied himself, resting his hands on the tree's trunk. He lowered his head and glared into his wife's eyes, now fluttering at finding herself trapped between the tree and her husband. "You will not say her name," he snarled, their noses almost touching. "Do you understand? Never!"

The tone in his voice made her flinch, but she didn't try to extract herself from her current position. Instead, she raised her chin a hint and met his eyes head-on. "Did she ever want to leave? Because I do. The only thing keeping me here is Georgiana." She spoke with an even and quiet voice, barely audible over the drumming of the rain.

Gritting his teeth, Graham tried to hold back the anger that slowly built within him. Afraid of what he might do, he focused all his attention on her eyes, staring into them as though they were a lifeline out of the dark. As black as they looked with heavy clouds blocking the sun, he could still see the small sparks of hazel that danced like stars in the night.

Lost in her eyes, he barely noticed as they changed. The stars vanished, and the night turned into an ocean of the purest blue he had ever seen.

He looked into her face then, at the golden curls framing her rosy cheeks, at her full lips that always carried a smile but were now drawn into a tight line. Her eyes narrowed, and she glared at him. "I know you mean well," she said, and he could hear the effort in her voice at keeping her anger in check. "But you are smothering me. I will be eternally grateful for what you have done for me, but I cannot forget what was. My heart does not forget simply because I spoke vows. And I thought you knew that. I thought you understood. I thought you were all right with this."

He swallowed. "So did I."

"I have always been honest with you," she continued, a clear reproach in her voice. "I told you from the beginning what kind of marriage this would be."

"You gave me your word," he interjected.

Again, the scowl returned to her beautiful features. "I gave you my word that I would try. I could not promise you more. I have no control over my heart. As much as I wish it were so, there is nothing I can do that would change how I feel." She gave him a quick shove, and he stepped back. "You cannot change how you feel either. Do not expect more of me."

Frustrated, he balled his hand into a fist, slamming it into his palm. He clenched his jaw, trying to fight off the desperate need to hit something, anything. "I'm not sure what to do." He shook his head as though mad. "I cannot go on like this. It is killing me."

She nodded her head, understanding, and yet, he could still see her own anger at the situation they found themselves in etched into her eyes. "Distance," she said. "We need distance. There is no other way. To me, you're a friend, a very good friend, but I cannot give you more. Believe me, I have tried. I just can't." She shook her head to enforce her words.

He stared at her, knowing what she said was true, and yet, he hoped he had misunderstood her. Knowing the pain it would cause him, he still could not refrain from asking, "Do you still love him?"

Her eyes opened wide, taken aback, before her eyebrows drew down. "Do not ask me this!" she hissed, suppressed pain lacing her own voice. "I told you not to speak of him!"

Running his hands through his hair, almost pulling them out with the roots, he paced up and down before her. "I take that as a confirmation then."

Her usually gentle eyes turned ablaze with anger as she came toward him. "How dare you?" she hissed, drawing back her arm and slapping him hard across the face.

Losing all self-control, he reached for her, but she evaded him. Her hands balled into fists, she attacked him, pummelling his chest, trying to rid herself of her own anger boiling just underneath the surface.

A distant part of Graham's mind told him to walk away, told him that he had walked away. But not this time. He had never fought, not for himself, for his own happiness. In the line of duty, yes, but not where his own heart was concerned.

Catching her wrists, he pushed her back against the tree, pressing into her. Her head snapped up, and her eyes widened as he bent his head down to her.

"Stop! You—" But her words were cut off as his mouth closed over hers. Kissing her like he had wanted, dreamed of for years, Graham lost all sense of his surroundings. He did not feel the hands that tried to push him away. He did not taste the blood as she bit his lip. He did not notice the deep blue eyes changing back to a midnight black, stars extinguished by the force that had her pinned to the tree.

32

AMENDS

hannelling all her strength, Rosabel shoved against him, but his hold on her was too strong. The anger she had seen in his eyes before had changed with each word they had exchanged. The moment before he had started toward her, there had been madness shining in them, and it had scared her more than anything she had ever experienced.

From what he said, she knew that he was not responding to her. His eyes rested on her, and yet, she could tell that he did not see her. Something she had said or done had carried him away to a place and time of his past. The words he said, he spoke to Leonora, and although she found herself at the receiving end of his anger, Rosabel was not immune to the pain that fuelled him.

As he kissed her with an urgency born out of years of desire held in check, Rosabel felt herself respond, welcoming his advances with every fibre of her body. But her heart screamed for her to stop him. As much as she wanted him, she also wanted him to want her back. Right then and there, all he wanted was Leonora.

Once again placing her hands on his shoulders, she strained to push him away, and for a second, his own grip slipped, and he freed her mouth. "Stop! I am not Leonora!" she said, turning her head away, trying to shake him out of his trance.

He did not hear her though. Pinning her with his body to the tree, his hands roamed her body freely, and she drew in a sharp breath as he began to lift up her skirts. "Please! You cannot really mean to force yourself on me!"

Instantly, his hand stopped, and the hem of her dress fell back to the ground.

Rosabel drew in a deep breath, her hands shaking as she pushed him away.

This time he moved. Taking a few steps back, his eyes shifted to her face, staring at her swollen lips and dishevelled dress. He blinked and rubbed his hands over his face. Again, his eyes sought hers, and he shook his head as though trying to rid himself of the vision that had taken him over. "I'm sorry," he mumbled. Unable to look at her any longer, he turned around and walked away a few steps. His shoulders slumped as he looked out into the rain.

Wrapping her arms around herself, Rosabel shivered; if from the cold or his attack she did not know. Her knees wobbled, and she sank down into the grass, resting her head against the tree. Her gaze fixed on his back, Rosabel felt a lump in her throat. She swallowed to dislodge the feeling, but the dread only slid down into her stomach, settling there like a block of ice.

As much as she tried, she could not hate him. He had crossed a line, yes, but he hadn't meant to. In a strange way, he was broken. He only knew how to suppress his feelings, had done so for many years. But once they broke free, he had no control over them. They took over his body and mind, leaving him defenceless.

Eyes shifting over his hunched figure, Rosabel wondered if he knew. Maybe he knew that if he let go, even just a little, he would lose control. Maybe that was why he pushed everyone away, because he was afraid of what he might do.

As strong as he had always seemed, Rosabel knew that he could not approach her now. She knew it would have to be her to take a step toward him. Drawing in another deep breath, Rosabel wondered if she could. If not, the only alternative would be to leave.

Could she forgive him and try to mend their relationship? Would he even be willing to do so?

Still unsure of what she would do, Rosabel pushed herself up, finding herself standing on shaky feet. Her wet clothes still held her in a grip of cold, intensified with each blow of wind that hit her. Overwhelmed, she turned her face away, resting her forehead against the rough bark of the tree. Could she leave him behind? From the corner of her eye, she saw Winter's reins tied to a branch a few steps from her. She could just take the horse and leave. But could she?

Glancing over her shoulder, her muscles loosened at the sight of his broken self, standing in a puddle as water dripped off the branches above him, running down the side of his face, like the tears he couldn't shed. He didn't move, rigid like a stone column, trapped by demons of his past.

Not sure where she drew the courage from, Rosabel felt herself place one foot before the other, slowly making her way through the slippery grass to her husband's side.

When the sun climbed the horizon the next morning, Rosabel turned her back, pulling the blanket over her head. She was not ready to face the world, much less her husband.

Without a word, they had ridden home once the rain had levelled off. Seated in front of him, his arms keeping her from sliding off the horse, she had shivered, her dress doing nothing to keep her warm. And while he had made sure she wouldn't fall, he had kept his distance, not wrapping her in his arms like he could have. She knew that he was miserable, and yet, she did not know what to do about it. How could she help him if she still did not understand what demons were lurking in his past?

After sending grooms after Storm, that still had not returned, he had escorted her up the stairs to her room. Promising to send for Bridget and have a bath readied, he had walked away without another look.

The distance between them had never been so insurmountable.

Still unsure what to do, Rosabel jumped up as the door to her room suddenly flew open. In marched Georgiana, small forehead in a frown. "Good morning," she said, climbing up on the bed. "Are you ill?"

Clearing her throat, Rosabel shook her head. "I'm fine," she assured the girl as much as herself. "I just didn't sleep well."

"Father left again," Georgiana said without preamble. Neither her face nor her voice could hide the disappointment aching in her heart. "Are we still to return home?" she asked. "To Westmore?"

Realizing that she had all but forgotten about that, Rosabel shrugged. "I don't know." Pulling the girl into her arms, she tried to comfort her but doubted that anything but her father's return could put a smile back on the girl's face. How long before the little girl would close her heart to him? Rosabel wondered. How many more times could he leave before she stopped waiting for his return?

As the carriage sloshed along the muddy road, Graham sat with his head resting against the back wall. Eyes closed, he berated himself, had been ever since her words had pulled him out of his trance.

"Please! You cannot really mean to force yourself on me!"

Burying his face in his hands, he shook his head. What had he done? No wonder she had run from him. Had she seen it coming?

He had drifted away into a memory, and he hadn't even noticed. Only the memory had ended differently. Back then, he had walked away. He had not only left Leonora, but Westmore too, giving her the distance they both needed. Months had passed, in which he had rarely returned home. Whenever he had, her eyes had followed him, reminding him of what would never be. He had never stayed long. Never uttered more than a syllable in her presence. Before he could summon the courage to face her again, she had died, and he had lost his chance. Every chance of ever winning her heart.

Still, to this day, the memory of her angry eyes and pressed lips were edged into his soul. The last words he had spoken to her had been in anger and had caused her pain. And now it was too late to even make amends. Had she ever forgiven him? If he could only have spoken to her one more time.

Taking a deep breath, Graham once more closed his eyes. Instantly, he saw Rosabel's face, eyes open in fear. He felt her hands on his shoulders, desperately trying to push him away.

At the same time, he smelled the fresh scent of her hair and tasted the sweet flavour of blueberries still clinging to her tongue. Her soft skin trembled under his hands, and he felt the beating of her heart against his chest. How he had wanted her!

Realizing what he had done, he had put a safe distance between them, trying to come to terms with his actions. Convinced she would run from him, he had jumped as her light hand had settled on his arm. Staring at her, he had heard her words of forgiveness but could not believe his ears. Seeing her shiver, he had wanted to draw her into his arms and warm her but had checked himself at the last moment. He did not want to repulse her, not again.

Instead, he had retrieved Winter, and with Storm nowhere around, they had both mounted the mare and headed back. Keeping her atop the horse while at the same time maintaining a safe distance had taken its toll. By the time they had reached the estate, his muscles had ached from the sheer effort of control. Leading her to her room, he had taken his leave and not looked back.

How he had wished he could climb into the warm bath with her! Hold her in his arms. Make love to her. But it had only been Leonora's memory that had stirred up all these feelings. He knew that now. Rosabel deserved more than a shell of a man. A man who could not control his urges. He needed to make sure she would be safe. Even safe from him. After all, he was her husband. Keeping her safe was the least he could do for her.

Realizing that the family he had once hoped would be his was now completely out of his reach, Graham came to a decision that he knew was long overdue.

33

WE ARE THE SAME

wo weeks passed without a word from him. Rosabel did her best to keep Georgiana busy, but her own thoughts wouldn't let her rest. Again, she spent nights tossing and turning, awake to the point of exhaustion. When she did fall asleep, her dreams teetered between pleasant and terrifying. In one moment, her husband would cradle her in his arms, smiling at her with love shining in his eyes, when in the next he would lunge at her, violently grabbing at her dress and pushing her down. Rosabel woke from these dreams bathed in sweat, frantically glancing about the room, assuring herself that she was alone.

Until the day that he did return.

Once again, he sneaked past them into his study, and only hours later did they learn of his arrival from Hanson. While Georgiana was happy to hear her father had returned, Rosabel could see the restraint she had put on her heart. The little girl was becoming guarded in matters of the heart, trying to protect herself from further pain. Unlike before, Georgiana did not insist on seeking him out, and so they remained in their rooms while he did not venture from his study.

Finally, they were under the same roof again, and yet, it did not matter. The distance had grown to insurmountable proportions.

After taking their breakfast alone the next morning, Rosabel and Georgiana walked out into the hall only to stop in their tracks. Right there by the front doors stood trunks and bags filled with their possessions.

"He is sending us back," Georgiana whispered, her little hand wrapping itself more tightly around Rosabel's. "I had hoped he wouldn't."

Rosabel nodded. "Me too."

For a long moment, they stood and watched as footmen brought more bags, setting up two piles. Frowning, Rosabel glanced outside. Two carriages stood by the front stoop. When all their belongings had been brought to the front hall, the footmen began piling them onto the carriages, careful to store Georgiana's items on the roof of the first carriage while Rosabel's found their way onto the second.

Fear gripped Rosabel's heart.

When Bridget approached, wearing a dress for travel, Rosabel left Georgiana with her and headed to her husband's study.

As she approached the door, her unease grew. What would it be like to see him again after what had happened? Stopping in front of the door, she took a deep breath and knocked before her resolve could falter. From inside, his voice called to enter.

Rosabel swallowed hard, trying desperately to keep her hands from shaking, and crossed the threshold.

Nothing had changed in this room. It looked as it always had. Even her husband bore no mark that would speak of their unfortunate encounter. Although she knew that her line of thinking was bar any reason, her heart had expected an outward sign for what had changed on the inside. Had it not affected him? Was she the only one to suffer nightmares? Uncontrollable trembling?

Clearly not expecting her, his features froze when he looked up and found her standing behind the chair on the other side of his desk. He swallowed before rising from his chair. "My lady," he spoke, but his voice held no kindness or even civility. Even a stranger he would have addressed in a more civilized manner.

Forcing her voice out in an even, unaffected tone, Rosabel faced him. "My lord, may I inquire as to the situation presented in the front hall? Why are there two carriages? Your daughter and I assumed you'd be sending us back to Westmore. We do not have that much luggage

230

that would have us require two carriages." Unable to stop speaking, Rosabel prattled on. If she didn't stop, he couldn't answer, and if he couldn't answer, he couldn't confirm the fear that had begun to grow in her heart the moment her eyes had fallen on the two carriages outside the door.

With an expression devoid of any emotion, he looked at her. Clearing his throat, he said, "You observed correctly, my lady. It is not because of the luggage that I ordered two carriages." He paused, and Rosabel could have slapped him for drawing this out. Was he doing it on purpose to torture her? "One carriage is to take you back to Westmore, where you will remain from here on out. Do not fear. You will be amply provided for."

Rosabel swallowed. "And the other carriage? What about Georgiana?"

For a moment, his eyes dropped to a sheet of paper in front of him, and Rosabel thought that he was ashamed of what he was about to say. "I myself will escort Georgiana to another place of residence. From today on out, you will not have to worry about her anymore."

Rosabel's knees buckled, and she gripped the backrest of the chair in front of her. All blood drained from her face as bright spots started to dance in her vision.

Closing her eyes, she took a deep breath to steady her nerves. "My lord, what are you saying? Georgiana is my daughter. You cannot take her away from me."

Not meeting her pleading gaze, he shook his head. "She is not, and the sooner you accept that the sooner you will be able to move on." He lifted his head and looked at her. "I have said all that I wished. If you please now get ready to depart. We'll leave as soon as everything is packed."

Leaving shock behind, Rosabel ignited the flame of anger that had so often burned in the months since her wedding. It had served her well, helped her keep her wits about her and not break down in the face of looming danger. "How can you say that? Never will I accept this." Stepping around the chair, she closed the distance between them and stepped up to the desk until only an arm's length separated them. "She is my daughter. You made me her mother when you married me. Those were your words. You married me for the sole reason of giving Georgiana a new mother. Did you forget that?"

Her words caused his muscles to tense as his jaw clenched. His eyes narrowed, and she could see that he had found his own source of anger. "I assure you, my lady, I do remember. And I hate to admit it, but I was greatly mistaken in attempting this. I was wrong to do so." He swallowed hard. "However, now my only choice is to make the best of a terrible situation."

Rosabel shook her head, unable to comprehend his words. How could he be so cold? Tears began to well in her eyes, and her voice caught in her throat. "First, you make me love her, and then you take her away? What have I done to deserve such a punishment?"

At her distress, Rosabel thought to see a hint of his resolve crumble. He caught himself quickly though, the coldness returning to his eyes. "I assure you, this is not meant as a punishment."

When he remained silent, Rosabel stepped forward. "Is this all you have to say? Do I not deserve more of an explanation? Would you have ever separated Leonora from her daughter?"

Instantly, he froze. His features hardened even more, and an angry glare came to his eyes as he regarded her with ill-concealed hatred. "I told you never to speak of her again!" he boomed. Slamming a fist on the top of his desk, he stepped toward her with burning eyes.

Startled at his sudden proximity, Rosabel flinched.

Seeing her reaction, he stopped, eyes dropping to the floor before returning to look at her. The seething anger had left his features as he said, "Do not worry yourself, my lady. You have nothing to fear from me. I assure you I am in control of my actions."

Swallowing hard, Rosabel nodded as images from that fateful day two weeks ago flashed before her eyes. He had towered over her then too, her strength no match for his. But none of that mattered. She knew she could not allow him to scare her into submission. She would spend the rest of her life hating herself if she let him separate her from Georgiana.

"I assure you she is my daughter in every way, and taking her away serves no purpose but inflict the greatest of pain." Tears stood in her eyes, ready to spill forth at a moment's notice. Another word from him, and she would not be able to hold them back.

"You are mistaken," he all but whispered, turning back to the papers on his desk.

All of a sudden, a shiver went through Rosabel as though a draft in the air had touched her skin. Only there was no draft. Nothing cold. Instead, a warmth spread through her, and for a moment, Rosabel saw the image of Leonora before her eyes; Leonora standing tall and proud, her eyes unyielding, her hand resting on Rosabel's shoulder, giving her the strength to fight, and even more importantly, to say what needed to be said.

Taking another deep breath, Rosabel revealed a secret she had sworn to herself she would take to her grave. "I love her as much as you do, and being away from her breaks my heart as much as it breaks yours. Do you not see? We are the same. Both of us love a child that is not our own flesh and blood."

His hand stopped sorting the letters strewn about his desk. Ever so slowly, his head rose, and he turned around. With eyes round as plates, mouth open in shock, he stared at her. "What did you say?"

34

BEYOND HOPE

Graham stood, staring at his wife, as the world came crashing down around him. He had heard the words she had spoken, and yet, he knew she couldn't possibly have said what his ears had perceived. How could she know? No one knew. No one except for Leonora, himself, and of course Georgiana's father. Not even Edmond knew the whole truth.

Examining her features, Graham frowned. There was no judgment in her eyes, only understanding and a hint of exhaustion. Yes, he had put a lot on her shoulders. She was right to be angry with him. But he was trying to make amends by freeing her of her responsibilities as his wife as much as he could. He would divorce her if he could be sure it would ensure a better life for her, but he knew it wouldn't.

As he remembered her words, Graham realized that she had not spoken them in anger. She had not thrown the truth at his feet in order to humiliate and shame him. She had only revealed her knowledge of Georgiana's fatherhood to make him understand her situation. And she was right. Sending Georgiana away would hurt him as much as she said it would hurt her, but for once, he could not be selfish. He had made this decision because he believed it would be the best course of action for Georgiana, and in the long run maybe even for all of them.

However, from the desperate hope in her eyes, Graham could tell that she did not see it that way. She was exhausted, yes, but determination held her upright, and he knew that she would fight him every step of the way.

Feeling his own energy resources depleted, Graham sank into his chair. Resting his elbows on the desk, he laced his fingers and bent his head. Just for a moment, he wanted to pretend that none of this had happened.

Silence settled over the room, and he almost believed that she had left if it were not for the warmth that radiated from her body. It flowed to him in waves, washing over him, comforting, soothing. He closed his eyes and held on to the feeling of peace that invaded his soul. It had been a long time since he had felt at peace.

She knew the truth, and she didn't judge him. Never had he spoken about this situation with anyone. More than once, he had been tempted, feeling the desperate need to voice his struggles and find comfort in another's understanding. And yet, he hadn't.

However, he knew he couldn't let that change anything. He had to put his emotions aside one last time and do what was best, what was right. He never should have agreed to marry Leonora in the first place. He knew that now. As much as he had loved her, she had only ever seen him as a friend. By pretending he would eventually win her heart, he had made them both unhappy.

Out of nowhere, a small weight descended on his head. A delicate hand brushed back his hair, again and again stroking his head, as the other settled on his shoulder. He held his breath as her fingertips touched his neck.

Instantly, goose bumps rose on his arms, and he had to suppress a moan that rose from his throat.

Graham knew he needed to stop her before he revealed feelings he hadn't even acknowledged to himself. He needed to get up and put some distance between them, and yet, he couldn't bring himself to look at her, afraid to find understanding replaced by pity.

"You must have loved her beyond hope," she whispered, her voice breaking the silence. "She needed you, and you didn't hesitate. You married her even though she carried the child of another man." Head still hiding in his hands, Graham wondered how she knew all this.

"You wanted to protect her, but you forgot what this would do to your own heart. And now you're a father, and your child's heart is the one to consider. I know you would never hurt her, not intentionally. You believe what you're doing is the right thing, but…"

He drew in a sharp breath. Could she really understand his motives? Did it matter? She still wanted nothing more than for him to change his mind, didn't she?

"But you're wrong," she said, confirming his suspicions. "What she needs are parents who love her, and I know that you do. Just like I am her mother, you are her father. If you could only see that. Do you really want her to live without family? All by herself? With no one to take care of her but servants?"

"I do not," he whispered and took a deep breath. Then he raised his head and looked up at her. As she withdrew her hands, he spoke, "That is not what I have in mind." He rose to his feet, and she took a step back. Again, shame flooded his heart, but he pushed on before he could lose his nerve. "You are right. Georgiana deserves to be with her family."

At his words, relief washed over her, and her features began to relax. Cringing, Graham berated himself for phrasing it the way he had and giving her false hope. "But we are not her family. I am not her father, and you are not her mother." Her face went white as his words pierced her heart. "She does not have a mother anymore. I cannot change that." Again, he took a deep breath, bracing himself for what was to come, knowing it was inevitable. "But she has a father."

For a while, she just stared at him, her mind working to make sense of his words and grasp the meaning they implied. Watching her closely, Graham saw the very moment as understanding filled her. Her eyes grew big, and all blood drained from her face. She swayed on her feet, and he wanted to reach out and steady her. Instead, he remained where he was.

"You…" Her voice rang too weak to form a complete sentence. Extending a hand, she held on to the bookshelf beside her. Closing her eyes, she took a deep breath and tried anew. "You want to return her?" she breathed, shock all but audible in her voice. "You want to take her back? To her father?"

Not saying a word, Graham just nodded.

35

A CRIPPLING FATE

*S*eeing his head bob up and down, Rosabel still couldn't believe what he was saying. She had known that Georgiana was not his child for a while now, and yet, it had been far from her mind, everyday life keeping her too busy.

Trying to understand what this strangely complicated situation felt like for him, Rosabel walked back around the desk and feeling her knees about to buckle sank into the cushioned armchair.

Watching him closely, she found him standing with his shoulders squared, chin raised as he looked down at her. His eyes remained calm, and not a muscle twitched out of place. Nothing betrayed that he was emotionally involved in this matter. In that very moment, his mask was perfect, and Rosabel feared that he, now more than ever, had made up his mind. This was his final decision.

"Why?" was all Rosabel's aching heart wanted to know.

Pressing his lips together for a second, he placed his hands on the desk, leaning forward. Then, as though changing his mind, he sat down, elbows resting on the table top. "As I said before, this is the best course of action for all of us." He sat back, regarding her with a levelled gaze. "You will come to see it in time." He nodded to the door. "I suggest you say your goodbyes."

Rosabel drew in a deep breath. Unable to fight, for her knees were still as soft as pudding, and yet, unable to give up, Rosabel shifted in her chair to get more comfortable, eyes gazing out the window as memories flooded her mind.

"I know what it is like to lose someone you love." Eyes distant, she spoke as though recounting the memory of another, not her own. At least for now, her voice held no sadness, no pain. Only the distance that time offered and for it rang all the more true. "My mother died when I was barely six years old. I had hoped for a brother or sister. Instead, I lost my mother; and all of a sudden, life changed."

As she stopped and her eyes closed for a moment, Graham knew he should interrupt her. He knew if he didn't, her words would affect him. And yet, he did not move. Did not speak up. He just sat there watching her and realized he knew nothing about the woman he had chosen for his wife.

Her eyes opened again, and she brushed a strand of hair behind her ear. Then her gaze turned to him. "All that was left to me was my father." He swallowed as her gaze seemed to drill a hole into his soul. "I know that he tried his best. He tried to smile and laugh. And he tried to make me smile and laugh, but in the end, it wasn't enough." A slight tremble shook her small frame. "He died not two years later. The doctor said he'd caught pneumonia." She shook her head. "But I knew that it had been his heart. His heart had stopped beating the day my mother died, and without it, he could not go on. Not even for me." Her eyes focused on him, and he fought the urge to look down. "I wasn't enough to keep him in this world. And like my mother's death, it changed everything." Her hands entwined, she held on to something, anything that would give her the strength to go on. "I was alone." Her gaze moved over his face then, and he felt himself wanting to squirm. "Maybe you know what it is like? To know that, all of a sudden, you don't matter anymore, that no one in this world would be willing to walk through hell and back for you, that no one loved you without condition, without restraint. It is a terrible fate. Crippling, and not easy to recover from." Abandoning their scrutiny of his face, her eyes looked into his as she leaned forward, emphasizing the words she was about to say. "Do you want that for Georgiana?"

Feeling the stare of her eyes like little needles piercing his heart, Graham swallowed.

Then he rose from his chair and without saying a word or even looking at her fled the room.

Dumbfounded, Rosabel stared at the empty seat as silent tears ran down her cheeks. For a long time, she just sat there, unable to get up, unable to form a coherent thought. What now? What would she do? Would he really take Georgiana away? Would she lose yet another loved one? After her mother and father now her daughter?

As the sun shone in through the window, mocking the clouds settling over her heart, Rosabel wept, all fight leaving her body. She had tried. She had fought so bitterly, and yet, it had all been in vain. What was she to do now? Again and again, the question assaulted her mind, and again and again, she pushed it away, unable to face the future that lay ahead.

Until a horse's whinny reached her ear.

Instantly, her head jerked up, tears brimming in her eyes. *The carriage*, her mind screamed. *He is taking her away.*

Jumping off the chair, Rosabel flew out of the study and down the hall. Setting one foot in front of the other, she ran as her heart beat in her chest as though trying to outdistance her.

When she reached the entrance hall, panting for breath, the entire luggage was gone. And Georgiana was nowhere in sight.

Brushing by Hanson, Rosabel almost tripped as she hastened out the door and down the front steps.

While one carriage still stood by the windows of the front parlour, patiently waiting, the other was slowly making its way down the drive. Without hesitation, her mind urged her forward.

The gravel churned under her feet, hindering her progress, but determination gave her tired limbs the strength they needed. Each step carried her closer to the door. Soon, the handle was within reach.

Before the carriage could pick up speed and leave her behind,

Rosabel lunged forward, her hand closing around the handle and yanking open the door. Holding on as though for dear life, she pulled herself forward and set a foot into the carriage.

Instantly, a hand grabbed her, pulling her in. Falling forward, Rosabel almost landed on the carriage floor if it weren't for her husband's arm steadying her. "What the blazes are you doing?" he asked, his eyes open wide in shock, matching Georgiana's.

Rosabel took a deep breath. "I'm coming."

He stared at her for a long time but didn't say a word as the carriage rattled down the drive, soon leaving Camden Hall behind.

While Georgiana happily prattled on about the adventures that awaited them, her parents sat almost motionless, staring out their respective windows at the scenery before their eyes, not seeing anything though as their minds kept them occupied.

Occasionally, Rosabel glanced in her husband's direction, finding him equally lost in thought, wondering what his plans were. Whenever her eyes fell on Georgiana, a delighted smile on her lips as she read or played with her doll, Rosabel's heart cringed at the mere thought of losing her little girl. How long had it been since she'd first thought of her as her daughter? Rosabel didn't know. Didn't care. Because it didn't matter. She was Georgiana's mother, and she would fight for her.

Again glancing at her husband, Rosabel once more wondered what he planned to do. Surely he had to know that she would not relinquish her daughter willingly. Did he plan to leave her behind at some point on their journey? Did he mean to lock her up when−?

Suddenly, Rosabel's mind stopped, realizing that she had no clue where they were headed. While she felt relatively certain that Georgiana had been named for her father, which would mean he carried the name George, she did not know who he was. There had to be a thousand *Georges* in England.

Silently cursing herself for not inquiring after Georgiana's father when she had the chance, Rosabel leaned back in her seat and crossed her arms, disgusted with herself. Watching Georgiana's eyes light up as they passed a small clearing where in the distance a doe was tending to her fawn, Rosabel knew she could not ask with the girl present. She would have to wait.

Oh, how she hated waiting!

36

ANSWERS REVEALED

hortly after darkness fell, they reached an inn, its lit windows shining like beacons in the blackness of night. Muscles sore from the rattling of the carriage and her own pent-up tension, Rosabel sighed as she took her first steps outside, stretching her tired limbs.

Georgiana had fallen asleep with her head in her father's lap. At first, he had seemed highly uncomfortable, trying to extract himself without waking her. When that, however, had proved impossible, he had settled into his seat, a hand on her shoulder. Out of the corner of her eyes, Rosabel had watched his posture relax before long, his hand occasionally caressing her head, stroking her hair absentmindedly.

More than anything else, this sign of his affection for his daughter, blood-related or not, had lifted Rosabel's spirit. There had to be a way she could make him see the error of his ways.

Gently, her husband carried Georgiana into the inn, up the flight of stairs and carefully laid her down on her bed. While Rosabel quickly removed the most uncomfortable items of the girl's clothing, such as boots and coat, her husband stood beside the bed, eyes focused on his

241

daughter's sleeping face.

Sighing in her dreams, a smile lifted the corners of her mouth, and her father's eyes lit up, a smile of his own curling his lips.

In the end, Rosabel had to take him by the arm and lead him out into the hall. Quietly closing the door, she turned to face him. A smile on her lips, she gazed into his eyes. "You love her. Do not deny it?"

Instantly, his face changed. The quiet, serene joy that had illuminated his eyes turned dark. His lips thinned, and he swallowed, brushing a hand through his hair. "Your room is next to Georgiana's." He quickly bowed to her. "I bid you good night."

Before he could take two steps, Rosabel brushed past him, stepping in his way. Holding out a hand, she stopped him in his tracks, his chest slamming into her outstretched arm. "If you insist on pretending that this," she pointed to the door Georgiana lay behind sleeping, "is not breaking your heart, I have to tell you that I do feel sorry for you, my lord." His eyes narrowed, but she hastened on before he could comment. "But I do insist you tell me where we are headed!"

A frown settled on his face. "I did tell you."

"You merely hinted at returning Georgiana to her real father," Rosabel corrected, squaring her shoulders. "But you failed to explain who he is and where he resides."

Crossing his arms, her husband eyed her carefully. "That does not concern you, my lady. You should not even be here."

"But I am."

"So?"

"So, tell me!"

Hesitating for only a second, he whispered a quick good night, brushed past her, opened the door to his room and vanished inside.

For a moment, Rosabel just stood in the hall, cursing herself for allowing him to run off yet again. However, as she turned to enter her own room, she realized that he had indeed not escaped yet. He had merely retired to his room, and Rosabel did not remember hearing a key turning in the lock.

A triumphant smile on her face, she stepped forward and without knocking pushed open the door and stepped inside.

Hearing her steps, he spun around, surprise visible on his face. "What the blazes are you doing in here? This is hardly proper," he said, fingers working to re-button his shirt.

Rosabel snorted, closing the door behind her. "I doubt that. I am your wife after all."

"That may be true, but your room is still across the hall," he said, pointing past her shoulder. "Do you need further directions?"

Her back brushing the door when she shifted from one foot to the other, Rosabel crossed her arms, fixing him with her eyes. "Speak of what you like, but I assure you I will not leave this room until I have answers."

Jaw tightening, he once more raked his hands through his hair, eyes frantically searching for a way out. "Why do you insist on knowing?"

Rosabel could hear the desperation in his voice. "Because she is my daughter."

"She is not—"

Lifting a hand, she stepped toward him. "I know, but she is. We can argue about this all night if you prefer, or you could tell me now, and we can both get some sleep."

Exhaling slowly, he closed his eyes. When they opened again, Rosabel knew she had at least won this battle. "We are going to London."

Rosabel nodded. "I suspected as much. But where exactly? Who is he?"

"He is an old friend." Wringing his hands, he started pacing. When he remained silent, Rosabel asked, "Fine, but what makes you think he would even take her back? If he cared about her at all, would he not have married Leonora back then? I still don't understand why they could not get married. I mean, I know his father had objections, but what could they have been? She was the daughter of a family of the peerage, a family of means. How could that not have been enough?"

Staring at her, he shook his head, probably wondering how she knew all that. "It was not that simple. He had…a duty. He could not marry for love."

"Fine, even if it wasn't for love, she was still a good match. Why would his father have objected? Was there some kind of family feud?"

He shook his head. "No, their families had been close for generations. Allies even."

"Then I don't see the problem."

Sinking onto his bed, he hung his head as though unable to hold himself upright any longer. "It was complicated. Their families had been connected for generations. They did not need to marry their children to achieve this. Instead, they sought other connections."

Rosabel nodded, every fibre of her being trembling with disgust at the marriage politics that more often than not destroyed every hope for love and happiness. Only too well did she remember the trouble her own parents had to go through merely to be together and how hard life had been for them because they had defied the rules.

"I see," she mumbled. "But I don't understand why you cannot tell me his name. His full name. I mean, I suspect he is named George." Instantly, her husband's head snapped up. "Georgiana is named after him, is she not?"

Rising from the bed, he came toward her. As he stopped in front of her, his shoes almost touching hers, his eyes burned into hers. "How do you know all this?"

Rosabel raised her chin, meeting his gaze unflinching. "I will tell you, after you tell me."

"Blasted woman!" he cursed. "I do not remember you being so stubborn!"

Rosabel smiled. "I didn't used to be." Eyes searching her face, he shook his head. Without trouble Rosabel saw in his expression what he wanted to know. "But everything changed when I became a mother." Her eyes looked deeper into his. "When you made me a mother."

He swallowed but didn't argue.

"Then tell me," Rosabel insisted. "Why can you not tell me who he is?"

"Because his life is not his own," he said, sadness ringing in his voice, and Rosabel could see that he was speaking from experience. "He has a duty to his country above all else."

"Don't we all serve our country?" Rosabel asked, wondering what he was trying to say. "In whichever way we can."

He nodded. "But not like he does. Not like he was born to do."

"Why?" she asked, a frown settling on her face.

"Because..." he took a deep breath, "he is the future king of England!"

37

A BLIND MAN

As they reached Carlton House, the residence of Georgiana's father, Rosabel moved as though through a thick fog. Ever since the previous night when her husband had finally shared the truth about his daughter's parentage and the complications surrounding her existence, Rosabel's mind had finally decided that this was all too much to handle. A small part of her wondered that it had not happened earlier.

As they walked the halls and corridors, spent almost an hour waiting in a front parlour and then proceeded to the study, Rosabel's feet moved as though with a mind of their own while her eyes refused to pay attention to the intricate furnishings around her, which was inconsequential anyway because her mind was unable to convert any perceptions into long-term memories.

Instead, Rosabel's eyes only saw the little girl with the golden curls. She remembered how her little arms wrapped around her neck in a heartfelt hug, how she used to skip the halls after finishing her lessons with Mrs. Rigsby and how her eyes glowed whenever they fell on her mother's portrait. All those memories and more kept Rosabel from acknowledging the harsh reality before her eyes. She was about to lose her daughter, and there was not a bloody thing she could do about that!

After all, he was the future king of England. Could she argue with him? Could she deny him his daughter? His own flesh and blood? When her own claim was rooted in nothing else but a mother's love. Nothing tangible. Nothing beyond reproach. Nothing recognized by law.

Silent tears ran down her cheeks as she saw Georgiana's eager eyes absorbing the palace around her. While she knew nothing of her own connection to the man they were about to meet, her father had told her that he was the future king of England in order to elicit her best behaviour. To Georgiana, such a revelation had only lifted her into her most beloved fairy tales of dashing princes and beautiful princesses, unaware that she was a princess herself.

Approaching double-hung mahogany doors, the footman guiding their way stopped and knocked. The sound echoed in Rosabel's mind, and she blinked.

As her memories wafted away, and reality reclaimed her attention, a cold shiver ran down her arms, and she shook herself involuntarily. Keeping step with her husband, Rosabel took a deep breath to calm her nerves as the doors were opened and they proceeded inside, Georgiana trailing after them.

Brilliant sunlight filtered in through the massive windows lining the west wall, bathing the study's interior in a warm glow of afternoon delight. A no less massive mahogany desk captured the centre of the room, framed by book cases touching the arched, two-story ceiling. Ornamental rugs softened the clear-cut marble floors, absorbing the slight echo of their footfalls as they approached the man sitting in the leather armchair, scribbling on a sheet of paper.

As they drew near, he lifted his head for a moment, recognition flashing in his dark eyes.

For a reason Rosabel could not grasp, she heaved a sigh of relief when she saw that Georgiana had inherited her brilliantly blue eyes from her mother.

For a moment, they stood before the desk, waiting to be acknowledged, and Rosabel tried to breathe as quietly as she could so as not to disturbed the silence that hung over the room, the only sound the slight scratching of quill on parchment.

Then the scratching stopped, and the future king of England nimble-footed jumped out of his chair and strode toward them, eyes brilliant and a welcoming smile decorating his features. "Kensington," he boomed as though trying to be heard in a crowded opera house. "How wonderful to see you! How long has it been? Ten years? Almost, I dare say!"

"Your royal highness," her husband greeted his old friend, and although his manners were beyond reproach, Rosabel observed the casual air that spoke of secrets told and memories shared. A part of her wished she were not in the room so that they could speak more openly.

Turning to her, the king's son winked at her husband. "And this must be your wife. I heard you remarried." There was a hitch in his voice as he said the word *wife*, making it clear that the feelings he'd once had for Leonora had not been lessened by her death. "Congratulations!"

"Thank you, Sir."

The king's heir bowed to her, mumbling "your grace", and Rosabel curtsied, hoping she would not fall flat on her face. "Your royal highness."

He smiled at her but instantly turned back to her husband. "Well then, what brings you here? I admit I was quite surprised to hear from you after all these years. Your letter left me wondering quite a bit."

As Rosabel watched her husband open his mouth to reply, her insides twisted into knots and she started to feel ill. However, before he could speak, a soft giggle echoed through the spacious room, and peeking behind her, Rosabel found her curious daughter steal a glance past her father's back at the man who was a real prince.

His hearing clearly unimpaired, his royal highness shifted his gaze down to the hint of golden curls appearing behind his old friend. Frown lines sprang up on his forehead, and he moved around his friend just as her husband took a step sideways out of the way. The second his eyes fell on Georgiana, taking in her striking blue eyes and angel-like hair, his mouth fell open, and his hand went to his chest.

For a moment, he just stared at her.

And everyone else stared at him.

Glancing at her husband, Rosabel saw his shoulders tense as he gritted his teeth, forcing himself to draw another breath. Judging from the pained look on his face, Rosabel thought he would gladly abandon his quest and return home.

But it was too late for that.

While Georgiana, overwhelmed by shyness, slid her hand into

Rosabel's, her biological father was still thunderstruck, unable to tear his eyes away from her. Rosabel's heart softened a little toward him as she saw the longing clearly visible in the way his eyes caressed his daughter's face. Had he ever even seen her? Rosabel wondered.

Clearing his throat, her husband's voice broke the magic of the moment. "I have come to return what is yours, sir."

Rosabel drew in a sharp breath at his words, and while Georgiana did not understand that her father was referring to her, the king's son jerked his eyes upward, eyebrows drawn down in a shocked expression. "Excuse me?"

Having trouble stilling the trembling in her arms, Rosabel squeezed Georgiana's hand, and the little girl smiled up at her. It almost broke her heart.

The future king glanced back and forth between his old friend and his daughter as realization began to dawn on him. He opened his mouth but shut it again as his eyes once more settled on Georgiana. He swallowed hard and then approached her. Leaning forward, a smile on his face, he said, "Seeing as you are your mother's daughter, I am sure you have a great fondness for horses. Is that so?"

Instantly, Georgiana's face lit up, and her head started bobbing up and down.

Seeing her answer, his smile broadened. "As I thought. You know, the horses here at Carlton House are among the finest in the country. Would you like to see them?"

Again, Georgiana had trouble containing her enthusiasm, her little legs fidgeting as though ready to run off.

"Marvellous," he beamed, glancing at Rosabel. "Then why don't you and your...mother go for a little stroll? Henry will show you the way. And later you can tell me which one you liked best. Deal?"

Georgiana nodded, eyes sparkling, ready to be off. "Deal!"

Curtseying, Rosabel and Georgiana followed the footman out the door and down the hall, leaving Georgiana's two fathers behind to sort out her future.

As Rosabel passed her husband, she tried to catch his eye, but he held his gaze firmly fixed on the floor. Placing her hand on his arm, she felt the tension in his muscles. Reluctantly, she turned to go, partly cursing under her breath that her earlier wish to afford them some privacy had been granted. She could only hope that her husband would change his mind. But did she dare dream of such an outcome?

As the door closed behind his wife and daughter, Graham turned to his old friend. Before he could say a word though, he found dark eyes searching his face.

"What is the meaning of this? You wish to return what is mine?" The Prince of Wales took two steps forward, peering into his face as though trying to decipher the answer to his questions. "You cannot be speaking about...?" His voice trailed off as his arm lifted, pointing at the door through which Georgiana had only just left.

Graham took a deep breath, recalling the duty he had to his family, and met his old friend's gaze without flinching. "Sir, I—"

"No!" The prince lifted a hand to stop him. Then he turned on his heel and started pacing the length of the room. "Why now? What has changed?" Again, he stopped right in front of Graham, eyes still searching. "Why?"

Graham swallowed. "Because it is the right thing to do, sir."

"Again, I ask you, why?"

Drawing in a deep breath, Graham steeled himself for what he had never said out loud. "Because she is...your daughter. Not mine."

The prince shook his head. "That little girl," he said, once more pointing at the door, "doesn't even know me. I am nothing to her." He placed a hand on Graham's shoulder, looking into his eyes, imploring him to understand. "You are her father. You have been since the day she was born."

Not knowing what to say, how to explain himself at a moment when he felt all answers slipping away, Graham remained silent.

"You love her," his friend said. "Like a father loves his daughter. Do not deny it." He took a deep breath. "And as much as it pains me to say this, she loves you, too. Like a daughter loves her father. Why do you want to take that from her?"

Remembering how his wife had asked him the same question, Graham shook his head. "Because I am not good for her. She deserves more. More than I can give her."

Again, the prince frowned. "But why now? Why did you not come to me two years ago? Right after Leonora's accident? Or three years? Or right after Georgiana was born? After the wedding? Why did you agree to marry her in the first place? Because I asked? Because you thought you couldn't deny me? I thought…," Graham could feel a slight tremble in the hand still resting on his shoulder, "I thought you loved her, too. Was I wrong?"

Not trusting his own voice, Graham shook his head.

"Then explain yourself," his friend urged, but hastened on himself. "I asked you because I knew you cared for her and that you would give your life before you'd let anything happen to her." Graham nodded, remembering Leonora's beautiful smile that had always made his heart beat faster in his chest. "You are an honourable man. A man who keeps his word. A man who protects those he loves." Again, he hesitated. "Although the thought nearly killed me, I hoped that she would find happiness with you. That over time she would give you her heart." His lips thinned into a tight line as his words ceased. And although he hadn't asked a question out loud, Graham could read it in his friend's eyes.

In answer, Graham shook his head. "She never could. Believe me, I'd hoped for the same, but you cannot give your heart away if it is no longer in your possession, can you? You should know." Just like Leonora, his friend had been forced to marry against the wishes of his heart, and it had never made him happy.

"I do, yes." His eyes softened. "I am sorry," his friend mumbled, resuming his pacing up and down the room. "I never meant for this to happen. I had hoped that somehow things would fall into place."

Graham nodded. "So did I. But at some point, we must face the truth. And that is why I am here."

Reminded of the purpose behind his friend's visit, the prince spun around, eyes narrowing. "And what is the truth?"

"The truth is that Georgiana is your daughter. Not mine. The truth is that you should have been Leonora's husband. Not me."

The prince nodded. "Yes, she is my daughter, and yes, I would have loved nothing more than to marry her mother. But I didn't. We all made our decisions. The reasons behind them do not matter now. The only thing that matters now is her happiness!"

"I agree."

"Then take her home and be the best father she could have."

For a moment, Graham closed his eyes, feeling his feet tremble with the need to move. More than anything, he wanted to open the door and leave. Return home. With his family.

But he couldn't.

He opened his eyes and faced reality. "Since Leonora's death, I've hardly ever been home. Something changed that day. I changed. I can't...I am not the man I used to be. I can't be a father to her. I've tried, but something..." He trailed off, not sure he himself knew what stood in the way.

"What about your wife? She loves her."

Graham could feel frown lines descend upon his face.

"Don't look surprised!" his friend chided. "A blind man could see the love between them. If she can be a mother to another woman's child, how come you can't be her father?"

Again, Graham frowned. "She asked me the same question."

"I assume she is furious with you," the prince said, a slight chuckle in his voice. "Are you not afraid she will never forgive you?"

Graham shrugged. "That is of no importance."

"It would make your life unbearable."

"That will not be the case. I've made arrangements for her to return to Westmore."

The prince frowned. "While you remain in London?"

"No, I've rented a place farther south."

"I see," his friend said, nodding his head. "I never knew you were such a coward."

Graham's head snapped up. "Sir?"

"I can see that your love for Leonora brought you nothing but pain," the prince said. "But she," again he pointed at the doors, "is not Leonora. As furious as she is with you for wanting to give away her child, she loves you."

Graham's eyes grew round as the words sank to his core.

"You did not know that?" his friend asked, again a chuckle rang in his voice as he once more placed a comforting hand on Graham's shoulder. "You truly are a blind man, my friend."

38

YOU WON, MY LADY

"Isn't he precious?" Georgiana asked, stroking the graceful neck of a white stallion. The second they had entered the stables, her heart had settled on the horse in the snow-like coat. Rubbing him behind the ears, she smiled as he gently took an apple from the palm of her hand.

As magnificent as the stallion was, Rosabel had only eyes for her daughter. Wringing her hands to keep from screaming in frustration, she stood a few feet away, watching as the late afternoon sun sparkled in Georgiana's golden hair. Her rosy cheeks off-set her deep blue eyes as a smile once more curled up her lips. How many more days would she be allowed to gaze at her daughter like this? Before she would be snatched away?

Tears threatened to spill, and Rosabel quickly brushed at her eyes, trying to fend them off.

What were they talking about? Rosabel couldn't help but wonder. Would the prince accept his daughter back? Or would he refuse her husband's proposal? Oh, how she wished she could eavesdrop on their conversation!

By the time the sun had dropped behind the horizon, painting the sky a deep shade of red and purple, Rosabel's head started to throb. A dull pain thumped behind her temples, and she desperately wished she could close her eyes to shut it out.

Footsteps echoed on the cobblestone path, and Rosabel spun around to see her husband enter the stables. His head hung low between his shoulders, and he all but dragged his feet as he made his way toward them. Eyes overshadowed, he gazed at her as though seeing something he had never noticed before. Returning his curious glance with a frown of her own, she watched a slight tinge of red spot his cheeks before he turned away.

Kissing her new friend goodbye, Georgiana flung herself into her father's arms, planting a kiss on his cheek as well. "Thank you for taking us here, Father. I've had the most wonderful time." As she turned her head and glanced back at the white stallion, Rosabel saw her husband's eyes close as he embraced his child once more.

Instantly, hope grew in Rosabel's heart. Had he changed his mind? Had the prince refused him? Entering the stables, his whole demeanour had been that of a defeated man while the way he had embraced his daughter had spoken of painful longing. Could it be?

"Can we come back here tomorrow?" Georgiana asked, introducing her father to the young stallion, whose nose once again inspected her hands for savoury treats. "We have become good friends."

To Rosabel's surprise, her husband nodded. "Of course, we can. I have agreed to stay a few days."

Overjoyed, Georgiana clapped her hands. "How wonderful!"

Keeping pace with her husband, Rosabel followed him as he led her through the intricate system of hallways to their guest rooms. After bidding Georgiana good night, they walked a few steps farther down the corridor before he stopped and opened the door to the adjoining room. Rosabel stepped inside and was surprised when he followed her, closing the door behind them.

Did he wish to tell her what had happened? Rosabel wondered, frowning. He had never volunteered information, and she had expected it to be incredibly difficult to obtain any tangible details with regard to his conversation with the prince.

Turning to face her husband, Rosabel folded her hands over her waist, forcing her muscles to appear calm and relaxed. Inside, she heard herself scream at him, but only a mildly interested smile appeared on her face. Proud of herself for having mastered her facial expression to such a degree, Rosabel watched him.

No air of calm hung about him. His eyes flitted from the door to her and then glanced over her shoulder.

Not turning around, Rosabel maintained her steady expression.

"His royal majesty asked for us to stay a few days," he said without preamble, lifting his eyes to meet hers. "He desires a little time with his daughter."

Rosabel exhaled slowly, feeling her heart leap into her throat. "Then he did not agree to your proposal?"

A smile flitted across his face as he stepped toward her. "You won, my lady." His eyes remained focused on hers, waiting for her reaction.

"We both did," she whispered as all the tension of the last few days dropped to the floor. All of a sudden, she felt as light as a feather, and yet, so tired that she could barely keep her eyelids open.

As exhaustion washed over her, her legs started to tremble. Unable to maintain her own balance any longer, Rosabel began to sway as the world became unhinged before her eyes.

Grasping for anything to keep from falling, her hand landed on something solid; something that moved higher up her arm and kept her steady. As her gaze focused, she found her husband's eyes staring into hers, worry creasing his forehead. "You need rest," he whispered, wrapping his other arm around her middle, escorting her to the massive four-poster bed in the centre of the room.

Day had long since given way to night, and a starless black wrapped the house in darkness. As flames danced in the stone fireplace, sending their comforting warmth into the room, Rosabel sank into the soft mattress, barely aware that her husband removed her boots. A warm cloak descended upon her, and her hands reached out to draw the blanket closer, draping it around her shoulders.

As sleep entered her mind, removing all worry and care from her soul, Rosabel felt the mattress shift as another weight settled into it.

The next few days, Rosabel spent in a constant state of wonder. With the threat of losing her daughter not hanging over her head any longer, she enjoyed the time they had together. Georgiana was delighted to have both her parents with her as well as a true prince, who doted on her like the dashing doubles she had met in her fairy tales.

Always observant, Rosabel saw the longing in the prince's eyes whenever he spoke to Georgiana or took her to the stables to see the white stallion. She also saw her husband's thoughtful eyes as he observed them as much as she did. Occasionally, he seemed to envy his friend's ease with which he delighted Georgiana while at other times Rosabel thought to detect a hint of guilt. Over what, she wasn't sure.

When they bid Georgiana good night on their second day and returned to the adjoining room, Rosabel was astounded when her husband once again entered, closing the door behind them.

As he saw her questioning look, a shy smile crossed his features, and Rosabel felt herself blush although she did not know why. "I suppose you do not remember this," he said, raising his eyebrows, indicating the bed behind her, "but we are to share this room." Slowly, his eyes returned to her face, once again waiting for her reaction.

When she had woken up that morning, the other side of the bed had looked relatively untouched, and he had already been downstairs, taking a stroll through the gardens with Georgiana and the prince. However, a distant corner of her mind remembered the presence she had felt when sleep had claimed her the night before.

"I see," she whispered, not knowing how to respond. Although her pulse sped up and her hands began to tremble, part of her noticed the slight tingle of excitement that ran through her body at the thought of sharing a bed with her husband.

Interpreting her silence differently, her husband pointed to the small settee situated by the fireplace on the west-facing wall. "If it makes you uncomfortable, I can sleep there." His eyes remained on hers, waiting.

In a strange way, Rosabel thought he was asking much more than simply whether or not she felt uncomfortable having him sleep beside her. A glimmer of hope shone in his eyes mingled with a touch of fear. Confused, Rosabel narrowed her eyes, unable to make sense of the emotions that coursed through him.

When he turned around, she placed a hand on his shoulder, stopping him. "I do not mind sharing the bed."

As he looked back at her, a flame burned within her, touching her cheeks. He stepped closer and nodded. "All right." His gaze slid over her, here and there stopping to linger. Rosabel drew in a deep breath, trying to steady her nerves. As though in answer, he cleared his throat, eyes snapping back up to her face. "I will step out onto the balcony while you change."

Once again, he turned to go, and once again, Rosabel stopped him. "Just keep your back turned," she whispered, unable to meet his eyes.

He nodded, facing the dancing flames.

After taking off her boots, Rosabel realized that she was stuck. Her mind had been too occupied to notice earlier, but without help, she would never be able to undo the laces in the back of her dress. "Eh," she stammered.

"Is something wrong?" he asked over his shoulder, keeping his eyes fixed on the opposite wall.

Pushing embarrassment aside, Rosabel found her voice. "I need help with my laces."

For a moment, he didn't move, didn't say anything. Then his shoulders tensed, and he inhaled deeply. "Can I look?"

Rosabel nodded before realizing that he couldn't see her. "Yes," she whispered, eyes shifting to the floor as he turned to face her.

"What do you need me to do?" he whispered.

Turning her back to him, a shiver ran over her skin. At first, relief filled her at not having to face his scrutinizing eyes, but after a moment, she realized that although she could not see them, she felt their touch as they ran over her body. Again, a shiver went through her, and she took a deep breath. "Undo the laces." Until his fingers brushed her back through the fabric, Rosabel wasn't sure if he had heard her; as feeble as her voice sounded to her own ears.

Starting at the very top, his hands moved down her back, here and there struggling to loosen her bodice. His warm breath brushed over the soft skin on her neck, raising goose bumps in its wake. He stood so close that the warmth radiating from his body touched her chilled skin like a balmy breeze on a summer's day. More than anything, she wanted to lean into him and feel his arms wrap around her.

Slowly, Rosabel felt the fabric's tight hug slip away as the cool night air touched her skin, which only moments later was set aflame when his fingers lightly brushed over it like the touch of a feather.

"All right," he whispered, and Rosabel opened her eyes, completely unaware that she had closed them.

"Thank you," she mumbled without turning around. The burning hot in her cheeks spoke of the red that had settled there, and she couldn't bring herself to face him.

For a moment, silence hung in the air. Then she heard him step back and walk over to the other side of the room. Glancing over her shoulder, she found him standing by the set of armchairs facing the stone fireplace. With one hand leaning on the backrest, he stood completely still, staring into the flames.

Hesitating at first, Rosabel quickly brushed away the thought that he might turn back too early and catch her with hardly anything covering her body. But he would not. She was sure of it. He wouldn't move until she told him to.

Stepping out of her dress, she carefully laid it over the chair's backrest standing in front of the vanity in the corner of the room. After removing her shoes and stockings, she took off her stay, once more drawing in a deep breath. Keeping her chemise on, she slipped into her nightgown and slid into bed, drawing the covers almost to her chin.

"It's all right," she said, forcing her voice loud enough for him to hear. "You can turn around."

At first, she thought he hadn't heard her. His shoulders remained tense, and his hand looked like it was gripping the back of the chair for support. Then a small tremble went through his frame and slowly, ever so slowly, he turned to face her.

When their eyes met, Rosabel instantly looked down at the delicate quilt keeping the cold at bay. Step by step, she heard him approach the other side of the bed. Without saying a word, he removed his boots and his outer coat. From under her eyelashes, Rosabel watched as he slid into bed beside her, keeping his breeches and shirt on.

Leaning over to the bed stand where the last candle burned, a tiny light in the dark of night, he extinguished it and settled back into bed. Only the glowing embers from the fireplace cast a last looming light across the room, dancing shadows in a world of darkness. "Good night," he whispered.

Lying on her back, the dark wrapping her in a safe cocoon, Rosabel's unease about the situation slipped away with each breath she took and each breath she heard him take not an arm's length away from her. "Will you still send me back to Westmore?" she asked, relieved that the shadows hid his face.

Hearing his head shift on the pillow, she waited, holding her breath.

"Do you want to return?" he asked instead of answering her

question.

"I like Westmore. It's beautiful, and I do miss Helen. I think I could feel at home there."

After a moment of silence, he said, "But?"

"But not without Georgiana." Once again holding her breath, Rosabel waited. Even if the prince had refused to take his child back, her husband could still refuse her access to Georgiana and send them to different estates. Ultimately, she had no say in the matter.

On the other side of the bed, Rosabel heard the ruffling of covers as he moved, turning on his side as he looked at her, the glow of embers dancing in his eyes.

Keeping her own gaze fixed on the ceiling, she felt his warm breath travel the small distance between them and caress her chilled cheek. A tremble ran through her as she drew in another breath, anticipation growing.

"Have no fear," his voice sounded in the dark. "I will not attempt to separate the two of you again." Rosabel heard herself exhale audibly. "I never should have. You are a good mother to her, and she deserves that."

Feeling her heart jump in her chest, Rosabel's lips broke into a smile as her eyes closed, savouring the moment. "Thank you," she breathed.

"You're welcome," he said, turning back around.

Again, silence hung between them, and although Rosabel's heart hammered in her chest, she could not walk away. Gathering her courage, she spoke into the dark. "What about you, my lord?"

"What about me?"

She swallowed, forcing the words past her lips. "Will you return to Westmore with us?"

Again, silence rang in the room. Then he once more turned around to look at her. "Do you want me to?" he whispered, the same hint of hope mingled with fear in his voice that Rosabel had seen in his eyes before. What did he want her to say? Did he want to come but at the same time wanted her to want him there too? Or did he want her to give him leave to stay away?

Rosabel's head swam as she contemplated the many ways this conversation could go. While afraid to offer herself to him and be rejected, Rosabel knew that only the truth would set her free. If she did not at least try, she would be left wondering. The past months had been torment enough. She needed to make her peace with the future.

She needed to see things settled. One way or another.

Bracing herself for what was to come, Rosabel spoke with her heart on her tongue. "I do not want you to leave again. Neither would Georgiana. Stay with us, whether at Westmore or Camden Hall does not matter." Holding her breath, Rosabel waited.

Was she serious? Did she really wish for them to live under the same roof? Graham wondered.

Then realization dawned. Of course, how could he have been so daft? The only reason she asked him to stay with them–not her, them– was because of Georgiana. After all, she was the girl's mother and wanted what was best for her. That, he finally understood.

But could he live in the same house with her and keep his distance at the same time? Feeling her closeness even now, Graham had to keep a tight grip on his emotions, lest they overwhelm him and make him do things he would regret later. Things he could not take back. Like the day, she had sought refuge under a tree in the rain. He had found her, though, and invaded her haven.

Again cursing himself in the dark, his hands curled into the bed covers. More than anything, he wanted to reach over and touch her, feel that soft skin tremble under his fingers once more. But he knew doing so would shatter their fragile relationship for good. She would be appalled and never forgive him.

"I do not yet know," he finally said, hearing her sigh in response. Of course, he thought, she felt conflicted. While she herself probably wished for them to continue living in different residences, she was willing to accept his presence for Georgiana's sake. How torturous these emotions had to be for her! He thought, well remembering the fine line he had walked daily during his marriage to Leonora.

"What will happen now?" her soft voice danced through the dark. "What about Georgiana and…her father?"

Although he knew how she meant it and understood the slight hesitation for what it was, hearing another man referred to as Georgiana's father felt like a stab to the heart. Involuntarily, his hand went to his chest, and he drew in a sharp breath.

"We will stay a few more days." He knew his voice sounded

clipped, but he couldn't help it. "Then we will return to Camden Hall, at least for now."

"And the prince?" she asked, her own voice as gentle as before. "Will he see her again?"

Graham's fingers dug deeper into the bed covers. He could barely keep himself from jumping out of bed as his legs trembled with the need to move, to run, to get away. Gritting his teeth, he tried his best to keep his voice level. "Occasionally, yes. I will not keep them apart. Whether Georgiana knows that he is her real father or not makes no difference to me."

Again, a sigh reached his ears, and he wondered if she did not like his answer, if she'd rather forget about the circumstances that had brought them here.

After a while she spoke again. "I do not know how to say this without sounding condescending." He could hear a tremble in her voice, and his muscles tensed, waiting for her to continue. "But I just need to say that…I am proud of you, of what you did for Georgiana. I know it was not easy for you, and I thank you for it."

Stunned beyond comprehension, Graham lay completely still, staring at the dark ceiling. Of all the things he had expected her to say, this had not been among them. She, who had every reason to hate him, felt the need to express her gratitude in such a way. She was proud of him! He shook his head, still unable to believe what his ears had heard. No one had voiced such a sentiment in a long time, not since the death of his parents many years ago.

In that moment, Graham knew that if he let himself, he could love her.

39

IDLE GOSSIP

n a strange way, Camden Hall looked different when Rosabel caught sight of it as they came around a bend in the road, passing the last group of oak trees obstructing their view. Like Westmore, it still had a looming darkness about it, with the grey stone turned almost black, the heavy curtains shielding the interior from the world outside and the dense forest just off to the east that seemed to vibrate with a myriad of things dark and dangerous lurking somewhere inside.

When her eyes touched the old manor on this beautiful spring day though, Rosabel felt a tiny jump in her stomach as though her body tried to tell her that it was good to be home. What was home? She wondered. Certainly not Camden Hall. Or even Westmore, for that matter. She had spent but a few months living on these estates. Was that enough time to call it home? Deep in thought, Rosabel shook her head. Then what had changed? She wondered.

Glancing at the peacefully sleeping girl across from her, head resting on her father's lap, whose own head had rolled back against the wall, eyes closed, for once no signs of inner turmoil on his face,

Rosabel smiled. Although things were far from resolved, life did look brighter. Somehow they would find a way, Rosabel was sure of it. Georgiana would stay with them, and maybe, just maybe, her husband would decide against separate residences. Taking a deep breath, Rosabel felt her heart flutter at the thought of seeing him every day. The vulnerability and deep emotions he had been unable to mask during their trip to London gave her hope that he didn't find their company as unbearable as he often let on.

When the carriage came to a stop, softly swaying back and forth as though they were at sea, her husband's eyes opened with a clarity that suggested he hadn't been sleeping after all. Frowning at his strange behaviour, Rosabel wondered why. Had he not wanted to converse with her? Again, a lump settled in her stomach, and doubt crept into her heart. Oh, how she wished for clarity! More than anything, she wanted to know where they stood, honest and open, without pretence.

Gently cradling his daughter in his arms, her husband stepped from the carriage, a shy smile playing on his lips as he passed her and their eyes met for the briefest of moments. Once again, Rosabel's knees turned to pudding, and she was amazed at how unpredictably these emotions seized her and how easily his behaviour affected her.

When night fell, Rosabel settled into the room she had occupied since arriving at Camden Hall with Georgiana a few weeks ago. Her bed welcomed her with open arms, and although tired from the days spent travelling, her eyes were drawn to the door connecting her room to her husband's. Was he sleeping? Or did he lie awake as well? Worrying her lower lip, Rosabel drew the covers around her, feeling their soft smoothness against her skin. Then she closed her eyes, imagining strong arms holding her, and soon she drifted off to sleep.

The door beckoned him to open it.

Standing with his hand on the handle, Graham's shoulders tensed, and every muscle in his body threatened to tear with the struggle coursing through him. Why did this have to be so difficult? Why was doing what he wanted equivalent to going against his better judgment? Gritting his teeth, a frustrated moan escaped his throat, and he leaned forward, resting his forehead against the cool wood of the door.

As he closed his eyes, his mind conjured up images of Rosabel; the way her lips curled up in that amused half-smile whenever she found him tedious, the glow that had come to her eyes when they had drawn near Camden Hall that day, and the slight catch in her voice as she'd asked him to stay with them. Once again, he wondered if she regretted her answer by now. Would she answer differently if he asked her again?

As doubts infiltrated his mind once more, Graham pushed away from the door, pacing the room. He linked his hands behind his back only to bring them forward a moment later, raking his fingers through his hair. He paced until he felt his pulse speed up and his tired body began to protest against this late night exertion. And yet, he couldn't stop. For if he stopped, he would find himself alone in his room again, and more than that he would realize that this situation was not going to change, as much as he wished otherwise.

Hours passed as Graham continued to pace the length of his bedchamber. His breathing quickened, and small beads of sweat popped up on his forehead. But only when his eyelids grew heavy, too heavy to keep them open, and he almost made contact with the wall, did he drop down onto his bed. The moment his head met the pillow, his mind abandoned its slippery grasp on reality, and he drifted off into a fitful sleep.

In the coming days, Graham tiptoed around Camden Hall, unsure how to fit into his old life that had so suddenly changed. Even more so when he realized he could not leave. As much as he knew he should, he wanted to stay. Again and again, he planned to leave on the morrow, only to conjure up ludicrous excuses to postpone his departure. A fortnight later, he finally admitted to himself that he had no intention of ever leaving.

However, finally having reached a decision, Graham was at a loss after all. Nothing had been settled, except for the fact that they were all to remain under the same roof. In addition, only he was aware of this fact. The other two concerned had not been informed yet. But how ought he to tell them when he could not be sure his information would be well received? Of course, Georgiana would welcome him. She would be delighted. Picturing her glowing eyes and radiant smile as she threw herself into his arms brought a deep smile to his own face.

But what about Rosabel?

Something had changed.

Glancing through the small gap between the row of books and the next shelf, Rosabel observed how Georgiana and her husband sat in an armchair, reading a book. Settled onto her father's lap, Georgiana's lips moved as she tried her best to sound out the words on the page before her. Occasionally, she stumbled, and her father would give her a hint. With their faces side by side, peering into the book, Rosabel noticed for the first time how alike they looked. Sure, Georgiana more strongly favoured her mother with regard to outward appearance; however, the shy, yet delighted smile that played on her lips echoed back in the one that lit up her father's face as well. Their eyes moved across the page in synchronization as though one mind controlled them both. Slight nuances in their facial expressions that had eluded Rosabel's attention before now almost screamed for her to notice.

And yet, she knew that Georgiana was not her husband's child. At least not biologically, but in every other way he so obviously was her father.

Throughout the following weeks, Rosabel more than once found herself turning a corner only to stumble upon father and daughter in intimate togetherness; at the pond feeding ducks, in the nursery sipping tea, in the stables discussing horses, even in the kitchen stealing cookies. With wide eyes, Rosabel observed the sudden change that had gone through her husband. From one day to the next, an impish quality had appeared in his demeanour that not only cast a spell over Georgiana. Wishing to join them, Rosabel had trouble keeping her distance and giving them the time they needed to reconnect. Occasionally, a slight pain echoed in her chest at not being included. In these moments, Rosabel felt reminded that she had only just recently joined their lives and that their connection did not run as deep yet. But she hoped it would eventually.

For now, Rosabel decided to simply enjoy the advantages of her husband's change of heart. While the house often echoed with joy and playfulness, it wasn't only their voices that could be heard. Suddenly neighbours were invited for tea or even a dinner party was given. In turn, they too went to visit their neighbouring estates. After spending most of her life isolated from the world around her, mostly by her own doing due to thoughts of inferiority, Rosabel delighted in her neighbours' company. Georgiana, too, began to thrive as burdens that had been placed on her small shoulders after her mother's death slowly disappeared.

"She is a beautiful child," Ellie said, coming up behind her. "And so sweet-tempered. We are all very fond of her." Glancing over her shoulder, she watched as Georgiana and Ellie's own younger siblings raced each other down the lawn and to the duck pond bordering her father's estate.

Feeling her heart swell with pride, Rosabel nodded. "I cannot tell you how relieved I am to see her like this. She has always been too serious, spending most of her time with adults, never getting to play and be wild." Watching her, Rosabel felt a stab of envy as she remembered the restrictions that upon her parents' deaths had been forced on her own life.

"Let's walk." Ellie drew Rosabel's arm through hers and led her friend down the small slope to the pavilion that had heard many of their secrets. Rosabel couldn't help but wonder whether her cousin had something important to say.

As they sat down on the marble bench, Ellie's fingers fidgeted with the seam of her dress.

"Is something wrong?" Rosabel asked, desperately hoping her cousin's answer would set her mind at ease. When Ellie remained silent, she pressed, "Is there news with regard to your desired engagement?"

For a second, Ellie looked up, then shook her head. "No, it is nothing of the kind, but you are right. There is something I need to tell you."

Again, their silence grew heavy.

"Say whatever it is," Rosabel urged as goose bumps crawled up her arms. "Your silence is making this unbearable."

Dropping the hem of her dress, Ellie nodded. "You're right. I apologise."

"So?"

"Well, this is still difficult to say," Ellie said, her fingers once more searching for something to distract her rattled mind. "It is about you and your husband. There's…," she took a deep breath, "there's a rumour going around."

Rosabel's eyebrows flew up. "A rumour? What kind of rumour?" As her pulse sped up, Rosabel concentrated on drawing one breath after another into her lungs. Please, do not let it be about Georgiana! She prayed, wondering how, if at all, anyone could have found out about the girl's parentage. And now of all times.

"I am not sure 'rumour' is the correct word," Ellie continued, clearly seeking to avoid the details that made her so uncomfortable. "But there are whispers."

"What about?"

Ellie drew in a deep breath before closing her eyes for a second. "Well, you have been married for almost a year now, and I suppose people expected you to be with child by now."

Letting out a breath she didn't know she'd been holding, Rosabel felt her muscles relax. "Oh, that. I thought it was something serious."

"It is," Ellie insisted, turning sympathetic eyes on her cousin. "Since your husband already has a child, people believe the fault lies with you. Believe me, if this continues on, you will find sad and pitying looks wherever you go."

"That may be. But it is of no concern for me. I have a child I love with all my heart. I do not need another for my life to be complete."

"Good." A relieved smile played on Ellie's lips as she took her friend's hand. "But I hope the rumours will not take away from the happiness you've finally found."

Returning her cousin's smile, Rosabel shook her head. "I won't let them." On the contrary, she was not only determined to hold on to the happiness that had already settled into her life but sought to gather even more. Her husband's smiling face flashed before her eyes as he gazed at his daughter. More than anything, Rosabel wanted to have him look at her with the same heart-felt devotion and unconditional love.

If only she knew how to make that happen.

40

HONESTY

As the moon cast an eerie light over Camden Hall, troublesome thoughts drove Graham from his bed. At first he paced the length of his room, up and down, up and down, until his hands raked through his hair in a desperate attempt to calm the erratic beating of his heart. But nothing worked. The thoughts kept coming, torturing him, and drew before his mind images he desired and yet, feared were out of his reach.

Pushing open the door to his room with enough force for it to collide with the wall, Graham cringed as a soft bang echoed through the night and down the corridor. For an instant, he froze in his tracks, listening.

When all remained quiet, he strode down the corridor, his angry footsteps cushioned by the heavy rug covering the hardwood floors. His mind still occupied with the hurtful rumours that had reached his ears at the baron's gathering, his feet carried him forward without direction. After a few turns and a staircase down to the ground floor, Graham was surprised to find himself heading for the kitchen.

A frown creased his forehead as he realized the oddity of his situation.

Never in his life had he spent much time in the kitchen. The only significant memory he could conjure to mind brought back the touch of Rosabel's soft lips against his as her trembling body melted into him.

Graham shivered, wondering if his subconscious mind had carried him here for more than he was willing to admit.

As he drew near, about to push open the door, the sound of a steaming kettle reached his ears. Instantly, he stopped, leaning forward to listen.

Light footsteps danced across the kitchen. A teacup connected with the table top and gave off a soft *clink*. Then water rushed from the kettle, pouring into the cup, and a soft aroma of mint and lemon tickled his nose.

Pushing the door ajar, Graham peeked through the gap, his heart beating as though he was a little boy sneaking out of his room after dark.

At first, he couldn't see anything. But then a soft rustling of fabric brought her into view.

It was Rosabel, and his heart jumped with excitement.

Knowing that courage would fail him any second, Graham pushed open the door and stepped into the room.

Rosabel spun around, eyes wide, and the teacup slipped from her hand, shattering on the kitchen floor, a deafening sound in the silence that hung about the night.

Cringing at his clumsiness, Graham stepped forward. "I apologise for startling you."

A hand to her chest, Rosabel shook her head, her breath coming quick. "No, my lord, do not worry yourself." Turning her eyes to the floor, she knelt down. "I will clean this up right away."

"I wish you wouldn't call me 'my lord'," Graham blurted out, instantly feeling heat creep up his cheeks.

Her eyes looked up, meeting his, and before he could die of embarrassment, Graham knelt down beside her, reaching for the remnants of the teacup. "Let me help you with this."

Shard for shard he took from her hand, and each time his fingers brushed against hers sent lightning sparks down to his core. Seeing the slight tremble in her shoulders, Graham wondered if his touch had the same effect on her, but he didn't dare ask.

Disposing of the shattered teacup, Graham turned to the kitchen cabinets for a new one but realized he had no idea where to look.

Seeing him hesitate, Rosabel strode forward, her movements steady and precise, and he realized that she had to have spent a great deal of time in the kitchen to be so familiar with it. Were her nights restless too? Did she come here when sleep eluded her? The one time they had met in the kitchen at night, she had been sitting here, drinking tea in her night robe as well.

"Would you care for a cup, my lord?"

Again, she called him 'my lord', and again, it burnt a hole into his heart. She had called him that many times before, after all it was appropriate, and yet, tonight he felt the heavy distance these two words carried. He wished she would call him something dearer.

"Yes, please," he mumbled, if only to have something to hold, something to keep his hands from reaching out and touching her smooth skin, sparkling in the candle light.

Cups in hand, they sat down at the large worktable, sipping the hot liquid, while carefully keeping their eyes from looking at the other. Graham could feel the awkward silence grow heavier and realized he needed to speak up now or would never find the courage to do so.

"I am quite relieved that we met here tonight for I happened to overhear a conversation at the baron's gathering today that sparked my concern." Taking another sip, he watched her face.

Although nothing much changed—neither did her eyes widen, nor her mouth drop open—Graham couldn't help but suspect that she was not ignorant of the rumour that seemed to be circulating at present.

"What is it, my lord?"

Clearing his throat, Graham rushed on as his muscles tightened around the hot cup in his hands. "People are beginning to suspect—and I suppose you know how idle gossip can grow out of control—that," again he cleared his throat, forcing his gaze to remain on her face instead of dropping down to the hot liquid slowly burning his skin, "you are unable to provide me with an heir."

Whatever he had expected her reaction to be—shame, embarrassment, anger, hurt—the simple shrug that moved her shoulders before she took another slow sip from her cup rattled him to his core.

Swallowing the sweet liquid, she turned her eyes to him. "And what is your concern, my lord? Do you wish for an heir? A child of your own blood?"

Shocked at her boldness, Graham searched her face. Neither anger nor resentment shone in her brown eyes as they looked at him with nothing but the desire to know the truth. That, Graham could understand. Relinquishing his tight grip on the hot cup, Graham leaned back in his chair. "Would you agree that if nothing else, there should always be honesty between us? No matter what the issue?" He hadn't known he would ask that question; his heart had loosened his tongue, bypassing his mind for approval. But once out, he felt relieved. He had to know.

At his words, the ghost of a smile curled up her lips before she lifted her cup once more to take a small sip. "Honesty," she mused. "Yes, honesty is never a wrong road to take." A full smile lit up her features. "Honesty, then."

He nodded as his shoulders relaxed. Somehow this small word had set the foundation for a bridge that could one day span the abyss still gaping between them. "Then, to be honest, I do want an heir, yes. Someone to carry on my name, my family's name. Someone I can trust to take care of Westmore and its people." As their eyes connected across the table, Graham saw no need to hold back. She was his wife, and somehow he knew she would understand. "Georgiana is my child in every way. I know that now." Her eyes lit up like the stars at night. "I know I cannot pass on my title to her. But if she were a boy, I would have no regrets about her carrying on my family's legacy. My blood or not, she is my child. A wonderful child." He shook his head as a tinge of heat crept up his cheeks. "I'd forgotten how lucky I was to be her father. I will never forget again. I promise."

Setting the cup down on the table, her hands still curled around it, seeking its warmth, his wife leaned forward as though wishing to be closer to him. If he reached out, he could touch her hand; but he held back, knowing that rushing her could destroy the fragile connection they had formed in the past few minutes.

"Nothing pleases me more than hearing you say this." Her smile lit up the room more than the two small candles standing on the table ever could. "However, do you mind if I ask what brought on this sudden change of mind?"

A shy smile dancing across his face, he averted his eyes. "I apologise for this thick skull of mine. You tried to make me see the truth time and time again, and I snapped at you. Again, I apologise. To tell you the truth," he looked up and found her eyes on him, not judging, just observing, "I am not entirely certain when it happened. But I remember seeing the anguish on my friend's face as he looked at her; his own flesh and blood, and yet, she could never be his. It broke my heart, and I realized how lucky I was to be the one who gets to raise her, see her every day, and have her call me 'Father'." Another radiant smile lit up her face, and struck by her beauty, Graham couldn't help but stare. Seeing her avert her eyes and fidget in her chair as though embarrassed, he shook his head, trying to clear it of the improper thoughts that had occupied it. "I apologise," he mumbled, realizing that his voice had to sound like an echo to her, considering how often he had apologised since they sat down at the table.

For a moment, silence hung in the air, and Graham could feel their connection slowly slipping from his grasp. Terrified of losing what he had only just found, he said, "Although you never held her as a baby, you loved her right away, didn't you?"

Another smile stripped all embarrassment from her features. "I did. I cannot explain it, but she captured my heart." For a second, her eyes drifted upward, became distant, and the dreamy look on her face told him that the memories she was replaying in her mind were among the dearest she possessed. Then her gaze returned to him. "I was always surprised to see you ignore her with such vehemence, but I know now that you were only desperate to protect yourself, your own heart."

Once again, he found himself staring at her. Did she really understand him? How he had struggled? Did she really not hold his actions against him anymore? Looking into her eyes told him that she truly did not. Amazed at her compassion, he realized that they had strayed off topic a little. Clearing his throat, he said, "I am sorry for bringing up this topic again, but I need to be certain of your feelings on the matter." He swallowed. "Even though you love Georgiana the way you do, the way every mother would love her child, do you wish for a child of your own? A child you yourself deliver into this world?" Again, he swallowed, afraid of her answer.

For a long while, she looked into her empty cup as though hoping to find the answer to his question in there. Feeling his heart beat against his ribs, he watched her. Would she be repulsed by his suggestion? Would she even contemplate sharing his bed if it meant for her to have a child of her own? Would it be enough of an incentive?

When she looked up, he found neither disgust nor repulsion in her eyes and breathed a sigh of relief.

"My lord, I promised you honesty, and honest I will be." His heart skipped a beat, and for a second, he was afraid it wouldn't start up again. "If you truly wish for an heir, I will not refuse you." Graham cringed, hearing the sense of duty ring in her voice. "While I do not feel the need for more children, I would welcome them. However, if you ask my feelings on the matter, I would prefer to leave duty and obligation out of it." She rose from her chair, and he hastened to follow. As she stepped toward him, her dark eyes gazed into his. "Should you ever decide to visit my chamber," she whispered, her warm breath teasing his resolve to keep his distance, "then let it be because of desire, not obligation." For a moment, she just stood before him, looking into his eyes as though words were unnecessary for what she wanted to communicate.

His eyes slid from hers down to her mouth, tracing the line of her lips. However, before he could make up his mind to kiss her, she turned around and without a look back left the kitchen, her footsteps echoing down the corridor.

More than anything, he wanted to follow her, but his feet wouldn't move.

41

RETURN TO THE WILLOW TREE

As fast as her feet would carry her, Rosabel walked down the hall. Would he follow her? His face had looked fairly shocked at hearing her words. She herself had been too, still wondering how she could have been so bold. Her cheeks still felt hot when she entered her room. Shutting the door behind her, she leaned against it and closed her eyes. How could she have spoken to him like that? She desperately hoped he did not think her an improper wife now! Had she just lost what little affection might have developed on his part?

Her mind still spinning with all the possible consequences of her lack of self-control, Rosabel retired. However, sleep proved elusive as her eyes refused to stray from the door, hoping for and yet, dreading it to open and reveal in its frame the one man who held her heart.

Minutes ticked by, then hours. But nothing. No footsteps. No knock on her door.

As exhaustion weighed heavily on Rosabel's tired limbs, her eyelids closed again and again as her mind lost control of them. Before long she drifted off into a fitful sleep, still unable to let rest the issues that already plagued her during the day.

Morning came too soon, and with it a return of her flushed cheeks whenever her mind recalled the previous night. Only sheer willpower forced her down the stairs and into the breakfast parlour. Would his eyes be cold when he looked at her? Rosabel cringed, and an involuntary shiver seized her small frame.

As the footman pulled open the doors, Rosabel took a deep breath and consciously raised her chin.

"Good morning," Georgiana's cheerful voice greeted her, and for a moment, Rosabel allowed herself to bath in the sight of the little girl before her eyes strayed to her husband.

Seated in his usual spot, he turned his head, and when their eyes met, Rosabel breathed a sigh of relief. His eyes were anything but cold! They were warm and glowing as though the sun shone through them. The hint of a smile danced on his features before he returned his gaze to Georgiana.

For a moment, Rosabel hesitated. Had her eyes deceived her? Had his cheeks turned a shade of crimson just then? The same as the flush that still burned in hers?

Taking her seat, Rosabel kept glancing at her husband from under her eyelashes, trying to interpret the many nuances that changed his handsome face as he conversed with Georgiana. Occasionally, she caught him glancing in her direction, which instantly resulted in more heat lighting up her cheeks. The flame of embarrassment burned hot, and Rosabel wished she could flee the room and not have her emotions so plainly visible for all the world to see.

When breakfast ended, and Rosabel had barely eaten a morsel, Georgiana dragged her husband out the door to the stables. A new foal had been born during the night, and she insisted on seeing it without delay. As they rushed by her, Rosabel stepped aside, and yet, the back of his hand brushed against her fingers.

A jolt went through her body, and her head snapped up.

Before he disappeared through the double doors, Rosabel thought she'd seen a smile as he looked back at her. A smile that lit up his eyes. A smile that touched her heart. A smile she had seen before when he had gazed at his daughter and Rosabel had realized how much he loved her. Had that smile really been meant for her?

Over the next few days, they stole hidden glances at one another. Whenever one caught the other's stare, they would avert their eyes and almost run from the room. Although Rosabel recognized her own insecure behaviour in his, she wondered if his reaction to her was of a positive nature as she hoped or if she was merely deceiving herself. All objectivity left her the moment his deep blue eyes found hers. Instantly, her heart would speed up and her palms would become moist. Under different circumstances, Rosabel would have worried about her current state of health.

The following Thursday started out as every other day. However, during mid-morning Rosabel turned a corner and almost collided with her husband.

Both trying to step out of the other's way, they ended up swaying for balance, and Rosabel felt strong hands grab a hold of her upper arms, steadying her. As she looked up at him, the by now familiar heat rose to her cheeks when she found his blue eyes glowing with…was that affection?

Rosabel shook her head, hoping to see more clearly.

"Would you like to accompany me on a horseback ride this afternoon?" His velvety voice resonated in her ears, and she leaned into him, his strong arms still holding her upright. "Or do you need rest?" A slight frown appeared on his forehead as he searched her face.

Trying to find her voice, Rosabel shook her head. "No, I'm fine." A weak smile pulled up the corners of her mouth, and she desperately hoped it looked reassuring. "I would love to go riding with you."

At her words, his eyes lit up, and a face-splitting grin contorted his handsome features. "Wonderful." Realizing that he was still holding her, he cleared his throat and stepped back.

Again, Rosabel thought to detect a hint of crimson colouring his cheeks.

As they raced across the fields, heading toward the tree line, Graham felt guilty for the break-neck speed he forced on her. However, after a few painful minutes of awkward silence, he couldn't help himself. Glancing over his shoulder, he saw her follow on Winter, leaning forward as though whispering into the mare's ear. She held herself well, and Graham was pleased to find her an accomplished rider.

Once they entered the forest, Graham realized his mistake.

Instantly, the horses slowed down to manoeuvre the uneven terrain, carefully picking their way through the thick underbrush and around tree stumps.

His wife, however, remained silent, eyes gliding over her surroundings as though what she saw was completely new to her.

Silence lingered like a heavy fog.

Graham did not know how much time had passed when his wife's voice reached his ears. "Is there a reason you bring me here?"

Frowning, he turned to her. "What do you mean?"

In answer, her eyes travelled past him, looking over his shoulder. As Graham turned around to see what had caught her attention, the blood froze in his veins.

How could he have made such a mistake?

Down the slope, he spotted the lonely willow tree standing in the open meadow beyond the tree line. The tree that had seen the worst of him. The tree that she had sought shelter under from the pouring rain. The tree that had not kept him at bay.

Raking his fingers through his hair, Graham did not know what to do. Ought they to turn back? Or continue on? Would she not demand an explanation either way? And even if she didn't, was the day not ruined by the memories the sight of the lonely tree conjured before their eyes? And what about the days that would follow? What would today's effect be on them?

However, before Graham could make up his mind, Rosabel guided Winter past him. The horse trotted down the small slope and headed straight for the willow tree, standing in the middle of the meadow like a lonely sentinel.

While he still stared at her slowly receding back, a thick drop of rain landed squarely on his forehead. Blinking, he wiped it away and only just then noticed the dark clouds covering the formerly blue sky. Individual drops came crashing toward the earth here and there as he urged Storm on, following after his wife. All the while, he couldn't help but wonder if this was some kind of cruel game. What were the chances of another downpour just when they accidentally stumbled upon the sight of their deepest rift once more?

Following his wife's example, Graham tied his stallion to a low-hanging branch. Then he turned to face her.

As the rain grew heavier, drawing a thick curtain around them, almost cutting them off from the rest of the world, she stood with her back resting against the willow's enormous trunk, eyes glowing in awe.

For a moment, her head rolled back against the rough tree bark, and she closed her eyes, inhaling deeply through her nose, absorbing the fresh aroma of wet grass.

Wondering how she could be so at peace, Graham drew nearer.

When his boots squished on a patch of muddy ground, her eyes opened and found his.

Stopping in his tracks, Graham froze. Ought he to turn and leave? Assure her that he was no threat to her any longer?

"You should come closer to the trunk," she spoke above the drumming of water droplets around them, "or you will get soaked through before you know it."

As though her words were his command, his feet continued their way through the high grass. Afraid of what he might see if he looked into her eyes, Graham stopped beside her and turned to rest his back against the trunk as well. Side by side, they stared out into the rain, each dwelling on their own fears.

"I love the smell of rain," she whispered into the silence that hung between them, eyes still staring at the curtain of streaming water encircling them. "It smells of new beginnings, of possibilities and new days to come."

More than her words themselves, it was the echo of hope in her voice that made Graham turn. Searching her face as she shifted her glowing eyes to him, he saw neither fear nor resentment. Could it be that she did not fear him? That he did not repulse her? Had this place not conjured most unpleasant memories for her?

Again, he looked at her, and again, he found a peaceful glow on her features. Her lips curled up into a shy smile as her eyes glided over him for barely a second before returning to the rain. Memories tickled his mind, and for the first time, he recognized the slight tremble in her frame, the delicate smile and the flittering eyes for what they really were.

A young woman falling in love, afraid to have her feelings rejected.

As the huge boulder that had held down his heart for countless years slowly lifted and disappeared into thin air, the corners of his mouth drew up into a face-splitting smile. Relief flooded his body. He had never felt so light, so weightless, like nothing could touch him.

Nothing but her.

Reaching out, he took her hands in his, feeling the slight tremble as his fingers touched her skin. She felt warm, welcoming, and did not withdraw her hands. Yet, Graham needed to be sure. "Do you mind?" he whispered, gazing into her dark eyes.

As she shook her head, he took a step closer, feeling the warmth of her breath touch his cheek, sending shivers down his back. Mesmerized he watched a single raindrop roll down the side of her temple, for a second pooling in the corner of her eye as though masquerading as a tear. Slowly it grew heavier until it spilled down her cheek, running all the way to the corner of her mouth. There it lingered, until the tip of her tongue snaked out, drawing it within.

A strangled moan escaped him, and he had to force himself to focus. His eyes still lingered on her lips, unable to abandon their post.

Slipping his arms around her waist, he drew her closer, his gaze finally returning to her eyes. She trembled in his arms, drawing in a sharp breath, but she didn't push him away.

Licking his own lips, Graham swallowed. "May I steal a kiss?"

A radiant smile illuminated her features, and it warmed Graham's heart. He could look at her beautiful face forever.

As quickly as it had appeared, it once again vanished though, replaced by frown lines creasing her forehead.

Graham's heart stopped as the blood drained from his face.

Her eyes swept over him as though trying to find an answer to an unspoken question. Then she drew in a breath and asked, "Are you sure you want my kiss? And not rather Leonora's? For I do not merely want to be her replacement."

For a moment, he closed his eyes as relief flooded his body. "It is your kiss I desire," he assured her, delighted to see the beautiful smile return to her features. "You need not worry. Although honesty compels me to tell you that a part of me will always love Leonora. I cannot explain it any better than this, but she is a love of the past. It is not gone, but neither is it the one thing I need in order to be fulfilled, to be happy." As another rain drop ran down her cheek, he lifted his hand and gently brushed it away, feeling her soft skin under his fingertips. "My love for you though is a love of the present and of the future."

Staring into her eyes, he saw her blink as though waking from a dream. Then her lips parted, and a soft question full of wonder and amazement travelled to his ears. "You love me?"

42

CONFESSIONS

As her heart beat echoed in her ears, Rosabel's eyes were irrevocably drawn to the man holding her in his arms. Gazing down at her, his own eyes shone like stars in the night sky, and he smiled at her with that hint of shyness hiding under his rather rough exterior that she had come to love. Her hands came to rest on his chest, and even through the damp layers of fabric she could feel his own heart beat quicken.

Shifting his eyes downward as though embarrassed, he quickly met her gaze again, his head slowly bobbing up and down. "I do. I love you." He sighed, and another heart-breaking smile set his eyes on fire. "It took me too long to realize, but now that I finally know," he shook his head for emphasis, "I do not want to waste another moment."

Unable to form a coherent thought, Rosabel basked in the light that shone from his eyes. A light meant for her. A light that warmed her to her core. A light that would see her safe for the rest of her days.

And finally Rosabel felt like she had found her place in the world. The one place where she was meant to be. The one place where she could be all she was. The one place that would never turn her out.

That place was home.

"I know what you mean," she whispered. "I feel like I have been waiting for this my whole life, and a part of me had already stopped believing that I'd ever find it." Reaching up, she cupped her hand to his cheek. "I love you too." He exhaled as though her words had finally set him free. "I have for a while now, but I couldn't be sure of what you wanted. It always seemed like you were stuck in the past."

Graham nodded. "I was. I couldn't let it go. I couldn't move forward, couldn't see what was right before my eyes because I was too busy regretting the past." For a moment, his eyes closed, and he took a deep breath. "When Leonora was unable to return my feelings for her, it was more than just the loss of someone I cared about deeply. All around me, I saw people in love. Sometimes it was a tragic love, but at least there was someone in the world who looked at them like..." He trailed off, trying to find the right words.

Rosabel took a deep breath, remembering the way her father's eyes had lit up whenever her mother had entered a room. "Like you're the only one who matters," she finished his sentence, and as he looked at her, she could see that he understood. They were the same.

He nodded. "I thought I wasn't worthy to be loved. No one ever had, and after a while, I started to believe that no one ever could." Brushing a damp strand of hair from her forehead, he looked at her with devotion shining in his eyes. "Until you came into my life. But I was so determined to protect myself from another disappointment that I didn't even look at you. And so I didn't see. I didn't see how you looked back at me, how your feelings shone in your eyes and spoke with all honesty. I'm sorry. I just hope that I will not disappoint you."

Snuggling into him more closely, Rosabel shook her head. "You still believe you're not worthy. You think that tomorrow or the day after, I will come to my senses and realize that I made a mistake, that I do not feel for you the way you feel for me." Again, she shook her head as she saw the truth of her words flicker across his face. "You once asked me how I knew the things I did about Leonora."

A slight frown settled onto his face. "How did you?"

"Up in the attic when I found her portrait, I also discovered a wooden chest." Drawing in a deep breath, she hoped the truth would not drive a rift between them once more. "Inside that chest, I found not only her diaries, but also letters. Most were from the Prince of Wales, but one was from you." Again, she took a deep breath, her fingers digging into his arms as though trying to prevent him from walking away. "At first, I hesitated. I thought I had no right to invade her privacy. But then something changed. I can't really say what it was, but deep down, I felt like she was giving me permission to learn about her past because of the one thing we shared, our love for Georgiana." Rosabel shrugged, recalling the conflicting emotions raging within her at the time. "She was her mother, and she loved her, but she couldn't protect her anymore. It was as though she wanted me to do it for her. So I had to know." Worrying her lower lip between her teeth, she looked up into his eyes, hoping that he would understand.

He nodded then, rubbing her arms to warm her, inside and out. "I am glad you did. I don't know what would have become of Georgiana, of all of us for that matter, if you hadn't. I'm sure Leonora would have given her permission. Do not worry yourself."

As the burden this secret had been on her heart and soul slowly slipped away, Rosabel felt lighter than she ever had. "Thank you for understanding. However, there is something else I need to tell you." Searching his eyes, she carefully chose her words. "You said you felt unworthy because no one ever loved you." His eyes darken, but she pressed on. "You thought no one ever could. But you were wrong." Relieved, she watched a tiny spark return to his gaze. "However, it is not me I am talking about, but Leonora."

Instantly, his eyes narrowed, and a frown creased his forehead. "What do you mean?"

"She did come to love you," Rosabel whispered. "Just a few days before she died, she wrote into her diary. I think you should read what she wrote. I know your marriage didn't start out as one of mutual love, but sometimes things change." Again, she cupped her hand to his cheek that had gone pale at her words. "I hope knowing this will help you believe that you are truly worthy of love."

For a moment, he just stared at her with blank eyes, and Rosabel was certain that he wasn't seeing her as his thoughts raced to make sense of what he had learned. Then after a while, he blinked, and his gaze refocused on the woman in his arms. The hint of a smile played on his lips. "Thank you for telling me. I…you don't know what…no, you do know what this means to me." He nodded. "You understand me like no one else. I don't feel like I have to hide from you. I can show you my worst fears and insecurities, and you still respect me. Thank you for that." Again, he ran the tips of his fingers over her forehead and down her temple, sending shivers through her body. He cupped her cheek and gazing into her eyes brushed his thumb over her lips. "You did not answer my question though?"

Realizing what he meant, Rosabel felt a warm blush creep up her cheeks. She tried to lower her head, but his hand held her in place.

"May I kiss you?" he whispered, his lips a mere inch from hers, his warm breath tickling her skin.

Starting to feel dizzy, Rosabel dug her fingers deeper into the thick fabric of his sleeves, pulling herself closer against him. A soft moan escaped him as his lips gently brushed hers for a split second. "May I?" he whispered against her mouth.

As the world began to sway around her, Rosabel managed a single word. As though in slow motion it travelled from her mind down her nerve endings until her mouth carried it out into the world. "Yes."

Without losing so much as a second, Graham's lips came down on hers with a hunger she had never known before. As his arms pulled her closer into him, almost forcing the air from her lungs, his mouth explored hers with a familiarity that shocked her, but only for an instant, before she revelled in it. Growing bolder, her hands ran through his hair, then down his cheeks and onto his strong shoulders.

Giving herself over to the moment, Rosabel barely noticed him shift until she felt the rough bark of the willow tree pressing into her back. His hands roamed her body freely, sending jolts of pleasure into every region of her being and making her gasp.

He broke the kiss, and a moan of displeasure escaped her lips.

"I'm sorry," he panted, brushing a loose strand behind her ear. "I hope I didn't scare you."

Seeing the concern in his eyes, Rosabel shook her head. She raised herself on her tiptoes and planted the softest of kisses on his lips. When she leaned back, the worry had left his eyes, leaving nothing but love and devotion. Again, Rosabel revelled in the emotions they evoked.

As he held her close, Rosabel could see the struggle on his face as he tried to keep his distance, and she was touched by his concern for her. And yet, a part of her wished he would throw caution to the wind and kiss her breathless again.

When the rain finally let up, they mounted their horses and headed home.

Although the skies still hung with heavy clouds in dark grey, waiting for the opportune moment to soak the earth once more, Rosabel's eyes shone as she took in everything around her. The sun was nowhere to be seen, and a heavy mist clung to the ground, slowing their horses' tempo to a slow trot. And yet, the world had never seemed so bright. Her heart overflowed, and Rosabel smiled, feeling the corners of her mouth lift up in a most unfamiliar way, as though she had never smiled before.

What would tomorrow bring? Rosabel didn't know. But whatever it was, she would face it with a happy heart.

After returning their horses to the stables and leaving them to the care of the groomsmen, they headed into the house, climbing the large staircase side by side. Occasionally their hands would brush against one another, resulting in shy glances cast at the other.

Coming upon their rooms, they stopped, and for a moment, silence returned. As Rosabel's hands brushed over her damp dress, her fingertips tingled, remembering what they had touched not too long ago. Aching to feel him closer to her, Rosabel drew in a deep breath. Now was neither the time nor the place. She turned to enter her room to change out of her wet clothes lest she catch cold. However, before she could take a single step, a strong hand settled on her arm, pulling her back.

Even through the damp fabric of her sleeve, Rosabel felt the heat from his hand as he held her back. More than willing she stepped into his embrace, his eyes shining down at her once more. Then his gaze flitted up and down the corridor, making sure no one was within earshot. He licked his lips, leaning closer until the tip of his nose almost touched hers. "I do not mean to be forward," he whispered as his breath caressed the skin on her cheeks and down her neck, almost like a trail of kisses, "but would you give me permission to visit your chambers tonight?"

Holding his breath, Graham saw the slight widening of her eyes, and his heart beat faster. "I won't hold it against you if you decline my request," he said, hoping he hadn't scared her by being so forward. However, holding her in his arms, it took every ounce of self-control he had not to sweep her off her feet and carry her to the bed, standing but a few feet behind her, beckoning him forward. "Although I'll be thoroughly disappointed," he added, hoping that honesty would not fail him.

She drew in a few quick breaths, her chest rising and falling with each, taunting him, before a shy smile lit up her face. Though she did not say a word, he could see the answer in her eyes and the barely perceptible nod of her head.

Planting a soft kiss on her lips, Graham forced his feet to step back. "All right, then I'll see you at supper."

Again, she nodded, then turned around and disappeared into her room.

For a few more moments, Graham remained where he was, staring at her door, until he could conjure the willpower to walk away to his own chambers.

43

GUILT

hile the rain had returned, pounding onto the window panes as though demanding entry, they sat around the dining table over roasted duck and steamed vegetables, listening to Georgiana's afternoon explorations. "The black one is Midnight," she explained, naming all six kittens from the new litter born in the stables barely three hours ago. Her face glowed as excitement coursed through her. And while Graham truly enjoyed seeing his daughter so happy, he had trouble hearing what she said as his attention again and again strayed to his wife, seated to his right, a mere arm's length away.

As her delicate hand came to rest on the white table cloth, his own hand twitched with the need to touch her. Gritting his teeth, he drew in a deep breath, fighting to keep his limbs under control. Instead, he looked up, eyes finding hers, and the breath caught in his throat.

She was so beautiful, and pure and honest. And he realized, had he not been blinded by Leonora's loss, he would never have dared approach her. He would never have thought himself worthy of such a woman. He still wasn't sure he deserved her, and yet, she was his wife.

285

His. And after tonight, he would finally be her husband in every way.

As Rosabel accompanied Georgiana to the nursery after supper, Graham retired to his room. Feeling his hands tremble with anticipation, he started pacing the floor until he caught something out of the corner of his eye. Right there, on the side table by the armchair under the arched windows rested a small leather-bound book. As he approached, the blood froze in his veins.

As though the ink was still fresh, as though she had only just written the words looking up at him from the smooth page, Leonora's presence suddenly lingered in the room.

For a moment, Graham was certain that if he turned around, he would find her standing behind him. The small hairs in the back of his neck rose as a shiver went down his spine.

Shaking himself as though shaking off her ghost as well, Graham couldn't help but glance over his shoulder.

But there was nothing. No spirit. No ghost. And certainly not Leonora in the flesh.

Exhaling deeply, Graham stepped forward as though walking on glass. Easing himself into the chair, his eyes were already playing with the words on the page. His mind raced. What would he find there? Had Rosabel been right about what she thought she'd read in Leonora's diary? Or had she misinterpreted her words?

Not certain if he wanted to know, Graham closed the book and leaned back, steepling his fingers and resting his head against them. Could he really not read the page that now lay buried before him? Would he ever get a good night's sleep again if he didn't? Would his mind be at peace not knowing?

Lifting his head, Graham reached for the diary. He had known the answer from the beginning, and yet, he had needed a moment to prepare himself. He opened the book, his eyes settling on the top of the page. The entry was dated a mere week before her accident.

Graham took a deep breath, feeling his hands tremble, and began to read.

Guilt has been my constant companion as of late. I hoped ignoring the truth would somehow erase it, but I now know that this was a hollow wish. Instead, I need to face the truth and learn to live with it.

Thinking back, I now realize that guilt is not a new companion after all. Whenever I look upon the face of my daughter, I feel guilty for keeping her in the dark about her true parentage. Should she ever set foot in the same room with her father, she will not recognize him as such. Nor will he recognize her. Never has he laid eyes on this beautiful child. Again, guilt floods my heart. While I hold nothing dearer than her radiant smile and sweet hugs and kisses, her father will never know the blessing of her presence.

More guilt crushes my heart when I think of my husband. (Graham took a deep breath, closing his eyes for just a second and bracing himself, before returning his eyes to the page.) *He is a good man. A good friend. Someone who deserves to be loved for who he is. However, from the moment we exchanged our vows, I knew that the love we had for one another was not of equal measure. For the past years, his sad eyes have followed me day in and out, weighing more heavily on my heart with each day that passed.*

Until now.

Now, a new guilt has made itself known. While he still looks at me with sad eyes, I have to admit, at least to myself, that my own eyes now see him in a different light. I do not know what has changed, but I am certain something has. All of a sudden, when he enters the room, my heart jumps in my chest. I feel myself blush whenever he looks at me, and my palms become sweaty when his hand holds mine upon escorting me into the carriage. In the beginning of our marriage, I was grateful for his consideration not to enter my bedchamber uninvited. Now, however, I find myself dreaming of his touch.

Do I have the right to love him?

I already promised my heart to another. Do I have the right to break that promise? He did not marry me. He could not. But does the law of man really affect the ways of the heart? Am I betraying my daughter by loving the man she believes to be her father instead of the man who really is?

As her words filled his mind, the emotions that had conjured them touched his heart. The sadness and desperation that rang off the page filled him with sorrow. How could he not have seen her struggle? All these years, he had been so focused on his own misery and failed to notice how deep her own ran. More than anything, he wanted to comfort her, assure her that all would be well. But it was too late.

Leonora was gone. There was no way back.

Instantly, guilt washed over him as Rosabel's face drifted before his eyes. If Leonora had never died, he would never even have met Rosabel. And yet, how could he not wish her alive?

His eyes returned to the shaky handwriting on the page, betraying her emotions far deeper than words ever could, and for the first time, Graham felt a connection to the woman he had loved for years on end.

The woman he loved to this day. And yet, his love for her had changed, too.

Regrets served nothing because they were only that, regrets. They had no power, no effect on the future or the past. A life lived with regret was a life wasted. He knew that now. More than anything, the time spent after Leonora's death had been a waste. Wallowing in self-pity, he had ignored the beauties life held.

Until Rosabel had fought her way through the wall he had erected around himself. With her gentle determination, she had smashed a hole through its solid bricks, bringing light back into his life.

Firmly closing the diary, Graham stood. Running his hand over the smooth leather of its cover, he finally said his goodbye to the woman who had been his life for so long. He placed the diary on the top shelf of his book case. Not hidden. Not forgotten. But remembered.

Then he turned to the door and with a smile on his face walked toward his future.

44

TO HELL WITH THE BLOODY VOWS

uietly closing the door to the nursery behind her, Rosabel tiptoed down the hall. As she passed her husband's chamber, her eyes darted to his closed door, and she wondered if Leonora's words would finally set his mind at ease. Her heart beat against her ribs, and she took a deep breath, knowing only too well how much depended on tonight. Would he be able to let Leonora rest in peace and move on? Would they have a future together? Or would the past still hold its sway over him?

Feeling her skin crawl, Rosabel paced the floor of her chamber, then and there stopping and peering out the window at the night settling over the land. The sky was covered in diamonds, and the moon shone almost at its fullest, its silver light drifting in through the curtains touching the delicate embroidery on her nightgown. From the fireplace a soothing warmth emanated, floating through the room and settling on her chilled skin.

"You look beautiful in this light."

Rosabel spun around, her heart jumping into her throat.

As her eyes fell on her husband's laughing eyes, however, she sank back against the wall, letting out the breath that had lodged in her throat.

"I apologise," he said, closing the door and coming toward her. "I did not mean to startle you." His hair was unkempt, yet not in a way that suggested he had been trying to pull it from its roots in sheer frustration. On the contrary, his eyes were bright and glowing and looking at her in a way that sent a tingle down her spine. He had removed his coat, and his shirt hung down unbuttoned. As he moved, it swayed, here and there revealing flawless skin.

"It is all right," she croaked. "I just...I did not hear the door open."

Standing in front of her, he reached out and took her hands in his. The heat from his skin ignited her blood. It burned hotter and hotter, racing through her veins, filling her with the strangest sensation. Never in her life had Rosabel felt safer than in that moment as her husband held her hands in his, looking into her eyes as though she was the only woman in the world.

Then a gleaming spark lit up his eyes as they roamed her body freely, and she felt the fire that danced under his skin when he touched her. Danger was lurking just around the corner. And yet,...

As his hands slid up her arms to her shoulders, exploring every inch of her, a shiver crawled up her back, shaking her limbs and making them tremble. The breath caught in her throat, and her pulse hammered against her skin as though trying to get free.

Only when his hand settled under her chin, gently lifting her head, did Rosabel realize that she had averted her eyes. "Are you all right?" he whispered, his gaze searching her face. The heat she had seen there replaced by concern. "You need to be comfortable." His breath tickled her skin as he spoke. "If you want me to go—"

"No!" The word had left her lips before Rosabel had even fully comprehended his question. Its vehemence shocked her, and she felt the warmth of embarrassment colour her cheeks. Her husband's face though split into a delighted grin as he cupped her face in his large hands. "I too am nervous."

Biting her lip, she raised her eyes to his, reading honesty in them, and felt her own muscles relax under his touch.

While his gaze never left hers, his hands slowly explored her body, noting every slight change in posture or intake of breath. Her heart still beating far beyond its usual rhythm, Rosabel revelled in the feel of his skin on hers. The shivers excited her, and she felt their pleasure deep within.

As his arms slipped around and settled in the small of her back, she melted into him, her own hands tentatively resting on his shoulders. When his embrace tightened, she gave in to the pull, feeling the length of his body pressed against hers. Occasionally, she glanced down, peering at the soft skin below her fingertips, only separated from them by a thin layer of fabric.

He pulled her even closer then, holding her in his arms, resting his chin on her shoulder and breathing in her scent. Rosabel felt his warmth envelop her and leaned her own head against his strong chest. With her eyes closed, all sensation entered her body through the soft nerve endings of her skin; the gentle touch of his lips on her neck, his hands stroking her back and up and down her arms.

Growing bolder, Rosabel's hands travelled over his arms before returning to his chest, her fingers slowly nearing the edge of his shirt. When she felt his skin brush against her fingertips, she gasped.

Instantly, his arms tightened around her, and a low moan escaped his lips.

Encouraged, Rosabel continued her explorations, revelling in his open response to her hesitant touch. When she lifted her head off his shoulder to look at him, he turned to her, one hand cupping her face while the other held her body close to his. For a moment, his eyes gazed into hers in sheer amazement as though he was seeing her for the first time. Then his arms tightened on her possessively, almost lifting her off her feet, bringing her closer. As he dropped his head, his hungry mouth found hers as though by instinct.

Losing themselves in each other's arms, they let go of the past and all its grievances. Under the lone willow tree that afternoon, Graham had confessed his love for her, but only now Rosabel understood what that meant. With every kiss, every touch and every whispered word, he opened his heart to her, and she welcomed him just as eagerly, returning the deep emotions he was so willing to share.

At some point in the whirl of emotions, Rosabel felt the world shift under her feet as though their love had changed its axis. Strong arms picked her up, holding her close, and carried her the few steps to the bed. Sinking into the soft covers, Rosabel reached out her arms and pulled him toward her, finding the absence of his kisses intolerable.

Careful not to crush her, he buried her body under his, kissing the exposed line of her arched neck. He nibbled her ear, one hand cupping her face. Then he lifted his head, and his eyes gazed down into hers. "I never knew what it felt like to hold someone you love," he whispered, awe shining in his unguarded eyes. "Had I known, I would have swept you off your feet the first time I laid eyes on you." A teasing smile played on his lips. "And to hell with the bloody vows!"

A soft giggle rose from Rosabel's throat as she brushed a lock of his dark hair off his forehead. "Had I known," she whispered, seeing the spark in his eyes ignite once more, "I would have let you!"

EPILOGUE

One Year Later

*T*urning the small rattle in her hand, Rosabel admired its smooth metal surface catching the sunlight streaming into the drawing room through the tall windows and sparkling like a million diamonds. "This is exquisite," she whispered, briefly lifting her eyes to Edmond, holding her new baby son. "And these patterns are so minuscule! That is true craftsmanship! Graham, look at this."

Absorbed in a game of chess with Georgiana, her husband barely raised his head, only glancing in her general direction. "I'm sure it is," he observed from a distance, manoeuvring his king into place. "Now, consider your next move carefully," he instructed Georgiana, the rattle all but forgotten.

Rosabel smiled.

More than ever, this small room held the family life she had always dreamed of. The life she had briefly had with her parents when she had been a little girl. The life she'd thought she would never have.

Rosabel could not be angry with her husband for not giving her his full attention. Instead, she stood and watched father and daughter, heads bent toward each other, battling over the small wooden board. Sometimes their foreheads would crease in earnest consternation, only to grow smooth in the next moment when laughter shook their bodies and gave colour to their cheeks.

"Do not mind him," Edmond interrupted her thoughts of peaceful awe. Cradling the infant in the crook of his arm, he walked over to her, slightly bouncing in his step and making soft shushing sounds as he went. "At least, this way I get to hold my nephew!" His face split into a grin as his eyes returned to the peacefully sleeping child in his arms.

Shifting her own gaze from father and daughter to the cheerful man holding her new-born son, Rosabel couldn't help but glance upward. Over the mantle, a new portrait had found its home. A portrait depicting a woman with deep-blue eyes full of affection and a dazzling smile that lit up the room. Her golden locks framed her face in a halo of light, and yet, goodness was not the first word that came to mind when beholding her image.

Rosabel had spent many hours staring up at Leonora's portrait, trying to piece together the woman behind it. And even though she had never known her in life, Rosabel was certain that the quality most befitting her daughter's mother was strength.

Emotional hardship had marked her life, and yet, she had never given up. She had walked her path, and even in death had guided Rosabel toward her own future. A future as Georgiana's mother.

Rosabel truly believed that Leonora had given her blessing and whole-heartedly approved of the new family bonds that had formed over the past year. Family bonds that included her brother Edmond just the same. From the beginning, he had referred to himself as her son's uncle, never mind that they did not share the same blood. But then again, neither did Graham and Georgiana, and no one would ever doubt that they were father and daughter.

"Do you want me to take him?" Rosabel whispered, gazing at her sleeping son. "He must be getting heavy."

Edmond shook his head. "As light as a feather." His eyes never ventured from his nephew's face as he slowly lowered himself into the armchair by the pianoforte. "If you don't mind," he added, his questioning eyes meeting hers.

"Not at all." Seating herself on the settee, Rosabel's gaze strayed back and forth between father and daughter and nephew and uncle. Her heart warmed as happiness filled the room, and Rosabel reminded herself just how lucky she was to have found a life she could love after all, not just one she could live with.

As her eyes returned to Edmond, she couldn't help but wonder if there was someone special in his life. So far he had not mentioned any lady in particular, but Rosabel hoped that whoever she was, she would find her way into his life soon. Watching him with her son, she was certain he would make a wonderful father. One day, she thought. Hopefully, one day soon.

ABOUT BREE

USA Today bestselling author, Bree Wolf has always been a language enthusiast (though not a grammarian!) and is rarely found without a book in her hand or her fingers glued to a keyboard. Trying to find her way, she has taught English as a second language, traveled abroad and worked at a translation agency as well as a law firm in Ireland. She also spent loooong years obtaining a BA in English and Education and an MA in Specialized Translation while wishing she could simply be a writer. Although there is nothing simple about being a writer, her dreams have finally come true.

"A big thanks to my fairy godmother!"

Currently, Bree has found her new home in the historical romance genre, writing Regency novels and novellas. Enjoying the mix of fact and fiction, she occasionally feels like a puppet master (or mistress? Although that sounds weird!), forcing her characters into ever-new situations that will put their strength, their beliefs, their love to the test, hoping that in the end they will triumph and get the happily-ever-after we are all looking for.

If you're an avid reader, sign up for Bree's newsletter at www.breewolf.com as she has the tendency to simply give books away. Find out about freebies, giveaways as well as occasional advance reader copies and read before the book is even on the shelves!

All the best,

Bree

Cursed & Cherished - The Duke's Wilful Wife

#2 in the Love's Second Chance Series

One night, she stole his kiss.
Now, he is determined to steal it back.

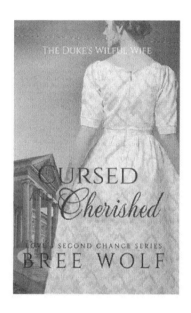

EDMOND DUNSWORTH, Duke of Cromwell, is bankrupt. The solution to his problem: a wife with a sizable dowry.
Not worried in the least, Edmond takes his pick. After all, what woman could resist his charms?

ANNA HANFORD, a merchant's daughter, is faced with a difficult choice: allow her sister to marry the duke and see her happiness shattered...or marry the duke herself.
Determined to ensure her sister's future, Anna makes her choice. After all, isn't marriage just a minor inconvenience in life?

Despised & Desired - The Marquess' Passionate Wife

#3 in the Love's Second Chance Series

Long ago, he kept her secret.
Now, she will save his soul.

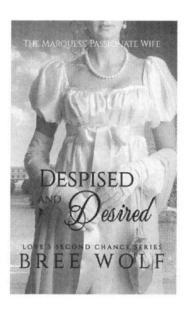

ELSBETH MUNFORD is set to marry the man she loves until an accident destroys her life. Her beauty tainted by ugly scars, Ellie resigns herself to a life of spinsterhood.

FREDERICK LANCASTER, brother to the Marquess of Elmridge, returns home from war. A hero in the eyes of others, he is haunted by nightmares. Unable to make his peace with the past, Frederick retreats into the dark until his brother dies and he not only inherits his title, but with it the obligation to produce an heir.

When two damaged souls find themselves tied to one another, will they pull each other under? Or will they help each other rise again from the ashes of their shattered lives?

Abandoned & Protected – The Marquis' Tenacious Wife

#4 in the Love's Second Chance Series

He forced her hand.
Now, she will deny him her heart.

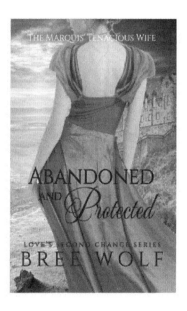

After what her father did to her mother, HENRIETTA TURNER's worst fears are to be realised when her uncle decides to marry her off to a Scot. Gentleman or not, Henrietta knows that at his core he is still a barbarian. What will she suffer at the hands of this savage?

CONNOR BRUNWOOD, Marquis of Rodridge, can't believe he fell head over heels in love with this thin, pale twig of a girl. However, the moment he saw her, he knew he had to make her his wife. If only she didn't hate his guts!

However, when his life is suddenly in danger, an assassin lying in wait, everything they thought they knew is put to the test.

Will Henrietta betray her husband or stand by his side? Will she take the opportunity to rid herself of him forever? Or will she risk everything to save his life…as well as her heart?

LOVE'S SECOND CHANCE SERIES

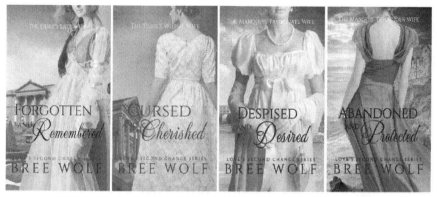

More to follow!

www.breewolf.com

A FORBIDDEN LOVE
NOVELLA SERIES

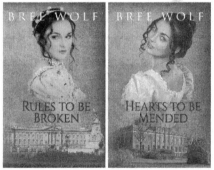

For more information, visit

www.breewolf.com

Made in the USA
Columbia, SC
26 January 2019